THE TOWER
AND
THE DREAM

Jan Westcott

THE TOWER AND THE DREAM

G. P. Putnam's Sons, New York

This book is dedicated to the ladies of our family, young and old, with the fondest of memories and with deep affection.

*But the High Chamber of Hardwick Hall is no
accident. The walls are hung with eight Brussels
tapestries purchased by Bess in time to design the
room to contain them exactly. Sacheverell Sitwell
has called it "the most beautiful room, not in England alone, but in the whole of Europe."*

—Nigel Nicolson
Great Houses of Britain

THE TOWER
AND
THE DREAM

Part I

THE mail from London had arrived about three o'clock in the afternoon, by special courier to the first earl of Devonshire, at his residence of Chatsworth in the County of Derbyshire. It had been received by the earl's oldest son, William, who sorted it and stood looking down at the last letter, engraved with the Stuart arms. He weighed it in his hand.

It was bitter afternoon. The hills were powdered with snow. Icicles hung, fat and huge, from the porch that protected the entrance.

William was still dressed in heavy outdoor clothes. With the letter in hand, he turned and ran up the stairway and through the twin galleries of Chatsworth. He found his father in the study.

"Father," he said, "there's a letter from Arabella for Grandmother. I'm going to ride over with it."

The earl raised his head; he waited.

"It is so cold, Father, so damned cold, that I had to stop the building. I had to stop it. No human being can work outside for long in this. I'll reach Hardwick before nightfall."

The earl said, "It's just a superstition, Will. A legend that she will not die while she is building."

"She hasn't been well! I'm going, Father." He turned and went to the door. Just before he closed it, the earl called "Take three grooms, William. In case of trouble."

It was six miles to Hardwick. When William reached the foot of the hill, the snow began to fall again, a whirling mass

1

of icy beauty. He and his escort dismounted, and, leading the horses, heads bent against the wind, they plodded up to the great mansion on the top of the hill.

The gates were not yet closed. William's grooms led away the horses to the line of stables. William crossed the slippery wide brick entranceway to the front of the hall. He looked up, through the snow.

"Hardwick Hall, more glass than wall," said the rhyme.

"How beautiful it is!" He said the words aloud. The tall towers were encased in white, and the glitter of light from the great windows made the entire front face of the house look like a fairy palace of carved ice and candlelight. He ducked into the cover of the shallow porch; a footman in livery opened one of the double doors.

"Good evening, my lord," he said, as though he were used to greeting guests arriving in the middle of the worst weather anyone could ever remember in the whole of their lives.

William was amused. But there was nothing wrong here at Hardwick. He heaved a sigh of relief. He said he would get changed out of his wet and icy clothes before he did anything else.

Upstairs, reclining among the cushions of her gilt bedstead, the countess watched the merrily burning logs in the fireplace. The room was hung in deep red velvet. Her long thin hands blazed with rings. Her counterpane was gold and silver squares; her bedgown of cloth of gold, furred with sables. She listened, listened to the wind; it howled in fury.

The countess closed her eyes, seeing behind her lids how the great house looked in the snow and storm. Many had been the times she had put on her heavy cloak to go out and see it on winter nights. The six towers did indeed seem to float.

The towers. They were mostly glass. There was only one stairway to the roof; servants who slept in the towers had to cross the roof to enter them.

"Digby," the countess said, opening her eyes to look at Mistress Digby, who sat by the fire, "Digby, we shall have to inform the men who sleep in the towers that it will be

2

too cold for them there tonight, and that they must sleep elsewhere, perhaps in the kitchens."

Mistress Digby jumped, for she'd been dozing. "Aye, my lady. But, madam, what about supper? Won't you have any supper now? A bit of soup? Some chicken broth, for instance?"

The countess sat up straighter, pulling her pillows higher. "Put some thick cream in the soup, Digby. And a few biscuits. And that soup must be hot, Digby! Very hot! To warm my old bones."

She lay back, eyes half closed. "And lace it with some wine, the strongest wine we have." She could hear the voice as if it were yesterday, the young male voice, and she smiled.

"I remind myself of the past, Digby," she said.

"Aye, madam."

The countess heard the door close gently. Across the room the fire burned bright, and in the huge warm bed her body felt strangely young and weightless as she stretched out her legs. *Yes,* she thought, *a bit of soup, and put some cream in it, and the strongest wine you have!*

CHAPTER I

October, 1532

"WHAT are you looking for in that cupboard, Bess?" Lady Zouch asked, severely.

Bess Hardwick jumped. "I didn't hear you, my lady! I want . . . I'm looking for some strong wine."

"It is kept on the sideboard only at mealtimes," Lady Zouch said. "For good reason." She was putting some thin wafers on a silver plate. With the plate in hand, she turned to fix Elizabeth Hardwick with a stern glance. "Suppose you tell me why you are wanting wine?"

"It's not for myself! No, madam, it is young Master Bar-

3

low! He has asked me for some hot thick soup, with cream and a little strong wine! He feels so weak!"

Lady Zouch sighed with relief. One never knew about the young, what they were up to, and it was a great trial to have the children of one's friends here in the London house. After the experience she had had last year, she never would have had another girl in the household to train if she hadn't felt so sorry for Elizabeth Hardwick—this child's poor widowed mother, a lovely young woman with four daughters and a son to raise in an old half-timbered manor house in Derbyshire. Last fall Lady Zouch's good nature had got the best of her, and she had offered to take one of the Hardwick daughters to London; Mistress Hardwick had sent her daughter Bess; she had arrived four weeks ago, with a long letter of thanks from her mother.

"Well, now," said Lady Zouch, "Bess, prepare the soup, and cover it, and bring it up to me. I shall add the wine." She swished out, her ample skirts jutting from her waist. At the door she paused. "I'm very worried about young Master Barlow, Bess. Very worried."

And, indeed, she was. She shouldn't have consented to have him visit! He was too frail. Too frail for school, and that was why his father had asked her to give the lad a look at London. Other women were jealous of Lady Zouch for having this fine house in the city that she was able to go to during the winter, instead of being immured in the country like most of the gentry, while their husbands thronged the court of their King Henry VIII. Lady Zouch proceeded to the small withdrawing room off her own chamber. She set down the tray of wafers and said to the tall man who had risen at her entrance: "Trouble, trouble. I've a very sick boy on my hands."

Bess went on down to the kitchens; she prepared the tray; when the first curls of steam came from the soup, the head cook poured it into the bowl for her and added the cream. Quickly he clapped the cover on the top and laid a napkin over the whole tray. Bess bore it off.

She proceeded upward very carefully; the stairs were narrow and twisting. When she arrived at Lady Zouch's door, she didn't want to hold the tray with one hand, so she lifted

4

one foot and tapped on the door with it. When the door then opened suddenly, she was standing with one foot raised, and she had never felt so foolish in her life because she was looking up into the dark face and eyes of the handsomest man she had ever seen in her life. Her lips parted in a little round *o*.

The deep dark eyes regarded her steadily, as though they could see behind her own. Then two big hands reached for the tray and took it from her.

"Thank you, sir," she stammered.

"Elizabeth," said Lady Zouch, "I present Master William Cavendish to you."

Bess curtsied.

"Elizabeth Hardwick from Derbyshire, here with me for a while, sir."

Cavendish bowed, smiled. He still held the tray. "This isn't for me?"

"Oh, no, sir! It's for young Master Barlow, who is sick!"

Cavendish looked down at her; Lady Zouch hastened over, lifted the napkin and cover, and poured some wine in the soup, and recovered all hastily. "There," she said. Taking the tray from Cavendish, she went to the door and handed the tray once more to Bess. She closed the door firmly.

Cavendish regarded his hostess. The girl had the long pale oval face, with dark velvet brown eyes, and the ivory skin, which went of necessity with the red gold hair. She had an elegant slim body. He asked casually, "How old is she?"

"Twelve," said Lady Zouch, snapping out the word. Then she added, "Bess will be twelve in six weeks." Lady Zouch frowned. Had she heard the faintest sigh of regret from him?

Young Master Barlow had his own very narrow, very small chamber, but it was a great luxury, and it was because he was a guest, and a rich one at that, Bess thought. Not that she would have wanted her own room; she had never enjoyed such a thing; at home at Hardwick, she shared a room with her three sisters, and shared a bed, too. Here she shared with Lady Zouch's two daughters; they were

5

older than she and more accomplished, and they fascinated her. For although Mistress Hardwick, like many ladies in the manor houses of England, carefully taught her son and daughters to read and write and do their sums, Bess had had no Latin, no French, no Italian, nor did she know how to play the lute, the viol, or the virginals. Lady Zouch's daughters did, and they spoke a pretty French; they had had a tutor. But Bess had no envy; she had only a great deal of interest; she was learning rapidly, and that was precisely why her mother had sent her here.

She bore the tray into the room. Robert Barlow was propped up in his bed, with its rather faded but heavy red damask curtains and spread. He was wearing a very elegant bedgown, which had been his last year New Year's present, he had told her. He looked pale and weary, with shadowed eyes, but they brightened at the sight of her, and he smiled; he had the most pleasant smile she had ever seen, she thought, and beautiful, even, white teeth. His servant had shaved him, and there was a nice aroma of soap in the room.

"You look so happy!" he said, and then a fit of coughing took him, and Bess, who was about to blurt out she had just met the handsomest man she had ever seen, forbore, forgot her own excitement at the encounter, brief as it had been, and put the tray down and leaned over him and rubbed his back. Finally the paroxysm stopped.

"Eat this before it gets cold," she commanded. "Don't talk, just eat!" She sat at the bottom of the bed, her feet swinging, and watched him, smiling. "Good," she said. "That's fine! You're going to eat it all. I shall tell you what I learned to do this morning. We took the fruit from within oranges today, very carefully, and then we will fill the orange with vinegar and spices, and tie it in a ribbon, with cloves stuck in it, as the kind of pomander men like. They are for presents! I'll give you one!"

"I would treasure anything you gave me," he said. He lay back and closed his eyes, the last view of her face impressed behind the closed lids. Lately he had been thinking of her every minute of the day and in his dreams. He heard her move and knew she would take the tray; he put his hand over hers. "Don't go away," he said.

6

She came back and he felt her settle on the bottom of the bed. His blue eyes opened.

"When I open my eyes and find you there," he said, "I think I'm already in heaven."

Bess made to speak and then stopped. She couldn't understand him. "You will get better!" She was positive!

He smiled at her. "I've been thinking of you and me, Bess," he said. Her arched light brows drew together faintly; she tried to divert him.

"Tell me what you know about someone called William Cavendish. You know so much about politics and people."

"I know more about George Cavendish, his older brother. George Cavendish was Cardinal Wolsey's 'gentleman-usher,' which means he stood closer to the cardinal probably than any other man; he was the one on whom Wolsey relied, his second in command. "George Cavendish served Cardinal Wolsey while he lived," he said. "But there is another man who used to be in the late cardinal's service, a man called Cromwell. And this William Cavendish serves Cromwell."

"I met him," she said. "Here. He is very tall and handsome; he wears a narrow sideburn and very close-cut beard, so you can see the shape of his face. How old is he?"

"About twenty-four, I guess," he said. "His brother George is more of an intellectual, a writer, a very respected and unique man. They say William Cavendish is a more exciting fellow, honorable but perhaps not completely scrupulous."

"He is very gallant," Bess said.

"He is married, Bess."

She made a mock sigh. "All the ones I like are married."

"Bess," he said gravely, "last week I wrote to my father about you."

She sat up straight, curled her legs underneath her, and looked straight into his eyes, those deep blue eyes, so honest, so loving, so terribly young. "God's blood, Robin," she whispered, "we're too young!"

He shook his head. "I love you, Bess. I love you better than anything in the entire world, or sky or sea. I don't have much time. I want to take care of you; I want to marry you."

7

"Robin," she whispered.

"You surely knew or guessed?"

"Yes, and I thank you." He could barely hear her.

"You don't have to whisper; what we speak of is perfectly honorable. A contract of marriage!" His eyes lighted and he smiled.

She was silent, trying to conceal the trouble of her thoughts. *What of me,* she thought? *I'm not in love. I like you, Robin, I like you, but—can I say that aloud? I must. But I can't.* Her voice trembled. "But my mother, Robin, my mother will think we're too young. So will your father."

"It doesn't matter what he thinks," he said. "I've made up my mind. I know what I want, and I have very very little time to do it in. You must understand that, Bess! You must not try to blink your eyes at the facts. And I'm surprised at you. You are romantic, but you are practical. They are remarkable assets. You can fly and you can walk. Do it all your life."

He was silent then, as though the effort of talking thus was too tiring. And he was thinking, *How shall I put it to her? Shall I be blunt and overbearing, or shall I try to woo her with soft words and a kiss on her cheek?* But he couldn't do either chained to this bed. He would have to meet her on her own ground, not lying here in disarray, in bed.

He was fairly tall, even pale as he was and thin as he was, nature had bestowed good features, a strong chin, and fine thick blond hair. The dress of the day, for men, was dictated by the king, and it emphasized the overbearing maleness of that king—in the heavy doublet, for instance, which broadened any shoulder to a magnificent width. "I'm going to get up, Bess," he said. "Take out that tray, and call Jack for me. Get your cloak, Bess. We'll go out for a walk."

She started to say he wasn't well enough to go out, but it would do no good. She left the tray on the floor by his door for one of the servants to pick up. She got her cloak, brushed the old white fur around the hood so that it looked as good as possible, and came down to the lower hall to wait. At the top of the curving steps, out of sight, she heard Lady Zouch bid good-bye to her guest, although the words

8

were indistinguishable. Then William Cavendish came running down and stopped short as he saw her.

"It was a pleasure to meet you, mistress," he said.

She dipped him a small curtsey. "Mine also, sir."

"Good-bye." He hesitated—the white fur about her face was not becoming; it was yellowed and cheap. Anyway, against the tendrils of red hair it was wrong. "When you grow up," he said, low, "I'd like to put sables with gold clasps around your head and shoulders." Surprised, she looked up into the dark eyes; they were reckless and glinting, and yet there was a hint of patronage in them, to which she took instant umbrage.

"Good God, sir," she said levelly, "I shouldn't want to wait that long." Then she blushed, for she had forgot he was older and, in her newfound liberty, being away from her mother, had used an oath. But William Cavendish grinned; he leaned over and kissed her on the cheek.

"I deserved that," he said, and then he reached for the door and was gone down the steps to the street.

Bess stood there watching him, the door open.

A pox on the man, she thought angrily. *He might just as well have said my cloak is not becoming; in fact, he did say it!* She scowled and turned that frown onto Robert Barlow, who was coming slowly down the stairs, holding to the rail. As he came further into view, though, the scowl left her face, and she smiled up at him. He looked so different! His cap, with a jewel and a little flat feather, sat rakishly on his thick blond hair. He was clean shaven because he wasn't old enough to grow a beard, but she liked clean-shaven men. They were young, like her. His doublet was red and black, and the sleeves slashed and puffed with white silk, so he looked as broad as a bear; his blue eyes shone at the sight of her.

"Oh, you look so fair," he said.

He came up to her, and his servant put his rich furred cloak over his shoulders. And suddenly Bess sighed with pure pleasure. What a delightful prospect—to go out walking, in London, with an escort like this! "Thank you for telling me I look fair," she said, wishing that clod Cavendish could hear.

9

"You're not only fair, my love," he said, regardless of the listening servant, "you are beautiful." He tucked her hand in his arm, and proudly Bess started down the steps and into the streets of this wonderful, wonderful city, her city, her London.

They sat, watching the river, the endless stream of river traffic, the noise, the cry of birds and boatmen. The sun shone, and the October wind was soft. Robert Barlow had taken her hand, and in their walk here, she had forgot temporarily that he had spoken to her of marriage. But now, suddenly, she knew that he was about to ask her again, and soberly she looked at him, sideways, and then averted her eyes. She sighed deeply. "Before you speak, Robin, I must tell you we are too young." She bit her lip, she didn't know exactly what else to say, but then she decided she had better continue. "I'm not ready for marriage." She glanced at him; did he know what she meant?

"I know that, Bess," he said, squeezing her hand. "You don't need to be embarrassed."

She sighed again, now in relief. "Oh, well, then—"

"But the subject is not closed." His voice was firm. "Bess, at the risk of being dramatic, which I despise, I must tell you something, too. I may not have long to live. Don't argue with me. I love you, and when I die, I want to have wed with you, and I want to give you security; I am a wealthy man, Bess, and I want to share it with you. We don't have time to wait."

Bess took her eyes from the river and looked down at the hand on top of hers. *What a tragedy,* she thought. *Suppose I, Elizabeth Hardwick, thought I wouldn't live, suppose I were mortally ill?*

"You see, Bess," he said gently, "there is just one thing I want from my life, and that is to know that I am taking care of you. I will die happy if I am sure that I, your husband, have provided for you. It's the only thing in the world I want. You are my life, my hold on life. You have become the purpose of it, ever since I met you six weeks ago. With you at my side, I am happy. But you don't need to get into my bed, Bess. You are too young, and I am too sick, my love."

10

"I can't believe it!" she cried. "You are only fifteen! You will get better!"

He shook his head. "I doubt it, Bess; but I am happy when I am with you. Bess, my dearest love, will you marry me and allow me to take care of you for the rest of my life, to hold and cherish, and to endow you with all my goods, forever and ever? You will be my immortality, you and your quick wit and your beautiful face and body. You will live, and I will have a hand in it! You will bear my name, and you will be comforted and secure in the future, by my doing."

She thought, *I can't believe it. It is the strangest proposal in the world, it doesn't seem possible; when I tell Mother, she won't believe me, either.*

"What will my mother say, Robin?" she whispered.

He patted her hand. "We'll ask her and see," he said.

CHAPTER 2

BUT first they had to tell their hostess, Lady Zouch. It was Sunday, that next day, and after a midday dinner, she took the two of them into her bedroom. The bed had been made up like a daybed, so Lady Zouch reclined comfortably against her striped satin bolsters, a woven throw pulled up to her waist. She gazed at them benignly; they were nervous, especially the girl, Bess. Lady Zouch thought briefly of Bess' mother, whom she had known as a girl. Ashby-de-la-Zouch and Hardwick Manor and the Barlow lands —all lay close.

She said aloud, "We are all closeknit, my two young friends. You can confide in me."

Robert Barlow cleared his throat. *He is not uneasy,* Bess thought with pride. She herself squirmed on her stool.

"Lady Zouch," Robert said, "this may not come as a surprise to you, but Bess and I are betrothed, and we wish

11

to be married, and so we think it best we go back home, and get our parents' consent and blessings."

Lady Zouch had not been prepared. She was astonished. She had noted well enough that Bess had taken care of Robert since he had come into her home; she had been grateful to the girl for undertaking this task. Again it had been her extreme good nature that had allowed her to consent to Robert's coming. He had always been a sickly child, frail, coddled, precocious; his enforced leisure had pushed him into voracious study and extensive reading. But this news was a thunderclap. What would his mother say? *She will blame me,* Lady Zouch thought. *What a calamity!*

"By my faith," she muttered. "By my faith! You do take me unawares, my dear young Robert."

For a moment there was silence. Lady Zouch took advantage of it. "Bess, you are only twelve years old!"

How in the world could we have foreseen this? Lady Zouch thought despairingly. *And I will be the unwitting villain of the piece. Surely there could be nothing physical between them!* Lady Zouch swiftly reckoned the surveillance they had had and decided it had not been good. But she had never suspicioned such a thing! This sick lad and a twelve-year-old girl. She looked sharply at Bess, whose head was bent over her needlework. Her fingers flew. She was knitting. Very often she was embroidering, but she could knit without looking at her fingers, and now she raised her head, her needles still clicking rapidly. For the first time, Lady Zouch appraised her, slowly. The pale ivory skin, the long oval of her face, the shining red gold hair, and the dark eyes set under lazy lids, heavy with lash. Quickly Lady Zouch remembered anew that Robert Barlow was a very wealthy young man. Bess was poor. It was common knowledge that her father had left each of his four daughters but forty marks as a dowry, a very, very small sum. It was common knowledge that her mother was having a difficult time making ends meet at the manor house.

Surely she was too young to have planned this! She had been a delightful young guest, quick to learn all the household duties for which she had been sent; she was cheerful, in fact she was gay, and although Lady Zouch had never perceived it, her daughters told her that she had a quick, biting wit. And said the most improbable and nonsense things.

Robert said, "It has been all my doing, my lady. I love Bess, and I have asked her to marry me, and she has consented. But only if her mother will permit."

"That speaks well for you, Bess." Lady Zouch threw out the phrase automatically, her mind on other implications. Of course, her mother would probably consent. *If I were her mother, I should consent,* Lady Zouch thought. *There are too many obvious advantages to this child and to the family to be related to the Barlows.* She looked at Bess again, and Bess received the look. She realized it was a look of respect, the look of one woman to another who has done well, acquitted herself in the game of life and men and sex with all honors. Bess smiled.

"It's customary to congratulate Robert, my lady, not me."

Lady Zouch giggled involuntarily.

"Bess," she said reprovingly, but Robert was smiling at Bess, lovingly. *She makes him laugh, too,* Lady Zouch thought. *She makes him laugh, and she is so sweet, too, and she is so sure!*

"Well," she sighed, "I do congratulate you, young Robin. You are a very fortunate young man." She added, "You'll be safe with Bess!"

He nodded. "There is something about her, isn't there, my lady?"

The hazards of traveling in the winter months—it was almost November—were not inconsiderable. From London to Derbyshire was at least four days' journey, and dangerous. Adequate armed guards were needed and runners who went ahead to be sure there was a proper place at the next good inn with good clean and aired beds and food and proper provisions and quarters for the horses, and a litter in case one of the party was not able to ride, plus servants and lastly a chaperone. Lady Zouch decided on the chaperone first. Her widowed sister-in-law. She would be rid of her for a month at least, and the Barlows would have to pay to send her home again.

"Much as we hate to leave your home and hospitality," Robert said, "we would like to be home by next Sunday."

* * *

13

He was extraordinarily efficient, Bess thought. From his bed in the mornings, he instructed both his servants and his tutor, who had accompanied him to London, and with whom he spoke Latin for an hour every morning. He gave all his instructions in Latin, so that he didn't miss a day of practice, and Bess envied him and made up her mind she would have her children so taught. Her needles clicked furiously. Everything proceeded fast, and in three days they stood on the steps, early in the morning; they were ready to leave.

Bess had looked around herself for the last time; in the crowded bedroom, then in the kitchens, then in the dining hall, then in Lady Zouch's bedroom to say good-bye. She knelt for Lady Zouch's blessing. When she rose her eyes were wet. "Thank you for all you have done for us," she whispered. "I will never forget."

Lady Zouch wept a little, too. "Good-bye, Bess."

Robert and Lady Zouch's sister-in-law rode in the litter. Bess rode a newly purchased mare, Robert's first gift. "I want to ride through the city, even the outskirts, to see it for the last time," she said.

"Oh, not the last time!" one of Lady Zouch's daughter's cried. "You'll come again, Bess. Soon!"

For none of them had any idea, least of all Bess, that it would be almost fifteen years before she would return to London.

English inns were already famous. Regardless of the weather and the long day in the saddle, Bess, like any other girl, was fascinated with the journey back to Derbyshire. Every night in a comfortable inn, with good food, with servants to plump up featherbeds, and clean linen sheets, to be waited on hand and foot—it was delightful! And during the days she pushed away the thought of the impending marriage, about which she was not at all sure, and Robert's obvious weakness, never more apparent than when he was forced to do more than he should.

"When you get home, you can rest up and recover," she told him endlessly. But when they reached Hardwick manor, when they topped the hill and saw the half-timbered house and the sprawling, untidy outbuildings, in need of

14

patching, Robert looked so pale and ill that Mistress Hardwick put him right to bed.

Bess was rather glad, for his wanness prevented her from enjoying the reunion with her family. After Robert was safely in bed in her brother's room, then all of them could gather round and talk and laugh and listen to all Bess had to tell them of London; none of them had ever seen it.

Then later, in the early evening, after supper, when the crude fireplace sent out both smoke and warmth, Robert descended the stairs, warmly wrapped in his furred cloak. Mistress Hardwick made a place for him by the fire, in the only chair, formerly her husband's, with two cushions behind him and one on the hard seat, and a stool for his feet. Bess' sisters had been banished to their room, and now just they four sat around the fire, Bess on a bench next to her brother James, representing the man in the family. James was sixteen. Mistress Hardwick sat on a low wooden chair without arms, which the village carpenter had made for her some winters before.

"Mistress Hardwick," Robert said, "as I told you when we arrived, Bess and I are betrothed and wish to be married." He implied that his future mother-in-law had had time to brood over the request and that she would now be ready to answer him.

Bess looked to her mother, not quite realizing her eyes were both startled and imploring; suddenly Bess was afraid this was all wrong, and she was ready to draw back. She drew in her breath sharply as her mother said, "Why, Robert, Bess is very young, you know that. She is only twelve!"

James stirred on the bench and was puzzled by this whole conversation; he thought Robert very odd.

Robert said, "I don't need to tell you, ma'am, that many, many of our age wed, postpone the marriage bed, but still wed each other."

Bess threw a glance at James, blushed, and James, eyes round, thought Robert sounded like an old man; why, he was younger than he, James!

Mistress Hardwick nodded her head slowly.

Impatient, Robert disdained his real reason, his love for Bess and his own ill, weak body. "I wish to provide for

15

Bess," he said. "I wish to endow her with all my lands, my two manors, and the lead mines that my grandfather willed me. Thus, you see, madam, it is no small offer I am making for Bess."

Mistress Hardwick said, "You have your father's permission for this?"

Robert didn't. But he answered firmly. "It shall all be in writing, indeed, all legally drawn and executed before the ceremony."

There was no need for Mistress Hardwick to announce that Bess' portion from her father was a mere forty marks. And in this year, the end of the year 1532, in England, when a butcher's son had become a cardinal and the lord chancellor of the realm, in this age of ambition, when the twin gods of money and education could bring untold rewards, it was impossible for Mistress Hardwick to say no to Robert Barlow. Nor in fact could her daughter, for she was a product of her time and its thinking. Athough she didn't know it, ambition stirred and motivated her every action. She drew a deep breath, a long sigh, she was saying good-bye to romantic dreams and shaking hands with the beckoning, realistic future. Money and security. Love came later. But not for Robert.

"I love Bess with all my heart," he said sternly.

Mistress Hardwick smiled with joy. "Robert, you are a fine young man, and Bess should be very very happy. To have won the love and respect of a man like you."

James said gruffly, "I congratulate you, Robert." He wondered if he ought to say jokingly that Bess had a temper as hot as fire, but decided against it. They were all too serious and adult for him.

Robert stood then and lifted Bess to her feet and kissed her cheek. "I'm going to ask your leave to go to bed now," he said. "And tomorrow or the next day, perhaps, my father and I will call upon you, here."

It was all done in such a rush and hurry: Mistress Hardwick thought she would go mad. But the papers were indeed legal and signed and attested to by her own lawyer. Christmas was coming, and so was Bess' wedding. Her three sisters refurbished their gowns. There was much polishing

16

and decorating of the old manor and its raftered hall as the girls and servants could manage. Although Robert wanted a small, quiet wedding, the list of guests grew daily.

"Well, we can't leave out the Vernons of Haddon Hall!" Mistress Hardwick would cry in despair. "They are lifelong friends. And we are all neighbors. Their feelings will be hurt."

So in the end the Vernons of Haddon Hall and the Knivetons of Mercaston and Leches of Chatsworth, the Frechevilles of Staveley, and the Foljambes of Barlborough all came. Bess was so caught up in the arrangements that she had had no time to think, even at night in bed with her giggling sisters.

The oldest was Mary, a ripening fifteen. Then Jane, a year older than Bess, her very favorite, and trailing behind at eleven, Alice. Yet even at this busy time, Bess couldn't help but note what an injection of money and a good marriage did to galvanize a household. Suddenly the Hardwicks were more important.

Gifts flowed in from nearby manors. Ladies called. Heads together, they chatted with the widowed mistress of Hardwick, bearing little offerings for Bess, little treasures like a new, knitted shawl and cap and a handmade shift with lace! Bess scrubbed out her old chest and polished it till it shone, so it could properly contain these wonderful new possessions. Every day Robert sent presents. From a fat pig for the wedding feast to four dozen wax candles; one day a cartload of ivy and fresh-cut yew, plus two men to twine it around the stairwell. One day a huge load of wood to be stacked by the fire.

And the young men from nearby manors called, too, carrying notes from their parents. In their presence the Hardwick sisters did their hair more carefully and used their homemade perfume with abandon.

Two days before the wedding, Sir Francis Leche of Chatsworth called to see if he could offer the services of his two horsedrawn litters, in case it should rain or snow. On that day Mistress Hardwick, her face flushed and rosy, greeted him with such a warm smile and a merry glance that Sir Francis, a widower, felt a stirring in the blood. Bess had never seen her mother so gay and happy, for just before

17

he left, he said, "Now, madam, since young James will stand up with Bess, it shall be my great pleasure to escort you. A very great pleasure, indeed," said Sir Francis, beaming down on Elizabeth Hardwick.

Oh, such happiness! It was four days before Christmas. There was just the lightest powdering of snow on the hills of Derbyshire. Little fat clouds sailed in the winter sky. Bess was married in the hall, with candlelight, in the morning at ten o'clock. The wedding feasting began at eleven, the wines flowed, the cake was dark with spice and nuts and raisins. There was venison and roast pig, and there was enough for the villagers, who carried their own plates.

At two o'clock Bess went upstairs. In her chest were all her new presents and a new dress. In her chest was a brass-bound box, locked. It held the legal papers that made her the lady of two manors, the possessor of five hundred acres of pasture and forest, and the sole owner of a considerable lead mine and its workings. It also held her forty marks, which Robert had refused to take. The key she wore around her neck.

Her sisters helped her out of her wedding gown and bound up her long red hair. On her finger she wore her wedding ring and her gift ring, a mass of table-cut diamonds. On the big bed lay Robert's wedding present, which he had brought from London. After Bess was dressed in her green wool traveling gown, Jane lifted the wedding gift reverently from the bed and put it around her shoulders.

"Oh, oh!" they all whispered.

It was a glowing green velvet cloak, lined in satin, and furred all about with thick lustrous fur. Bess stroked it. It smelled good, too, of some kind of whispering perfume. "How does it look?" she asked. Jane sighed in envy. "Oh, Bess!" she said. "You look like a princess!" Then, "Look, Bess. See how I've done your hair?" Jane was proud of her handiwork. She held up the tiny polished glass, which they all shared. "See how the curls fall from that back knot?" Bess bit her lip. How she wished Jane were coming with her!

"I'll miss you," she quavered, the excitement suddenly gone, and only now the realization she was leaving her

18

home, her beloved old manor, those hills and rocky paths she knew so very well, the stream at the bottom of the hill where the flowers grew so bravely in the spring. "Don't cry!" Jane waved her finger in front of Bess' nose. "Don't dare! Princesses don't cry!"

Bess managed a wavering smile. She pressed the fur to her cheek. "It's sable," she said aloud. And then she did smile, a brilliant smile. "You see, Master Cavendish! You see!"

"Who's Master Cavendish?" Jane asked.

"Just a man I met," Bess said, "in London," her eyes sparkling.

But her three sisters hardly heard her. They said together, solemnly, "Bess, we wish you all happiness! A happy life, a happy Christmas!"

"Thank you all for giving me such a wonderful wedding!" She blinked hastily, and with the tears standing in her eyes like stars, she turned and went down the hallway and down the steps to her waiting Robert. *I am married,* she thought. *I am Mistress Robert Barlow, of Barlow Manor and Oldcotes.*

CHAPTER 3

THE manor at Barlow was one of the largest and most impressive of the dwellings in Bess' world. Robert's chamber was paneled, and it boasted a new chimney of brick and a wide hearth that didn't smoke. A narrow door had been cut in the paneling to allow access to a small room next.

Mistress Barlow preceded Bess into the room. Bess' eyes roved over the room. It was perfect! There was a small window seat under the two narrow, heavily leaded casements; it looked as though the big plumped featherbed and shiny quilt were brand new; there was a low chair and a polished chest at the foot of the bed.

"I love it!" She turned around again.

Mistress Barlow set her chin a bit. Robert came into the

room from his own, and he said, "Everything in it is yours, my love." He had weighed taking Bess to one of her own manors and reluctantly decided that it would not do. She was too young and inexperienced, and he was not well enough. This small suite of rooms should serve them well enough. His tutor, who had used to sleep on a trundle in Robert's room, had been banished upstairs. Here they could be alone and yet surrounded by aid should they need it. He only devoutly hoped that his mother would try to get along with Bess, and that his brothers and sisters would not resent her. His younger brother had heartily approved of his disposing of his manors as he wished, but his mother had not! She had fussed at him for two weeks.

"We'll have our supper up here, before the fire, Bess," Robert said. "Put on your slippers, and I'll do the same."

Mistress Barlow left them. Out in the hall she met her husband. "He's like an old man with a pretty face," she whispered. "He treats her like an old man's toy."

"Shush!" Master Barlow held up a warning finger.

But Mistress Barlow was too annoyed to hold her tongue. "It's wicked to give away his inheritance to a stranger! It should have gone to John. I don't understand you, Arthur. I'll never understand you. How could you? Disinherit your other son!"

"Oh, madam," he said wearily, "pray desist. Yours and mine younger son is far from disinherited. He will have this manor and these lands."

"It isn't right," she said stubbornly. "And you have daughters."

"And I've a wife, worse luck, who can't hold her tongue. You should be thanking the Lord that your poor sick son has something to live for in the last months of his life."

Mistress Barlow didn't believe that, and neither did Bess. It was only Master Barlow and Robert who could see the truth.

At Christmas the manor was alive with guests and relatives. Every night it seemed to Bess there were delicacies to eat, from fresh roasted venison to quail and squab. On New Year's Robert gave her a heavy gold chain and a curiously carved gold ring set with pearls and a fiery opal.

Mistress Barlow's eyes snapped when she saw Bess wearing her finery and showing it to all her new family.

After New Year's the January days fell into a pattern. She and Robert had a light breakfast together, milk and a bit of cheese and bread. During the morning his tutor came and they spoke their Latin for an hour, while Bess sat by the fire and did her needlework. She had made a sketch of Robert's room, and she was embroidering it for a pillow cover for his mother, whose birthday was the end of the month. Robert was fascinated with it, as the colors and each day's stitches brought the sketch to life.

"You are so talented," Robert exclaimed. "And you have such beautiful hands. I'd like to cover them with rings."

Pooh! thought Mistress Barlow, overhearing this and entering the room. "Robert, it's such a nice day—do you know it is really warm outside in the sun?—maybe you should take the air, and while you're gone, we'll clean and freshen this chamber." *One would think his wife could do it,* she told herself.

Bess' face lightened with joy at the prospect of going out. She was beginning to feel shut in like a rabbit in a trap.

"I would love to go out. I'd like to ride over and see my new manor." Mistress Barlow threw a piece of wood on the fire with violence.

"That will be too far for Robert."

"Oh, then, of course," said Bess, contrite. "We will just stroll around the garden. I love gardens, Robert. That's something you don't yet know. At Hardwick, I had my own garden; I had flowers and herbs, all laid out in neat paths with grass between."

"We will ride where you wish," Robert said. His face was flushed with two red spots on his cheekbones. Then he relented. "Mother, we'll take two docile mares and just jog along, and I'll come back if I'm tiring."

He did tire, but he forbore to say so, because Bess was so happy. The manor of Oldcotes was small and old, but it was well kept, and looked cozily prosperous. Smoke curled from its two chimneys, and all about it was neat and the gardens were heavy with yews. Ivy clung to the old walls. Behind it stretched its pastures. Bess dismounted and laid her gloved hand on the earth. *It's mine,* she thought.

21

It's mine. Those thick woods in the distance. Mine. My own land.

Robert waited in the old hall while the tenant farmer's wife brought them some steaming ale.

The hall was tiny. The stairway, wooden, made a right-hand turn onto a small gallery.

"Explore," Robert said. "I'll sit here and rest."

She was gone a long time, he thought. Then she reappeared on the gallery and pressed her nose to the one leaded window. She came slowly down the shallow stairs and turned to look up.

"Someday we shall live here," Robert said.

"Aye, I hope, soon," she said. "I would tear out that wall, Robert, and build a wing directly off this hall and the same width. The ground floor would be a withdrawing room, just for privacy and eating together, and the upper story—both having the new fireplaces, one chimney would suffice—would be our bedroom. The vista would enlarge this hall, and the gallery would be very attractive, thus coming over the entrance to the new private parlor."

"Why, Bess!" He looked up, from her to the old gallery.

"It has graceful lines, you see," she said.

"Why, Bess," he repeated, "you are a budding builder!"

"You're joking me," she said. "It's just something I thought of when I saw the upper story. There's no light, Robert. There's not enough glass, naturally. It's old. But I love the half-timbered manor house; they are beautiful, and besides that I was born in one." She smiled and sipped the hot ale. Then suddenly she realized he looked very pale. "We ought to get back," she said, "while it's still warm and the sun's high."

When Robert dismounted in the courtyard at Barlow, he staggered a bit, and his mother came hurrying out to seize his arm. They put him to bed. But he managed to eat some dinner, and then he fell asleep.

"His chronical distemper is always worse in winter," his mother whispered to Bess. "But he ate rather well. For Robert."

Bess sat by the fire, reading from the Book of Job that Robert's father had given her for New Year's. But Bess was not too much of a reader, and soon she took up her needlework again. She was troubled, though, so deliberately

22

she thought about the manor house, seeing again its neat outbuildings, all so well cared for, from the dovecote to the stables to the small washhouse. The barn had been full of fresh-smelling hay. And the house itself! It was comforting just to remember it, to know it was there, welcoming, a haven.

That night Robert wakened with chills. Bess threw on her bedgown and came hurrying into his room. She took two hot bricks from the hearth and tucked them into the foot of his bed. She took two more quilts from the chest and laid them over him.

He was still shivering.

"Shall I get you a hot toddy or—"

He shook his head. "I might get sick if I drank something," he muttered. "I feel as though I would vomit if I drank anything."

Bess got a towel and basin and put it next to the bed. He was lying on his side, his knees drawn up, and he was still shaking. Bess pulled aside the quilts and slid into bed, cuddling up against his back and holding him tight. "There," she whispered, "I'll make you warm."

"Sweetheart," he murmured.

Bess could feel the warm bricks under one foot and edged it closer to him. She kept the quilts close around the pillows and around their necks. She thought he was not shivering anymore.

"I missed a bedfellow," she whispered. "I felt lonely! In bed all by myself."

"I'm harmless, sweetheart." She could hardly hear him.

"Go to sleep, go to sleep. We're just like the prince—" She stopped. She had been about to say they were just like Prince Arthur and Queen Catherine; they'd been put to bed together but Catherine swore she was untouched and virgin when she married Henry, after Arthur's death. For Arthur had died. *Suppose Robert died? Oh, no! He wasn't that sick. Look how he'd ridden today!* She hugged him. "Go to sleep," she whispered. She would keep him safe.

Robert died on the night of January 29. He and Bess had been married for exactly six weeks. On February 6 Bess and her mother-in-law and the women of the family waited in

23

the small severe Norman church of St. Lawrence, at Barlow.

The chapel was called Our Lady's Quire. Outside the snow was falling gently. The funeral procession wound across the hill. It was bitter cold in the chapel. Bess stood under the shadow of the tomb of Robert and Margaret Barlow. Their life-sized figures towered over her. When she looked straight ahead, she looked at the stony handclasp. It made her tremble, the sight of it.

Robert's open tomb lay just beside their figures. She could read the inscription, already carved in the stone. There was a blank space beside it, for her name. *Someday Elizabeth Barlow will be inscribed above—no, below—Robert's name,* she thought. *Someday I will lie here.* But it wasn't possible! She hung on tight to the hand of her sister-in-law, whom she hardly knew. She edged closer to her mother-in-law, taking sides with the living against the dead. *Poor Robert,* she thought. *Oh, oh, my poor Robert.* The tears flowed down her cheeks and dripped over her chin. It had been so quick! One moment he had been whispering to her, and the next moment—the next moment he was dead. There was nothing there. Nothing. Bess put her hands over her face and sobbed.

Part II

CHAPTER 1

April 14, 1547

"IT'S a most wonderful beautiful day, Jane," Bess said. "And if we're going to ride over to Chatsworth, to congratulate Mother, you'd best get up. I've been up since five."

It was seven now. If she went straight to her table, she could start the day's accounts. She pulled out her stool and opened the ledger. *April 14,* she wrote in her sprawly untutored hand. *Just imagine, she thought, it's been 15 years since Mother married Sr. Francis Leche. I can't believe it. Fifteen years. Where have they gone? Well, they've gone into rebuilding Oldcotes. They've gone in a spate of marriages.* James had married Elizabeth Draycott; he lived at Hardwick manor and managed it poorly. Mary had wed Richard Wingfield and lived in Suffolk. Alice had married the son of her stepfather's eldest brother, Francis Leche, and she lived at Chatsworth, too. Jane was a widow, Mistress Godfrey Boswell. Dear Jane! What would she do without her?

Jane and Bess and two grooms set forth at nine. There was a bit of chill in the spring wind, but the sun shone and Bess was glad to be ahorse and free, for the day. It would be good to see all of them at Chatsworth.

"I only hope Mother doesn't rail at me for not finding a husband," she said to Jane.

25

Jane was silent. Bess was so difficult to please, she thought. She had turned down four suitors that Jane knew of, and there had probably been more. Bess was a wealthy widow. Even had she been ugly as sin, she'd have had suitors. For those two prosperous manors and the acres of private park and woodland. She even managed the lead mines and rode over twice a week to see the workings; she paid her men and kept all the accounts. *She is remarkable,* Jane thought. *I could not have done it!*

Bess reined in her horse. *Why,* Jane wondered. Then she realized they could look down from this little hill onto Bess' peaceful slumbering fields; fat cattle grazed, and beyond, where Bess had enclosed land, were the sheep; from here they were just dots, lots and lots of dots, all worth their weight in silver for their precious wool. It was an achievement and no wonder she was proud. *Whereas James, at Hardwick—well, even Mother was worried about Hardwick,* Jane thought.

Bess spurred her horse again. "I told Mother," she said firmly, "that I wouldn't marry again till I find someone to love." She smiled at Jane, and Jane wondered whether to confide in Bess or not.

Instead she said, "I agree, Bess. I agree!" How long would it be before they got to the gates of Chatsworth? Not long, she hoped. For perhaps a man called Kniveton would be there, too.

When they could see Chatsworth, they could also see there were a great many visitors, for there were horsemen ahead and the figures of people on the lawns. Jane was in a hurry, but Bess was not. She checked her horse completely before the shallow ford in the river. It spilled down around the hill on which Chatsworth stood.

"God's death," said Bess. " 'Tis the most beautiful site for a house!" Her eyes drank it in hungrily. The contours of the land, sloping down to the encircling water, running clear and full of noisy splatterings. What a lovely sound! The sound of water, running, cascading, and how beautiful the banks. The spring flowers, the violets, the white of the hawthorn. Bess said, "I love this land!"

She doesn't need a husband, Jane thought. *She's in love with*

26

the land; she really is. Jane was in love with Thomas Kniveton. Would he be here today?

The county was gathering, coming to Chatsworth. Sir Francis and his wife were waiting to greet their guests; Lady Leche was waiting anxiously to see her daughters. James wasn't there yet; James would be late; he was always late. Lady Leche was worried about her daughters, Jane and Bess. Both widowed, both still so young, Jane twenty-seven, and Bess, twenty-six. Neither with any children. Lady Leche was dismayed with Bess, especially.

"Here they come!" she cried, and as they did indeed come nearer, she forgot her misgivings and was instantly proud of them both. Both so pretty, one dark, one with that so very fashionable red gold hair; the same color as their adored Princess Elizabeth, indeed, the same coloring did her Bess have.

Lady Leche saw now with extreme pleasure that Thomas Kniveton had rushed forward to assist Jane from her horse. Lady Leche beamed approvingly as they sauntered off together for a stroll after they'd properly greeted her. Anyway, she wanted to talk to Bess.

"Come to the herb garden with me. There'll be no one there, I hope." Arm in arm they started forth.

They rounded the house in a wide sweep and came to the garden behind, on a gentle slope, enclosed in berry bushes, now green. Lady Leche was framing her first question to Bess when her daughter said, "Mother, your garden thrives, but what of the house? It looks neglected."

"Our lease is up, and we are going to put it on the market."

"God's death," muttered Bess, "I wish I could buy it!"

"By my faith!" Lady Leche exclaimed, using her strongest oath. "By my faith, Bess, have you taken leave of your senses?"

"It's in disrepair, Mother, no one could use any other term," said Bess severely. Then she glanced at her mother. *It is too big for her; it is probably best to sell it.* But oh, my, her heart longed for it. She said, "Don't fret, Mother. The land itself is worth too much for me."

27

She was silent. Lady Leche said, "Bess, you should stop thinking about houses and think about a husband!"

"Oh, I do," said Bess. "I think about finding a husband, but be damned if I can." She laughed. "I keep telling myself that impatience is always a mistake or brings mistakes and trouble with it. That's all the comfort I have to give myself. I wonder—I am getting older, and people are beginning to feel sorry for me. Then I think, I'll show them! But what good would it do to parade around with a husband I don't want? God's death, what good would that do?"

"You would have children," Lady Leche said. "You swear too much, Bess."

"I know. I'm grown up, Mother; I've learned to take care of myself, and to swear. I'm lucky to have Jane, and shan't have her long. I envy her, Mother, she's in love."

Lady Leche patted Bess' hand, and took her arm again. "Come," she said, "we must go back. The Barlows have come."

Master Barlow took Bess in his arms and kissed her. "You look as fair—fairer than ever, Bess! Thank you for your christening present to young Anthony; you have to come over and see him. He is a beautiful baby."

"I'm sure he is," said Bess warmly, looking up at his rugged lined face. *The manor house at Barlow must be overflowing with children,* Bess thought. Did they sleep in Robert's room, and crowd into her little room? Did they have their lessons there? If only her dear Robert had lived!

"When I think of all of you there, happy," Bess said, "I weep a few tears for Robert and myself, and our lost youth."

Master Barlow cleared his throat. "You gave him something so precious, Bess, that I will never cease to be grateful."

Bess said, "Where is Mistress Barlow?"

"Over with your stepfather and our guest. We have a very important guest. He is here on the king's business, and he is staying with us for a few days." The slightest frown crossed Master Barlow's forehead. "His wife is not with him," Master Barlow continued. "She wasn't able to leave London."

He was steering Bess toward the ample figure of Mistress

Barlow and her stepfather. There was something vaguely familiar about the tall, magnificently dressed man with them, whose back was to her.

"Has he stayed here before?" she asked.

"No. This is his first trip into Derbyshire. He was the late king's right-hand man for the dissolution of the monastaries and convents, Bess. It is he who sends their inventories to the king and later their treasures." Master Barlow spoke in a matter-of-fact voice, so that no one could tell whether or not he approved of Henry's despoliation of the former chapels, the abbeys; it was a dangerous thing to speak slightingly of Henry's ruthless suppression. They had all embraced the new faith, the Church of England. It was only wise. And he wasn't sure how Bess felt. They said she had welcomed the new church, because of its simplicities.

"He must be a very powerful man," Bess whispered, for they were very near now.

"We were delighted to offer him our hospitality," said Master Barlow, which meant that they didn't dare refuse it.

Mistress Barlow saw Bess and kissed her. Taking Bess' hand, she drew her in front of the very tall, very dark stranger, dressed in the latest style, his boots of the softest leather, the breadth of the wide shoulders enhanced by the width of the doublet and the full sleeves, and the rest of him encased in such tight hose that he might as well be naked, Bess thought. These were the styles evolved by a king, designed to show off the magnificence and threat of the male animal. His eyes rested on her levelly.

"We've met before," he said. The brown eyes swept her again and came back to rest on her face. "But where, Mistress Barlow?"

Bess said, seeing that narrow hall in London, "At the house of Lady Zouch, Sir William. You were Master William Cavendish then; I was Bess Hardwick."

"Ah! Of course. I remember. You were a young maid, up from the country." He smiled, it was a flashing smile in that so dark face. He put her hand on his arm. "Come," he said. "We must talk about old times, and you must take me for a walk up the hill, so I can look down on this beautiful river valley. I've never been in Derbyshire before."

Master Barlow watched them go. When they were out of earshot, he whispered to his wife, "I told her he was married!"

CHAPTER 2

BY the winding path that Bess and William Cavendish took it was roughly a mile to the top of the hill that encircled Chatsworth, and the winding serpentine Derwent River at its foot. In the early spring sunlight, the land so tender and yellow-green, it was enchanting.

"You are related to the Leches of Chatsworth?" he asked, looking down at the low-lying manor house.

"Lady Leche is my mother. Sir Francis is her second husband."

"Ah."

"And my older sister married my stepfather's nephew."

"And where," he asked, "do you live, then? Here?"

"No," Bess said. "Look—way, way over beyond that far hill with the cloud sitting on top. I live on the other side. But not under the cloud." She laughed. "I am a widow, sir. I live with my widowed sister, I left my old home years ago, a few years after my mother married Sir Francis."

He glanced down at the curve of her cheek. Then she had been a widow when her mother remarried, and presumably she had been living back in her old home. He wondered how old she had been, so he asked.

"How old were you when you left home?"

"Sixteen," she said. "Quite old enough."

He was astonished. "You've been a widow for these many years, then? It's incredible!"

"I'm twenty-five," Bess said, calmly subtracting a year from her age. "Believe it or not, sir, I'm a lady of business; I run my two manors." She said nothing about the mine; why should he know she owned a mine?

30

"I do believe it," he said. "And I can believe your coffers are groaning."

"Just fretting a bit," Bess said. "Not really groaning."

He was enchanted by her smile and the laughter in her dark eyes. "In London, you'd have lasted a week after losing your spouse. Then you'd have been eaten alive!"

"Best for me to stay right here, then," Bess said. "I can't spare even a nibble; I'm too thin."

"It's all the fashion," he said, "to be thin. For women; the Lady Elizabeth has your exact coloring, and she is very slender."

"And how does she dress?" Bess asked, with great interest.

"Very, very—plain. The king calls her his Miss Temperance. She often wears plain gray, which, of course, makes her hair more startling."

Bess thought of the length of plain gray woolen in her chest.

"Lord, lord," he said, "I can see you're already sewing up a gray dress."

Did he find women so transparent, she wondered, or did he know too many women? She looked up at him, speculatively. "What do you do at court?" she asked bluntly.

"February, a year ago," he said, "upon the death of Sir Anthony Rous, I was made treasurer of the king's chamber." Did she know how important that was, he wondered? That it was not merely a palace treasury but really a national department of finance?

"I paid a thousand pounds for the office, but don't tell anyone," he said lightly. She probably wouldn't believe that, either, even though it was perfectly true.

She said, "Do you have children, Sir William?"

"Two," he said. "Almost grown. You behold a man of thirty-nine years, plague take it." He grinned down at her, companionably and she laughed, for he didn't look almost forty to her. He looked immensely strong and lithe and young, just as handsome as he'd been at twenty-four, and she knew he was the most compelling and attractive man she had ever met in her life, and she'd never forgotten him. She sighed openly.

"What's the matter, sweetheart?" He took her hand.

31

"All the handsomest men are always married," she said. "It's such a pity!"

She gave him such a merry glance that he exclaimed, "God's blood, madam, you make me feel fettered." He held up his hands. "Chains, around them. Or I'd make violent love to you!"

"Why are you here?" she asked. "In Derbyshire? Surely there are no more abbeys to inspect, and—" She stopped, wondering how to put it right and not offend him.

He said seriously, "I'm here buying property. I've just sold some of my properties in Herefordshire and Cornwall, and am purchasing here and in the county of Nottinghamshire."

"You think land here a good investment?"

"How serious you are." It amused him. "Yes, I do think it good, very good indeed. I'd like to buy this." He waved his hand.

"Ah, so should I," said Bess longingly. "And it may soon come on the marketplace."

"I know," he said and let his eyes go over the whole valley slowly, carefully.

She saw with surprise that he wanted this land as much as she did, she could tell easily by the expression in his eyes and on his face. He leaned down and took a handful of the soil and crumbled it and let it fall to earth, back to the earth.

"Look at the way the clouds blow over the hills," Bess said. "Like streamers of smoke."

"Aye."

"I've always lived here," Bess said. "I love it."

He was silent. Then he said, "I'm hungry. Let's go back." He was rather abrupt.

"Of course," she said obediently.

"God's blood," he said, "how meek you are suddenly. I'm not old enough to be your father."

"You mistake," Bess said. "I'm hungry, too. In fact, I'm starving."

Jane saw them coming. Jane was sitting on a bench side by side with Tom Kniveton, and she had just stood up to

32

go to help her mother and the servants serve their guests. She waved to them, thinking what a pair they made.

The long trestle tables had been set up, because it was such a beautiful day and warm enough to eat outside. Bess brought Sir William a pewter basin and napkin. He washed and thanked her. But when they sat down to eat they were separated, for there were a number of men who wanted to talk with Sir William about the king, their new king, Edward VI, son of Jane Seymour, who was only nine years old, and who had been on the throne only a few months. Henry VIII had died January 28. They wanted to ask many questions, about the Protector Somerset, Edward Seymour, and about his brother Tom Seymour, and what of Dudley, how powerful was he, and what of the politics that were being played in the council itself, and what did he think, that the country would not stagger and grow faint with such a young monarch—did it bode ill for England?

Bess hung on his answers. He did not commit himself but said that all men mourned their King Henry VIII, and that the council was as wise and careful as men could devise, and that Catherine Parr was rumored to be pregnant, and had wed Tom Seymour secret, and true, Dudley was power-ful—yes, that was true. Yes, he had himself heard the late king name the succession. First, of course, his dearest treasure, his son Edward, their present beloved King Edward VI, then his firstborn daughter, the Lady Mary, then the daughter of Anne Boleyn, the Lady Elizabeth.

When he said her name, there was a sigh. The Lady Elizabeth. Everyone smiled and nodded. Then the little Lady Jane Grey. "Her father is one of my best friends," Cavendish said. "I've known him for years. She is extremely brilliant, like the Lady Elizabeth. She studies Latin and Greek. She is much with her tutor. She is a Puritan, like her cousin, the king."

Yes, the protector is a very strict Protestant. But people know that the Lady Mary still has her confessor. Well, times change. Yes, times change, but change is not bad, it is inevit-able.

Inevitable? Bess thought. *But it hasn't been for me. There's been no change; I've matured in body and mind; but change?* She had been leaning forward to catch his words. For a brief moment their eyes met and fell away. *Perhaps change is coming,* she thought, *and I'm ready for it.*

CHAPTER 3

SIR William Cavendish, sunk in thought, started suddenly, and his barber nicked his chin. He used a fairly mild oath, and both men dabbed at the cut with the two ends of the towel. Sir William wanted to keep the blood from his new shirt, which his valet had been surprised to see him wear this morning. Dressed finally, in the softest suede riding jacket, with his jeweled dagger gleaming at his hip, he pronounced himself satisfied. He left the manor at Barlow with one groom. *Thirty-nine,* he thought, *is a damned dangerous age.*

At the top of the last hill, he looked down on the manor of Mistress Elizabeth Barlow. He was properly impressed with her husbandry. Yet at the moment it was not this he had come seeking. He had wrestled a bit with his conscience, but not much. In the hall of Oldcotes he waited impatiently, and when Bess came down the stairway, he bowed just as though they were both at court.

"I came, Mistress, to ask you a favor. It is such a beautiful day that I wanted you to ride out with me and show me your country." And he was thinking, *With two wives behind me, and quite a number of casual mistresses, I feel just like a damned boy!* He took her hand, the long white fingers were elegant in their grace; his brown fingers encircled hers. "You have the most beautiful hands," he said.

Bess said, "That's a nice compliment, sir."

His aplomb suddenly deserted him, and he stared at her. She said, "I'd love to go out riding this morning."

She pulled an embroidered bellpull that she had done herself.

While her cloak was being brought, he prowled restlessly about the hall, saying nothing, for he could imagine pricked ears at every doorway. But just before they left, he asked, "That wing—" He gestured toward the arched doorways, the wide windows on each side of a fine fireplace, with carved supports for the mantel—"did you have that done?"

"Aye," she said. "You like it?"

"I like it very much. Very effective—look how the sun pours in." She smiled up at him, and he put his arm around her and squeezed her shoulder with one big hand. "God's death. You're a clever girl!"

From an upstairs window Jane watched them go. They were without the sign of a groom; they were riding slowly, side by side, heads turned toward each other. Jane thought, *I should warn her. But how?* It was about as easy to instruct Bess— Jane couldn't think of a parallel. She went on down to the kitchens. "We may have a guest for dinner," she said and turned on her heel quickly before the interested cook could question her.

They didn't appear for dinner. Jane never knew whether they ate or where. But that evening, with Bess propped up in her big bed in the new bedroom over the new wing, Jane attempted to talk to her. It was useless. Bess just smiled at her dreamily.

It is some kind of magic, Bess thought, as April disappeared into the first week of May. "We've known each other three weeks," she said.

"Aye."

It was warm in the sun. There was no wind; the sun slanted in under the edge of a drooping tree. They were lying close. *It will be now, and soon,* Bess thought.

"I love you, Bess," he said. "I love you more than I thought it was possible to love. I have no words for it, Bess, my dearest, my dearest love."

"I love you," Bess said. "I adore you."

She had not told him that she and Robert had never really shared a bed. Lately she had kept that to herself because she was ashamed of her inexperience. It was nobody's business, Bess thought, whether or not she was a

35

virgin. She had planned to tell him just before he entered her, but the onrush of her desire for him was so overwhelming, she couldn't think nor talk but only cry out for him.

"My God, why didn't you warn me?" he whispered afterwards. She lay quiet in his arms. He found his handkerchief and wiped the smear of blood from the inside of her white thigh.

"I forgot," she said, and he hugged her and kissed the side of her lips.

He looked down at her body, and the curly red triangle of hair. "Sweetest sight I ever saw," he said as he folded the blanket across her so she wouldn't get cold.

The following day he would complete arrangements for the purchase of two properties; then he must make a quick trip to London and bring back a skeleton staff to manage them. He went back to London for part of June and returned the end of the month for the last week of June.

He had instructed her, and Bess had thought she and he had been careful; but on the first of July, when she awakened, she felt a little odd, a bit dizzy and she had some feelings of nausea. She got back in bed and fell asleep, and when she wakened for the second time, it was nine o'clock. She was amazed. She felt fine! She hopped out of bed, completely naked, and went over to the window. It was a most beautiful warm day; the sun poured in on her white body, and she welcomed it as warmly as she did her lover, turning around to let it fall on her back and bare buttocks. She looked down at her breasts, and suddenly, in a wave of remembrance, she said aloud, "My God! When did I have my last?" She sat down on the edge of the bed and tried to figure.

She was quite undismayed when she told him, that day, the first of July. "I'm afraid I'm sure," she said.

He used a variety of oaths. He was rapidly turning over in his mind what to do, what they could do, and he said, "Well, don't worry, darling. Don't worry." He had a dozen manors, a remote one in Cornwall. She could go there. He explained all this; they sat there, holding hands, while he explained. And she wouldn't have to go yet; there was

36

plenty of time. And what of the baby? Well, Bess said, she would keep it and legally adopt it. What did they care what people thought? After all, there was plenty of money. Plenty. And no one would truly know. Why shouldn't a lonely rich widow adopt a child?

"Well, that will all come later. The important thing is that you depend on me," he said. "I'll arrange everything; you are not to fret your beautiful head about anything. Bess, I'll take care of you, and I love you."

That night, a July night rich with summer, and still light at nine o'clock, a village courier picked his way across the hill. Bess read the hastily scrawled note. "Dearest," it said, "I've been summoned to London. Remember what I said; don't worry. I'll be back as soon as possible."

Four weeks later, about nine o'clock, an August storm of such violence descended that even Bess was frightened. She and Jane had been sewing because a great and important event was to take place in September. Jane was going to be married. To Thomas Kniveton. The thunder had begun rumbling early in the afternoon, and one by one, great high-piled storm clouds raised their heads across the hills. They muttered and stalked the skies, and then, by common consent, seemed to pick out the small valley at Oldcotes to vent their fury.

Jane insisted they come away from the empty fireplace and down into the main hall, under the stairs. Bess caught up two pillows and they sat there trembling while the whole house shuddered, and great sheets of lightning lit the hall with an unearthly light. Out in the garden a great tree fell, with a crashing and splintering of branches that made Bess cry out in dismay. Was it the great oak she loved so dearly?

She rushed to the window. Lightning lit the garden, but all she could see were branches tossing. She turned back to Jane; her face was as white as the queer light that filled the hall right after the thunderclap. Jane was terrified. Bess was never sick! And Jane knew that the sudden illness of a well person was the most dangerous.

In the light of the one candle, Jane reached out for Bess' hand. "Are you sick?" she asked. "Bess?" she asked again. She was completely unprepared for the answer. It came like the thunderclap of the storm itself. "I'm going to have a baby," Bess said.

Jane didn't believe her ears until she suddenly realized that it was quite quite true and why had she been so blind? Of course Bess and Cavendish were lovers. It should have been so patently obvious.

"God's death," whispered Jane, who never used any oath stronger than "by my faith." Then she realized that Bess, her Bess, was crying. Tears were streaming down her cheeks, her whole body was shaking. And Jane could hear the incredible words she was saying over and over. "And he's deserted me! He's left me! He left the very day I told him!"

"It's not possible," Jane cried. "Oh, by my faith, how could he?"

"Easily enough," Bess said. "He's done it! The lying bastard! If I could get my hands on him, I'd kill him!" And then she used some language that Cavendish had used, and Jane sat horrified, wringing her hands. Suddenly Jane stood up. The storm was receding. She said, "At least we haven't been struck by lightning." She picked up the solitary candle. "Let's go upstairs again, Bess."

Like a sleepwalker Bess did as she was told. She followed Jane up into her pretty bedroom and sat disconsolately on the edge of the bed while Jane relit the candles she had been using to sew by. When she could see Bess' tear-streaked face, she said calmly, "Bess, it's not the end of the world. There are plenty of friends who will help. You can always go up to Mary in Yorkshire; you don't need to use your own name. We will all help you."

"God's death, don't dare tell Mother!" Bess stood, white with passion.

Jane blurted, "You'll make yourself sick. You'll have a miscarry."

Bess began to laugh. "Do you think I want the bastard's bastard?"

"Oh, Bess," cried Jane helplessly. "Stop! Please stop!"

Bess wiped her face with her hand. She had a mirror hung over her table, with her brushes and pretty jars and pots of powder and perfume. She could see her reflection, her hair awry, her white face twisted. She muttered, "I look like a witch. But I'm all right now, Jane. I'm glad I told you. It's been too much, keeping it all to myself. And it isn't the baby, Jane. It's him and his perfidy." She hissed out the word. "It's that that's been keeping me awake at night; I spend all my time hating him. Now I'm going to forget him. I'm going to forget him!"

I'm going to forget him, she said, to herself, every morning. *I'm going to make myself a new life. I'll go to Yorkshire and leave the baby. Leave the baby. My son.* Sitting by the window, outside it was raining gently, her own eyes would fill with tears. *Leave my baby. Oh, God, how can I? . . . But I will.*

She dreamed of Cavendish. Waking sudden, in the warm summer night, she would sit up in bed, startled from sleep, hearing his voice, seeing his smile, feeling his touch. *Be damned to you, Cavendish,* she would whisper, and turn over in bed, and bury her face in the thick soft down pillow. She grew thin. It worried Jane. She had had trouble getting Bess to put a panel into two of her dresses, for the very very near future. And yet Jane sensed that in the bottom of her heart, Bess hoped.

But there had been no word from him. No letter, no dusty courier, nothing.

On the fourteenth of the month, it started to rain early in the morning. It rained for three days. Bess wandered about the house, and Jane, anxious to complete her wardrobe and her wedding arrangements, tried to hide what she was doing from Bess. It seemed wicked to Jane, for her to be preparing for a wedding while Bess prepared for the birth of an illegitimate child. Jane admired her. In no way and by no word did Bess show any feeling. She was calm; only her natural gaiety was missing, except once in a great while, her barbed dry wit would flash forth as of old.

August seventeenth dawned rosy with sun. Such a delight! Even Bess looked happier as she came trotting down the big stairway, her feet sounding quick and sure on the low worn wooden treads. She was going out in the garden. "You'll get your feet wet," Jane cautioned.

"Good," said Bess.

She went out to the kennels, and the dogs barked and barked and ran in circles to greet her madly. She walked up and down the wet grassy paths in the herb garden, she

39

gathered some rosemary and basil, some mustard, and took them into the old dark kitchen. At nine she went to the stables and watched while her horse was saddled. She rode off into the hills with her two favorite hounds, cantering, letting the dogs race ahead. At eleven or so Jane saw her coming back, the dogs still racing ahead, barking. Bess rode up to the front of the manor house, slid down from the saddle and hitched her horse. The dogs fawned around her, the sun was shining bright and it was deliciously warm. Bess leaned down to pat them when her ears caught the sound of a steady *thrump, thrump.* She frowned. She looked down the lane, to the fork where it met a rutted, still-wet road. Whoever was coming was riding fast, for all that.

She shielded her eyes against the sun. A lone rider. She sighed. He wouldn't come alone from London. From London he would have an escort. It wasn't safe to ride alone. She turned and went up the one shallow step to the threshold; the door of the manor stood open to admit the sunlight. And she didn't turn around until the sound of the hoofbeats told her that whoever was coming, was coming here, up the lane.

She turned then, curious, unfastening her hat clumsily, for she still held her riding crop. She never went out in summer without a hat, to protect the delicate white skin that went with her red head. She scowled suddenly. By the Lord God's death, it was he! It was he who was coming, she couldn't mistake; he was too close!

She rushed out into the small court, enclosed by a low wooden fence as Cavendish flung off his horse.

"I'll set the dogs on you!" she screamed.

The dogs bounded forward at her command, snarling. Cavendish used the butt of his riding whip, back and forth, back and forth, in front of him.

"God's blood, are you mad?" he shouted back, coming toward her, the dogs snarling and backing from him.

"Get away from here! Get out!" screamed Bess in a passion.

One dog took hold of Cavendish's sleeve, and he brought the handle of the whip down on its skull. The other dog barked frenziedly. Bess rushed forward in a flurry of skirts, brandishing her own whip. "I'll use this on you!"

40

He raised his arm and caught the blow on the side of his upper arm; the lash flicked his face and he seized it, wrenching it from her, threw it at the other dog and grabbed her into both arms, holding her tight, both arms at her side.

"What in God's name is the matter with you?" he muttered and lifted her easily and carried her into the hall and banged the doors shut while the dogs still yelped outside.

Jane, brought running from the back garden by all this shouting and racket, stood transfixed in the far doorway leading to the kitchens.

Bess was encircled in his arms; he could feel her trembling. "I couldn't come sooner," he whispered. "I couldn't write. I never thought you'd doubt me."

Bess shivered, shivered. Was it true? Was he really here? She looked up at his dark face. Her mouth quivered.

He kissed her gently, with increasing force, his arms so tight around her Bess thought the manor was tipping sideways. He whispered, "I came to marry you. My wife, Bess, my wife died."

Her dark eyes widened with sudden fear. "You didn't kill her?"

"God's death, Bess!"

"You might be caught, I meant," she breathed.

He held her off and looked into her eyes. "I didn't kill anybody, Bess, you knew she hadn't been well for years. I told you."

"I know, but—I don't care if you did," she cried passionately. "I thought you'd left me!" The tears sprang into her dark eyes, brimming over, and he picked her up again and cradled her in his arms.

"My poor darling," he muttered. He saw Jane, and he said, over Bess' head, "Mistress Jane, I've an escort following me—of ten men; they'll be here shortly." Then without speaking further, he carried Bess upstairs into her bedroom and shut the door. Jane heard the bolt slide shut with finality.

CHAPTER 4

THERE was silence from Bess' bedroom but plenty of noise in the court and stables, with Cavendish's escort arriving. And there was a lot to do, but Jane hummed merrily, all the gay songs she knew, and in the back of her mind she was planning Bess' wedding, wondering where it should be, and how pleased their mother would be, for, no doubt about it, Cavendish was quite a catch! Nonetheless, Jane was shocked; they were alone upstairs, and it was very improper, but that is the way people were nowadays, people like Bess and Cavendish, they did much as they pleased, without regard to the conventions that she, Jane, had been brought up to observe. But so had Bess. It was something in the air, Jane thought; there was a great deal of doing as one pleased.

So when they finally reappeared, it was dinnertime, and Jane said brightly, "You must be hungry," and then she blushed a deep red. Cavendish laughed and gave her a kiss.

Everyone else dined in the hall, but Bess and Jane and Cavendish dined separately, in the new room. Cavendish poured the wine at the sideboard and brought it to Jane and Bess and toasted them both; then after they were served, he said with a bluntness that made Jane blush again, "There's a need for haste, Mistress Jane. Bess and I will be married, and we want you to come with us."

Jane said, "At Chatsworth? At Mother's?"

Cavendish shook his head. "We'll send a letter to your mother. We are going to be married at Bradgate. We'll leave tomorrow morning early, they are expecting us. It's all arranged."

Jane's eyes grew bright with astonishment. Bradgate! And they were expected! Jane had never entertained a hope that she would ever see the inside of Bradgate. After dinner she recklessly packed the two fine dresses she had made for her trousseau and hoped they would not be too warm and that they would be good enough for the high society in which she was suddenly moving. For Bradgate was the seat, near Leicester, of the marquis of Dorset, bearing the family name of Grey. The first marquis had been the oldest son of Elizabeth Woodville Grey, the most beautiful woman in England, and the woman King Edward IV had later married despite all convention. The present marquis, her grandson, had married Frances Brandon, the niece of Henry VIII; thus, it was royalty itself that Jane prepared to visit. Her hostess would be the Lady Frances, niece to the former king and whose daughters were named in the succession to the throne.

Bradgate was new. It had been built about thirty years before by Thomas Grey, second marquis of Dorset. The moat and the curtain walls were decorative only, for it was unfortified, as befitted this age. The hexagonal towers rose graceful. The moat shimmered, like a placid reflecting pond, and a rushing trout stream was part of the stretching gardens. In the late afternoon, its brick walls were rosy with sunlight, its low hills a background. Jane cried, "How utterly beautiful!"

It was a jewel, poetic. Bess reined in her horse and looked at Cavendish. Her eyes shone like dark fire. "Someday," she said, "sweetheart, someday!"

She sucked in her breath, and Cavendish nodded slowly. "Someday," he agreed.

Bradgate had twin courts. In the inner one, their hosts awaited them, coming out the studded doors as though the young king himself had arrived. Henry Grey was as fair as his beautiful great-grandmother, his hair pale gold, his blue eyes warm with pleasure and greeting. Lady Frances was ample, beside her slender husband. They introduced two of their children, the Lady Catherine Grey and the Lady Mary. Their oldest daughter, Lady Jane Grey, was ten years old. She was now in the household of the queen dowager, Catherine Parr, and her husband, Lord Seymour. Lady Frances kissed Bess, hugging her to her ample figure. This was a great household, one of the greatest in the realm. There were so many servants it would have been impossible

43

for Jane or Bess to count them, and the same with its huge stretching suites of rooms, the galleries, the halls, the intimate private chambers.

Lady Frances said, shaking her auburn head, "You know I adore your husband-to-be. This will be a celebration."

The marquis had remonstrated, "He's only been a widower two weeks."

Lady Frances cried, "By my faith, my uncle the king was wed the very day Anne Boleyn was beheaded. Keep up with the times, Henry. Don't lag behind."

She herself escorted them to their rooms, so the travelers could wash and change from riding clothes. While Bess changed, she heard the sound of other arrivals, and when she finally descended to the first floor, she realized that Lady Frances had invited everyone from the nearby countryside. Everyone! Even Lady and Lord Zouch! Imagine!

There was more food than Bess had ever seen in her life. Including quivering custards and jellies and fresh-caught trout and tiny little birds, roasted, and comfits and sweetmeats and flowers of sugar to nibble. And wine. It flowed.

"Be careful," Cavendish warned her, frowning slightly.

"It's been my experience," he whispered, "that pregnant females, when they eat and drink too much, get sick."

Was she owl-eyed? "They vomit," he added.

At midnight, the musicians on the gallery were still playing. Jane was valiantly resisting the amorous advances of a very drunk younger son from one of the nearby manors. The party was becoming excessively gay, the dances wilder. At one thirty Lady Frances climbed up on a bench, and the musicians played three long blasts on horn and trumpet. " 'Tis time!" Lady Frances cried. "The groom has signaled!" There was a roar of applause and clapping. The great doors at the side of the hall were thrown open.

They gave onto the chapel. Within, candles burned. Everyone streamed in, and the colorful brilliant dress of men and women glowed against the plain walls.

"Imagine being wed at two in the morning," Jane thought.

The marquis himself took Bess down the aisle between all the guests, crowded close. At the altar Jane stood at her side, and when the brief ceremony was over, the marquis himself escorted her. The bride and groom had gone first.

Lady Frances whisked Bess away after Jane had kissed her and wished her much, much happiness. At the top of the great curving stairway, they paused for just a moment and then went on. In the big bedroom where she had dressed for the festivities, Lady Frances and two maids undressed Bess and put her in bed. Lady Frances kissed her. "I wish you happy, happy, happy!"

She laid her gift to Bess at the foot of the bed, a shimmering satin bedgown trimmed with lace.

"Thank you, thank you, Your Grace," Bess stammered.

Lady Frances was out of the room with a wave of her hand; Bess thought, *She looks as fresh now at two thirty in the morning as she did when we came!* She was as hearty as a thick foamy glass of ale. Bess sat in bed, the sheet over her hips, her hair falling about her bare shoulders. She sat there, scarcely breathing, so she could hear what was happening outside her door.

In the distance she thought she still heard the music. There were lots of footsteps, running, pounding; in one of the sudden silences she thought she heard the distant wail of a child crying. Then suddenly she heard Cavendish's voice.

"No, you don't," he was saying. "No one needs to put me to bed, thank you. Not at my age, sirs."

The door opened, and when he saw Bess sitting up in bed, he banged it shut hastily and bolted it.

"Did you look under the bed?" he asked.

Bess shook her head in astonishment.

He came over, lifted the ruffle, peered underneath. "You can never be sure," he said and went over to the table where two candelabra burned, pulled out the chair and sat down.

"What are you doing?" Bess asked.

He had been carrying something, and now she saw it was a pocketbook; he flipped it open and dipped a pen. Bess hopped out of bed and came to stand behind him, her hands on his shoulders.

He wrote, *Memorandum: That I was married to Elizabeth Hardwick, my third wife, in Leicestershire at Bradgate, my lord*

45

Marquess' house, the 20th of August, in the first year of King Edward VI, at two of the clock, after midnight.

He closed the notebook and stood up. "I'm a very methodical man, sweetheart," he said.

"Don't tease me," Bess said. "I am so happy I could die of joy! And I command you, sir—Lady Cavendish commands you—to come to bed right away."

CHAPTER 5

CAVENDISH was worried about the state of the realm, and he was worried about Bess. When Henry VIII had died more than two years before, the transition to government by council had not gone smooth, and young King Edward's uncle, Edward Seymour, had seized the reins and become Protector of the Realm. Naturally, he was going to be opposed in his ambitions, and the man who challenged him was John Dudley. It was Cavendish's duty, as treasurer of the King's Chamber, to steer an even course between these two powerful men, as they struggled for control of the young king, the council, and the country.

"Men will die right and left," Cavendish predicted to Bess. "Never confide, never gossip, my love." He sat with the baby Frances on his knee. She'd been named for Lady Frances, and Lady Frances was her godmother. That was safe enough, for the young king liked his cousin Frances.

From the next room came the wail, high and thin, of a sick child. Bess winced bodily, as though a blow had been struck at her.

Cavendish said, "Today the little king wrote in his diary that 'the Protector Somerset had commanded the armor to be brought down out of the armory of Hampton Court, about five hundred harnesses, to arm both his men and mine own men withal, the gates of those to be rampired.'"

Cavendish bounced his little daughter. She was eighteen

months old. "Today also, Bess, the Protector was deprived of his office and sent to the Tower." Bess did not answer.

"Dudley claimed the Protector was trying to closet the king away from his council with armed men, and Edward seemed to believe it. Try to remember, Bess, he is not yet twelve years old, has all the autocratic stubbornness of the Tudors and is a fanatic besides. He is a dangerous boy, Bess. A very dangerous boy. And he is a king."

Bess pushed back her chair with violence and stood. *They can all go to the devil,* she thought. *I care not at all!* How was it possible that for the last twenty-four months she had thought it important? How was it possible she had reveled in moving among the court, getting dressed in her finery, watching her little baby girl grow so fair and pretty and bright? How was it possible she had delighted in finding herself pregnant again, so soon? They were so popular, the two of them! So gay! It had been a triumph of the greatest magnitude for her; she was living at last, in the very thick of power and gossip, of intrigue and hatred, of envy and love. And what could stop either one of them? Nothing! Nothing!

She had not even been too disappointed when her second child was again a girl. She herself had chosen her name. In honor of the princess Bess admired the most of all the royal family. The Lady Elizabeth, sixteen years old, somehow a tower of cautious strength and wisdom and wit. Bess named her baby Temperance, for that was the name the little king called his sister, Elizabeth. Miss Temperance.

Bess' baby was two months old. She was lying in her cradle in Bess' room, for Bess was afraid to be far from her; she couldn't bear the thin cries coming through the closed door. She left Cavendish and went into her room and bent over the thickly padded cradle, with its pink satin quilts that were tied to the side so the baby wouldn't smother.

Every time Bess looked at Temperance she thought her heart would break. *Oh, Lord, help her,* Bess thought every time she knelt by the tiny child. *Help her; she can't breathe!*

The tiny little face looked up at her mother, and Bess slid her arms under the swaddled baby and lifted her. She was aware that Cavendish had come to stand close behind her; she could feel him physically, his height and breadth

47

and strength looming over her. "Go away," she whispered.

She heard him suck in his breath. He had been wrestling with the problem of Bess' inability to accept the terrible fact that Temperance was too frail, too sick. He was tempted to say bluntly, harshly, that she must accept the fact that if Temperance survived through her first two years, the critical years, it would be a miracle. But he couldn't. He turned away and left her cradling her baby in her arms, her baby, who had gained almost no weight since birth, the poor little doomed baby with the beautiful name. "Temperance," crooned Bess. "I'm here. I'm here."

Temperance died the first day of December, 1549. Bess was inconsolable; she was literally mad with grief. Closeted in her room, she wept. When Cavendish tried to comfort her, she turned away, as though it were his fault, his fault that she had had a baby who died. "I can't bear it," she would whisper, "I can't, I can't!"

"You must," he said. "Bess, you must. You have Frances. You will have other children."

"Never—" she said. "I can't bear it!"

After ten days Cavendish, in desperation, sent for Jane. Now Mistress Jane Kniveton. Jane arrived on the seventeenth of December. Even though Bess knew she was coming—for Cavendish hadn't dared to surprise her—when she saw Jane, she burst into tears.

"Oh, come, sweetheart," he said. "Don't drown Jane."

Was there impatience in his voice? She didn't answer him. But that night, when he came in late from a long stormy council meeting and wearily tried the door of her room, he realized she had bolted it from the inside.

William Cavendish was a typical man of his times, the essence of them. Honest, but not scrupulous, self-made, intellectual, he was part adventurer and part planner and thinker. The two sides warred considerably while he mastered his temper. Then he went quietly down the hall and to his own chamber and fell instantly asleep, thinking he had solved the problem. For he had decided, during that long moment outside Bess' locked door to attack the problem with his wits and not his brute strength.

48

"If it weren't Christmas," Jane said to him the following day, "if it weren't Christmas, maybe the grief would be easier for Bess to bear."

"Aye, she's literally out of her mind with grief," he said.

"I'm worried," Jane blurted.

"God's death, so am I!" But he squeezed her shoulder under his big hand and said, "Just do your best, each day. Try to divert her if you can. Get her out of this house."

Jane succeeded in getting Bess to walk out, and to show Jane some of the shops, where she could buy brilliant wool and satin and ribbon and that great luxury, a pair of gloves. And sweetmeats and a bird pie fresh from the baker's ovens. The cold air brought some color to Bess' cheeks, and when they got home, Jane said, "Bess, my dear love, you look much better for fresh air."

Bess managed a smile, and Jane took heart.

Three days passed, and Cavendish confronted his wife one night after supper. Jane had excused herself, on his earlier request. "While Jane's gone," he said, "I want to ask you, frankly, Bess, to tell me why you've locked your door each night."

Her dark eyes were pools of sullen resentment. She didn't answer.

"I'm only forty-one years old, Bess," he said, with a grin. Then he described his symptoms in pithy and graphic terms, ones that ordinarily brought a giggle to her lips. But she just stared at him stonily.

"You want me to have another woman, then?" he asked casually.

For just a second he saw a flash of real anger in her face.

"I'm waiting," he prodded.

Bess said, "I cannot lie in your arms knowing my little baby is dead. I cannot enjoy life when she has been placed in her grave, and I cannot bear to think of going through this again. I don't ever want to have another child. And that is the truth."

"All right," he said and stood up and came over and kissed her gently. "Have a happy Christmas, Bess. Goodnight." He turned and left her, and she heard him clattering down the narrow stairway and heard him shout for his coat. He would have been gratified to see her suddenly stand, pick up a brass vase of pine branches and hurl it across the room.

Now Bess had something else to worry about. What was he doing? He didn't appear for supper the day after Christmas, and the next night he arrived early in the morning, taking the steps two at a time. He changed his clothes and was gone again. Since Jane had not been taken into his confidence, she didn't know what was going on, only that Bess was weeping less and was instead extremely irritable. At least she was more human, Jane thought.

New Year's Eve he never came home at all. In the morning, the next day, New Year's Day, he appeared at nine o'clock. He came into the private withdrawing room. Jane and Bess were having late breakfast, some cheese and bread and ale.

"I wish you a Happy Year," Bess said, her hands clenched around her napkin. Then she said, "And what have you been doing?"

He grinned. "Gambling." He took out his purse and poured a golden stream of money on the table. "Happy New Year to you both," he said. "I'm going to go to sleep now."

Bess had planned a fine New Year's Day dinner. She was going to serve it at one o'clock. But he was still asleep, and his body-servant wouldn't call him even on his wife's orders, because he himself had commanded that he not be disturbed. So at three he appeared, freshly washed and dressed, looking, Jane thought, excessively handsome.

He acted as though nothing were amiss. He was extremely genial, talkative and solicitous; he poured their wine, jumping up and going to the sideboard to refill their glasses. Bess simmered; she ate hardly at all. After the meal had been cleared away and the comfits and nuts had been put on the table and the fire freshened, Cavendish gave Jane her New Year's gift. Jane exclaimed with delight at the long heavy golden chain with jewels; and he put it over her head and gave her a kiss.

"I don't have any jewels for you, my love," he said to his wife, "I have something else."

50

Bess felt a kind of shiver. Was he teasing her? He acted as though he didn't care a bit about that locked door. Maybe he didn't. Men got bored with their wives. He was unfolding a large paper, and now he brought it to her, and laid it on her lap. She looked down at it, and read it and even then she couldn't encompass it, quite.

Then she said, "Is it real?"

He laughed. "Yes, it's real. All attested, signed and paid for."

"I'm going to faint," she said, but a little tiny smile appeared on her mouth, and her eyes lit with her old fire. "Oh, Cavendish!" She bit her lip.

"Christ's blood, don't cry," he said. "Or I'll throw it in the fire!" She folded it against her bare breast, for she was wearing a very low-cut gown.

"You might, I wouldn't trust you!"

"But what is it?" cried Jane, who couldn't stand the suspense.

Bess' eyes went to Cavendish, standing tall by the mantelpiece, cradling his wine cup in one hand, his eyes smiling at her.

Bess said, in a whisper, "It's a deed, Jane. It's the deed to Chatsworth." She pressed her lips together and widened her eyes to keep the tears from showing. "It's the thing I wanted most in the world. Chatsworth." She could see the land plainly, in her mind's eye: the rippling river, the rising hills, studded with outcroppings of rock.

Cavendish said, "We'll build a house there, Bess. A beautiful house. There. Framed by the rising hills, ringed by the river. A house," he said carefully, watching her, "a big house, for a whole big lot of children." His eyes were a glitter as Bess tried to meet them squarely.

"I don't want any more children, Cavendish," she said.

"Oh, Bess!" Jane cried.

"I've already told Cavendish that," Bess said, irritated.

Cavendish poured her a cup of wine, and handed it to her. "Drink deep," he said, "each to his own; Bess can drink to no children, I'll drink to my son."

He watched her; had she had enough wine? He didn't want her drunk. He took the empty cup from her fingers, set it down, and abruptly took her in his arms.

51

"Jane is here," she whispered, warningly.

"Jane won't mind," he said aloud, and Jane grew pink and stepped to the fire and gazed into it.

Cavendish bent his head and kissed her. Bess closed her eyes.

"I'm afraid," she whispered. "I'm afraid, Cavendish!"

"No, you're not," he murmured. "Not my Bess. Never afraid."

"Please, Cavendish."

"I won't do anything you don't want."

I love him so, she thought despairingly. *Damn him.* He lifted her, cradling her in his arms. *And what would Jane think?*

"You betrayed me," she muttered and caught the flash of a smile, and his face lighted with his quick grin. Satanic, Bess thought; he was looking down at her with pure amusement at her accusation, and he reached out and opened the door.

"Good-night, Jane," he said politely.

"Good-night," Jane said weakly. The door had closed on them. *They are both mad,* she thought. *Living with them is like seeing a miracle play. Only better.*

CHAPTER 6

AS Cavendish predicted to her, Bess' next child was a big healthy boy. She wanted to name him William, but Cavendish said no, they would name him for the late king, because that would be the safest. All the heirs to the unsteady throne had one thing in common: a father named Henry. So Henry Cavendish it was, and Bess was thrilled, delighted, ecstatically happy when the young woman she admired most in the world, the Princess Elizabeth, consented to be his godmother. She held Elizabeth's letter in her hand, shaking her head in admiration.

"How beautifully she writes. What an elegant hand."

Her children would write like that, she vowed it. All of them. And the ceremony of the christening was scarcely past, she thought, with her beautiful boy held in the arms of the young princess, the ceremony was scarcely over before she told Cavendish she was expecting another child. Before the fire, they toasted each other and their growing family, and Bess wore a huge new ring, a great emerald set with pearls, her New Year's gift. For Cavendish she had a special gift. A canvas of needlework, a great canvas of Bradgate, which she had drawn and worked herself. It would someday hang over the mantelpiece in the new Chatsworth.

If you had asked them, they would have disclaimed ambition. They would have said, why, no, we just want a big family and a great new home and stretching parks about it, because that is just what everyone wants nowadays. And if we move on the edge of exalted circles, why, we have arrived by our own efforts.

Intrigue and gossip and fear were rampant at court. But Cavendish and Bess made friends, seeking out those whose ambition was based on ability, and not on dreams of power. Men and women similar to themselves. One of those men was William Paulet, Marquis of Winchester, who held the office of Lord High Treasurer, and whose financial genius would serve England for twenty-two years. The other was a young man named William Cecil, brilliant, caustic, witty. He was one of the king's secretaries.

Bess learned to play cards. Cavendish taught her and she was an apt pupil. She loved it, loved the feel of the cards. She learned to play whist, and she learned to gamble, although she was never as gifted as Cavendish, who, she thought, had an uncanny instinct for the cards.

They played whist with the Herberts; he had been created Earl of Pembroke. His wife's sister had been Catherine Parr, the Dowager Queen, who had died in childbirth. And the shadow of bloody things to come had already cast itself forward on Catherine's husband, Thomas Seymour, brother of the protector. He had already been beheaded on Tower Green. Accused of treason. Treason.

53

It was an unsteady time. Cecil himself had spent two anxious months in the Tower and had been let off with a fine. The struggle between the ambitious Dudley and the Protector Somerset was growing more bitter. When Bess was seven months pregnant with her latest child, Cavendish came home late one October night to tell her that Dudley had won, and that Somerset was in the Tower on charges of treason and felony. On the same day their friend William Cecil, was knighted.

It was apparent now that the Earl of Warwick—the family name Dudley—was now all powerful at court. The young king created him Duke of Northumberland. The court gasped. The Tudors had never, never, given a dukedom to any but the royal family.

Money knows no politics. Cavendish and William Paulet continued in their posts; valuable servants of the state's economy, they continued while others changed. The little king was a very strict Protestant. The Puritanism of his beliefs covered the ladies up at court, and they were as bare of ornament as the stripped and austere churches. The Greys moved nearer to the Dudleys. Dudley, the new Duke of Northumberland, was all powerful in the realm. The Princess Elizabeth and the Lady Jane Grey dressed severely in gray; the Lady Jane, studious and brilliant, had a voluminous correspondence with the Protestant reformers in Germany and Holland; she and the little king, her cousin, would pore over them, together.

It was a bitter cold December, the winter of 1551. Early in the month Bess bore her fourth child. A boy! She was ecstatic with joy. For the child was big and lusty; from the very minute of his birth, rosy with health, eyes shining. He looked just like his father.

"This time," said Bess, firmly, "the baby's name will be William."

Cavendish agreed and picked William Paulet and William Herbert for godparents, a safe choice. He bought Bess new hangings for her room, so when her friends called after the baby's birth, she could receive them in new splendor.

She received in bed. It seemed to Cavendish the room was always crowded with females and men, filled with presents and fat purses of gold.

On the fifth day after Bess' confinement, Frances Grey appeared. She was now the Duchess of Suffolk, because the male line of the duchy was extinct. So the Lady Frances and her husband Henry Grey were permitted the honor of bearing her father's title. Lady Frances, the duchess of Suffolk for two days now, viewed Bess' second son with envy and sorrow, for she had lost her only son and had to be content with her three daughters. She brought a purse heavy with gold and asked to hold the baby. She was barely thirty-one, but had had no children since the birth of Mary ten years ago.

The New Year came. The court was rife with rumor. What was going to happen to the former Protector Somerset, the king's uncle on the Seymour side? "Northumberland's ambition will not permit him to leave Somerset alive," Cavendish said to Bess.

On January 22, 1552, Somerset was executed. It was an icy bleak day. If the citizens shivered in the cold, so did the denizens of high places shiver for their lives.

Bess kept her children inside the house; it was too cold for a little tot outside in the snowy streets. The river was frozen solid, and men crossed it afoot and on horseback. Cavendish wrestled with what he should do. As a member of the king's council he was being drawn near and nearer to Northumberland. The little king had fallen desperately ill of pox and measles.

It was obvious to everyone that Edward VI did not have long to live; it was a question of time only. Cavendish took Bess down to Chatsworth for the summer and fall. He was passionately fond of hunting and hawking, and for weeks he was in the saddle every day, and at night he and Bess pored over plans for their new house, picked the site, and that fall the foundations of Chatsworth were begun.

But when his holiday was over, Bess insisted that she return to the city with him. For old Chatsworth was hardly livable; it was old-fashioned and cold; the fires smoked and the drafts made most of the rooms untenable. So Bess packed up, and five days later, in October, found herself back in her beloved London.

The little king had recovered from his measles and pox;

the sickness had left him with a racking cough. The court celebrated Christmas and New Year as usual, only underneath the tensions were beginning to grow and the rifts began to appear, and suspicion kept every man's tongue quiet.

Cecil and Cavendish and Paulet moved in their same old circles, the council met daily, with Northumberland at its head; but as the first months of the new year began, the king's health was the primary subject of each man's thoughts. The successor to the throne, in Henry's will, was his first daughter, the Princess Mary. Up in the country, where she dwelt, her priests were with her, for she was as devout a Catholic as Edward was a Protestant.

The king was failing. There were no more festive social activities at court. The nobility and gentry lay quiet, like waiting shadows that winter. Instead of parties Cavendish's brother George stayed with them in London; he had finished his long book on the late Cardinal Wolsey, whose long reign of power he had shared so intimately. Before the fire, on a winter evening, he would tell long tales to Bess about the great cardinal, about the building of Hampton Court, about the great banquets, about the varied dealings with other countries and other courts and the early life of the Greys. The Greys had originally sponsored Wolsey, having discovered him at Oxford, teaching their son, the present holder of the title. "That is how William and I met the Greys," George explained.

In the long dark evenings, they would talk about those days, when Cromwell had first joined Wolsey's train, and how William Cavendish had been involved with Cromwell, and then Cromwell himself had fallen helpless before the wrath of his master Henry VIII.

"We have survived rough waters," Cavendish said, lifting his glass to toast his brother. "And there's another wave coming."

Under Cromwell's eye Cavendish had supervised the dissolution of the monasteries, the money flowing back through his big hands to his master, Henry VIII. For that work, those endless tallies, the long journeys, the ferreting out of hidden wealth, all to be poured at the feet of the king; for all those years of work Cavendish had received endless grants himself—of confiscated abbey lands, of rich pasture, of small outlying convents. If Edward died, Mary Tudor would become queen. She would hardly look with kindness upon the name of Cavendish, except that George had been the faithful friend and intimate of Cardinal Wolsey, who had suffered for her mother, her dearest mother, the Queen Catherine of Aragon.

"You may keep us safe yet," Cavendish said.

George answered, "It was you who testified in my behalf before the council eight years ago. I'll be glad to repay the favor."

Bess looked from one to the other. "Do you think," she asked, low, "do you think that Northumberland will try to stop the Princess Mary from inheriting the throne?"

It was George who answered her. "I think so. Yes. But he will not succeed. For the people know that the Princess Mary is the rightful and lawful heir to the throne."

Bess did the household accounts every morning. *May 2, 1553*, she wrote in her rather unformed hand. She gave a little sigh, thank heaven it was May.

May 2, wrote William Cecil, the king's secretary. The council was meeting, and Cavendish gratefully felt the sun across his shoulders, as he sat at the table between William Herbert and William Paulet. He had seen the king that morning and the chill was still with him. If the little king lived another month it would be amazing, Cavendish thought. His black brows drawn, he speculated on the month ahead; two days ago Bess had told him she would bear another child in late November. In his pocket a huge pearl ring awaited her. He could hear her voice this morning as she'd said, "And if I have another healthy son, I'll be the envy of every lady in London!" She was happy; he would have to keep her so.

At the head of the table, Dudley, duke of Northumberland, heartily hated for his arrogance and feared by his foes and friends, was ending the meeting. "And before I do so I—" he said, and a volpine smile played across his face. Cavendish thought, *What the devil is he up to?*

"I want to announce a betrothal, nay, two betrothals," Northumberland continued. Next to Cavendish, William

Herbert, earl of Pembroke, stirred and one of his knees hit Cavendish. He gave Cavendish a brief glance of apology but did not interrupt Northumberland. Northumberland glanced around the table again. "After all, it is the month of May," he said.

He's too damned genial, Cavendish thought. Here comes some deviltry. And when it did come, he wondered why he hadn't thought of it before.

"My son Guildford," Dudley said, "and the daughter of my dearest friend, Henry Grey, the duke of Suffolk, the beautiful Lady Jane Grey, will be wed in a double ceremony on Whitsunday—the other couple to be the Lady Catherine Grey and the son of the earl of Pembroke, Will Herbert."

He beamed around the table. Cavendish looked at him squarely without smiling. He pushed back his chair and stood up. "My congratulations," Cavendish said in his most clipped tones. It was an old, old gambit to marry one's son to one of the heirs to the throne. Northumberland should have known better, and so should Will Herbert.

Whitsunday was the last Sunday in May. The double marriage would take place on the beautiful spreading grounds of the Dudley mansion, by the riverside. Bess wanted to go.

"You don't know it, but you're far too ill with your latest pregnancy," Cavendish informed her.

"The little king is delighted that his cousin marry Guilford Dudley," Bess said. "I hear that everywhere, so it must be true."

"The little king is delighted," Cavendish agreed. "But the ghost of his father has got both of those men already beheaded."

Bess laughed.

"It's not a laughing matter," Cavendish said grimly. Then he patted her shoulder; he didn't want to worry her. What was the use of that? As a member of the council, which was meeting now every day at Greenwich, he was dressed and ready to leave her that morning.

"You're wearing a sword!" Bess said.

His black brows drew a bit. "Just a precaution, my love," he said and offered no further explanation.

But the explanation was very simple, indeed. The power

of Northumberland grew daily, his retainers and hirelings were everywhere; men who didn't agree with him were hardly safe; disliked as he was for his insufferable arrogance, he was justly feared. Now it was certain the young king was dying, it was merely a matter of weeks before Northumberland would try to seize the crown. He was already in a fairly impregnable position. His own men controlled the palaces and the Tower; he had a small fleet of six heavily armed ships, ready to sail at his bidding. He was undoubtedly the best soldier in England. There was no single man strong enough to stop him. Therefore, they must combine forces. And yet everything proceeded now as Northumberland wished it, all went as he had carefully planned.

The king was dying. He was racked with pain. Propped up in his big bed, his eyes fevered and intense, with the lords of the council crowded into his chamber, he spoke.

"You have been summoned to witness my will."

He was too weak to read it, so Northumberland read it, the king nodding his head. As his divine right to order the succession, Edward passed over his two half sisters, the Lady Mary and the Lady Elizabeth, they were both bastards.

Once again Cavendish saw plainly in his head the huge figure of Edward's father. Henry must be stomping the halls of heaven or hell asking for just an hour's return to earth to set things straight.

The men of the council looked quickly about at each other, eye meeting eye. So therefore, Edward's will continued, the crown will pass on to his cousin, the Lady Jane Grey, and her heirs male. The Lady Jane was legitimate, she was the holder of the Protestant faith, she was the proper successor to Edward's crown. And it was his royal right to leave it to her. Northumberland handed the will to Archbishop Cranmer, for him to sign it. Cranmer drew back.

"Sign it!" the king commanded.

Cavendish, next to Cranmer, saw that the archbishop's hands were trembling so that he almost dropped the parchment.

"Sign it!" Edward cried.

Cranmer laid it down on the table, Cecil handed him the

pen. Cavendish looked down at his thin fingers, shaking, as he scratched his name, in witness to his king's last will and testament.

Edward sank back onto his pillows. The council filed slowly from the room. Northumberland watched them go: All of them had been witness to their king's will! All of them were as guilty as he!

Cavendish and Paulet rode away together, and by the riverbank they stopped for a few moments. They talked very briefly. When Cavendish put spurs to his horse, he inclined his head toward a boat in midriver.

"We're being observed, my friend," he said. "It will be reported back to Northumberland that you and I spoke in private here." He grinned his satanic grin, and Paulet's heavy-lidded eyes opened wider than usual and then fell back into his peering gaze.

Cavendish rode slowly home; it was hot; it was July fourth. Before he had left the palace of Greenwich, where the court lay and where the council met, Northumberland had sent off messengers to the king's two sisters, to summon them to court, where he would have his hands on them. Cavendish was not worried about Elizabeth; canny, cautious, the princess would stay where she was. But what about her sister Mary, the next in line to the throne?

He greeted Bess, taking her in his arms, looking down at the pale cheek. "Are you sick, my love?" he asked, suddenly anxious.

"I must be bearing another son," she said, "because he is behaving damnably already, Cavendish. I feel queasy and faint with this heat."

He squeezed her hard. "For God's sake, take care of yourself." He was about to say he had enough to worry about already, but he forbore. There was no use worrying her, anyway it was nothing she could solve; only he could solve it, how to keep his family safe and free and to realize his ever-present dream of the future, for which he had worked so hard all his life. Chatsworth, rising tall and beautiful, a big family, an earldom, all those things loomed ahead, and he was not going to let Northumberland take them away from him, from Bess, or from his children.

60

July seventh dawned just as hot; Cavendish was up at five, and at five thirty a messenger arrived with a notice that the council would be meeting that morning, at Syon House, instead of Greenwich. Syon House, Northumberland's mansion on the river. Cavendish said good-bye to Bess. He said, "The king must have died last night. But 'tis evident they are trying to keep it secret from the people for a few days."

He kissed her good-bye; but his manner upset her and she spent the whole day wondering and fretful.

When Cavendish got to Syon House, there was a barge coming up the silvery river. Cavendish walked to the grassy landing. He could make out Henry Grey, his old friend, and Lady Frances' auburn head and plump figure, and their oldest daughter, the Lady Jane Grey. He knew the Lady Jane had been at Chelsea; sometime during the night she had been summoned, and now she was arriving, setting her feet on the landing, dressed finely, her mother was bearing her train. *God's death,* thought Cavendish, *what are they doing to her? And to themselves? I could never, never have foreseen this, even as much as a year ago! Never! My old friends, embarked on destruction.*

His face was set as he bowed. Then they passed by him.

Cavendish joined the council. They waited there, all of them, for Jane, and when she came, Northumberland told her again that she was the queen. The lords of the council all knelt, Cavendish included. According to her cousin's will, she was their queen.

There isn't much time, Cavendish thought. *Not much time.* Northumberland explained that tomorrow Jane would go by royal barge to the Tower, and there be formally installed as the reigning monarch, and be presented with the crown and the trappings of royalty, including the crown jewels. So it was Cavendish and Paulet's duty, as lord treasurer and king's treasurer respectively, to present them to Jane. And the council would meet the following day in the Tower.

Cavendish and Paulet rode off, before others. At the gates of Syon, Northumberland's son, Robert Dudley, at the head of about three hundred horses, was ready to ride. Cavendish took the bridle of Robert Dudley's horse. "Where are you going, young sir?" he asked genially.

61

"To fetch the Lady Mary," Robert Dudley answered. "We've just had word she's arrived at Hoddesdon on her way to London."

When Cavendish arrived at the Tower, men were slaving and sweating and swearing as they hoisted two great guns into position. This was hardly a usual action.

Neither was Cavendish's action. Before he handed the huge casket containing Henry VIII's jewels to Paulet, to be put under guard in the state chamber, he took out a thumb ring of the former king, and put it in his purse. He and Paulet had time for a word alone.

"I'm going to warn the Lady Mary," Cavendish said.

Paulet nodded.

Cavendish made his way through the city to Goldsmith's row. He had discarded the idea of sending one of his own servants to Mary. It was too dangerous. Northumberland probably had men watching. Instead Cavendish entered his favorite shop, where he had dealt for many years. Within the shop the owner's son came to greet him.

"My wife is going to present me with another child," Cavendish said, "and so I've come for a pretty bauble."

It was done very swift and easy, almost under the eyes of an apprentice. "Young Jack," Cavendish said, "let's see how much money I have." He spilled out the contents of his purse, covering the ring with his hand. "Now," he said, "I might not have enough gold. Better send for your father."

Young Jack waved his hand, the apprentice disappeared, and although he was gone only a few seconds, it was time enough for Cavendish to place the heavy huge ring in young Jack's hand. "Ride to Hoddesdon today, as fast as you can, boy, and warn the Princess Mary to turn around and flee north. Her life is in danger. Show her this ring. She will know from whom it must come. She should recognize it."

Jack Guildford wasted no words. He slipped the ring into a small leather pouch which he took from behind the counter. Hs eyes gleamed and his pleasant smile never changed.

"I'll be delighted, Sir William," he was saying, as his

father came into the shop. "Just delighted. Anything I can do to serve you, I do willingly."

"You're a good lad," said Cavendish warmly. "A good lad. You should be very proud of him, Master Guildford."

Outside in the street, a servant of Northumberland who had followed Cavendish waited patiently for him to come out. When Cavendish emerged, he doggedly followed him home. Just after both men had left the street, young Jack Guildford led his horse out of the stable doors behind the shop.

Cavendish sat on his stool, within the draped bath, his feet in a big basin of water, while his servant washed him. He heard Bess' footstep, and she came into the room; he couldn't see her because of the screens and drapes of white linen. She spoke to his body servant, "Why are you packing?"

Cavendish said, "Because tomorrow the council must stay in the Tower; he is packing linen, and the things I will need."

His mind was on young Jack Guildford, putting hot dusty miles behind him on his way to Hoddesdon. He should reach there before dark, and before Robert Dudley, with his troop of three hundred horses. Poor little Lady Mary. A little stubborn woman, whom Northumberland could clap into prison, her only crime that she was the firstborn daughter of Henry VIII and a papist. Yet she was their rightful queen. Even if Northumberland succeeded in having Jane crowned, at least the poor little Lady Mary wouldn't pay with her life—if she could get away.

Cavendish called to Bess. "I laid something on my chest for you to see. Be careful of it, the ink is still damp."

Bess stood beside his big bed and picked up the handbill by the edge. She uttered a gasp and then a cry. The handbill said that both the late king's sisters were bastards, and one of them a papist, and that the Lady Jane Grey was their queen. Bess looked at it as though it were not real.

"I didn't think this could happen anymore," she said. "To go back to the days of lawlessness, to go back to fighting and civil war, to go back to—" Cavendish was tired of being patted dry, and he took the towel, wound it around his middle, and stepped out of the bath. Bess looked white and shaken, and he knew she was afraid. Everyone was afraid of Northumberland, and everyone knew he was the power behind the throne.

"There's nothing to fret your head about," he said.

"Don't do anything, Cavendish," she said earnestly. "Don't do anything to cross Northumberland! He'll have you killed!"

At five o'clock the following morning, when the first streaks of color were in the skies, Jack Guildford made his leisurely way up toward the Cavendish house, and was stopped by two men. They asked him why he was going to that house so early in the morning.

Jack Guildford explained that Sir William had ordered a jewel for his wife to be delivered at that hour, because he was himself leaving very early, for his council meeting.

The two men searched Jack Guildford quickly and efficiently. He bore no recent evidence of his hard ride, he was clean and neat, and he carried nothing but an obviously new gold chain, with a green jeweled heart swinging from its end. They let him go.

Cavendish was being shaved, and Jack was ushered into his room. Cavendish's face lighted into a wide, relieved smile; he reached his big hand from under the towel around his shoulders and shook the boy's hand and thanked him heartily for delivering the jewel so early in the morning.

Cavendish left the house after breakfast; by now the sun was up and the city was beginning to stir. Before Cavendish reached the Tower, the yeomen of the guard were calling out at each market place and square and before the churches that Queen Jane was their new queen—God save Queen Jane! The people stared at the heralds and were silent. After each pronouncement by the heralds, the men and women sullenly turned away, and the guards cheered alone in unnatural voices.

The morning was full of curious drama within the Tower,

within the walls where royalty stayed on state occasions and where the council met. Jane sat on a thronelike chair; her long green eyes both excited and fearful. Paulet himself bore her the casket of the jewels of Henry VIII. Her delicate hands lifted the trinkets, glittering, expensive. Who would notice there was a jewel missing, unless one read the inventory? Cavendish nonetheless felt his heart give a big thump when she closed the large casket. Now the crown itself was presented. It was placed on her head, to see if it fitted well enough. Cavendish saw plain the expression of dismay and fear as she realized she was wearing the crown itself. Then Paulet, under Northumberland's eye, presented another crown, the crown matrimonial for her husband, Northumberland's son.

Jane Grey then behaved like the Tudor she was. "There will be no crown matrimonial for my husband," she announced. "I shall create him a duke." Her mother-in-law cried out as in pain, and Northumberland's face grew red with anger.

That affected Jane not at all. She looked at them down her patrician nose.

It's a family fight, Cavendish thought. *Everyone's furiously angry.* It would have been comical, if it hadn't been tragic. Meanwhile, outside the great doors, an army of servants were waiting to serve the council its dinner, and Cavendish, who had been up so early, was ravenous. While everyone waited, Jane sat immovable on her throne. Cavendish thought, *I've known her well since she was an infant. This whole scene is incredible!* Jane's mother-in-law was screaming with passion—she adored her sons—and this chit was defying her. Jane grew more pale, and determined. Cavendish bit his lip hard to keep from smiling.

"My dear son," Jane's mother-in-law began again, when there was an imperious knocking on the doors that even Northumberland couldn't ignore, and now there burst into the room quite unceremoniously, a harried messenger. He bowed and offered a letter.

Northumberland ripped open the single sheet, stamped and sealed with the insignia of the king's oldest sister, Mary Tudor. Northumberland stared at the few lines and threw down the letter on the table in front of the council members, who all leaned forward to try and read it sideways, or upside down, whichever way they were sitting.

Northumberland snorted, "The Lady Mary claims her rights!"

At this Jane's mother burst into tears. In frustration over arguing with Jane, the girl's mother-in-law also burst out in loud sobs. The two women cried, Jane looked stony—and frightened. Northumberland was thinking that at any minute his son Robert Dudley should be riding into London with the little Lady Mary as his prisoner. But Cavendish knew that by now Mary should be safely thirty miles farther north, and riding hard, perhaps disguised, as indeed she was.

Northumberland, with little ceremony, ordered his wife and the mother of his son's wife out of the room, and Jane chose to leave also. The council sat down to its long-deferred dinner.

It was the middle of the afternoon before they were finished, and since Northumberland wanted to go and argue again with Queen Jane about a crown matrimonial for his son, he dismissed the council, and Cavendish was escorted to his room; it was set high, with a drop below to the stones of the Tower court. There was no way out.

He sought out Paulet on the excuse he had left an account book with the lord treasurer. A guard took him to Paulet's narrow chamber. Cavendish came in, closed the door, and prowled over to the window. Narrow as it was, he leaned out.

"I could lower you down far enough for you to drop onto the grass," he said conversationally.

Paulet came over beside him and stuck his head out. He scowled a bit. "My legs aren't what they used to be, Cavendish," he said.

Cavendish grinned. "As you say, quite often, we two are sprung of the willow instead of the oak."

Paulet laughed.

"We're prisoners here, you know," Cavendish went on.

"Aye," agreed the lord treasurer. "And when the time comes to get out, you've found a way."

66

The next day brought the news Cavendish was waiting for—the news that Mary had ridden north to the great castle of Framlingham and that she was safely there and that from all over the country men were flocking to her standards. "A full-fledged revolt," Cavendish said to Will Herbert, in the privy; it was difficult for the members of the council to speak together privately; they seized any opportunity.

But the revolt was not a secret; Northumberland's spies kept him and the council well informed. It was obvious that something would have to be done to stop Mary and to take her prisoner.

Solemnly the council sat, to take action. The windows were open, the hot, hot July sun burned down. Queen Jane, at the head of the table, looked sick and faint.

Northumberland said that Henry Grey should lead a quickly mustered army out of London, north, to find and capture Mary.

Jane burst out, "No!" With that she suddenly lost control of herself and began to sob. Her father quickly went to her, putting his arms around her, and she spoke through tears and against his shoulder.

"Do not take my father from me! Do not take him away!"

Cavendish said, "My lord," and he spoke directly to Northumberland, "it is my feeling that you should go yourself."

Northumberland gave an involuntary start.

"You are our best soldier," Cavendish said.

"Aye," said Paulet. "I concur!"

"I, too," cried the earl of Pembroke, as Cavendish nudged his foot under the table.

It was imperative to get Northumberland out of London. *While the cat's away.* . . . The refrain kept going through Cavendish's head. He didn't underestimate Northumberland; it was going through the duke's head too, with frightening monotony. *While the cat's away* . . . Northumberland's eyes went around the table, slowly, and he didn't like what he was thinking.

They were adamant that he should go—all their voices were raised to tell him so, in flattering tones they extolled his great reputation as a soldier, reminding him of the bloody repression in Norfolk a few years back.

"Well," he said, "since you are resolved to send me, I and mine will go, not doubting of your fidelity to the Queen's Majesty, whom I leave in your custody."

Jane gulped and swallowed; Cavendish's dark eyes were on her unflinchingly. Northumberland went on and on about the council's fidelity.

Cavendish was annoyed. He said in his clipped tones, "Oh, come, now, my lord. Which of us can wipe his hands clean?"

Northumberland grated, "I pray God it be so."

"Let us go in to dinner," Cavendish said. Once again it was the dinner hour, and once again he was hungry and anxious to have no more talk. He rose and the council slowly filed from the room.

When Northumberland rode out of the Tower with his men, Cavendish watched from the top of the leads. The crowds were silent. There were no "Godspeeds" from the watching people.

"It cannot last much longer," he thought.

Northumberland rode north, proclaiming he was going to take the Lady Mary. He left the men of the council well guarded and in virtual prison. The next day Cavendish lowered Paulet out the window of his room, and while he crouched against the wall, Cavendish ran down the steps and engaged the guard in conversation while Paulet crept out.

When it was discovered that the canny old lord treasurer was missing, there was a great cry and hullaballoo. It was seven in the evening and still broad daylight, and suddenly all the gates clanged shut and the Tower was locked and the huge keys taken up to Queen Jane. Then a body of soldiers clattered out of the guardhouse to find Paulet.

But he had a good start, and he accomplished what he wished; he had gotten clean away with the contents of the privy purse.

Cavendish thought, *He who holds the purse strings. . . .* He was waiting in one of the lower rooms, with Sir Edmund

Peckham, keeper of the king's privy purse. The plan was very simple. In the excitement, when the guards reappeared with Paulet, as indeed they would, Sir Edmund was to slip out, retrieve the money from Paulet's house, where he had taken it, and ride north to Mary with it.

At midnight with a few torches the wily lord treasurer appeared in a company of soldiers; they were returning the treasurer to safekeeping. Cavendish and Peckham rushed to the gates, and in all the comings and goings Peckham slipped safely out into the darkness, making his way on foot to Paulet's house.

Will Herbert was becoming increasingly restive. The lords of the council could easily see all their heads rolling on Tower Green if Mary appeared at the head of her troops. It was not difficult to assess the feeling of the country. They wanted their rightful queen.

On the eighteenth of July, at the morning meeting, after a night of whispered conferences, Cavendish rapped on the table. There was silence, and he spoke. The faintest smile hovered over his mobile mouth. For he was not of the oak but of the willow.

"My lords," he said softly, "as one of the lesser members of the council, I propose we offer a reward for the duke of Northumberland, one thousand pounds to any noble, five hundred pounds to any knight, and one hundred pounds to any yeoman, who can bring the said duke to justice. And after that I propose we, as a body, repair to my lord of Pembroke's house to continue our meeting."

In the silence he continued: "None of us has consented heartily to Edward's will. And we are restrained here, virtual prisoners. We should leave together, en masse, and go at once to my lord of Pembroke's house, to Baynard's castle!"

It was all done then quickly and legally. Northumberland was proclaimed a traitor. The lords and their attendants assembled; the guards melted away, leaving a sinking ship. In terror and fear Henry Grey himself went to Jane and tore the royal trappings from her chambers.

From Baynard's castle the council proclaimed Mary as their queen. Between five and six in the evening, they rode out of Baynard's castle. They were making for the cross.

At St. Paul's the crowds now filled the streets to see what was happening. Garter king at arms began to read to the massed people, "And so we proclaim Queen Mary—"

He got no further. At least if he did no one heard him. "God save Queen Mary!"

Cavendish listened to the mighty roar of approval. Caps sailed through the air. The council was supposed to go on to St. Paul's. The choir was already there. When they arrived there, pushing through crowds gone mad, the *Te Deum* was already being sung in great waves of voices and organs; the church bells were pealing, and soon every bell in London was pealing out the news.

The bells—first in the distance and then nearer and nearer as each church in the city answered. Bess heard them. Like everyone else she rushed into the street. The city was going mad, she thought, mad with joy! People were seizing each other and dancing around in the streets. Over their heads windows were flung open; coins were raining down onto the streets; the children screamed with excitement and raced in all directions.

"Bring out the tables," Bess screamed; the servants were all outside with her, her staid dresser was jigging about in the arms of a footman. Bess ran back into the house, two of the men after her, and they lugged out a trestle table and wine and cups.

Then they brought food and more wine, and because it was beginning to get dark, they brought out faggots and wood from the kitchens and lighted bonfires; all along the streets the bonfires burned and everyone who had any musical instruments brought them out too, so that by the time Cavendish finally pushed his way home, he could see ahead of him the same scene he had seen throughout the whole of London. Never in his life had he seen the city so, and never again would he see it, he thought.

In front of his house, the fire burned bright, and in its light he saw Bess dancing, skirts flying, and everyone was shouting and laughing. Finally Bess saw him. And then with the last breath in her lungs, she stopped, pointed at him.

"Cavendish!" she shouted. "Cavendish! Isn't it wonderful? Queen Mary!"

CHAPTER 7

THE first of August dawned very hot, and close. About four o'clock a figure slipped into Bess' small withdrawing room next to her own bedroom, threw off her veil, and sank into the nearest chair.

"Oh, my lady," Bess cried. "Your Grace!"

The Lady Frances, duchess of Suffolk, had done a great deal for Bess. From the moment of Bess' wedding, to guiding her through the intricacies of the court of Edward VI, she had helped Bess. Lady Frances described to Bess the dramatic scene that saved Jane Grey's life.

"I went on my knees," Lady Frances said. "And with my hands clasped, I prayed Her Majesty for the life of my little girl! And my husband!"

"What did she say?"

"She said, and I wept as she spoke, she said that she was convinced that my little Jane was the dupe of Northumberland and not his accomplice. And she said she would spare her and her husband and my husband!"

"God bless Her Majesty," Bess murmured. She made the sign of the cross against her breast. The Lady Frances was a bit annoyed at that gesture. She and her family were ardent Protestants. Evidently people like Bess Cavendish could change religion at the wave of a hand. But that was the middle class for you, Lady Frances thought. Survival came first; ideals were the province of the nobility, the true old nobility.

"My dear friend," Bess said, "I thank God for the wisdom and clemency of your dearest cousin, the Queen's Majesty."

Bess was indeed grateful to Mary Tudor. For in this the beginning of her reign, she was trying hard to heal the wounds, not make fresh ones. Cavendish and Cecil and William Paulet all continued on in their posts. Life at court opened up for Bess again in all its dazzling splendor and

71

excitement. It was true that she and Cavendish moved on its fringe; they moved as the servants of the state and its monarch and not as her intimates; they attended functions, but not small parties. There was a difference. Ambitious, Bess saw herself hurdling this final hurdle, so that the queen might lean close to her, and borrow her hand-kerchief, for instance!

Bess' eyes glittered. Cavendish was only slightly amused by her plans. But he didn't say much; when he wasn't preoc-cupied with his duties, he spent a good deal of time with the children. On August 22, Northumberland was beheaded for his presumption. The Lady Jane Grey stayed in ward in the Tower, for after all she had dared to call herself a queen. Her husband Guildford Dudley stayed prisoner also, and young Robert Dudley, but Henry Grey was freed.

The Lady Frances could welcome her husband back home again. She had already her daughter Catherine. Will Herbert, her father-in-law, had had her marriage to his son annulled on the grounds it had not been consummated. "Will Herbert breathes easier, now," Cavendish said cyni-cally. Will had been on the edge of the plot and Mary the Queen had forgiven him. But Will Herbert had decided that Catherine Grey was an unsafe wife for his young son and he had sent her back home.

Queen Catherine of Aragon, Henry VIII's first wife, had been a devout Catholic. So was her daughter Mary. Not only did the new queen restore the Catholic faith to Eng-land, but she betrothed herself to the king of Spain, the arch enemy of England; his ambassadors and representa-tives thronged the court, and poured advice into Mary's ears, and generally intruded themselves into English affairs.

Politically it was dangerous, and Cavendish worried, fretted that even some of his most hard-headed friends were gathering together, whispering; some didn't like the religion that had been forced upon them, most hated the Spaniards, and there were rumblings of rebellion. The ardent Protestants in England had another candidate for the throne, the young Princess Elizabeth, good Protestant that she was.

Cavendish himself steered very, very clear of all entanglements. So too did the Princess Elizabeth, who had learned caution and patience at an early age. Cavendish hoped devoutly the hotheads would not involve the princess; he would hate to see that red head entering the Tower by the traitor's gate.

"There is nothing we can do but wait," Cavendish told Bess. "It is easy to judge Mary harshly," Cavendish said, "but truly no woman, no child suffered more than she."

But he was not at all sure that the new reign would prosper; he looked across at Bess, blooming with her latest child. Lord, she was beautiful! How long would he be able to keep her with him, in London! He said, "Come, I'll take you out to dinner."

Bess had a little carriage, hung and fringed in red, with the Cavendish stags on each corner. Through the crowded filthy streets they picked their way; the flocks of birds, almost underneath the wheels, interrupted from their pecking, wheeled away from them angrily. Older people shook their heads. "They ride, whose parents were content to walk," they said in disapproval. It was difficult to make one's way through the narrow streets. Bess wanted to eat in Mr. Gillan's cellar and have oysters. She ate from the top of a hogshead; the candles flickered; she stuffed oysters and onion relish into her mouth, washing it down with red claret. The room was crowded with men. "Am I the only female here?" she asked Cavendish, her mouth full.

"It doesn't matter," he said. "You'll set a style."

The cellar was whitewashed and clean; it was cozy, in the candlelight, and it rumbled with men's laughter and talk. Bess was supremely happy. She had just had a brilliant thought. She was going to ask the queen herself to be godmother to her latest child.

Bess' third son was born November 28, on a cold starry night. And the queen did indeed stand as godmother. He was named Charles; looking back Bess thought he had the glitter of fun and laughter in his eyes from the moment of his birth. Everyone called to see her, gifts and money piled up on her big bed. Cavendish laughed to see her when he came home at night, her hair tumbled, her eyes alight, wearing a rich new bedgown, her hands blazing with the rings he gave her. Proud as a peacock she was as she leaned back against the pillows, sipping her wine.

"Not too much dragon's blood," he said, taking the cup from her hand.

"I have three sons, Cavendish, and one beautiful daughter!"

She smiled at him, and he took her in his arms and kissed her.

"No, you don't," she said, wriggling away from him. "Not until New Year's, at least!"

At Christmastime he took her to court. The huge room, ceilinged in gold colors, painted with all kinds of brilliant colored animals and flowers, was a sea of beautiful gowns, flashing jewels and everywhere men in the green and white of the Tudor livery. The music played, the dancers leaped and cavorted, and wines were heady. On New Year's day Cavendish gave her a heavy gold chain with a pearl cross. He noted the gift in his pocket book on the last day of the year. He added a last note. "But I am not sanguine," he wrote on December 31, 1553, "about the New Year."

And it happened sooner than he expected. In January, the first full-fledged rebellion, the first plot to oust Queen Mary and her Spaniards and the old religion burst into bloody flower. By February 12, little Lady Jane Grey and her husband had lost their heads on Tower Green, followed by Henry Grey, who had died for his religion. Northumberland had already died, and Wyatt would die; the Princess Elizabeth was in the Tower, suspect. They said that when she entered and stepped onto the slimy stones at Traitor's Gate, she slipped on the stones, wetted by each tide. They said her red head was bent, and that she had knelt there a moment, to gather courage. Then she had stood and gone forward, the same way her mother had entered. The people feared for their young princess. The city was quiet, sullen, tense.

"Mary Tudor," Cavendish said, "is the most stubborn of all the Tudors, including her father. As soon as the roads are passable, I'm going to send you and the children home to Chatsworth."

CHAPTER 8

THE foundations of Chatsworth had been laid for two years and the walls were slowly rising. Meantime Bess and her family lived in the old manor house, so familiar to Bess because it had been the dwelling place of her mother and her second husband. And Bess returned to Derbyshire in triumph!

Didn't she have money and a handsome husband and four healthy bright handsome children? And wasn't she already expecting another child? And didn't she have her husband often home with her?

Foreigners were surprised that most English gentlemen couldn't wait to shake the dust of the city from their heels and retreat to their country homes. Cavendish was no different. He loved to be ahorse, he loved the hunt and his precious falcons; he was most happy when he was standing watching the workmen at Chatsworth, writing to different men in the county whose new houses he had seen, asking about a particular plasterer whose work he admired, stuffing himself full of fresh fish and then sitting by the fire in the evenings while he pored over the plans of Chatsworth and while Bess stitched quickly and neatly on her newest canvas. And the children! He beamed with pride on his children. He had always wanted a big thriving family. Now he possessed it, and Bess was ripe with another. He had already decided on Eton for his boys.

"They will be the first of a long line," he predicted. And he was right. There was a great deal of social life in the county and new buildings. There was Vernon Hall, in all its new magnificence, and Sir John Thynne was refashioning the old priory of the Black Canons, and their friend John Revell was building onto Ogston Hall. Their owners couldn't wait to give parties, hunts, balls, christenings.

On March 31, 1555 Bess had another daughter, and

Cavendish insisted she be named Elizabeth. Bess chose for her godmother the young Lady Catherine Grey, because she felt she owed the Greys so much. Her poor widowed friend Lady Frances and her daughter Catherine Grey were the only family left. It was so sad, Bess thought. She welcomed them to Chatsworth for the christening, but it was the last contact she had with the court for four years. That winter Cavendish forbid her traveling to London, for she was already again big with a new baby. Happily Bess planned an enormous and gala christening; the county would come from miles around; the godmother would be her own mother, the baby's grandmother, and the godfather their dear friend Sir George Vernon of Haddon Hall. And Bess, always with an eye to propriety and politics thoughtfully named her newest daughter Mary, after the queen.

She was radiantly happy. Chatsworth was rising, stone by stone. Her children never had a moment's illness; they grew strong and tall and quick of wit and body. There were six, but there seemed a dozen when one entered the old sprawling manor. There was so much for the lady of the manor to do that Bess was eternally busy, and when her favorite sister Jane's husband died, nothing would do but that Jane must come too, and bring her two children. The draughty old house, with its leaky chimneys and old-fashioned rooms was cold in winter, wet in summer, and full of laughter.

Mary was born the March following the birth of Elizabeth, only a year separated the two girls. By August the four towers of Chatsworth were begun—there were to be four. By August Bess, who had had her husband home for two months now said to him, "God's blood, Cavendish, you've done it again. I think I'm going to have another baby next March. I'll be damned if I think you shouldn't stay in London longer."

That winter the household accounts, which Bess carefully kept, showed that they ate well. Turbot, whiting flounders, sole and once in a while a barrel of oysters. A loin of pork cost one shilling, four pence, and a quarter of mutton two shillings. Six larks for lark pudding, cost four pence. They ate lots of butter, cream and fresh eggs, ginger, mace, cinnamon and cloves; from the garden came mint, thyme,

76

and pennyroyal; spinach, peas, beans, artichokes and cowcumbers. The children ate oatmeal, and their spice cakes were stuffed with raisins and currents. Bess drank malmsey and Rhine wine. And in the winter, when the beef had been killed off, they ate venison, for the red deer roamed Chatsworth park. The manor brewed its own beer and ale. When Cavendish came for Christmas, he brought eighteen yards of green satin to line Bess' litter and a six-yard long tablecloth woven with the story of Abraham. He also brought down a new goshawk, which he had bought at Smithfield.

In March, once again, the manor made ready for Bess' lying in. The new baby was a girl.

From the very moment of birth she was frail, and fretful. Bess named her Lucrece, from the story of Rome that Cavendish had read to her; he often read to her and the children in the winter evenings.

It was a cold and bitter March. The winds howled. The little Lucrece had her oldest sister Frances, who was nine and her aunt Jane Kniveton stand as godparents, and stout John Revell of Ogston Hall nearby as godfather.

Lucrece lived only a week. Bess, who always had difficulty believing anything could go wrong for her, was stunned with grief. Jane worried, remembered vividly the time eight years ago when little Temperance had died. But when Bess looked up into Cavendish's face and saw the bright tears standing in his eyes, she suddenly threw her arms around him and hugged him. *She has grown up, Jane thought. It is she who will comfort him this time.*

Cavendish went back to London two weeks later and then returned the end of June. Stone by stone, Chatsworth was growing; though it was patterned after Bradgate, it was built of Derbyshire stone instead of brick, and Bess and Cavendish were particularly fascinated by the beginning of a separate smaller building in the garden, a bower, Bess called it. August 20 was their tenth wedding anniversary, and the gardens and lawns flowered with trestle tables and sagged with food, and the county came for miles around. On September fifteenth, Cavendish made ready to go back to London.

The journey took four days and three nights, but Cavendish, traveling without womenfolk, might easily have made it in less time. Bess looked up at him astride the big horse. He looked so handsome!

"Keep out of trouble, sir, I warn you!"

She waved good-bye as the small troop of men rode down the graveled drive. Bess stood and waved, then finally turned to look over at the rising walls of Chatsworth.

It rises in noble beauty, she thought proudly; she had a child at each side. Holding hands, together they walked back to the old manor house.

Cavendish sent messages and letters once a week. Therefore, it was a surprise to see a weary horse and rider in the middle of the week. Bess had no premonition of disaster, only curiosity spurred her forward across the hall to see who had come and why. When the messenger blurted out that Sir William was deathly ill, she at first couldn't believe it; then the whole hall swerved around her, she grasped at the stair rail, her dark eyes wide with terror.

Jane helped her plan, quickly, for the trip to London. "I cannot take the baby," Bess said.

"Of course not," Jane said.

"I can take little Bess," she sobbed. She was only two and a half, and would miss her mother more than little Mary, who would have her Aunt Jane and her nurse. "And I'll take Henry," Bess said, throwing clothes in a heap on the bed while Jane methodically packed them. Henry was the oldest boy, he was almost seven.

When Bess set forth the next morning, Jane didn't see how it had been done. Bess and the two children were in the litter; mounted men rode ahead; there were two footmen in livery who would run ahead as they approached each town, to make sure of good lodging and to make sure the inn's rooms were ready to receive the weary dust-laden travelers. Bess crossed the Trent the first day, by ferry at Shardlee. Jolting along in the litter with the two children and two servants, she thought they would never reach Northampton that second day. It was drizzling; she crept into bed that night and cried herself to sleep.

The next night they reached St. Albans, where Bess bought shoes for the running footmen and a pair for little

Bess. The innkeeper warned her of the dangers of approaching London.

"God's death," raged Bess. "You mean they'd set upon a woman and her two children?"

"Aye, my lady," he said, nodding solemnly.

"Then I'll hire four stout armed rogues myself and hope we meet with the cowards!" cried Bess. She paid ten shillings for her four rogues, and riding as hard as they could with the litter, they reached London just before nightfall. Picking up her skirts in both hands, Bess ran up the long flight of stairs, down the hallway, and then came to a dead stop before the heavy closed doors of Cavendish's room. Panic struck her. Her hand reached out to knock and fell back.

"Oh, lord, oh, lord," she prayed silently. "Help him, help me, let me make him well." Timidly she raised her hand again and knocked on the oaken door.

When she saw him, propped up on pillows in his big bed, her first feeling was one of relief. He didn't look so sick! She flung herself at the side of the bed, fell on her knees and took his hand, his big strong brown hand, and cried, "Oh, Cavendish, Cavendish, I was terrified!"

Her red head was bent over his hand, he could feel her tears dripping onto it, and he smiled his quick smile and disengaged his fingers from her and patted her on the shoulder. "My poor little Bess," he said, low. She climbed up on the big bed, her eyes devouring his face. He looked almost the same. If he were paler, the pallor was hid by the close-cropped dark beard; but there were shadows under his eyes and he looked thin.

"You haven't been eating enough, my dearest," she said, lovingly holding his hand to her cheek.

He smiled, but the smile didn't touch his eyes. He said, "Go get washed, sweetheart, and changed, I know you're weary, weary. Then bring the children in, if any of them are with you."

The way he said it struck her dumb with fear. Afraid to ask him any questions, she stumbled out of the room, trying to say with gusto, "As soon as I wash, I'll be back!"

Cavendish lay back among the pillows. With his customary deliberate planning, his mind went evenly over the events of the past two weeks; he resolved to say nothing to Bess tonight, but to wait until she had recovered from the rigors of her long journey, undertaken with heart tense and fearful.

The next morning Cavendish was still asleep when Bess rose. Even with her fatigue, it had been hard to woo sleep, and it had come too late. Lying sleepless almost till morning, she had planned her campaign and her menu. What he needed was food and care! All night visions of oysters and delicate sole, calves' foot jelly and the lightest of Rhine wine, sparrows pudding and capons and squab—all night she listed all the delicacies she would have bought and fixed for him, aye, if she had to spoon feed him herself! For four days Cavendish let her play this game. He watched her as a father watches the lovable antics of a child. But the sixth evening, after supper, when the October day had drawn to a close and candles were burning on the tall candelabra, and the fire was low and cozy, Cavendish broke the bubble.

"I am going to die, Bess," he said. "And therefore there is much I want to instruct you about, my dearest wife. Many, many matters. So I have here to hand pen and ink; I would wish you to sit at my table and listen well, and write when you need to."

Bess sucked in her breath as though she couldn't get enough air into her lungs. Her dark eyes were enormous, pleading; she held out her hands to him, for she had been sitting on a stool by the fire.

"My heart's given out, Bess," he said. "I've overused it, I guess. I've always lived hard, Bess, and now it's like a coiled snake inside my chest, Bess. The first day, my dear, I had six such attacks."

"Cavendish," she quavered.

"Don't weep, darling, please. Emotion is difficult for me. You will be brave, I know you will."

Is he really saying this, she thought wildly? Was this a nightmare? Could it possibly be true?

"First," said Cavendish, summoning a smile, "one of my rascally clerks has absconded with a thousand pounds of the queen's money. Do not pay it back yourself; let the lawyers catch him."

80

"Cavendish," she whispered.

"Don't talk, my love, just listen. You will be well off, probably better off without me. You wouldn't want me to live on this way, would you, Bess? My oldest daughter, Dorothy Cavendish, by my first marriage, she came to me three weeks ago; she is in trouble, I pray you will help her."

"Of course," Bess whispered. "Of course, my love."

"I want you to finish Chatsworth, Bess, just the way we planned it. Of course I have made a will, and you have a fine lawyer." He looked across at her, his eyes half closed. "You should summon a priest for a private mass for a very sick man, Bess. The authorities and our queen will think it odd if you don't." Then he added, "Better times are going to come for you and England, Bess."

That was the sixth of October. On the evening of the thirteenth at eight o'clock, Cavendish was sleeping. Bess opened up the big household account book and picked up her pen. Every day Bess did the household accounts.

She said aloud, "I can't do it. I can't." She laid down the pen and stared at the wall in front of her as though she were made of stone. She sat there unblinking. Till suddenly she shouted, "God's death!" She picked up the household book and threw it against the farthest wall; then she put her head down in her arms and began to weep, bitterly and endlessly.

The long, long tear-filled night was good for Bess, relieving in part the terrible tension of sitting and discussing calmly with Cavendish the fact that he was going to die. She tried to keep her distress to herself.

"You're remarkable," he said to her. "And you are going to have a remarkable life, Bess. We have had ten wonderful years! I leave our six children in your hands; you will make earls and countesses of all of them!"

"How is that possible without you?" Bess cried.

"Don't ask me, sweetheart. But you'll find the way."

"My life is over," Bess sobbed.

"At thirty-six?" He grinned a real grin. "Nonsense, Bess, men will be after you. I leave it to your good sense to make a good marriage. I'd like to see you trailing your finery through the court as one of the first ladies of the land!"

Bess said, "Oh, how can you, Cavendish? How can you? When you know what you have been to me and how we have loved?"

He said somberly, yet with a glint of humor in his eyes, "I can because I get pleasure from thinking of you, living on, happy, adventuring. I would like to go on, adventuring at your side, but I can't, so it gives me a bit of immortality to think of you, going on, the way we have together; I'll always go with you, darling; I'll always be there, cheering you on, with a pat on your beautiful bottom. If the lord and the angels permit me, I will!" But the speech had tired him, and he leaned back and closed his eyes. "Call John, Bess, I have to piss."

"I'll fetch it, my love," she said; evidently the pot Cavendish used had been taken from the room. She left him, and the door was closed softly. He lay there a moment, resting, eyes still closed, when her words came floating back to him: "I'll fetch it, my love."

Cavendish pushed himself up and sat straight. A heavy frown crossed his dark face. And a fury of impatience gripped him. That his wife should see him thus and have to bring him a pot! He threw back the bedclothes and stood. Ten feet away was his chair behind a screen. He started toward it, anger propelling his powerful legs, and he had reached it, almost, when the pain exploded in his chest and the whole of his upper body.

He whispered, "Oh, no. No." Then he crashed forward, full length, at the foot of his bed.

Bess heard him fall. She ran, hurling herself onto her knees beside him, cradling his head on her lap, crying her bitter, tragic cries of love and despair.

The candles were guttering very low that night; it was almost midnight. In her room Bess opened for the first time Cavendish's pocket book. Vividly she remembered her wedding night and his sitting there calmly, writing his notes; she turned the pages slowly, here were notes of the births of all the children and all the principal memoranda of their life. Bess smoothed out the blank page, dipped her pen and wrote these words:

That Sir William Cavendish, knight, my most dear and well beloved husband, departed this present life on Monday, the 25th day of October, betwixt the hours of eight and nine at night, in the year of our lord 1557. On whose soul I most humbly beseech the Lord to have mercy, and to rid me and his poor children out of our great miserie. Elizabeth Cavendish

Bess buried Cavendish five days later in the church of St. Botolph in Aldersgate, in a stately funeral. Then she shut the London house, and like a wounded animal in mortal hurt, she crawled home with her children to the safety of Chatsworth.

Part III

CHAPTER 1

August, 1559

SIR William St. Loe was inspecting, with approval, the long gallery at Haddon Hall. He had walked the length of it, had turned and retraced his steps. When he came to the head of the wide, wide stairway, he paused; from this point he could see out the nearest huge window to the rolling Derbyshire hills.

He was a frail man, slender. He wore a short black cloak and a narrow white ruff; his natural grace enhanced his elegance; his eyes were dark and intelligent; his dark beard was flecked with gray, but the single most imposing fact of his whole appearance, impressed on the onlooker by the briefest of glances, was that Sir William was a gentleman.

It was three o'clock of a sunny summer day, and he had enjoyed a much deserved rest, and he felt much better than he had two hours ago. As captain of the guard, and butler of the royal household, he had been prepared two hours ago to ride out with his royal mistress, but when Elizabeth had taken one glance at his face, she had said, "St. Loe, you've caught my cold. I'm recovered. You'd best retire and rest."

He managed a smile down at her face. "Is that a royal command, Your Grace?"

She nodded her imperious nod, and when he bent to kiss

her hand, she said, laughing, "No, no. Keep your cold; I don't want it back."

He stood looking after her, watching her helped into her saddle by Robert Dudley, her master of horse, watching carefully to see the look that passed between them, his eyes suddenly wary and cautiously veiled. But then, ahorse, she waved at him, and automatically he smiled back and raised his hand.

They were old old friends, Sir William and Elizabeth Tudor. He had been, officially, the gentleman-in-residence to the Lady Elizabeth, the young redheaded daughter of Henry VIII and Anne Boleyn. And in his long service to her he had never failed her, not even during the long days and nights in the Tower, after Wyatt's rebellion. They had questioned him and questioned him: Never a word incriminating the young princess had been forced from him. Now for a little more than eight months the Lady Elizabeth had been Elizabeth the Queen.

Sir William took out his napkin and blew his nose. Then he started down the wide shallow steps, passed through the great doors, and out into the gardens that stretched around this country home in Derbyshire. Across the hills was coming a small body of men and women on horseback. Sir William shaded his eyes with his hand and squinted into the sun. No figure could be distinguished, so he paced back and forth on the wide terrace above a yew hedge, watching the horses come closer. The figure now coming into view was a woman in pale lavender riding dress, and for the life of him Sir William couldn't remember what color dress Elizabeth had been wearing. But she was very partial to that color, he remembered vividly she had worn it on her state entrance into London, that cold winter day last November. And now as the riders came into clearer view, he thought it was indeed the queen, for he caught the glint of her red hair and the graceful way she sat her saddle. He took another turn around the terrace, and when he swung around and started down the steps to greet her, only then did he realize that it was not the queen at all but another woman he had never seen before. He came to an abrupt stop and, forgetting his manners, stared up at her face and figure.

Bess was still too far away to see that he was indeed staring. By the time she reined in her horse, he had come forward and taken the bridle from her; smiling up at her, he assisted her to the graveled drive and then did the same for Jane; the rest of the little company were two grooms and two children. The grooms had tumbled off their horses, and each lifted down a child. The little group then stood before the elegant suave Sir William, a habitué of court and close friend to royalty. He made an instant impression with a graceful little bow. "Sir William St. Loe, madam, at your service."

Bess ran her red tongue over her lips; this must be some very grand man, very important. "Lady Cavendish, sir, and my dearest sister, Mistress Kniveton." She paused, dipped him a curtsey, and remembered her children. She took Frances' hand. "My oldest daughter, Frances Cavendish, Sir William."

Bess looked at Frances, who now also remembered to curtsey.

Bess continued, "And oldest son, Henry Cavendish . . . Sir William." In her confusion she had forgotten his name. Her oval face paled a little. "I brought my children to have the great honor of meeting their queen!"

Now her smile flashed out and she shrugged her shoulders. What did correctness matter? She was so excited!

She said breathlessly, "Isn't this a great great occasion, sir?" Sir William St. Loe felt the ground heave under his feet, and his head swim. He sighed and, bemused, bent a long, long look on her, until he finally said, "It's a great occasion, ma'am!"

Late that night, while his body servant packed—for the queen was moving on the next day in this progress to see and greet her subjects—Sir William sat at his table, writing. He still had his cold, he blew his nose often, reminding himself he was scarcely a romantic figure. Yet at the end of the letter he wrote in his beautiful clear handwriting, "I sign this thine, who is wholly and only thine, for all time." Sir William had fallen deeply and irrevocably in love. Her face floated before him, he heard the sound of her low laugh. And the beautiful redheaded Lady Cavendish was a widow!

The letter delivered by courier, reached Bess two days later. She was out in the garden; the project for the summer had been an artificial pond with two little waterfalls fed by the river, and all the children had helped and brought stones, and the boys had caught fish in nets to stock it, and Jane had supervised the planting around it. Bess sat down on a bench, shading her eyes against the sun to read. Her eyes grew large, the smallest smile tugged at the corners of her mouth. As Jane sat down beside her, curious, she passed over the letter without a word.

Jane read it once and then again. She laid the single sheet on her lap. "I liked him excessively," she said.

"Mary, don't go near the edge," called Bess, to the toddling child. Mary was three.

Then Bess said, "I don't suppose he's serious. A widow with six children."

Jane said, "He sounds serious to me. I think you have a suitor on your hands, Bess. And now you're going to face a decision, once again." Jane was thinking that Bess had refused all offers of marriage since Cavendish had died. She was about to speak again, when she realized that Bess was reading and rereading another letter. Her face looked white and still; she raised her eyes and looked unseeingly at the rising hills, deep, deep green in summer.

"What is the matter?" Jane breathed.

Bess didn't answer. She was back in the past. The letter she had just read had come from Elizabeth's court. It had come from one of the queen's maids-in-waiting, Lady Catherine Grey. Four years ago the little Catherine Grey had been fifteen when Bess had asked her to be a godmother to little Elizabeth, born that year, 1555, in March. She wrote to Bess that her mother, Frances Grey, had just died; Frances Grey, who had been Bess' first friend at court and who had put her in bed on her wedding night with hearty bursts of giggling to wait for Cavendish. Now she was dead. Bess wiped her eyes. "I shall never marry again," she said.

If Sir William St. Loe had heard these words, it wouldn't have made any difference to him, for once he set his mind to something nothing would divert him; he had possessed an unswerving will none the less forceful because it was quiet. Sir William arrived at Chatsworth three days later, having made the excuse to his royal mistress that he wished to look after some of his property in the west country. For no male member of Elizabeth's court would ever have the temerity to confess he was running after a woman.

He found a very subdued Bess.

During those three days Bess had had another letter from Catherine Grey, setting forth in uneven sentences that the queen had ordered a magnificent funeral for her mother, the queen's cousin. Elizabeth had been disgusted with Frances Grey's marriage to a man fifteen years younger than she and had forbidden her the court. "She married her head groom! God's death!" Elizabeth had exclaimed. But now she decreed that Frances should have a state funeral and be buried in Westminster Abbey, with great banners of arms, eight dozen escutcheons, and eight banner rolls, Catherine Grey wrote disconsolately, blotting the ink evidently with her tears, for the paper was all splotchy. "But the queen hath befriended me," added Catherine Grey, "and I am to stay under her protection. I mourn the last of my family."

Sir William was so sympathetic that Bess gave him the letter to read, when he had asked why she was so sad, not merry, the way he had first glimpsed her. "You looked to me like the kind of person whom life could never subdue. As though you were more than a match for the largest dragon."

Bess smiled. "It's this," she'd said, and when he had read the letter, he laid his hand over hers.

They were sitting outside; before them lay the vista of the slowly rising walls of Chatsworth. Bess looked down at his hand, the nails neatly clipped and clean; his grip was gentle yet strong.

Bess was thinking of that February day when Catherine's sister, the Lady Jane Grey and her father, Henry Grey, and her husband, Guildford Dudley, had been executed on Tower Green. "It was so dreadful a winter," she whispered.

He tipped up her face with his other hand and looked into the somber dark eyes. "I was there, too," he reminded her with the faintest smile.

Bess saw the glint of rueful humor in his eyes.

He continued, "The Lady Elizabeth was straitly confined; she couldn't even take the air on the leads till weeks later; we were desperately afraid for her. In my nightmares—I had them—I could hear Wyatt screaming. I had carried a letter to him, you know, from the Lady Elizabeth. Robert Dudley was next to me; he used to scratch on the stone; I could hear him." He paused. "We've survived. Better times are coming for England."

"Aye," said Bess. "My husband said that to me before he died."

"The ambitious men will find they have a stifler now. Her Majesty is more than a match for them; she is, indeed, my Bess, the lion's cub. She is here, you are here, I am here, and so, I fear, is Robert Dudley." Had he diverted her? He thought so, for she flashed him an inquiring look.

"Is Her Grace in love with him?"

"He is married," said Sir William.

"But—" said Bess.

"No *buts*," said Sir William. "He is married, and your queen is much too cautious and intelligent to do anything foolish. I suggest that you forget everything but that it's a warm sunny summer day."

He wanted to explore the foundations and the slowly rising walls of Chatsworth, so they put on boots and clambered over the stones amidst the workmen like children, Bess explaining as they picked their way around half built walls. And when Sir William left two days later, Bess was astonished how alone and forlorn she felt as she waved good-bye to him. He was galloping back to court, to all the excitement and gaiety, and here she was, left alone in Chatsworth, like an old shoe.

Sir William had disappeared from sight, and she was buried in the country. She clenched both fists. "God's death!" She was very sorry for herself. Sir William would have been very delighted to know it.

She received a note from him three days later. "My dearest Chatsworth," he began, and a little smile tugged at Bess' mouth.

"He has such a sly sense of humor," Bess said to Jane.

90

Jane was doing petitpoint and didn't look up. "He is such a gentleman," she said. "He would be good for your sons, Bess."

Bess' three boys were now eight, seven, and six. When they entered the old manor it was like a summer storm, with Bess providing the lightning to their thunder. "The only time I've seen them human was when they came in from their ride with Sir William," Jane continued.

"If you're telling me I need a husband to control my sons . . ." Bess began dangerously.

Jane interrupted. "That's what I'm telling you," she said placidly. "And what's worse, Bess, because you have difficulty controlling them, you overdo it with your little daughters. You order them around, and the poor little things—" Jane frowned. "I've missed a stitch."

"You're missing your brains," snapped Bess.

Jane abandoned her needlework, she'd have to pull out the wrong stitch. "There's no one would want you to marry again more than Cavendish, Bess," she said matter-of-factly.

"The citadel is falling," said Sir William tenderly. "The fort that parleys always surrenders. But you know, Bess, falling in love with you is like falling in love with a building."

Bess giggled. "But you are a staunch rock. Even the queen says that."

"So we should make a fine pair. Bess, I have drawn up a new will, leaving all my lands in Gloucestershire to you, and all my other property—to you, my bride."

"Oh," breathed Bess, "but—"

"My two daughters are well married and well off, they need nothing more from me. You have six young children, and you are much younger than I am. I have considered, and this is the right way. I have also here an indenture which promises one thousand pounds to Anne Cavendish, in case she rejects the marriage which I intend to try to make for her."

This problem had been worrying Bess; Sir William had many contacts that Bess did not have.

"Oh, if I could get her well married."

"We will, but first I want to get you well married."

Sir William took her in his arms. Almost timidly Bess

returned his kiss, so timidly that he held her off and laughed. "Bess," he said, "let's try again."

But Bess was still uncertain. Jane thought she was acting like a child. "You can't expect to feel the wild love and desire you had for Cavendish," she said. "Any woman could feel the great attraction Cavendish had for women, Bess; all he had to do was walk into a room."

Bess bit her lip and her eyes grew huge.

"He's much older than I, much older, Jane."

"So he'll be less demanding, probably. By my faith," Jane said, from the superior vantage point of two husbands, "the workings of sex are the same, Bess. You'll find out."

"Will we be married at court?" Bess asked Sir William.

"Hardly." He smiled at her fondly. His interview with Elizabeth had not been smooth. "Her Grace did not take kindly to the idea of my getting married, Bess," It was an understatement. Elizabeth had been annoyed and waspish and had left her sting. In fact, Sir William had been so annoyed that he had not kissed her hand when he left her. "But," he shrugged his elegant shoulders, "I have a week with you. We can be wed right here."

"A week?" cried Bess.

"That's all," he confessed.

For the first time Bess had locked horns—distant this time—with Elizabeth Tudor.

Jane thought it was a lovely wedding. All the county came from miles around, and what, after all, was more touching than a country wedding in the sweet, sweet summer?

"You can be married in the garden amongst all our oldest and dearest friends," Jane said and happily made all the arrangements.

As for Bess, she discovered that Sir William's body was thin and steely, like his will, and that he made love with careful authority. On her wedding night, she fell asleep in his arms, deeply ravished by his love and deeply content.

"I did right," she whispered to Jane. "We are happy!"

But the week went all too fast, and once more when she stood in the doorway watching him mount, to ride off to the court and queen, she felt very, very sorry for herself.

When he came back, she would have to make him understand that she was his wife and that the queen would have
to take second place.

If Sir William had known what Bess was thinking, he
would have laughed most ruefully. The princess he had
cared for and watched mature for a dozen years would
allow no prior claim. She was making his life miserable with
little sideways taunts and displays of temper when he was
in her presence. So he was in a particularly bad frame of
mind when he returned to his room to find his younger
brother waiting for him, a younger brother of whom Sir
William had always disapproved and whose actions had
shamed him often. Sir William noted his brother Edward's
expression, and he snapped, "What trouble are you in now,
sir?" He was hot and he stripped off his doublet and threw
it on a chair, waved to his servant to remove it and remove
himself. When that was done, he turned again to Edward.
"What did you say? I was preoccupied and didn't listen."

Edward said furiously, "I said I was in no trouble whatsoever!"

"Thank God for that. I have enough troubles." Sir William threw his length into the only comfortable chair, and
looked across the room to Edward, who in his anger was
pacing up and down the small room.

"You've lost your mind!" Edward came to a stop.

"Don't point your finger at me, or I'll have you thrown
out," Sir William said. "You worry about your mind, and
I'll take care of mine. Is that what you came to tell me, by
the way?"

"Marrying a young widow, and—"

"She's not so young, she's thirty-eight."

Edward muttered, "I heard she was only twenty-eight;
she looks only twenty-eight so one of my friends—"

"Your friends are all liars and stupid," Sir William said,
now lazy.

"This friend lives in Derbyshire and knows—"

"Nothing," said Sir William, enjoying himself slightly,
because Elizabeth had been badgering him all day, and now
he was getting some of it back. Then he bethought himself
that Edward was a poor target and a poor opponent, and

93

he sighed. He looked Edward over from head to toe, his eyes lingering on the narrow chin and foxy look under his reddish hair. He said thoughtfully, "It isn't all your fault. Our blood—it is running too thin. Father should have married a woman like Bess Hardwick to put some strength back into our line."

"Now you're attacking our poor mother!"

"She has always been a weak and querulous woman, and no one knows it better than you, Edward." Sir William sighed again, deeply, and thought of Bess and wished he were with her right now. Anyway he was tired and sleepy, and it was almost midnight, and besides that, he had lost at cards. "What did you come for?" he asked and yawned.

"I came to tell you that I'm going to sue! I'm going to get a lawyer!"

Sir William looked at him, honestly puzzled. "Have you gone mad?"

"You've no right, no right whatsoever, to leave all our family property to your latest folly! To get married and leave all—all —to your bride! Bride!"

Sir William said, "I must remind you, Edward, that it is all my property. Mine. To do with as I see fit. No lawyer would take your case, if you can call it a case. I could leave you some property, if it pleased me, and if I chose, in the goodness of my heart, to so endow you. But I don't choose, Edward. And nothing under the sun could make me so choose. So you'd best go."

"You'd disinherit your only brother!"

"If any were left to you, you'd just dissipate it, as you well know and as I well know. I'm sleepy, Edward. I wish you would take yourself off. Do me the honor of congratulating me, and say good-night like the gentleman you are supposed to be."

"Jesu!" Edward clenched his fists in impotent anger. "You are so rigid."

"Aye, and I've been commended for it many times."

"There's nothing I can say that would make you change your mind? What of your daughters?"

"I have informed them both, and they are well satisfied, Edward. Does it surprise you?"

"My friends—my friends cannot believe this could have

94

happened!" Edward could hear in his head the dark mutterings of his friends, when they had learned that there would never be any money coming to their bedfellow and card friend from his wealthy brother. "He couldn't have left you nothing. Nothing at all," they had said again and again.

"You're not going to leave me even a little memento. Why, look at the chain you're wearing."

This remark made Sir William laugh. "God's death! That's what Her Grace would say if she saw you wearing it! She gave it to me. She'd snatch it from you and disinter me, if I left you this. Oh, Edward, Edward, I'm ashamed of you." He shook his head. "I'm sorry for you, too. But there's nothing more I can do for you. You will have to do for yourself now. Why don't you try?"

He rose and put his hand out to Edward, and Edward did take his hand. "For God's sake, straighten yourself out! Give up your squalid friends! Remember you were born with a fine old name!"

But Edward didn't answer him. He went to the door, and it closed on him, his footsteps receded. Sir William frowned. Edward still had the same repulsive wet hands, with the limp grip; he was just the same as ever. Disgusting.

Sir William called his personal servant, and he undressed and washed and went to bed. The interview with Edward receded from his mind; he had had many like it before. But if he could have seen the man with whom Edward was at the moment in deep, close conversation, he might not have slept so soundly and so dreamlessly.

When Sir William arrived at Chatsworth a week later, and was accompanied by a whole retinue of servants and personal attendants, Bess' heart leaped with joy.

"Surprise, my dearest love!"

"You're going to stay!"

"Aye," said Sir William, his eyes glistening with excitement. "I'm going to stand for parliament, from Derbyshire. What do you think of that?"

"I think it's wonderful!" Bess cried. "It's simply wonderful!"

That fall Sir William was returned as the member of parliament for Derbyshire with no trouble whatsoever. Not only was he a man of well-known integrity, but everyone knew he stood close to the queen in her affections, and what sort of man could be better trusted with the interests of the county? To gain the election, everyone of consequence had to meet Sir William, and Bess had thrown herself into this job with all her natural enthusiasm. When she introduced him to her friends, she was so proud of him.

He was so urbane. A master of every situation. And he knew almost as much about horses as Cavendish had. From where she worked at her accounts on her big table, she could look out over the series of ponds that Cavendish had constructed to drain off the overflow water from the pebbly bedded Derwent River that wound through the grounds of Chatsworth. She could see him coming toward her with the three boys. Bess had had to admit that Jane had been right about the boys. They responded to Sir William's very soft-spoken authority with a respect that astounded Bess. They were all four coming toward her window. She pulled the last piece of paper for her signature before her and dipped her pen and dashed off her name.

Elizabeth Cavendish.

She had picked up the sander before she realized what she had done. She looked down at the firmly written name. Then, taking up her pen again, she drew a thick dark line over Cavendish. With a trembling hand, she wrote below the crossed-out Cavendish, Saint Loe. Bess sanded the signature, and wiped her eyes with her hand. She turned her head to see Sir William enter the room.

"What's the matter, my love?" he asked, seeing her face.

Bess laid her hand over the signature. Then she folded it quickly, to get it out of his sight. "Nothing," said Bess. "Honestly. Nothing is the matter."

But Sir William found her strangely subdued the rest of the day. She went up to her room soon after dinner, and when he entered it later, she was propped up in bed, reading, leaning back against the piled-up pillows, her red hair tied back. The candlelight played across her white, white skin.

Sir William closed the door. "Do you feel ill, my dearest?" he asked.

"No. No." Bess closed the book on her finger.

He walked over to the window. "The moon is rising." It was shining down onto the ponds, making them silver. He swung around. "Is something worrying you? Plaguing you?"

Bess looked across at him. There had been something else worrying her. She blurted, "I'm afraid of getting pregnant."

Sir William grinned. "Oh," he said.

Bess burst into speech. "You see, I had eight children in ten years, and it never bothered me, but now, I think, well, I think—" She stopped suddenly and then, "I never realized before we were married that you would be so—" she stopped, and Sir William laughed.

"Bess, Bess," he said. "I'm afraid that only oversexed men fall in love with you."

Bess was astonished.

"The others would be too wary of that fire, too unsure and too fearful." Bess didn't understand him. "You know nothing about yourself, Bess," he said. "You never weigh, never look inward, you've never had time, I expect. Plato says: 'Know thyself.' I'm not sure whether that's right or not. If you probe too much of yourself, you may doubt too much. You don't doubt at all, do you?"

"I don't read very much," Bess said defensively. "I've never read Plato."

"You don't understand a word I've been saying," he said and shook his head and smiled at her lovingly.

"Do you mean you'd like a baby?" Bess said, her eyes enormous.

Sir William said, "What man wouldn't want a son by you?"

Bess sighed. "That's a fine compliment, sir, I do think, and I do take those words kindly."

Sir William grinned, and took off his bedgown.

Bess made room for him in her big bed. "But I do read. See?"

He laid down the book of Psalms. "Why do you read them, Bess?"

"Because they're so beautiful." She smiled, and he took her in his arms.

"You're beautiful," he whispered.

"But I wish, wish so much," she whispered back, "that you'd take me to court with you, after Christmas."

97

Sir William went back to London the day after Christmas, determined to fulfill her wish. During the New Year's festivities, and under the avalanche of New Year's gifts the queen would receive, she might be more apt to look and listen to him kindly, even though he were speaking of another woman. He took with him three finely bred horses, one of them a high-spirited gelding.

Sir William presented his New Year's gift to the queen on bended knee, and she was charmed with the delicately wrought jeweled cup. He asked for his gift that his new wife be made a lady of the bedchamber.

Elizabeth said, "I find great fault with your long absence, sir. I'm going to talk with you later and chide you further."

Sir William had risen. It was not an auspicious beginning. He said very gravely, "Your Grace, when you understand the cause and the truth, you will not be offended."

Elizabeth frowned. "Very well. Very well." It was a bit snappish, her tone, but not bad, he decided. And his chance came on a nice mild day, when he rode at her side on the new black gelding. Elizabeth much admired the horse. Late that night, Sir William wrote to Bess.

"The queen yesterday," he wrote, "her own self riding by my side, craved my horse. I gave him to her, receiving openly for the same many goodly words. You are going to be made a lady of the bedchamber!"

CHAPTER 2

LONDON! London again! London after three years away! Such bliss! And she was coming for a full month, and she was to be a lady of the bedchamber. Her red hair freshly washed and curled, her little ruff freshly starched and framing her face, her best diamond earrings sparkling like her eyes, Bess came to Elizabeth's court for the first time.

It was a young court, it was gay, it was highly intelligent.

And when Bess entered the presence chamber for the first time on Sir William's arm, her old, old friend Sir William Cecil came forward and kissed her. "Oh, I am so glad to see you again." Bess cried. And there was Lord Herbert.

"Here is the best whist player in skirts," Will Herbert said, giving her a big kiss and hug.

And there was William Paulet, the treasurer.

"Bess!" he cried. "Bess! Welcome!" he held her off and looked at her. "More beautiful than ever. More dazzling than ever."

All this while Elizabeth was watching. As Bess came forward, through the greetings, Elizabeth watched narrowly. And when Bess finally stood before her, and curtsied deeply, Elizabeth said nothing.

Bess murmured, "Oh, Your Grace, this is such a great honor you do me. I am overwhelmed." She raised her huge dark eyes and looked up into Elizabeth's face.

In spite of her dislike for the wives of her gentlemen, Elizabeth found this hard to resist. Her smile flashed forth, so did the smile of the man standing to her left, Robert Dudley.

"Welcome, my lady."

"Thank you, thank you," Bess breathed.

Bess and Sir William had two rooms in the palace and an anteroom; they were very fortunate. Bess, as a lady of the bedchamber, had gradually attained some entrance to the intimate care of her queen. The whole court talked of almost nothing but the man whom the queen should choose for her husband. Of course there were suitors from foreign lands, but it was quite obvious to everyone that their queen preferred the company of Robert Dudley. They had known each other from childhood, together they had spent grim time in the Tower; it was Robin the queen doted on. It all made for much gossip.

"She has vowed to me," Sir William said, "that she will never marry."

Bess said, "It might be that she never expects to have children. She doesn't have a proper flux. Sometimes it is fifty days between."

For the queen could keep no secrets. Those who attended

the bedchamber, from the ladies to the laundresses, knew the intimate details of Elizabeth's body. They also knew countless other likes and dislikes.

"She has an extremely sensitive nose; she is most particular of any noisome odor."

But Bess also knew now how hard Elizabeth worked at her papers and at her table and at the council table, and how she paced and fretted; she knew of the raging headaches and the devastating colds and the intense weariness after long sessions with Cecil, when she would finally cry, "No! God's death, no!"

There would be a clatter. What had she hurled? Suddenly she would appear, her full skirts swinging, her brow furrowed. "God's death! If he is right, I shall have done it all wrong!"

She was sparing in food and drink, but already her closet bulged with clothes; she spent hours on her toilette, and she could dance the night through.

Bess' month had been extended. She received mail every week from Chatsworth, for all her family wrote voluminous letters.

"My Aunt Linacre has come back to Chatsworth!" she exclaimed, looking up from Jane's letter.

Sir William had never met Aunt Linacre and so Bess explained, again, all about her, how the children loved her and how well they obeyed her and how she was their mother's favorite sister and Bess' favorite aunt and how gay and fat and loving and bright she was and the most magnificent cook and needlewoman and gardener!

"I'm so happy she's come back, and she says she will stay. And then maybe Jane could come and visit us. What do you think?"

Sir William smiled at all this enthusiasm. "I think she might," he said.

The day before Jane was to arrive Bess picked her way down the hall. Outside her door was still the leftover food from dinner the night before, for she and Sir William had dined privately.

"God's death!" cried Bess, looking at the mess. "The dogs

have got into it!" She stepped around the large tray and pushed open the door. Frowning, she looked at the man waiting inside the room.

"Who are you?" she asked.

He was tall and redhaired, and he seemed vaguely familiar. "I'm Edward St. Loe," he said, "and I've come to congratulate my brother and have the pleasure of meeting his new bride!"

Bess said, "Why, I thought your face was familiar." She came forward, and he leaned down and kissed her.

"What excellent taste William shows, my lady!"

"Thank you, sir," said Bess. "I'm happy to meet you. Sit down and we'll share a cup of wine. I'm weary, sir. I've been with the queen for five hours." She was intensely proud she could say that.

What preening, thought Edward St. Loe. *What conceit, she flaunts it, I don't like her.*

Bess had gone over to the sideboard and got out two cups. He came to her side. "What kind of wine do you prefer?"

"The malmsey," said Bess, flashing her big smile. "I've always preferred it."

She poured the two cups and handed him one.

"To your health and your happiness, my lady," he said, bowing.

"Yours, sir," said Bess, raising the cup. He was looking at her, with his rather foxy eyes.

"Very good," he pronounced. "You know how abstemious my brother is. I thought perhaps he'd pick an inferior wine." He grinned at her, and his smile reminded her of Sir William, and she relaxed a bit and prepared to like him.

"I'm sorry Will isn't here," Bess said. "Perhaps he'll arrive any minute."

"Oh, I saw him in his office. It was you I wanted to meet."

Bess frowned, drawing her light brows together. He almost sounded as though he hoped Sir William would not appear. They measured each other quite openly.

Edward said, "Oh, my lady, my brother insisted I come, to pay my respects, to the new Lady St. Loe."

Bess didn't believe a word he said.

101

"After all, I should come, you know, to welcome a new member of the family. And my mother, who's not well, I bring you her welcome and words of affection."

"That's very kind of you," Bess said stiffly.

He sat down. "And how do you like being at court, after the country?"

Bess said, "Oh, I love it. Of course, I meet many strange and odd folk." She sipped her wine.

He was twirling his cup, it was obviously empty.

"Help yourself, sir," she said.

He rose with alacrity and poured himself a generous cupful and came toward her. "For you, too?" he asked.

"No, thank you."

"Oh," he chided. And he smiled at her, and when he smiled, he did remind her of Sir William, and again she tried to allay her dislike of him. "Come," he prodded, and willy-nilly Bess held out her half-empty cup.

"That's better," he said. "Enjoy it with me, and then I'll leave you, my lady. You probably want to rest."

Bess was thinking longingly of her soft bed and her pile of cushions, and her warm satin quilt.

She sipped at the wine and sighed. "It will make for a pleasant doze, I agree, sir. And I am happy that you came; it was kind of you."

His eyes went over her. She looked so young. They said she had beautiful carriage and she did. Her breasts were high and perfect, and their outline was perfectly plain under her tight gown. Under his gaze Bess ran her tongue over her mouth. How could she get rid of him?

"I must ask your forbearance, sir," she said, "but it is time for me to retire to my room."

He laughed in a familiar manner that managed to be insulting. "Of course." He rose and set down his empty cup. He leaned over to kiss her good-bye, and Bess shrank away from his breath.

"Thank you for coming," she said as civilly as she could. And when the door closed on him, she heaved a big sigh of relief and stuck her tongue out at the door. She made a face. "Ugh," she said aloud. Then she forgot him. She scampered into her room, threw herself on the wide bed. Jane was coming tomorrow!

102

CHAPTER 3

"YOU'VE been here just a week, and everybody loves you, Jane," Bess said happily.

Jane smiled her little deprecating smile.

They were finishing a quiet dinner, the three of them, having sought the privacy of their own chambers to dine together, for Sir William had had an arduous day and was weary. He lifted his half-finished wine cup to his lips and then set it down without tasting it.

"I don't feel very well," he said, frowning slightly.

He rose and put his hand at the bottom of his ribs and rubbed. He was usually so correct, Bess had never seen him do such a thing. Alarmed, she jumped to her feet.

"You get right to bed," she cried.

His face looked quite white. Jane took his arm and started toward his bedroom, and suddenly Sir William said, "No, leave go, Jane. I'm going to be sick."

He made hastily for his room, and the garderobe within; his servant was in there with him, Bess knew, but they could hear him retching. After a few minutes, he called out weakly.

Bess went in, to find him partly undressed, in bed in his shirt-sleeves, smiling weakly at her.

"I feel a bit better," he said. "I'm sorry, Bess." He sighed and leaned back against the pillows. "I think I can sleep now, Bess."

She came over and bent to give him a kiss, then backed from the room, quietly, for his eyes were closed.

At the door, she heard him say to her, "Don't worry, Bess, there's nothing to worry about."

But it had frightened Bess, the sudden illness, and the violence of the retching she had heard, and his white, white face. She went over to the sideboard and poured herself another cup of wine.

"By my faith, I was frightened," she said.

Jane said, "I hope there was nothing wrong with the meat." She poked at the remains on her plate, and held up one piece and sniffed it. "It smells perfect," she said.

"It was tough," said Bess. The hand that held her wine was still shaky. "I was terrified," she whispered. She finished the wine and helped Jane pile all the plates on the tray, and then they both carried it to the door and set it down outside for the servants to remove. Her wine cup was half empty and she decided to refill it.

"This will calm me down," she said.

Jane didn't want wine. She put the bottle back on the sideboard and helped herself to a sweet cake. She was deciding how to comfort Bess, and also wondering if the two of them would be sick, when Bess suddenly said, "Oh! Jesu!" She grimaced as a pain knifed through her vitals.

Jane cried, "Bess!"

One glance at Bess' face told her to get Bess into her room. She leaped to her feet and put her arm around her sister. Bess staggered. She groaned, and then she fell onto her hands and knees on the floor. Her face was not white; it was gray. She lay doubled up on the floor, writhing.

Jane fled for a pot. She returned with it, kneeling beside Bess, but Bess was not retching, only crying helplessly.

"Bess! Bess!" sobbed Jane.

Sir William rolled out of bed and came to the doorway. Horrified, he ran toward Bess, knelt on the floor. Bess was saying something.

"What?" he cried. "What?"

Bess muttered, "I'm dying."

The room swayed around Jane. "She's been poisoned," Jane cried. "Poisoned!"

Bess wrapped her arms around her own body; her breath was coming in short, short gasps.

Jane ran to the sideboard and poured water into a cup; it was still hot. Frantically she rubbed soap in her hands, and came running back. "Lift her up," she said.

Sir William tried to right the struggling Bess. He got her head tipped over his arm. Jane held the soapy water to her lips.

"Drink, Bess! Drink! You must vomit!"

Bess heard her from a great distance. She tried to drink. The soapy water ran down her chin, but she gulped at it and gulped again.

"Drink!" Jane kept saying.

Bess couldn't answer, but she kept gulping. Finally, she tried to push them away, and when Sir William released her, she turned on her hands and knees and began to vomit.

Jane threw towels over the stream of yellow vomit. "Hold her while I get more soapy water," she cried, her voice trembling.

Sir William tried to hold Bess propped up as she was on her hands and knees. When Jane came back he rolled her over and again held her head up so she could drink. By now Sir William's valet and two more servants had arrived, one was sent for a doctor. Before he came, the rumor was already flying through the halls of Westminster that Lady St. Loe was dying, or dead, poisoned by her brother-in-law.

Jane and Sir William thought she was going to die. When they finally got her in bed, when the retching had ceased, the pallor of her gray face seemed to increase, and she had trouble breathing.

"My chest, my chest," she muttered in uneven gaspings. "It's stony."

The doctor was so upset his flat cap had come awry, and Bess' female servants sat in the corner crying. Sir William staggered around, feeling as if he were going to faint. But they packed Bess' body with warm bricks and piled her with quilts and kept her almost upright on the doctor's orders, so to help with her labored breath.

During the night Bess seemed to go into a coma. Jane watched her every hard-drawn breath as she fought for life. Jane sat there through the night, too terrified to weep, too horror-struck to think; mindlessly she crouched on her stool, holding Bess' hand, as if she could keep her thus from stepping forth into the unknown vastness that seemed to stretch before her.

"Don't die, Bess," Jane kept whispering in the silent room. "Don't die." She had sent away the servants; there was nothing to do, the doctor said, but pray, and keep her warm.

Sir William—who they had decided had also been poisoned, but very, very slightly, for he'd drunk almost no wine, and Jane had had beer—Sir William had laid down a pallet in the corner and was resting there.

"I can't leave you and Bess, Jane," he said. He had wept silently, and Jane had put her arms around him, and they had clung together in their fear and misery.

Thus the night passed, dragging its leaden black hours endlessly, it seemed to Jane. When the first light of dawn came, Bess was still breathing. Sir William struggled up wearily from his nightmarish daze. He touched Jane on the shoulder.

"I think she breathes a bit easier," he whispered, his voice shaking with relief.

"I can't tell; it's still terrible," Jane whispered back.

The doctor had been in and out all night, and now he reappeared with Elizabeth's personal physician and two ladies of the bedchamber who came to bring the queen's deepest sympathy and to inquire about the patient. And by the end of the day, it seemed as though Bess might live. Once she asked for water, which she vomited, and once she squeezed Jane's hand. But for most of the day she lay there, semiconscious, still gray.

It took Bess three weeks to recover. For two weeks she lay in her bed; it was difficult for her to eat, and the doctors kept purging her constantly. She grew very thin, but gradually the palest color came back to her cheeks, and there finally came a day when her servants could wash her hair and brush it free of all the tangles, and when she could sit up in her anteroom, wrapped in the new robe Sir William had bought for her, her feet resting on a stool.

The next week she was able to write her letters again, voluminous letters to her sons and her daughter Frances and her mother and all her relatives and her aunt.

Dearest Aunt Linacre, Bess wrote, *I don't know what we would have done without you, and without knowing you were there with my dearest beloved children, so that Jane could stay here with me. I know Jane has written you all about my illness, so no more need be said. But I have been thinking that the little garden which is*

106

beside the new house should be made a great garden this year, and I think you should sow it, as you did before in Oldcotes, with all kinds of herbs and flowers, and some pieces with mallows and eglantine. I love them, and so do you! I'm sending this letter by Crompe [Bess' agent] plus three bundles of garden seeds all written with William Marchington's hand, and by the next carrier, you shall know how to use them at every point.

That day Bess was able to spend two hours with Master Crompe, who came up from Derbyshire every four weeks while Bess was in London, to bring the accounts, the tally sheets, and to do all the business that Bess normally transacted from Chatsworth. For Bess was by now a very wealthy woman, with huge holdings of land. Every penny not needed during the last fifteen years had been put back into land and manors. After Crompe had left, Bess, weary, received another letter, by special messenger.

"It's from my mother-in-law." Bess cried. "Listen." She read aloud to Jane.

"And many have said to me they hearsay that Edward St. Loe has gone about to poison his brother and you, and I have told them I know nothing. Here is great talk of it."

"I can imagine," Bess interposed.

"A lady came to me and asked me if I knew anything. But I told her I was sure you were poisoned when I was at London, and if you had not had a present remedy, you would have died. I know she came to see whether I would say aught about Edward. But he bears you good will that he came to see you in London. His good friendship to you and to me is all the same. I pray you, madam, send me word when this devil's devices began and how it came to light. Thanks be to God you know it."

"She's trying to save the family honor," Bess said.

But it was too serious a matter to be kept in a family, and investigations now began. Sir William employed an old friend, an astrologer, to see if he could find the guilty one. But Bess, still half sick, told him that she thought she wanted, as soon as she were well, to go back to Chatsworth.

CHAPTER 4

THE walls of new Chatsworth were now about twenty feet high. The towers at the gateway were half built, and the octagonal towers at each corner were almost ready for roofing. The building eighty feet from the main house was twenty feet high, a rounded graceful "bower"; the drawings called for a flat roof, where the view over the countryside was spectacular, and where a lady could walk and dream and take the air in private, and nap and do needlework way above the mundane life. The stairway to the flat roof was already in place, a narrow curving graceful flight of stone steps, and Bess would often go up to the top, in summer, standing poised on the last step, and draw in her breath in delight not only at the view but the soon-to-come days when she could spend the summer nights up here, way up in the sky.

"I wish you'd come down," Sir William would say. He was afraid of heights. "I'm sure you'll stumble!"

"Not me," said Bess, holding her hat with one hand. When Sir William sat reading on a summer afternoon, he could see Bess' hat go bobbing along in the distance, as she talked to the workmen, inspected the gardens, or walked in the already fragrant grassy paths between the banks of eglantine in the growing main garden. She would return with her basket full of roses and peonies in the spring, and gilly flowers and sweet-smelling stock in the summer. But there were also drawn up and laid out the formal gardens that her age loved so much—the lines of yew and box, and little fountains, the close-cropped grass, the graveled walks and the statuary.

Sir William also made the acquaintance of Aunt Linacre; she fascinated him. She was as round as she was tall, and to prove the pudding, her cooking was superb; she made the most delicious soups; the meat turned out to be tender, and there would be tiny pieces of light dough floating on the top, and pieces of fresh vegetables, barely cooked; Sir William had never seen anyone put lettuce in soup before, but Aunt Linacre did. She had an imperiousness that amused him and a quick, quick tongue.

"Aye, she'd even put you down if you gave her the chance," Bess said happily, for she was so pleased that Sir William liked Aunt Linacre. Lots of men didn't; she was too much for them and too ready with a retort.

Bess spent the summer preparing the trunks and chests and selecting the servant who would accompany her oldest two boys to Eton that September. But as August drew to a close, her eyes began to get bigger every time she looked at them, as she contemplated this kind of separation for the first time.

"Henry isn't ten yet, and William is only eight!" she would wail.

"It'll be good for them," Sir William repeated stoutly.

"Well, to make sure they're good and healthy before they go, let's take them to Buxton Springs for the baths."

This amused Sir William mightily for he had never seen two boys possessed of so much good health and high spirits. They were always in trouble, and they made the life of the workmen on new Chatsworth a daily gamble.

"All right," he said. "For one thing, it will get them off those high walls; the workmen will be delighted."

So the first week in September, off they went, the whole family, to the springs at Buxton. Bess was convinced the baths did everyone a great deal of good.

"I don't know how much good it did," Sir William said, "but at least they're clean and they didn't drown."

But October 21 finally came—the morning of the great day that they were to set forth from Chatsworth into the great world, alone save for one servant, exposed to all their fellows, on an equal footing for the first time, to be introduced to Latin and mathematics. Bess cried and hugged them, while they squirmed.

"Good-bye," Bess called, waving. Henry was mounted on his pony, and William was riding post behind the carefully picked body servant, a retainer in his twenties, sober and smart. He was able to keep their accounts, which he would send to Bess every month.

"Good-bye, good-bye," she called.

Aunt Linacre and Jane and the rest of the children waved and shouted. Sir William had already gone back to his duties, but he had stopped at Eton and spoken to the bursar, who was an old friend.

They were out of sight, and tears stood in Bess' eyes. Aunt Linacre said, "You should be smiling; they're getting too much for you, Bess."

And when, three days later, Bess received the first message from their attendant, she looked up from the letter in joy.

"They stayed at an inn their first night and entertained the two sons of Sir Francis Knollys! The queen's kin!" she cried proudly. "They had a breast of roast mutton, costing ten pence, one little chicken and bread and beer." Bess put the letter down. "I hope that was good enough for the queen's very own kin."

Sir William wrote from London that all men there were pressing the queen to marry, and that she was irritable and pale. He wrote, too, that Robert Dudley was laying schemes with his family and with any friend, some ecclesiastical, to press the queen into marrying him. But Sir William could not forget, and neither could anyone else, the sentence that had been reported back to England, the sentence that had been authored in France: The queen of England is going to marry her master of horse, who killed his wife in order to be free.

Scandal. Of course, Robert Dudley had been exonerated of any crime by a coroner's jury, which had heard all the evidence, but it didn't matter. Guilt clung to him, and the people never tired of saying, "But how could his wife have fallen and broke her neck, down those stairs, as they say, when the little ruff around her neck was not even disarranged?"

Sir William said he would come home for Christmas with the boys and take Bess back with him in January. At Christmastime, Bess marveled over the books the boys brought home to show her.

110

"Cicero's *Letters to Atticus*," she exclaimed, while they corrected her pronunciation.

"Lucian's *Dialogues*, King Edward's *Latin Grammar*, and Aesop's *Fables*!" Bess was very impressed and looked at her sons with eyes shining with love and pride. "Tonight you will read to me, Henry, out of the *Fables*. But how, how in the world did you manage to go through three pairs of shoes? And you haven't a decent shirt left."

At court, on the eighteenth of January, Bess sat at Sir William's side, in the great presence chamber in Whitehall, while a long, long play was performed for the whole court and the queen. It was called *Ferrex and Porrex*. It was written by Sir Thomas Sackville, a relative of the queen through her mother and a very close friend of Elizabeth. It was the first English play ever to be written in blank verse.

Bess thought it was wonderful. It was horrifying and tragic. Ferrex and Porrex were sons of King Gorboduc and they fought over the succession, and the younger one slew his older brother right on the stage.

Bess gasped and put her hands over her eyes. Then the queen mother, who loved her elder son the most, slew her younger son, and in awful wrath, the people rose and killed the king and queen, and then the nobility, outraged and vengeful, bloodily laid waste to the common people and their lands, and the whole realm was wasted and ravished.

At the play's end Bess sat stricken and wiping away the tears of horror. This is what would happen to England unless there were a legitimate heir. To be sure.

Back in their rooms, Bess explained what the play meant to Sir William. He laughed.

"It never ceases to amaze me that a preconceived idea blots out any propaganda. That play was written expressly to show the dangers of having heirs! The writer is the queen's good friend. He wanted to show that heirs are more dangerous than none."

"Oh," said Bess.

"I know all the dangers of an unmarried virgin queen, my love," he said. "But I know Elizabeth Tudor exceedingly well. And I much doubt that she will ever exchange the

111

coronation ring on the fourth finger of her left hand for a wedding ring."

"But she loves Robert Dudley."

"She is already married to England."

"She goes to his room," Bess whispered. "She will rise from her bed and cast a shawl about her shoulders and slip away."

Sir William said, "How much intimacy she permits, we don't know, but I would wager you it is she who is satisfied by it, but never him."

The short month of February slipped away, in cold and frost, little mourned. March brought the news that there had been arrested three men, on charges of conspiring by witchcraft the death of Lady St. Loe. On March 21, they were sent to the Tower. But there was no evidence connecting Edward St. Loe to the deed, except that one of the men resided near him at Knighton Sutton.

"The whole thing stinks to high heaven," Bess said. "Those poor fools are made the culprits, and that knave Edward St. Loe will go unscathed."

Bess was not on terms of great intimacy with Elizabeth, but the queen liked her and kept her that spring at court, in the capacity of lady of the bedchamber. Bess was happy and paid no attention to some of the women who were jealous of her, until in the late spring, her brother-in-law Edward began to get active again. He very neatly spread the rumor that the trial of the three men in the Tower was a farce, because it was actually the Lady St. Loe herself who had connived to poison her husband and got too much poison herself in the trying.

Bess' enemies gleefully repeated this choice bit of gossip. "She dotes on money," they said. "Stranger things have happened!" But Sir William was outraged and wrote a long lengthy denial of the charges, which he had attested by his lawyers.

Bess said, "Pooh. What does it matter what he says, he's such a silly villain. Except I'd like to have died," she added speculatively.

112

Sir William thought she looked as though she wondered what that would have been like.

Bess sighed, "Here I am, forty years old."

Sir William now scrutinized her carefully; she never mentioned her age. What was coming next?

"Here I am forty years old," Bess repeated, and a smile was lifting the corners of her mouth. "And what do you think, sir? I'm going to have a baby."

Sir William was so thunderstruck and delighted he could only open his mouth and stare at her.

Bess laughed. "Well?"

Sir William leaped to his feet, and gathered her into his arms, hugging her tight. "Why, Bess! Why, Bess!" Now all sorts of words tumbled out of his mouth, endearments, happy words of delight, and finally he held her off and looked at her face. "Why, you bloom, my dearest love! And you look about thirty years old!"

Bess smiled radiantly. Sir William was so bright and always right. She settled back happily into her chair, and they both lifted their glasses, which Sir William had just poured, and drank to the health of the new life.

CHAPTER 5

ON July 30, 1561, in the evening, between eight and nine, a violent storm of thunder and lightning terrified the city of London. In June the spire of St. Paul's had been destroyed by lightning and now this new storm shook the whole palace, and Bess, alone in her rooms except for her servants, was terrified. It was a bad omen. Of what she was not quite sure.

She was packing because the court was moving to Ipswich. But the enormous barrage of sounds and crashes from the heavens above put the maids in an uproar, and they huddled in the corners of the room, their skirts over their heads.

Torrential rains fell until midnight, pounding against the roofs and windows, and the maids thought the world was coming to a watery end. But finally at midnight, the rains began to lessen.

"Everyone go to bed," Bess commanded. "We'll pack in the morning."

Relieved that their days had not ended, everyone did sleep, although Bess wished heartily for Sir William, but as the butler of the royal household he had gone on to Ipswich.

The queen's train set out two days later. Traveling with the queen was not only Bess, as lady of the bedchamber, but Sir William Cecil, her indispensable first secretary, Robert Dudley, and many of her court, including the Lady Catherine Grey. On Saturday night, August 9, at Ipswich, Bess retired early to her chamber; Sir William was playing cards.

At the timid knock on the door Bess rose rather wearily, for it was hot, and she had already undressed and bathed, and she was alone.

When she saw that her visitor was Lady Catherine Grey, she let her in and climbed back onto her bed. She had no warning of what was coming. In fact she yawned openly to show the Lady Catherine she was not disposed to talk very much.

Lady Catherine arranged herself on the stool by Bess' bed; her draperies fell around her like a toadstool, Bess thought. Bess hadn't had much to do with the Lady Catherine, for she was but a lady of the presence chamber. Bess supposed she resented this, being the last living heir to the throne, in the act of succession of Henry VIII.

Bess said kindly, "You look so pale. It's the heat, I expect." *I wonder what she wants*, Bess thought. For Catherine hadn't said a word up to now, except "May I come in?"

Catherine's eyes filled with tears. Bess felt sorry for her, everyone did. She had had a wretched life, her poor little sister and her father had died by beheading, for treason, now her mother was dead, and she had no one in the world who cared about her.

114

"You are young," Bess said kindly. "My lady," she remembered to say, for this girl was a Tudor, "you will find happiness."

"You were kind enough to me when I was fifteen, and after the execution of my father and sister, to name me a godmother," Lady Catherine blurted.

"Aye, and your little godchild is now six years old," Bess said, thinking of her little Elizabeth.

"So I ask you now for further kindness and help!"

Bess drew her feathery brows together. "My lady," she said warningly, "You should go to your queen and your kin for help."

"I cannot!" Catherine Grey sobbed.

Bess sat up straight in bed. "Oh, my God!"

"Last December, when the queen went out hunting at Eltham, I told her I couldn't go because of a toothache! I tied up my face! Then, when Her Grace had ridden out of Westminster, Lady Jane and I stole out and walked along the sands by the river's edge, to Cannon Row!"

Bess leaped out of bed. "Lady Jane who?" she asked.

"Lady Jane Seymour, my dearest friend who died last month and was the only witness to my marriage to her brother," Catherine said piteously.

"God's death!" cried Bess. She leaned down and half lifted the bulky draped figure. "Get out! Get out!"

"No! No!" cried Catherine Grey. "I must tell someone. I wed Edward Seymour, and I am going to bear his child in a few weeks!"

Bess shook her by the shoulders. "You silly little twit, I should wring your skinny neck! How dare you make me privy to this? This is treason! Treason!" shouted Bess, beside herself with rage.

She was shaking the girl back and forth, and Catherine's neck wobbled dangerously on her slight shoulders. "How dare you?" Bess sobbed. "Get out! Go throw yourself on your knees before your queen and confess!"

"You tell her! And beg for me!" Catherine Grey had fallen to her knees, hands over her face, now that Bess had let go of her. "You tell her," she moaned.

"You stupid little coward, get out of here! Get out of here, or I'll kick you out! And don't tell anybody, ever, that

115

you came!" Bess had hold of her and was dragging her toward the door. At the door Lady Catherine stumbled to her feet, Bess opened the door and put her hands in her back and pushed. She slammed the door. Then she stood against it, holding it closed, swearing and crying at the same time.

Bess didn't sleep all that night until early in the morning, and then only after three glasses of strong wine. Sunday appeared, bright and sunny and hot. Bess attended Elizabeth, everything was as always, but in the afternoon Bess looked so white, with deep shadows under her eyes, that Elizabeth sent her to her rooms. Bess confessed she had a frightful headache.

And she did. Her head pounded and throbbed; she had no one to turn to, she didn't dare tell Sir William and draw him into this. Her only hope was to keep absolutely quiet and pray that her name would not be mentioned, for the queen's terrible wrath would fall on all who had knowledge. But over and over in Bess' head she heard,

"I am going to bear his child in a few weeks!"

It couldn't be long before all would be discovered. And when Elizabeth found out that Catherine was pregnant —and by a Seymour, of all the noble names in the realm —the royal anger would strike in every direction.

Bess' maids put cold cloths dipped in lavender water on her aching temples. Dusk finally came, the room mercifully darkened; it was Sunday night.

The palace slept, if Bess did not. Robert Dudley slept sound, his body servant Tamworth snoring at his feet on his narrow trundle bed. The door opened very quietly, and the shrouded figure of a woman crept into his room.

Tamworth started from his sleep and saw the female figure; he crept out of the room. Did he think it was the queen? Robert Dudley now wakened himself; in the night light he saw the figure and sat up straight in bed. Catherine Grey whispered, "Oh, sir, I've come for aid!"

Now there were two people who turned and tossed all night: Bess and Robert Dudley. He had got rid of Catherine Grey as soon as he could, and as quietly as possible. At the first of dawn on Monday morning, he was up and dressed,

116

and at that early hour he requested to see his queen. There was only one thing he could do: report immediately what had come to his ears. He told Elizabeth the whole story, as he had got it from the weeping Catherine.

"She was accompanied that day in December, the day we hunted at Eltham, you remember, she was accompanied by the Lady Jane Seymour; there were no other witnesses to the marriage, she says."

"And the Lady Jane Seymour is now dead!"

Elizabeth's eyes were flashing gold with rage. "And who else was privy to this secret marriage?"

"The Lady St. Loe," Dudley said. "Catherine Grey told me that she had told Lady St. Loe. The Cavendishes were close to the Greys."

Elizabeth now rose to her feet, and threw her hairbrush across the room. "God's death!" she cried. "That the two of them should dare!"

The sound for which Bess had been waiting for thirty-six hours now came with a thunderous rapping on her white door and "In the queen's name!"

Bess stood frozen. Sir William leaped for the door in complete amazement. The lieutenant of the guard bowed briefly, stepped inside, and announced in clipped tones that the Lady St. Loe was under arrest and would be lodged that day in the Tower, to await investigation.

Bess couldn't speak; her eyes fastened piteously on the young lieutenant, who averted his own blue eyes from hers and looked to Sir William.

"I didn't—" began Bess.

Sir William cut her short. He didn't know what had or could have happened, but he wanted no revelations before the ears of others. He said icily, "You may retire, Lieutenant."

The lieutenant hesitated.

"My love, you had best pack a few things and write a note to Jane, apprising her."

Bess' knees were trembling so she could hardly stand. She now looked imploringly at Sir William. Couldn't he do something, she thought! Anything!

117

Then she watched while he took the lieutenant by the arm and escorted him to the door. "You may leave us now," Sir William said in his calmest voice.

The lieutenant started to speak.

And Sir William said gently, "You may retire. You have done your duty. Now I shall do mine. As captain of the guard, I shall escort the Lady St. Loe to the Tower myself."

CHAPTER 6

THE lion's cub had unsheathed her claws. Elizabeth Tudor was not only enraged but fearful. The weakness of her position was the fact that she was unwed, and that there was no heir of her body to the throne of England. In her father's will, after her came the names of Jane and Mary and Catherine Grey, Henry's grandnieces through his sister. The little scholarly Lady Jane was dead, executed for the part she had unwillingly played in Northumberland's scheme to seize the throne. Lady Mary was a dwarf. Only Catherine Grey remained an heir. Were there other sinister forces behind this marriage of a Grey to a Seymour? Elizabeth appointed Archbishop Parker to investigate whether a marriage had or had not actually taken place. Catherine Grey and Bess St. Loe were shut up in the Tower; and the man in question, Edward Seymour, now in military service in the Netherlands, was sent for in haste. The first trial took place on September 21, and three days later, Lady Catherine Grey further enraged her sovereign by giving birth to a healthy son. Was this boy the heir to her throne?

Elizabeth wrote: *You shall also send secretly to Alderman Lodge for St. Loe, and put her in awe of divers matters confessed by the Lady Catherine, and deal with her so she may confess to you all her knowledge in the matter. It is certain that there have*

118

been great practices and purposes since the death of Lady Jane that she had been most privy to.

Day after day Bess was questioned. Sir William was worried, all kinds of rumors circulated through the court: that the extreme Protestants were behind this marriage of two such stalwart believers, that even members of the council and Sir William Cecil himself were behind this marriage, and that it was all part of a huge plot and that Bess was part of it, too.

Sir William had sent for Aunt Linacre. Bess was allowed a companion and a servant. The day Aunt Linacre arrived Bess had been questioned by both Alderman Lodge and Sir Edward Warner; when she saw Aunt Linacre, she burst into tears.

"Hush, dearie, hush," Aunt Linacre whispered as Bess clung to her.

"I am innocent and there is no way to prove it," Bess sobbed. She sat down on a wooden stool, and put her hands over her eyes.

Sir Edward Warner had been very hard that day, looking at her with blazing intentness, he had asked, "You understand, Lady St. Loe, that the only witness to this so-called marriage is dead? Lady Jane Seymour is dead, it was she who obtained the priest, no one knows his name and he is not to be found! It is only you, Lady St. Loe, who can tell us the truth. Was there a marriage? Was there a priest? What happened that day in December at Buston Street in the lodgings of Edward Seymour? What happened?"

"I don't know," cried Bess. "I don't know! I wasn't there!"

"You weren't there? So you say. But you were privy to this marriage. Don't deny it. You knew about the marriage and you kept silent."

"I was afraid!" Bess blurted.

"Ah. And how long have you been afraid? How long have you kept this secret? We know you kept silence, Lady St. Loe. How long were you silent?"

"God's death!" cried Bess. "I've told you over and over! I only learned of the marriage on the ninth of August!"

The investigation dragged on, for the legitimacy of the boy born to Catherine Grey was of great moment. Aunt Linacre tried to divert Bess.

119

"I brought a letter from Sir George Pierrepont. He told me it concerns the betrothment of Frances and his eldest son."

Bess wiped her eyes and ripped open the letter and read it. *"Dear George,"* she read. She blew her nose. "I guess I should accept; for Frances, it is a good match. Cavendish would approve. Sir George is very literary, too; Thomas Becon dedicated his book *The News Out of Heaven* to Sir George." Bess sighed. Frances was thirteen, and a pillar of strength already. At the thought of her, so far away—everyone seemed very far away to Bess—her eyes filled with tears again.

Sir William fretted and worried and got the ear of the queen, but the claws were still showing. She was adamant. Lady St. Loe would stay in the Tower till the whole investigation was over. She would stay and Catherine Grey would stay, and also the cub she'd whelped. Then Elizabeth realized she'd used the word cub, and she threw her paperweight at Sir William, who ducked neatly and was relieved when she ordered him out, out!

Sir William wrote to Bess every day, or sent a little gift. He sent a songbird in a pretty cage, and satin pillows for her bed, and perfume and wine. Bess had yearned after a gift to the queen, an hourglass of crystal with glass sand, bound in gold, in a black velvet case. Sir William asked where Sir Thomas Heneage had bought it, and he ordered one for Bess. To appease Elizabeth he paid to the crown the thousand pounds still owing from Cavendish accounts, which Bess had refused to pay because Cavendish had said not to, and anyway she was averse to handing out such a sum of money, just for nothing, as she phrased it.

Sir William couldn't see Bess very often, for it angered the Queen, and thus would do Bess harm. And he didn't dare tell her Bess was pregnant, for fear she would shout that Bess could also have her baby in the Tower as Catherine Grey had done. In desperation Sir William sought out the powerful earl of Shrewsbury, who had arrived in London. A man of unquestioned integrity, and trusted completely by Elizabeth, Sir William asked the earl, as the principal peer of Derbyshire and Yorkshire and lord high steward of the realm, to get leave to question Bess himself. When Sir William thought of Bess shut up in the two little rooms, without leave to walk outside on the leads, even to get a breath of air, he was afraid the confinement and relentless questioning would do harm to her beyond repair, for she was a spirit who couldn't be caged, he was sure.

Aunt Linacre had brought needlework, grospoint, petitpoint, and crewel. She brought paper and pens and ink and many letters. Bess fitted up a table and kept a hand in her affairs, as she had always done. She wrote innumerable letters to all her family. On the last day of October, she was busily writing to Frances when a guard knocked on the barred door.

"Questioning again," Bess said to Aunt Linacre. "I'm glad these clothes came."

Bess had sent for the dresses she had worn during her last pregnancy with Lucrece, about five years before. She was wearing a loose yellow velvet gown. Its ruff just reached her collar bones, framing her red head, and it was cut quite deep in the front. Bess deemed it alluring. When she had shown it to Cavendish, he had pursed his lips.

"Don't you like it?" she had asked.

He had leaned down and kissed her. "It put me in mind of instant and forcible possession, or more bluntly, rape." And he had grinned at her and squeezed her shoulder with his heavy strong hand. Now, facing the barred door opening slowly, she thought of him and of the past; it had been so short a time, she thought, and yet so long, so long. *I am different*, she thought, *so different*. A great sigh rent her as the door swung open full. There stood her guard.

"I am ready," she said with dignity.

She walked down the hallway as usual, with a guard, silent, on each side, as though she were marching to her doom. Their measured tread seemed to say that nothing less than execution awaited her. *Don't be foolish*, she told herself. *They can't kill you for this.* But deep within her she knew they could quickly kill her if they thought she was guilty of intrigue against the crown itself. She shoved the thought away. The two guards stopped before an open door, and Bess stepped inside. She was astonished and she was afraid. For there were three men around the table at the window.

121

Not only Sir Edward Warner and Alderman Lodge but another man. She wet her lips and tried to still the rapid thumping of her heart.

Sir Edward Warner said, "His lordship, the earl of Shrewsbury." Bess had known his father but she had never met his son, the present earl. She dipped him a curtsey. "Your lordship," she murmured.

He hardly looked up. He was reading the sheets and sheets of evidence and conversation, questions and answers. When he finally did raise his eyes, they were glacially blue and penetrating and swept her briefly with no expression at all that Bess could see.

"He's a monster," she thought.

"His lordship will take over your questioning," Sir Edward said unctuously, for he was honored to be in the presence of one of the wealthiest men in England, and one of its premier earls.

Shrewsbury didn't respond nor raise his head. He was still scanning the documents in front of him. Bess judged he must be about thirty-three or so, with a narrow lean face, tanned, dark-haired, he was, very elegantly dressed, and suddenly he did raise his head and the glacial blue eyes regarded her narrowly without expression.

"Lady St. Loe," he said.

He was sitting and Bess was standing, like the prisoner she was. She straightened to her full height and looked back. "I must make a good impression," she thought, "like a perfect lady!"

Shrewsbury leaned back in his chair and laid his arm lazily along its back. "You say here, Lady St. Loe, in your testimony, that you learned of this so-called marriage between Lord Hertford and the Lady Catherine Grey on the night of Saturday, August ninth, when she came to you in your room."

"That is true, my lord," Bess whispered.

"Ah," said Shrewsbury, "then you must have been taken by surprise."

Bess said, "Oh, I was! I was!"

Shrewsbury frowned. Bess shivered. What was coming now?

"Yet in your testimony here, Lady St. Loe, you say that you wept."

"I did weep," Bess cried. She looked at him piteously, then dropped her eyes. For a month she had steadfastly maintained that all she had done was weep and that in three minutes Lady Catherine had left her. Bess didn't want the world to know what she had really said. "I wept," Bess repeated, gazing at the earl. Would he believe her?

Evidently not. His upper lip curled slightly. "So you wept. Why?"

"Because I was afraid."

Shrewsbury frowned and leaned forward, placing his hands on the table. "Lady St. Loe," he said softly, "that doesn't seem reasonable. You were taken by surprise, yet you say you just wept and were frightened. What did you really say to the Lady Catherine Grey? What did you actually say to her, when she confided her secret, if secret it was to you?"

"It was secret to me, I mean it was unknown to me. At that time."

"So when she told you, you just burst out into tears, said nothing?"

Bess sucked in her breath. Her dark eyes met his for one startling moment, for suddenly those glacial blue eyes were not unreadable; they were very readable to Bess; for one moment there was a naked and plain communication between them. Bess thought, *Cavendish was right; it's this dress.* But her eyes showed their surprise and comprehension. Suddenly there was no expression whatsoever in his eyes save distant and faintly curious measuring.

"I gather you wept for the poor little Lady Catherine," he suggested.

"I did not!" snapped Bess. "I wept for myself and because I was angry!" She was breathing faster, and in her mind's eye she saw the scene on that Saturday night very plain.

"You were angry?" prodded the earl.

How dare he patronize me? Bess thought. "God's death," she spat. "Aye! She said she'd gone out, after a lie about a tooth-ache, with Lady Jane Seymour. I was lying in bed, and I rolled out of bed almost on top of her, sitting there, and told her to get out! I pulled at her. And then she sobbed she was going to have a child by Edward Seymour!"

There was silence in the room as the three men looked at her, visualizing this scene between two women.

Bess plunged on. "I had my hands on her and I shook her and I said, 'You silly little twit, I should wring your skinny neck!'"

Bess was breathing hard.

Shrewsbury lifted a patrician eyebrow. "And then?"

"And then," Bess shouted defiantly, "I shook her till her head wobbled. I said, 'How dare you make me privy to this? This is treason! Get out! Go to your queen and cousin, and get on your knees and confess!' But she was afraid, afraid. And she went down on her knees and begged me to tell the Queen's Majesty." Bess paused for breath. But what was the use of stopping now? "I said, 'You stupid coward, get out of here, or I'll drag you out,' and I was dragging her by her hair and shoulders. At the door she got up, and I gave her a push, and she fell out the door, and I slammed it!"

Bess drew a deep long breath and faced the three men, her eyes flashing. *I'm going to faint,* she thought. *I feel sick. What will they think of me?* Her eyes fell, and she was now conscious of pain, and she shivered; a bad cramp wrenched at her back and stomach. She felt her knees trembling.

"May I go now?" she whispered.

The earl of Shrewsbury looked across at her as though she were very far away.

"Call the guard," he said. "I have finished my questioning of the Lady St. Loe."

Bess thought she would never get out of that room. She felt as though she couldn't breathe. But actually it was only a minute before the door opened, and her guard appeared. Bess summoned all her presence of mind. She managed to curtsey.

"Good day, gentlemen," she said with as much dignity as she could muster, as her own revelations of what she had done rolled around in her head. *My reputation is ruined,* she thought drearily. *But I don't care! They can all go to the devil and be damned to them!* Swallowing the lump in her throat,

124

she followed her guard docilely out of the room, and the door closed.

The earl of Shrewsbury leaned back in his chair, his blue eyes remote. He didn't speak for a minute; in his veiled eyes was the vision of Bess, in that loose draped gown, her belly swollen with her baby. Sir Edward Warner cleared his throat. He was waiting for the earl to speak.

Shrewsbury tore his thoughts from Bess. He said, very bored, "The Lady St. Loe tried to keep that disgraceful scene a secret. But there seems to be no doubt but that she is telling the truth."

"You handled her masterfully," said Sir Edward, currying favor too obviously, for the earl gave him a glance of distaste.

He rose to his feet. "That's quite a compliment, sir," he said. "Any man who can handle the Lady St. Loe masterfully should be very proud of himself."

The earl excused himself. Sir Edward Warner stared after his lithe figure. *What did his lordship mean by that,* he wondered?

Bess had tried to hurry the guard, but he plodded woodenly, and she thought she would never get to her room; much as she hated it, it now represented a sanctuary. When she finally attained it, the guard shot the bolts, and she looked around for Aunt Linacre, to tell her what had happened and to get some comfort, when she realized she was all alone. Aunt Linacre had seized the opportunity of Bess' absence to take the air, and bribe one of the guards to bring them some wine and fruit. A bowl of apples and a little wine would do a lot for both of them. Bess turned around in a circle, as if Aunt Linacre must be hiding from her.

She grimaced with the sudden onslaught of another severe cramp. And then in fear she realized what was happening. At her feet was a little pool of blood. Terrified, Bess flung herself at the barred door, and pounded on it with her fists.

"Help!" she screamed. "Help! Aunt Linacre, help! I'm

having a miscarry! I'm losing my baby! Somebody come and help me! Somebody come!"

CHAPTER 7

ON May 12, 1562, the commission Elizabeth had appointed ruled that there had been no marriage between Edward Seymour and the Lady Catherine Grey. Seymour was fined fifteen thousand pounds, for seducing a virgin of the blood royal. Catherine Grey and her little son were kept in the Tower.

Sir Edward Warner reported that he had travailed with the Lady St. Loe, using all ways and means to bring out secret practices and secret dealings, but had made no progress.

Bess had lost her baby, and the earl of Shrewsbury had told Elizabeth he was sure she had told the truth about the night of August 9. Elizabeth relented, but just a bit, for it was not until March 25 that she gave Bess her freedom. Bess had stayed in the Tower for thirty-one weeks, from August 20 to March 25.

Sir William had suffered agonies. He worried and fretted over Bess and her health. He mourned over the loss of his child. When that early spring day finally came, Elizabeth had ordered him on a week's tour of the royal dwellings, so he could not take Bess back to Chatsworth. He procured a fine litter and provided two newly purchased horses, and outriders and retainers and servants, and arranged everything for Bess' comfort. That week he fretted even more, but at least he knew she was journeying safely to Chatsworth and her children, and that she was breathing the fresh air of freedom. When he finally arrived at Chatsworth himself, the end of the week, he came bursting into the old manor house, still half fearful at what he would find.

Bess came running to him, and threw herself in his arms.

He hugged her and hugged her. But she looked thin and pale. She never ate much, anyway, he told himself, being like the queen, having a bit of chicken or fish and some bread and lots of salad, which she loved, then she would push away her plate. He held her off and said, "Oh, my Bess. I've been so worried about you, my dearest love."

Bess said, very subdued, "It was a dreadful ordeal." She sighed deeply. "And I had, as you said once, time to think and time to realize things about myself."

"Oh, darling, sweetheart," he muttered, "that's what I didn't want you ever to do. Doubt yourself."

"Well, I do now," Bess said. "I realized there, in that horrible room in that awful, awful prison, that it wasn't my fault at all! It was those graceless Greys! I never should have befriended them!"

Sir William looked amazed. He realized then that a big fire was burning on this April morning, and he realized that the whole room was in disarray.

"What is happening? he asked.

"I'm burning their portraits!" Bess said. "Aye, I've torn all of the Greys out of their frames, and I'm burning them! I never want to see their faces on my wall. And when we finish we'll drink a toast! May their souls rot in hell!"

Sir William felt a great wave of relief and laughter; he felt weak with the combination. In the fireplace he could see the edge of Henry Grey's face disappearing in the flames. He cried, "Oh, Bess!" He flung his arms around her again. "You're just the same. Thank God. You're just the same as ever."

Bess and Sir William were grateful and happy to be able to spend the summer at Chatsworth. The roof of Chatsworth was almost ready to go on, it would probably be completed by the end of summer, and the interior was protected enough to permit the paneling of the first and second-floor rooms; the whole of Chatsworth was to be paneled complete, in oak. Nonetheless, Bess and Aunt Linacre and Jane and the embroiderer—for Bess, with her increasing income, had now employed steadily what she called a "broiderer," who drew the designs, or helped Bess draw them, and who was a professional in the craft—all

127

were indefatigable in their needlework, for Bess wanted Chatsworth's walls covered with hangings and curtains.

Nothing valuable that had ever been brought into the house ever went out of it. In the attic, stored in heavy chests, was booty of all sorts, much of it dating from Cavendish's time of service in the despoilation of the abbeys for Henry VIII. Now, practically standing on her head, her full-skirted rear stuck up like a hen's, Bess was pawing through one of the chests in search of a magnificent set of copes and chasubles from a very famous abbey; she had forgot which one.

It took two men to carry it downstairs when she finally unearthed the remembered treasure. When they finally got it down into the room they used for the embroidery and spread it out on the trestle tables that stretched the length of the room, everyone gasped in admiration.

The broiderer ventured the opinion that the work was of French nuns, of which there was nothing more marvelous in concept, color or design.

"I know where they came from," Bess cried. "I remember Cavendish saying they came from the Abbey of Lilleshall."

They would cover a whole wall, and Bess envisaged them strung on a heavy rod, across the space between, on each side of the fireplace in one of the two galleries at new Chatsworth.

"But they are saints," Aunt Linacre said, studying them.

"Aye," said Bess. "But their dress and figures are so full of color. How about if we cut out the heads?"

The broiderer nodded.

"We cut out the heads, and substitute the faces of Greek gods." Bess cried. "And we'll broider their names just above their heads—like Apollo and Pan—and we'll have a satyr in that small one with the bare legs."

By the time Sir William strolled in to see what was happening, the broiderer had finished carefully snipping out the heads of the saints. The room was full of people, there were even a few grooms whom Bess had taught to ply a needle. When Sir William learned that Bess planned to put Greek gods onto the top of the bodies of the saints, he was amused.

"Whatever made you think of that?" he inquired.

"They're so handsome," Bess answered happily. "And they are going to look perfect on each side of the fireplace and hearth in the main gallery. Remember the plasterer is doing the great crouching figure of Atlas, to hold up the mantel. It will be glorious," said Bess.

Chatsworth was indeed beginning to assume its final shape. Its four stories were almost complete; from the third to the fourth story great windows stretched; Bess watched them being put in, laboriously, day after day, and she complained bitterly they were using too much lead. But the workmen shook their heads and muttered the whole huge window would come crashing down if it were not well leaded between each tiny pane. And Bess had to be content.

"But it won't let as much light through as I wanted!"

"You'll have to build another house, then," Sir William said, teasing her.

"I will!" she answered. "I will!"

Inside some of the decorations were begun: the white wainscotting and elaborate plaster friezes in the high great chamber and gallery.

On this late summer day the heather and the bracken turned the sloping hills into purple and gold. As the river neared the house it twisted like a glittery snake and framed the grounds like a hoop. The gardens were a series of terraces, descending to the stone walls, the walks went through box and yew and holly and rosemary; fountains sprayed, and the air was fragrant with lilies and roses and eglantine.

Sir William loved the herb garden; he told Bess he had never tasted such gooseberries as grew in the gardens at Chatsworth. He ate them with thick cream, relishing every mouthful.

Yet Bess thought he was getting thinner and more frail. She mentioned this to Aunt Linacre, who said, "I thought you'd never notice it, Bess."

"I'm worried!"

"Aye, so am I," Aunt Linacre said, which hardly gave Bess much comfort.

Bess had been occupied with Chatsworth and her children. The children were growing up, from redheaded Henry to little Mary, who was exceptionally determined and bright; as the youngest she held her own with a tenacity that amazed her mother. Elizabeth was now eight and getting leggy; and though her face was thin and sharp with childhood, it was not difficult to see the beautiful bone structure, the wide-set eyes, and the mass of thick auburn hair. She was a quiet child for a Cavendish, Bess thought; there was something remote about her, too, at times; she was completely self-possessed and knew exactly what she wanted.

Frances, Bess' oldest child, was fourteen and betrothed to George Pierrepont, the marriage Bess had arranged last year when she was in the Tower. Frances was gay and enchanting and clever and happy. *She is like her father,* Bess thought, her eyes on her lovingly. *She will always be happy.* She took and used what she had and molded it into something she wanted.

The three boys were at Eton, Charles, the youngest, at nine, had joined his brothers.

"They are growing up so fast," mourned Bess. And Aunt Linacre said, "Not fast enough for me." When they were all at home, old Chatsworth bulged, not only with children but with their body servants, their tutors, and their friends and their endless pets.

"If that dog of yours pees on the floor one more time," Aunt Linacre said to Charles, "out he goes, never to return!"

In October the boys went back to school, but Bess would not leave Chatsworth; she was determined to spend the winter and the Christmas season in Derbyshire. "I was in the Tower last Christmas," she said. "This year I'm going to be at home. And watch the snows fall on the hillsides."

Sir William didn't blame her; he arranged to be at Chatsworth as much as possible. But he asked, "Bess, you're not afraid to go back to court, are you?"

"No." Bess looked down at her hands. She thought, *First that cur Edward St. Loe put it about that I tried to poison my husband, and then I told Shrewsbury what I said to Catherine Grey, and everybody will know it by now.*

Sir William said, "It's no permanent disgrace to have been placed in the Tower; it even happened to me."

"I know it," Bess said. "But that lecher, Shrewsbury—"

Sir William was aghast. The haughty patrician earl of Shrewsbury! "He deemed you innocent, he said you had told him the truth."

"He's a monster," Bess said. "I never want to see him again."

CHAPTER 8

"BESS will be a widow again before this year is out," Aunt Linacre said to Jane. "You mark my words, Jane. But don't tell Bess."

Aunt Linacre had had the faculty of being right so much that Bess and Jane were apt to take her predictions for the gospel truth, but this time Jane demurred. "Oh, no, Aunt!"

Aunt Linacre then used the gambit she always used to cow both of them. "Think how long I've lived and how much I've seen," she said darkly.

Jane worried and fussed all day. She could hardly keep her mind on the problems of her son, who was in love with a farmer's daughter, and on the problem of Frances' wedding, which was occupying Bess. Frances would be sixteen March, 1564, and she was to be married in June to young George Pierrepont. Every time Jane saw the young couple together, her heart beat fast with the memory of the wonder of young love, for these two were in love, it shone like magic all about them, as they went hand in hand through the spring days.

Bess had given the young couple a rebuilt manor house and five hundred acres of land, a little to the north in the shadow of Sheffield Castle. When they thanked her profusely, she shook her head. "I shall give all of you, all my children, the land which your father and I bought together. You shall all share it, male and female alike."

"Since we are going to live very near to Sheffield Castle," Frances said, "we should invite the earl to our wedding."

131

"He won't come," Bess said. "My mother invited the fifth earl to my wedding, and he didn't come. Then Cavendish insisted we ask him to stand godfather to Temperance, and he acquiesced; but since then we have had little or no communication."

Poor little Temperance, Bess thought; she wrenched her mind from the past. Frances was right; they should ask the earl; she was right just as her father had been right; the earl was the most principal noble of Derbyshire, and they should invite him to the wedding.

"He won't come, though," Bess predicted.

She was right; he sent a brief note, declining, but he also sent a magnificent present, a huge platter of silver, with its complement of knives, from Italy, all hand wrought, each handle different and each blade shining and sharp. They were brought by a neatly liveried messenger, with the Talbot embroidered on their sleeves. They bowed to Frances and announced that they came bearing the gift and good wishes of his lordship, the earl of Shrewsbury, who would indeed welcome them as his neighbors.

"He does everything perfect," Sir William said. As the two messengers refused any refreshment, saying politely they had orders to stop at one of his lordship's dwellings nearby instead. "Even to instructing his servants, so that they don't give you any inconvenience when you are busy with a wedding."

Bess thought, *Piss on his lordship.* "I think the gift too much, as though he wishes to impress us," she whispered later to Sir William. "He should have sent a more modest gift and come to the wedding."

"But it is his wife, Bess," Sir William said. "She is very ill."

No wonder, thought Bess, *living with him, and having six children by him. Poor soul.*

Frances' wedding day was a perfect June day, with little fat clouds chasing each other across the hills in the sunny blue skies. The bride and groom were so happy that everyone was happy, and Bess couldn't remember a more joyous day, so joyous she and Aunt Linacre and Jane and young Bess and Mary all cried happily into their handkerchiefs at various times during the ceremony and the festivities, and of course at Frances' leavetaking. Later Bess sat in bed and had a glass of wine and wiped away the last tears, and said to Sir William, "It was just beautiful!"

Sir William was leaving for London the next day. Bess said suddenly, "I hope you won't stay too long."

He assured her he wouldn't. But he didn't want to say that he was going to ask the queen for leave to come back to Chatsworth for two months because he wasn't feeling very well.

Sir William returned from court in late July, and never went back. He was becoming more thin and more frail. And although at first Bess was sure he needed just fresh air and good food and rest, in the early fall even Bess, with her blind optimism, could see that Sir William was getting worse every week. In fear and love Bess tended him. By October he was confined to bed. He had some pain and the doctors gave him purges and took blood.

In October the news came that Lady Shrewsbury had died. Sir William could not attend the funeral and found even writing a letter of condolence to the earl a chore, but he insisted on doing it in his own hand. Aunt Linacre cooked her wonderful soups for Sir William, and Bess and Jane fed him and read to him and made him as comfortable as they could, with smooth-made beds of fresh linen and big pillows, sweet-smelling with lavender, and freshly aired his chamber, even in winter, for they had moved him into a room with a new fireplace so the fires could be kept burning constantly.

Sir William died ten days before Christmas. The snow was falling as the tears were falling from Bess' eyes, steadily. She couldn't stop her weeping. Over and over she kept repeating, "I have lost my dearest, truest friend in all the world. In all the world," sobbed Bess.

Sir William had told her he wished to be buried beside his father, in the church of Great St. Helen, in Bishopsgate. There he was laid to rest. Bess said to Aunt Linacre, "My life is over."

On New Year's Day, Bess received a letter of condolence from the queen. The letters had poured in from everyone of consequence. Bess put them all away in a casket covered with velvet. It was January 1, 1565. It was ten o'clock at night, and the snow was falling; the children were in bed, subdued and quiet. It had been a sad New Year's Day. In Bess' room Aunt Linacre and Jane and Bess sat close to the fire. Aunt Linacre reached in her capacious pocket and drew out the cards. Every New Year's night, Aunt Linacre told them the future with her cards. And it was done in secret, for it might be deemed witchcraft, Aunt Linacre was so clairvoyant.

"I have no future," Bess said. But she took the cards and shuffled them the way Aunt Linacre had taught her, taking the deck in one hand and pushing the cards through each other with the other hand.

"Lay out twelve cards, face down," Aunt Linacre said.

Bess did, laying the bright-colored cards face down on the little table on Aunt Linacre's lap, the table she used for fine sewing.

Slowly Aunt Linacre turned them face up.

"You are going to come into a great deal of money," Aunt Linacre said.

Bess sniffed and blew her nose. "From Sir William's estates."

Aunt Linacre said, "Now here are Frances and George, happy and maybe with a child."

Aunt Linacre studied the cards. "It looks like a granddaughter for you, Bess. And I wouldn't be surprised if she wouldn't be named for you."

Bess tried to smile.

"It may be longer than a year away, though," Aunt Linacre said. "Now take ten more cards and place them in a circle around."

"Your affairs will prosper, Bess. Here is the ten of diamonds right next to you. Money, money, money. And your children, here they are, they are all well, and happy. I foresee no troubles with your family, no sickness, only good health and growing."

Bess sighed. "That's good," she said.

"You are going to be thinking about a bride for Henry, but I shouldn't if I were you. The cards say to wait. Wait for two years at least. But someone will ask you about marrying their girl to Henry. It won't be right. For him."

Bess and Jane looked at Aunt Linacre with great respect. "I'll wait, Aunt," Bess breathed solemnly.

Aunt Linacre hesitated. "There will be suitors for you, all around you, Bess."

Jane asked, "Do you see a marriage for Bess, Aunt?"

Aunt Linacre threw Jane a glance of deep reproach. Jane knew well enough Aunt Linacre disdained questions. But this time Bess was amazed at her answer to Jane's question.

"No," she snapped. "I see no marriage." Aunt Linacre looked at Bess' oval face, so near. She gathered up the spread-out cards, picking up the knave of hearts last. She said, "No marriage this year, Bess." Again she looked at the shadowed face. True, she'd seen no marriage, but she'd seen plain a lover. Of course she wouldn't tell Bess that. The cards must have been wrong.

CHAPTER 9

BESS and all the other occupants of Chatsworth missed Sir William sorely. Now that he was gone, Bess and Jane and Aunt Linacre realized how much they had looked forward to his arrivals from court, full of delightful news and exciting pieces of gossip, not only from London but from abroad. They missed his kindness and his wit, and they missed looking after a man. In the spring, even with the gardening and the excitement of summer coming, when all could be outside and not confined to the dark and often cold house, life at Chatsworth was not the same.

There was in residence at Chatsworth a tutor for Bess' younger daughters. The schoolroom was at the end of the second floor, a sunny cheerful room, and Bess began to sit in on the French lessons. It would be good for her to learn French, she thought. She found it very exciting.

The girls' tutor was a young man, about twenty-five, named Henry Jackson. His mother had been a Frenchwoman, and he spoke French fluently and with a nice accent; he led Bess along very neatly, with simple sentences and obvious phrases, which he repeated so that soon she was able to follow him.

"C'est très simple, ce n'est pas difficile," he would say, over and over, till Bess could say it herself, without thinking.

The exciting news that fall was that Mary Queen of Scotland and the Isles had come back to her kingdom from France, a young and, they said, beautiful widow. Henry Jackson was explaining to the children the line of descent.

"Ce n'est pas compliqué," he began, and Bess smiled because she was really beginning to follow. *"Margaret, la soeur de votre roi, Henry VIII. . . ."*

Bess nodded, proud she could understand. Margaret Tudor, the sister of your King Henry VIII was the wife of James IV of Scotland. Thus, Mary Stuart's grandmother is the aunt of your own Queen Elizabeth.

"Elles sont cousines."

Bess nodded happily.

"Mais, ecoutex bien. . . ."

Bess listened carefully. Henry's sister had married twice, the second time to the earl of Angus, by whom she had had a daughter. This daughter had married the earl of Lennox, a Stuart, and was now living in England with two sons. These sons bore both Stuart and Tudor blood and were thus of royal lineage. It was the older of the two sons of the duchess of Lennox whose name was being proposed as a husband for the young, beautiful Queen of Scots.

Henry Jackson went over more of the lineage and history until the two little girls seemed to understand this history lesson in French. Bess beamed on them both.

Henry Jackson saw that both of his young charges were beginning to squirm. *"Maintenant,"* he said, smiling at both of them, *"vôtre leçon est fini, est conclu."*

Bess thought the way he used two words, one following another so they could all understand, was exceedingly clever. She rose obediently as the class was dismissed, and her attitude of learning amused Henry Jackson, and he grinned.

The two little girls scampered out. Henry Jackson said to Bess, "Tomorrow I shall explain that Queen Mary of Scotland has quartered the arms of England on her flag, and try to explain to them the ill feeling between the two queens because of Mary's aspirations to the throne of England, that she is Catholic and claims she is the true heir. I will go into more of the background of the history."

Bess said, "I am truly beginning to follow you."

"You are an apt pupil, my lady," Henry Jackson said, "but you should speak more, in French; not only understand but speak."

"I could speak French with you."

"Indeed you could; I should be honored! *Enchanté!*" he bowed.

Bess felt as though she were already at court in France. She smiled dazzlingly on Henry Jackson, and they arranged that three times a week, for an hour, Bess would speak French with him. Before they parted he gave her some French poetry of Villon to memorize.

Bess' son Henry was fourteen that summer. Lanky and redheaded, he was often moody and difficult and resisted Bess' efforts to control him. William and Charles had a natural insouciance; they laughed more than they fussed. That summer a neighbor offered his daughter to Bess as Henry's bride. Solemnly Bess discussed this with Aunt Linacre. They turned down the offer with soft words; Henry was too young yet, and too volatile. And too wealthy, Bess thought privately. With her means, a splendid bride could be got for Henry.

When October came, the boys went back to school, Henry to Cambridge. It was a rainy fall, and when she wasn't at her accounts or her correspondence or watching the workmen at Chatsworth, she was busy with her French and annoyed Jane and Aunt Linacre excessively by inserting French words into her conversation at every conceivable point, so that she was speaking a jargon of English and French. Three times a week she spent an hour with Henry Jackson.

Bess was not a flirt; she was far too direct. But she treated men with an open camaraderie that many found enchanting. And one day in December, when Bess was rattling along in French with her verbs all mixed up and her eyes alight with the excitement of a new language, Henry Jackson suddenly couldn't resist, and he said, when she had finished her sentence, "*Je t'adore!*"

Bess stopped smiling and looked at him in complete astonishment. Had she heard him correctly? During this hour she was forbidden to use English, and she searched her mind for the right words in French. She said rapidly, "*Vous êtes fou!*"

He was advancing on her, and Bess turned her back. She said, "You've spoiled it, Master Jackson. Now I'll have to send you away."

She bent her head, for she was upset and disappointed. How had this ever happened? He put his hands on her shoulders, to turn her, but Bess shook her red head sadly.

"No, Master Jackson; we were friends. Now you will have to go. I want you to leave me now."

The words were spoken in so final and yet dispirited a tone that Henry Jackson obeyed her; she heard him going to the door and heard his footsteps receding slowly down the hall.

As soon as she decently could, Bess herself rushed from the room and sought Aunt Linacre.

"And he told me he adored me, and I had to tell him he must leave, and now we've got to find a new tutor in two weeks, and—God's death!"

Aunt Linacre said, "It's your own fault, Bess, for being alone with him so much."

Bess muttered, "*Ce n'est pas ma faute.*"

"Stop that silly French!" Aunt Linacre cried. "It is your fault!" Nonetheless, she was very relieved. The cards had been right after all. Henry Jackson was Bess' indicated lover, only nothing had happened; Bess had had too much sense. What a scandal it would have been! Aunt Linacre said darkly, "Remember your friend, Frances Grey, and her marrying her head groom—years younger than she. And how everyone laughed at her." Aunt Linacre sighed. "But you did right, Bess."

138

Bess stared at her in amazement. "Did you think I'd do anything so silly as Frances Grey?"

Aunt Linacre didn't dare confess what the cards had shown. "Of course not, Bess," she snapped. "But you ought to get rid of him as quick as possible." For who really knew what Bess might or might not do?

CHAPTER 10

SHEFFIELD CASTLE raised its bulky stone to the north of Chatsworth by some ten miles. Its lord had arrived from London, looking for some hunting and a few days in the saddle away from his cares, which he deemed many. For a conscientious man he had too much money, too many possessions, too much spreading land, too many children—and no wife. Not only that, but the weather had turned vile; it was bitter cold for the second week in December; this presented a problem for his comfort in the hunt for red deer, and his tenants were complaining bitterly about the lack of wood. He informed his bailiff at Sheffield Castle, which was just one of his many residences, that the farmers and tenants would be permitted to cut wood. And cold or not, he would sally forth for the red deer, and he would distribute it among the needy. His bailiff was pleased, then he whispered that young Gilbert was in trouble.

"What kind of trouble?" snapped the earl.

"The head cook's daughter," explained the bailiff, intending to say more, but the grim look on the face of Lord Shrewsbury forbade further speech, and the bailiff knew he had said enough.

"You may send young Lord Talbot to me," he said, and while he waited for his second son, he tried to remember how old he was and came to the conclusion that Gilbert was thirteen.

When Gilbert arrived, fully ten minutes later, his father was already vastly annoyed.

"What kept you, young man?" he asked, his blue eyes resting on Gilbert's smooth face and shaggy, tawny hair and his direct blue eyes, which always held laughter.

"I was reading," Gilbert said truthfully. "In bed. It's so damned cold, Father. I don't see," Gilbert went on, "why we have to stay for Christmas in this old cold stone pile. Why can't we go to London?"

"Your trouble is that you are too fortunate," the earl said, and looked troubled. "Too fortunate," he repeated. "Gilbert, don't you know that your very position precludes your taking advantage of the cook's daughter?"

The earl said these words with such deep distaste that Gilbert looked abashed, and the direct blue eyes, so like the earl's, fell before the eagle glance that had been bestowed on him. The earl in that glance had divined that the adventure had not been much of an adventure and that Gilbert was still innocent. The earl sighed with some relief, for thirteen was rather young, even for a Talbot.

The earl continued, now lazily. "When you are fifteen, Gilbert, it is my intention to send you abroad. There you may have all the adventures you please. Just be careful, though, and don't come home with the French disease." The earl then vividly described the effects of the French disease, and by the time he had concluded Gilbert looked as horrified as the earl could have wished.

His good humor restored, he then informed his son that he could accompany him on the hunt that day, and Gilbert left the room, wondering where he had put his heavy riding boots.

The earl hunted that day, and for four days thereafter, taking Gilbert, and Francis, his oldest son, and Grace, who was fourteen; the three youngest he wouldn't expose to the cold.

But on the fifth day, the earl, having risen early, as was his habit, having had a bite of breakfast, munching a piece of bread and cheese, before the huge fire that blazed in the old, old stone fireplace, dressed warmly in a furred lynx jacket, and staring into the bright flames, standing there, all alone, he came to the conclusion that his duties as lord

140

of the castle were done; there was enough meat and more for the tenants in the village and the huge complement of castle servants and residents. Moreover, out the narrow window hung silvery icicles, so cold had been the night of the twenty-second of December. He had come to a decision, and he gave orders that he would ride to a lodge of his, but a few miles distant, in the Derbyshire hills. It lay near to the manor of Chatsworth. Accompanied by two grooms, he set forth.

He rode direct to the lodge, had an early dinner, bathed, changed his shirt, and then, pulling on his heavy gloves, and with a fresh horse, the earl of Shrewsbury rode direct to Chatsworth.

When he arrived, alone, in the December afternoon, about two o'clock, he was met in the old raftered hall by Aunt Linacre. She was plainly astonished to see him, and she gave him a warm welcome, of course. But no, the earl would take no refreshment, even though it was bitter cold, he had wanted the fresh air. And he had come to see the Lady St. Loe. Where was she?

The earl, with his direct manner, looked about the hall, as if Bess should appear on the instant.

Aunt Linacre said that Bess was at new Chatsworth, with her new plasterer, who was so gifted—he was an artist!

"In this weather?" queried the earl. And before Aunt Linacre could explain, he was out the door.

Outside again, he looked across the sloping valley to the house rising in the distance, already four stories with its towers; it did indeed look romantic, and the conception of the architecture was new and lovely. Its windows glittered with ice, and the series of ponds that Cavendish had constructed looked like mirrors set in white velvet, for light snow lay on the hills of Chatsworth.

It was too far to walk, the earl decided, and he put one big-booted foot in the stirrups and turned the horse's head; because of the snow the pace was slow, and it seemed to take forever to reach the curtain walls of Chatsworth. Within them, the already fashioned, beautiful gardens lay hushed with snow, the yews stuck out a few green leaves like planned decoration.

The wide double doors stood open. Within, it seemed

141

colder than outside. The earl climbed the shallow steps, and emerged onto Chatsworth's first gallery; it boasted two. At the far end stood Bess, wrapped in a furred cloak, with little fur boots. The earl came to a standstill, for Bess was speaking. Not to the intruder, but to the man who was bent over his plaster saucer, a big lead one, and Bess was saying, "Then use beer! If the water is freezing when you mix the plaster, use beer."

The earl of Shrewsbury smiled, his blue eyes lighting with amusement and admiration. Although he was six feet tall, he moved lithely and quietly, and Bess didn't hear him coming, she was so intent on her idea of using beer to mix the plaster that she heard nothing until he was right beside her, looming over her. "What about warmed ale?" he suggested.

Startled, Bess turned, raising her eyes past the earl's big shoulders, even bigger with the heavy lynx fur, to his face. And when she saw who was standing over her, she was more astonished than Aunt Linacre. In a flash of remembrance, she recalled the last time she had seen him.

"Lord Shrewsbury," she stammered. "Welcome to Chatsworth."

The plasterer rose to his feet and touched his cap. But the earl didn't see him; his blue eyes were fastened on Bess' face; he reached out his gloved hand and took hers. "You'll catch cold out here," he said. "How long have you been here?"

"About an hour," Bess said.

"Then I'll take you back, now," the earl said.

Bess started to say no, but he had taken her arm. He had also told her own plasterer, and his two assistants that they should leave off work now, and Bess found herself descending the stairs to the cold empty hall below; the wind was whistling through the open doors.

When his horse saw them, he let out a loud plaintive whinny. Bess said stiffly, "I'll walk, my lord."

The earl shook his head. He picked her up and set her in the saddle and mounted himself. "Hang on tight," he said, "for he may slip on this ice. I'll walk him."

Bess did indeed hang on tight. And the horse did slip; it was a perilous journey, but accomplished in safety. At the doors of old Chatsworth, the earl lifted her from the saddle.

They walked to the front doors; it wasn't till they reached them that Bess realized he still had one big arm around her, as though to comfort her and hold her close against the cold.

The earl's unexpected arrival had galvanized Aunt Linacre into instant action in the kitchens, where she was directing the entire staff, her wooden spoon making fine flourishes in every direction and barely missing kerchiefed heads.

"It is a great and unexpected honor to have his lordship as a guest," she kept repeating, as she looked askance at a sauce being stirred. By the time he and Bess arrived, she was waiting for them at the doors. And when the earl perceived her, he let go of Bess, but not hastily, just releasing her slowly, and he asked for a groom to take his horse to the stables, out of the cold.

Aunt Linacre said, "Of course, my lord," and also that he must want for food and drink himself and that it was being prepared, their supper, with special attention for their honored guest.

The earl inclined his head and thanked her, and meantime Bess hadn't said a word, just looked from one to the other as though she were hypnotized. Finally, she made a gesture to take off her cloak, and the earl reached out and removed it from her shoulders; she felt the touch of his hands, curiously and instantly exciting, and she looked up at him, meeting his eyes.

Aunt Linacre's sharp eyes observed them both. She thought, *Why he's plainly mad about her, if she plays her cards well, she will be the Countess of Shrewsbury.* And then she thought, *Cards! Cards! Maybe I should have warned her! But no, that is past. That French-speaking knave Jackson leaves today.*

But still, she had a premonition of something, and she felt the blood rising in her face and a nagging pain in her head; she had felt this way before lately, and she was a bit afraid. *I eat too much,* she told herself. *I must begin to be less gluttonous, I must.* She drew a breath and smiled, and said aloud, "Let us go into the warm room, where we can be comfortable." She wanted to sit down.

Aunt Linacre and the whole household called it the

143

"warm room" because Bess, a few years ago, had had the paneling renewed and the plaster mended and a new fireplace built, with an overhanging mantel that threw out the heat. And she had hung the hangings that were to go into new Chatsworth when it was finished, or some of them, so it was cozy and colorful.

The earl had removed his heavy furred coat, and was dressed in a brown velvet riding habit, which suited his long lean figure perfectly. Aunt Linacre forgot her discomfort in the presence of such a man, although she saw why most people thought him arrogant and haughty. When Jane arrived, he barely acknowledged the introduction; he was polite but frosty. And when Aunt Linacre said that supper would soon be ready, he said that he would enjoy it, but he would leave afterwards.

Bess said, "Well, then, my lord, I should like you to meet my children."

Jane said she would fetch the boys and Mary and Elizabeth, and Aunt Linacre excused herself to tell the servants to serve, so for a moment Bess and the earl were alone.

Bess said, "You don't need to stay if you don't want to."

The earl shook his head, in annoyance at himself. "I'm too used to having my own way. I came to see you. What I would like is to sweep all these women out of my path." He looked down at her speculatively. "Why are you so tongue-tied?"

"I can't think of anything to say," Bess said.

He laughed. "A rare woman. But you don't have that reputation."

Bess felt her face pale. "I keep remembering—in the Tower, that day—I didn't want to tell you, or tell anybody. At the time I was frantic with anger. But later, when I told about it, it sounded . . . disgraceful." Bess drew the word out slowly, using it only because she couldn't think of a better one.

"Aye, it did," he agreed.

Before she could answer him, Jane reappeared with Mary and Elizabeth. Bess was pleased to see how sweet they looked, and she was glad the earl was now so courtly and kind, quite different from the way he had been with Jane.

144

Then the boys appeared, and he greeted them with a quick handclasp; Bess could see that the boys were awed and impressed and that they liked his direct manner, curt though it was.

It was too cold to eat in the hall. So the children were released and scampered away to eat with their own servants, in the schoolroom. Bess and Jane and Aunt Linacre and the earl sat down to supper on a hastily put up trestle table, which the maids had spread with fine linen. The earl now took the trouble to give them the news from London, since he had returned but a week ago, and to make himself agreeable to Jane and Aunt Linacre. He told them the court was aghast and incredulous because the queen had actually suggested that Robert Dudley wed with Mary Queen of Scots.

"It will make Mary wild with anger," Bess said. "I warrant that's why she did it!" Bess laughed; she could imagine Elizabeth laughing at her own coup. "She won't marry him herself, but she suggests that Mary marry him!"

Bess forgot her shyness, and got up and fetched the wine from the cupboard and poured the earl another cup. She watched him eat and drink; he had a healthy male appetite, she decided, and suddenly she smiled at him across the table, and she said happily, "Oh, it is good to have a man to feed. We're so glad you came to visit us!"

The earl raised his cup, his blue eyes bright. "Thank you, and a toast, to all of you."

Outside, in the darkening afternoon, the snow had begun to fall, lightly at first and then thick, thick. So that an hour later, with Bess holding his furry jacket, in the hall, she suddenly looked out through the narrow window.

"Why, it's snowing," she cried. "It's snowing very hard!"

Bess and Jane had aired, cleaned, and removed from the chamber all of Sir William's personal possessions months ago. But in the chest at the foot of the bed was a warm bedgown and quilts and towels. The fire had been lighted and the curtains drawn, and the bed freshly made up with linen sheets and bolsters, and hot bricks had been slid between the cold sheets to make the room ready for the overnight guest, for it would have been foolhardy for the

145

earl to have set forth on a night like this. Bess brushed the bedgown and hung it over the firescreen to warm; another servant appeared with hot steaming water. Bess sniffed at the towel to make sure it wasn't musty, but it smelled fresh with the lavender she had packed into the closet.

Aunt Linacre and Jane had said good-night to the earl in the hall outside the door, which stood open. Bess, before the fire, heard them say good-night, saw the small curtsey Jane dipped, and then the earl came into the room, which seemed to Bess welcoming and cozily warm.

"You rode over with not even a groom," she said, "and you are accustomed to a body servant, I know, and would you want me to call for Henry's? He is a fine young man, who attends them at school."

The earl smiled at her earnestness. "I can look after myself," he said. "I can even shave myself!"

Bess laughed. But she was not convinced. He probably never took off his own boots. "Are you sure you don't want Jack?"

He didn't answer her; he reached behind himself and closed the door, gently. Bess went over to the sideboard and lifted the white linen napkin which covered a pewter bowl of apples; she inspected them critically, they were well washed and shiny red. She lifted the stopper on the decanter to make sure he had the finest wine the household had to offer; the silver cup was gleaming with polish. Wisps of steam came out of the water ewer; the bedroom's convenient chair was hidden discreetly by a wicker screen. She was as satisfied with the hospitality of old Chatsworth as she could be. For although Bess had money and lived well, all her extra money had gone into new Chatsworth, and more and more land. She knew that in the earl's eyes she lived simply and plainly, in an old half-timbered manor house.

She turned and gave him a smile. "We have done the best we can, for an unexpected guest, my lord."

He had moved from the door to the fireplace and removed his coat and hung it over the back of a wooden chair by the fire. In his shirtsleeves, the bedroom suddenly took on an intimate atmosphere, and Bess thought, *He is very attractive.*

146

"I liked your children," the earl said, in his direct and honest manner.

"I have an older girl, she is married eighteen months, to Sir George Pierrepont. I have six children."

"So do I," he said. He grinned. "I know what it's like!"

Bess said, "Last year each of those boys went through four pairs of shoes, to say nothing of resoling and boots!" Then she stopped, for she thought that people criticized her for thinking of money; it was because they were jealous that she had it, of course. But she was troubled; the earl couldn't have a very good opinion of her; he had the reputation of being scrupulously patrician. *I wonder why he came,* she thought. *He will probably marry some meek creature who says "very well, my Lord, precisely."*

The candles flickered, and a log in the fireplace snapped loudly. There was a shower of sparks and, fearful, Bess rushed over to the hearth, and picked up the homemade broom and swept them neatly back. She straightened up, flushed from the heat.

"That always frightens me!" she exclaimed.

The earl had been watching her, and now, without preamble, his arms went around her like steel, and the fire that blazed up in Bess was far more dangerous than the shower of sparks. Her eyes closed tight, and she felt the length of his body against hers.

Her arms were around him tight, her legs braced against his. *This is why he came,* she thought. *He knows it, too; I want him inside me. Bad. And why not? Why not?* Bess made a token effort to free herself against his strength. He lifted her by wrapping his arms around her so her feet swung clear of the floor, and he carried her over to the big bed.

Aunt Linacre still didn't feel well. She turned in her bed, clumsily, despising her own bulk and her flopping breasts. Sleep would not come. Finally she got up and went to her door, wrapped in her warm woolen bedgown; the garderobe was down the hall, and if she used it, maybe she could get to sleep.

The hall was shadowy, but she thought she saw a figure. She realized that it was that French knave Henry Jackson.

147

He was coming back from the schoolroom, which lay in darkness.

"What are you doing here?" she hissed.

"I forgot one of my books," he whispered back.

Aunt Linacre was standing right beside the door of Sir William's former room. And Chatsworth manor was very old and saggy. At this precise moment the door that the earl had closed with a latch only swung slowly inward.

"Jesu!" The word escaped from Henry Jackson's parted lips like smoke.

Aunt Linacre reached down and softly closed the door; it took great presence of mind, and she could feel her heart hammering like an anvil in her great chest. How she spoke she never knew. "Get to bed," she whispered and gave him a look which he didn't see. But he obeyed; he tiptoed down the hall like a thief, and so did Aunt Linacre, tiptoeing as best she could, to get away from what she had seen with her own eyes, her very own eyes. And it was her very own Bess, too, whom she'd seen, and Bess' very own white legs cradling the earl, for Aunt Linacre had seen plain the little knitted green lace stockings that she herself had knitted for Bess for New Year's—only Bess had surprised her knitting them, and had begged her to give them to her right away. Little knitted lace green stockings to the knee. She hadn't bothered, in her passion, to take them off. The cards had been right. Aunt Linacre lay on her side and wept.

CHAPTER 11

AUNT LINACRE slept almost none and was up before dawn, in the winter darkness. She went into the kitchens where the fires were already glowing on the big hearth; it looked just the same and just as comforting, as if the events of the previous night had not, nay, could not have happened. She had a cup of warmed wine with spices and honey and water. She sucked the brew greedily. The cook and her helpers said it had stopped snowing, the weather was much warmer and promised to be more clement.

At six Henry Jackson set forth with loaded saddlebags. Aunt Linacre came into the hall to bid him good-bye, and kept her face emotionless, for she was pretending that if the earl of Shrewsbury had seduced a maid under their roof, it was really none of Henry Jackson's business. Aunt Linacre was clinging to the only hope she had—that he hadn't recognized Bess. How could he in that flurry of legs and tumbled bed quilts? Nonetheless, when Henry and his horse turned out of the old gates of Chatsworth, she said aloud, "I hope we've seen and heard the last of you!"

She went back to the kitchens and had another cup of watered wine and some bread and butter, and she commanded one of the maids to take hot water up to the earl's chamber, but to remember to knock and wait to be bid to enter. But surely her disreputable niece had had the sense to leave the chamber!

"Don't forget to knock!"

The maid staggered out with the water. When she reappeared without it, Aunt Linacre said, "What happened?"

The maid looked astonished.. "What happened, mum? Naught happened; his lordship bade me put the water on the sideboard. And he thanked me, mum."

"Then he must be getting dressed," Aunt Linacre said, and began to set out some meat and cheese on a pewter platter, and she sliced some pieces of the finest bread. She had just finished doing this, for she was making even, thin slices, when the earl stuck his head around the door and said, "Good morning! May I come in?"

Aunt Linacre jumped. "Of course, my lord! But I was going to serve you this in the warm room—the parlor where we ate last night!"

"No, no," he said, coming into the big kitchen. He sat down on a stool before the table, on the side of the fire. "I like it here." He smiled at Aunt Linacre, who found herself studying his face; it was undeniably a very masculine face, aquiline, the mouth a bit too large, but firm; he was clean shaven, and his blue eyes looked back at her openly.

Aunt Linacre tried to smile back politely. Then she said, "Of course, my lord, sit down."

149

"I already am," the earl reminded her, and while Aunt Linacre poured him some ale, which he said was what he wanted, he began to eat, with good appetite, Aunt Linacre observed, her beady eyes narrowing, and stormy. She gave him a quick glance, but he didn't notice. He was saying with his mouth full that he had to get back to Sheffield as soon as possible, for after all it was the day before Christmas, and his children were all at Sheffield.

She must pretend she knew nothing; she brought him the water to wash when he had finished eating. He washed his hands and wiped his mouth, laid down the napkin and stood up. When he was standing, he towered over Aunt Linacre, who was only about five feet tall. She looked up at him, and he took her hand in his big one and thanked her. Together they walked out into the hallway.

"I told the Lady St. Loe that I had to leave early. Pray bid her good-bye and a happy Christmas for me, and thank her for her hospitality."

He didn't even choke over that word, Aunt Linacre thought.

"I'll tell her, my lord." Then she realized she must say something more, so she continued, "Bess will be sorry not to bid you good-bye and a happy Christmas, so I'll say it for her." *And am I glad to see the last of you, too!* she thought.

While they were standing there, with the earl putting on his great big furry jacket, Bess appeared at the top of the stairway. She had on a warm gray wool morning gown, with a white ruff. She stood up there, looking down at them.

"Oh, you are going already," she said, and she started down the stairway, looking, Aunt Linacre thought angrily, positively dewy-eyed. She came up to them.

"I just told Mistress Linacre to bid you good-bye for me," the earl said.

"Have a happy Christmas, my lord," Bess said.

He took her in his arms lightly and kissed her cheek, like any gentleman taking leave of a friend. "A happy Christmas and a fine New Year," he said.

"Thank you," Bess said. Then he went to the door, and the groom who had been sent for his horse was there, waiting, holding the big horse. The earl gave a final wave, and the door closed.

150

Bess turned away to go out to the kitchen herself. Aunt Linacre snapped, "Well, I guess that's the last we've seen of him! He'll not come riding over after Christmas, I take it!"

"No," said Bess. "He must be at court at New Year's, of course. He told me, Aunt."

"Oh, of course! To present his gift to the queen as befits one of the most principal peers! And no doubt he has a few lady friends at court, too!"

Bess drew her feathery brows together thoughtfully, remembering her lover. "He might," she admitted.

Aunt Linacre spit out a "God's death!"

Bess regarded her, surprised. Aunt Linacre had never used such an expression.

"How can you talk so trashily?" Aunt Linacre cried.

"Well, I think it's probably true," Bess said, confused. "I'm going to get something to eat."

She ambled out to the kitchen, with Aunt Linacre bouncing along after her. When she reached the kitchen door, even with the cook and maids in the room, she said to Bess' back, "I think he's an arrogant monster! Like the Talbot hound!"

Bess stopped dead. She turned to look at Aunt Linacre, whose black eyes were snapping. Bess blinked. "Aunt," she said placatingly, "that's what I thought when I first laid my eyes on him and he laid his on me."

Aunt Linacre could hardly restrain herself, but she did. She said, "When you've finished eating, Elizabeth, I want a few words with you. In private!"

Bess didn't eat much. She fortified herself with a glass of wine. Was it possible that Aunt Linacre guessed? How could she? No, it wasn't possible. There had been no one in the hall when she had returned to her own room in the middle of the night; there had been no sound in the old manor house, no sound at all, except the creaking of the old bones of old, old manor timbers.

Bess drank the wine, with a piece of cheese. Then she thought she might as well beard the lion in her den, and she marched to the warm room where Aunt Linacre inevitably spent mornings in the winter. Bess closed the door

151

behind her and went over to the fire. Aunt Linacre was knitting furiously.

Bess said, "What is the matter, Aunt?"

Aunt Linacre looked at Bess, standing there in front of the glowing fire, and she suddenly couldn't believe what she had seen, and almost as though she hoped Bess would deny it, she blurted tearfully, "The door flew open last night, and you were seen!"

Bess cried, "Oh, Aunt!" She thought wildly she must have mistaken her aunt's words. "What are you talking about? Who was seen?"

Aunt Linacre felt her head splitting in two. She dropped her knitting and put her hands to her temples. "You were seen! You and the earl! By me and by Henry Jackson!"

"God's death," whispered Bess. She didn't know Aunt Linacre was feeling pain; she thought she was holding her head in sorrow, anger, and dismay. Bess rushed over to her and crouched beside her chair and put her arms around her.

"Oh, Aunt," she whispered.

"I couldn't believe my eyes," sobbed Aunt Linacre. "My beautiful Bess, lying in bed with a man implanted in her, and a man you hardly knew!" The tears ran down Aunt Linacre's cheeks.

"Jesu!" implored Bess. "I never meant to hurt anyone! If I had dreamed you would know—" Her mind flew to Henry Jackson. But she shoved that thought aside. She could deal with that later. "Aunt," she whispered, "I pray you forgive me for upsetting you so dreadful." She sat back on her heels, and Aunt Linacre took her hands away from her eyes and temples and looked into Bess' face.

Bess' head was whirling with dismay and guilt and doubt. "A man you hardly knew!" Aunt Linacre's cry came firmly again into her ears. The euphoria that had been hers last night and this morning—just his touch and kiss and the brief closeness to him—had bound her again into last night's passion and love. Love? She couldn't put words to it, there were no words anyway, but she had felt wonderful, happy and alive this morning. Not guilty; happy. Jolted now by the reality of Aunt Linacre's horror, she thought. *Oh,*

he is so straitlaced and proper! Was I wrong? He was so loving!
But what does he really think—that I'm a whore? God's death!
"I'm sick," moaned Aunt Linacre. "Sick!"

Bess commandeered two grooms with a litter, and with
dispatch they got Aunt Linacre up the stairs. Bess and Jane
undressed her and put her into bed. They propped her up
with her favorite pillows, brought her herb tea. Bess sat
beside her and held her hand, and finally she fell asleep.

On the day before New Year's, she announced she would
get up and get dressed. That day, in the morning, with Bess
sitting beside her bed on a stool, Aunt Linacre said, "It is
truly because I cannot bear you should throw yourself away;
why Bess, it was plain to me you could have caught him,
proper! And you would be the countess of Shrewsbury! I
forgive you, Bess, my dearest, but I don't forgive him. The
arrogant monster!"

Jane, at the door, heard this. Jane knew what had happened, how could it be kept from her? She came in, to the
other side of the bed; she held out a box, wrapped in a
pouch. "This just came by armed messenger, wearing the
badge of the Talbot!"

Aunt Linacre's beady eyes glistened. "Open it, Bess," she
urged.

Bess opened the pouch and took out a carved box. There
was a single heavy sheet of paper, folded over three times
and sealed. She broke it open, read the one line of writing.

It contained only these words. *I adore you. Shrewsbury.*

Then Bess opened the box. On the velvet lining lay a
huge heavy collar of oriental pearls.

Aunt Linacre looked at it a long time. Finally, she
nodded. "He's in love with you, Bess," she said.

But Bess was silent. What did it mean, she wondered?
What did he think of her? And what would he expect, the
next time he came? If he came. Would he?

Aunt Linacre insisted she was well enough to get up. But
when she did, she didn't feel as steady as she thought she
should. She didn't tell this to either Bess or Jane, and after
dinner she thought she would go back to bed, except that

153

she suddenly remembered it was New Year's Day. The thought of that magnificent gift—although the words of the note were those of a lover and not a prospective husband—even so, Aunt Linacre wanted to lay out the cards for Bess; she was full of hope for the future, in spite of the fact that Bess had behaved so stupidly. So she stayed up, she took off her shoes and put on slippers, and she sat in her big chair surrounded by pillows, with her feet up on a stool and the whole lower half of her body tucked up in a hand-knitted blanket of softest wool that was Bess' New Year's gift to her. Underneath the little hand-tucked white cap that Jane had given her, her eyes sparkled; the candles burned cheerily, so did the fire. Bess was wearing green velvet, very pale in color; her red head glowed, and the sight of her pearl collar gladdened Aunt Linacre's heart; it was a gift worthy of her adored wonderful Bess.

Jane lay the table board on Aunt Linacre's lap. Aunt Linacre put out the queen of hearts, representing her Bess, in the center. Bess shuffled the cards. Aunt Linacre took them and fanned them face down. "Pick twelve cards, Bess, and lay them in a circle around the queen."

Solemnly Bess picked twelve cards and laid them face down around the bright, staring queen. And just as solemnly and slowly Aunt Linacre turned them face up. One by one.

Her face paled. She had turned six cards. Her hand reached for the seventh. It was the queen of spades. No! Aunt Linacre thought and hastily turned up the next card to see if it would change the meaning of the dread queen. It didn't; it was the knave of spades. Biting her lip, Aunt Linacre turned up the rest of the cards. They were all black.

Drawing in her breath, she studied the board. She said calmly, "You see all these nasty little black cards, Bess; they mean a nasty cloud of trouble, Bess. But they are little cards, they are like flies and gnats; they will bite and make you squirm and hurt you. Oh, Bess," she said, and her eyes filled with tears. There sat the dread queen of spades. Sorrow and death, with the miserable knave attending. Aunt Linacre put her hands to her head. "I'm going to be sick," she muttered. She could feel the blackness rising. Was it

154

she herself who was to bring the sorrow? She herself who was going to represent death? Aunt Linacre fainted.

When she regained consciousness, she was in her own bed. The room was filled with gray dawn. She remembered perfectly clearly what had happened, and she was perfectly sure what had happened, for she had tended her mother in her last illness. Aunt Linacre knew she had had a stroke.

She raised her right hand, she wriggled her right foot and her leg. Then she tried to lift the left leg. She sighed deeply; she was paralyzed in the left leg. She wondered whether she could speak.

"Bess?" she asked.

Relief swept through her; she could talk! "Bess, I'm awake. My head feels free of pain."

"Oh," Bess cried. "Oh, Aunt!"

She had been sitting in a chair, wrapped up against the chill of the room, even though a fire burned. Cold had descended on Derbyshire, and it was snowing again.

Aunt Linacre felt Bess take her right hand. She patted and squeezed Bess' hand. She whispered, "Oh, my dearest Bess. Never in your life have you ever given me any hurt, only joy. My dearest Bess, my dearest love."

"Oh, I have, I have," sobbed Bess. "It is all my fault!"

"No, no," said Aunt Linacre. "Always you have been joy and love to me."

CHAPTER 12

BESS and Jane tended Aunt Linacre and tended her with devotion. Bess spent hours in the kitchen trying to encompass soups as good as Aunt Linacre's own. But Aunt Linacre did not improve. Bess and Jane rubbed and massaged her paralyzed leg, and there were days when she sat propped up in her chair, knitting rapidly, but there were other days when her head ached, and when she was dizzy, and when she couldn't eat—so for the first time in her life she was losing weight.

On the first day of February, when Aunt Linacre looked more pale and wan than usual, Bess sent for her mother.

Lady Leche arrived the fifth of the month, riding a spirited mare, disdaining the litter that jolted behind, full of luggage.

Her riding dress was maroon velvet; a feather hat swept her brow. As elegant as always, now in her sixty-fifth year, she alighted from her horse with the grace of a young woman, and Bess cried, "Oh, Mother, you look as beautiful as ever!"

She was so glad to see her! She and Jane poured out their troubles and their fears, and carefully left out Bess' adventures with the earl of Shrewsbury. "Don't tell Mother!" Bess had cried.

Lady Leche had a cup of wine in the warm room, and washed her hands, and divested herself of her riding cloak, and listened patiently to the flood of words from her daughters, who interrupted each other so often that only a mother could have followed this account.

"Jane said that, Bess," she reminded her. "Now, when did these headaches start?"

When she had got it all straight, she ascended the old sloping steps to Aunt Linacre's room, opened the door, and went across to her sister's bed. "Oh, my dearest Marcella," Bess heard her say, as she took Aunt Linacre in her arms and kissed her.

Lady Leche had brought jellied soups and her own marchpane cakes and a new handworked blanket and three new bedcaps for her sister. She sat with Aunt Linacre hours every day, talking of the past and asking Aunt Linacre's advice. James, for instance, might lose old Hardwick Hall, if something were not done to help him. He was simply unfit to manage a manor and the farms. Aunt Linacre and Lady Leche talked long about this, recalling James as a young man. Charming and lovable, he had been, too. So lovable.

156

They took watered wine together in the afternoons. Lady Leche, head bent over her needlepoint, never showed worry or impatience, Bess thought with great admiration. Yet it was all obviously doing no good, for Aunt Linacre now was dwindling in strength, ate almost nothing, and suffered severe headaches. One morning when she woke up she could not talk. Bess was terrified. But by afternoon, some garbled speech came from her lips, and by evening they could understand what she was saying.

Her first clear words came about eight in the evening, when Bess was sitting alone with her. She opened her eyes, for she'd been dozing, saw Bess, and said, "Bess, I am very sick, my dearest."

Her eyes looked into Bess' face, deeply, as though she were imprinting on her mind forever the beloved face of her beloved niece. Overwhelmed at that bestowal of naked love, Bess started to cry.

"Don't," Aunt Linacre said. "Just hold my hand, Bess."

Aunt Linacre died three days later. She was buried the second day in March. The next afternoon Lady Leche rode away; she had been at Chatsworth three weeks, and Bess had had the whole family to put up, to sleep on pallets and to feed on trestle tables. Spent and exhausted, she kissed her mother good-bye, hugged her, made her promise to come back soon, very soon.

It was a cold March day, with the wind gusty and spots of rain blowing against the windows. The afternoon was dark. The old manor house was quiet and still; the boys had gone back to school.

Jane said, "We must go over Aunt Linacre's room, but not today, Bess. Not today. I gave mother the jewelry, so she can distribute it, as Aunt Linacre told her; she has it written down." She would have continued, only Bess' face was so white and sad that she said, "Bess, why don't you go to bed?" She knew it was Bess' habit, when trouble, cares and the world threatened, to retreat to her bed; from there she gathered up her forces to sally forth once more.

"Aye," said Bess, "I'm going now, Jane."

Bess' bedroom had been made into the most luxurious retreat one could manage in the old house. The walls were hung with heavy tapestries, the fireplace was new and gave out plentiful heat and cheer. The quilts and pillows were covered with satin, and on the table by her bed were her favorite book of Psalms and Calvin's book on Job.

Alone in her room, Bess rubbed her stomach. It was the first day of her flux and her stomach ached with that familiar ache. She rubbed her hands over its distended shape, tenderly.

Undressed, she changed the blood-soaked linen for clean, and spread out a pad on the white sheets. Gratefully, she slid into the big bed and pulled up the quilts, sinking back against the pillows, sighing with relief, at having her legs up. At her elbow was her favorite malmsey. She poured herself a generous cup and sipped it. It was so dark an afternoon she had lighted a few candles. The fire burned bright; Bess leaned her head back against the pillows and closed her eyes. She was safe again, temporarily.

Eight miles to the south, the earl of Shrewsbury was listening to the news of the shire; he had just returned from London. When he heard that the Lady St. Loe's Aunt Linacre had been buried the day before, he exclaimed that he was sorry to hear it! "I shall ride over and offer my condolences," said the earl gravely, concealing the fact that he had been intending to ride over anyway; it was the reason he was in Derbyshire. He had been trying to get to his manor of Wingfield for the past six weeks, but the press of his duties at court had forbidden it. Chafing in London, those weeks had gone by slowly, indeed. He reached Chatsworth at four thirty in the afternoon.

Jane met him in the old hall where he had said good-bye to Bess and Aunt Linacre just ten weeks before. The earl didn't seem haughty at all to Jane, this time. He took her in his arms and kissed her, like an old friend.

"I'm so sorry, Mistress Kniveton," he said warmly. "Please accept my heartfelt condolences." He squeezed her hand, and Jane looked up at him gratefully. He seemed so big and strong and dependable. She bit her lip.

"Thank you, my lord," she said, low.

"The Lady St. Loe," the earl continued, "how is she?"

"Bess went to bed," Jane said. "She is—she is—"

"I can imagine," the earl said, cutting in because it seemed Jane would never find the right word. "But if you'll tell her I am here, I would like to see her."

Jane hesitated. She gave the earl a worried look, which he didn't understand at all, having no notion that Jane knew what had happened between him and Bess on that December night. Jane was upset because she had almost told him to go upstairs, and then she realized what she had almost done, and in a flurry, she said, "I'll go up and tell Bess you are here. Please go into the warm room, my lord."

Jane fled up the old shallow steps, and hurried along to Bess' room.

Bess was lying back on her pillows, eyes closed. *I'm numb,* she thought, *but I'm not going to think, or plan, or anything at all, till tomorrow; I'm safe here now, tonight.*

Jane opened the door then, and when Bess saw her, suddenly she realized that never again would it be Aunt Linacre who opened the door and stuck her head around and said, "Bess! I want a word with you in private!" And Bess' lip trembled, and the tears rolled down her cheeks.

"Don't cry, Bess!" Jane implored, coming to the side of the bed.

Bess looked at her through her tears. She mopped at her face with her napkin.

Jane said, "The earl of Shrewsbury is here! He wants to see you!"

Bess retreated back against the pillows and pulled the quilt up around her naked body as though she were searching for cover.

"I can't see him now!" she cried piteously. "Tell him I can't!"

Jane was appalled. "Bess! He's ridden all the way to bring his condolences!"

Bess wriggled down into the feather quilt. "That's what he told you!" Suddenly she sat up straight and reached for her wine and drank the rest of what was left in the cup. Jane came around the bed and took the decanter away and put it on the sideboard.

"That's enough dragon's blood," she said, using Cavendish's expression, and Bess cried, "It's all Shrewsbury's

159

fault, and mine, and I won't see him now! And you go down and tell him so!"

"Bess! Aunt Linacre—"

"Well, it's mostly his fault," Bess muttered sullenly.

Jane thought, *I can't do anything with her.* She shrugged her shoulders. "It's your doing, Bess," she said as she closed the door.

Jane descended the steps slowly. The earl was pacing back and forth in the hall, not trying to conceal his impatience. When he saw Jane, he took a step toward the stairs, as though he were going to bound up them three at a time.

"Is she all right?" he asked, seeing Jane's face. "Is she ill?"

Jane said, "She is in bed, my lord. She cannot see you."

The earl looked at her for a moment, not comprehending this nonsensical statement. What was the matter with Bess? He scowled. Jane was blocking his way up the steps, and he made a motion to put her aside forcibly, when something made him look upward to the small balcony on the second floor. It was only about ten feet long, and there, leaning over the railing, was a child.

It was young Elizabeth, eleven years old. She had heard part of her mother's words to her aunt, and curious, she had followed her Aunt Jane to the top of the steps to see what was happening. Her steady dark eyes, set wide apart, were on him.

"Mother doesn't feel well, my lord," she said.

The earl retreated, and Jane came all the way down the steps. He looked down at Jane.

"Bess cannot see you, my lord," Jane said again. And Jane thought, *This is a blow, and one he never expected.* She met the angry, icy look in his eyes.

He said, "*Cannot*, Mistress Kniveton? Or *will not?*"

When the earl snapped out a question like that, he was accustomed to getting the truth. And he got it.

"*Will not*, my lord," Jane said evenly.

He inclined his dark head, he didn't bother to speak further, or to be polite, or to say to give Bess his sympathy. He said nothing but walked to the old door and opened it and left Chatsworth. Jane stood in the hall, thinking there was nothing she could have done; between these two per-

160

sonalities no one could intervene. She went slowly back upstairs, putting her arm around Elizabeth, for she understood well enough if it hadn't been for the child standing there, watching, the earl might very well have simply pushed her aside and gone up to see Bess.

"Go find Mary," Jane told her, "and I will come and read you a story. You pick one out, Bessie."

Elizabeth smiled wanly and went off down the hall to find her sister; they were separated by only a year and were very close.

Jane went on to Bess. "He's gone," she said. *Gone for good, my girl,* she thought, *and I hope that's what you want.*

Now Bess' eyes filled with tears again for another reason. Now suddenly, there was nothing else in the world she wanted but his arms around her, and the comfort of his sympathy. Then she blinked away the tears and shook her head. "I couldn't see him, Jane," she whispered. "My breath reeks of wine, and I'm all undressed, and I just can't, couldn't, handle him!"

Jane didn't answer her, there was nothing to say. She left Bess, who now regarded the closed door; Bess slipped deep under her quilts and pictured the earl galloping away, angry, vowing never to return.

Oh, well, Bess thought, *he deserves it!*

CHAPTER 13

THE person about whom gossip swirls is very likely to be the last one to hear it. Bess had almost forgotten about Henry Jackson; he had gone back to his home in Yorkshire for Christmas, and she had hired another tutor.

Henry Jackson had liked and admired Bess, and for six weeks he said nothing. But when he went down to Oxford —he was a fellow of Merton College—he went out one night to a tavern, and over many tankards of ale with his cronies, and many stories, Henry had suddenly said, "But you should hear what happened to me! I was dismissed for making an advance, so it was called! And she was alone with me three times a week, to study French! And the night before I left, I was in the hall with her aunt—Aunt Linacre everyone called her—and Jesu! The bedroom door swung open, and there she was, a man plunged into her, taking his good pleasure, and I knew it was her because her witch of an aunt had been knitting these stockings she was still wearing—they were green lace knitted stockings to the knee—she'd been knitting them in the school room!"

"The Lady St. Loe, you mean? Who was the man?"

Now Henry Jackson fell silent. He didn't dare mention the name. "I don't know who it was," he lied. And he was abashed, for he really hadn't meant to start a scandal. He'd had too much to drink, he knew; he pushed back his stool and excused himself. For three days he worried a bit, and then he forgot it.

It was juicy scandal, and it spread rapidly. Shrewsbury didn't hear it, because he never listened to gossip; if anyone tried to tell him a bit of scandal, he would lift one languid hand to stop the teller and say he didn't want to hear it. Shrewsbury did hear, however, that Lord Darcy had been calling on Bess very often, and also Sir John Thynne, a dashing bearded pirate of a man, who was building Longleat, a magnificent classical dwelling; the earl could imagine Bess would be enchanted with it, and he could see them together, fascinated, birds of a feather, talking of Chatsworth and Longleat. Whenever their names were coupled, Shrewsbury tried to shut his ears.

Thus April passed, and it wasn't till the middle of May that Sir John came riding to Chatsworth, and with a paled face, said to Bess, "Bess, my sweet, there is the most lurid scandal being repeated all over about you!"

Bess gasped, and Jane's head flew up—she'd been knitting—and she stared at Sir John in horror.

Sir John cried, "My God, Bess, don't tell me you've been sleeping with your daughter's tutor!"

"Are you mad?" Bess shouted back.

He grinned. "Why should you, when you have me to

162

sleep with, if you'll only signify you'd be willing?" But he was relieved, for she'd borne a guilty look at first.

"That miserable knave," Bess cried with passion, leaping to her feet and raising both fists.

"Bess had to dismiss Master Jackson, the girl's tutor, Sir John," Jane said evenly, trying to control the rapid pounding of her heart. Bess was so angry God knew what she might say. Jane continued, "Master Jackson must have spread this lying tale to get back at Bess for dismissing him."

"I'll kill him!" cried Bess in a fury.

Sir John grinned. "That's less legal than slander, Bess, my sweet," he said. "You'll have to sue him, though, I think. Or do you have a good friend at court?"

Bess thought despairingly of the earl. But surely this scandal wouldn't drift all the way to London. "No," she said.

But it was not drifting; it was flying and growing. Lady Leche heard it the same day Bess did; she sat down and wrote a long letter, an appeal for help. The earl was back in London, and although he had a huge town house plus rooms at court, he had taken lodgings at his favorite tavern, where with a few servants, he could have more freedom. He was with his secretary the last week in May, reading his mail, when the letter from Lady Leche was delivered to him.

A letter from Bess' mother, he thought to himself in wonder; he began to read rapidly. "God's death!" he muttered, when he was halfway through. He went back to the beginning.

My lord, Lady Leche had written, *there has come to my ears the most dreadful slander and calumny of my dearest daughter and dearest departed sister, Marcella Linacre, a scandal evidently begun by a dismissed tutor, Henry Jackson, and one so dreadful I cannot bring myself to put it on paper. I appeal to you, your lordship, to acquaint the Queen's Majesty with this slander against one of Her Grace's former ladies of the bedchamber, and to do all in your power to clear the name of my sister Marcella Linacre, whose honor has been completely besmirched by this knave, Henry Jackon. My dearest sister lies in her grave but six weeks, and I am distraught complete with this dishonor to my family. I beg you, my lord, to use your influences, which are so many in the shires here and in London and with Her Majesty, to help your poor distressed friend in Derbyshire.*

163

"God's death!" muttered the earl. He glanced at his secretary and he said, "Have you heard any gossip about the Lady St. Loe?"

"Aye, my lord."

"Well," the earl snapped. "Tell it to me!"

The secretary gaped. "My lord, it's said that the Lady St. Loe has fallen from high." He grinned. "Anyway, it seems she had a witch of an aunt, and that she was not only lying with her daughter's tutor, but that there were other men, and the aunt and Jackson saw them." The secretary glanced at the earl from under his lids, because Shrewsbury usually would have stopped him long before this.

Shrewsbury said, "Go yourself and fetch me, immediate, Sir Charles Wood." He rose and paced to the narrow window. Wood was the best lawyer in England, Shrewsbury thought. But he also thought, how in the devil had Bess got herself into this? Jesu!

Bess and her mother and, indeed, the whole Hardwick family were voluminous letter writers. Bess and her mother wrote each other once a week, so Bess was surprised to receive a letter from her mother, delivered by the village courier, about three days after she had received the usual weekly communication. But then she was only momentarily surprised; she came running to Jane, holding the letter at arm's length, gingerly, as though it might explode.

"Mother must know!" She threw it down on Jane's lap. "You read it!"

Bess then flounced to a chair; she knew very well she was going to get a severe lecture at the hands of the impeccably dressed and impeccably mannered Lady Leche.

Jane pried open the seal and unfolded the letter.

"It's short, Bess," she said, trying to be comforting. "It says: 'I have just been closeted with Sir John Thynne. He told me of his conversation with you. Myself, I have warned you before, about being alone with your daughter's tutor! And I warned you about making an enemy of Edward St. Loe, who perhaps has helped spread this slander. You should have offered him some money from the estate, as I told you before. Sir John also told me he had offered to marry you, right away. You should give this serious thought, for you need a man to protect you. Lastly, I have written to Lord Shrewsbury, imploring his aid. I pray God his lordship will see fit to help you, and throw the weight of his influence behind you and our whole family, who are suffering beyond measure under this dreadful slander. And I pray that you, Bess, will conduct yourself with circumspection, in every circumstance, during the next months. Do not be alone with any man, even your plasterer at Chatsworth, and look kindly upon your devoted suitor, Sir John. Tell Jane I will write her soon, and that I would come were it not that Sir Francis has a bad, bad cold, and needs me here.' "

Bess heard almost nothing except that her mother had written to Shrewsbury. She uttered a cry of despair. Her mind raced around, in all directions. Imagine what her jealous enemies were saying and how they must be laughing, and then she came about again to the earl.

"My God, Jane," she whispered. "Suppose he believes it?"

"He can't believe it!"

"I don't know," said Bess despairingly. "He might." She drew a long, long breath. "Think of how I behaved with him!"

It was the twenty-fourth of May. In London the earl was trying to clear up all his affairs so he could leave for the country the first week of June. Men wearing the badge of the Talbot had quickly picked up Henry Jackson and deposited him in prison. Under examination by Sir Edward Wood, he had shamefacedly confessed what he had told about the night of the twenty-third of December last. In his dry manner, Edward Wood, alone with Shrewsbury, revealed the substance of the interview.

In fact, Wood was reading from the deposition he had taken. "Due to the angle at which Jackson saw into the bedroom, with the bedcurtains half drawn, he said that he identified the Lady St. Loe by her green knitted stockings, which Mistress Linacre had been knitting. I then asked him if he knew that Lady St. Loe had received the stockings, and he said he did not; he had assumed it only. I pointed out that the stockings could have been given to Mistress Linacre's maid, who is a woman about thirty, and with whom Henry

Jackson confessed that he had had sexual relations, himself. As to the man in the case, he said positively he did not know and could not identify. It could have been any of the men in the household, taking advantage of an empty bedroom."

"Of course," said the earl calmly. "Now Her Grace has appointed a commission which will deal with this, a high commission. And in view of the nastiness of the slander against not only the Lady St. Loe but her dead aunt, the Commission will hear only Henry Jackson's admission that he is guilty of slander. The findings of the commission will remain secret."

Wood nodded. "It can be done, my lord. I will advise Henry Jackson to confess he is guilty of slander against Mistress Marcella Linacre and the Lady St. Loe."

Sir Edward rose, and the two men shook hands. When the door closed, Shrewsbury threw himself into his chair. Green knitted stockings. Jesu! On that night of December 23, when he had finally released Bess, she was lying flat on her back, and she had smiled at him and whispered, "Hand me a pillow."

The pillows had all been pushed onto the floor. He had reached down and picked one up, lifted her and put a fat bolster under her shoulders. And then he had thought, the door! And he had got up and gone to that door, which was closed, and shot the bolt. Standing there, looking at the tumbled, shadowy bed, with only the head curtains partly drawn, Bess had said, smiling an angelic smile, "I am still tingling with love, all the way down to my toes." And she had lifted one foot and wriggled her toes in those ridiculous little stockings, just to the knee, and she had looked down at her toes as though they didn't belong to her at all.

The earl stirred and got up and walked over to the open window, to look down into the busy courtyard of the inn. But he saw nothing of the bustle of men and grooms and horses below him. He thought, *Thank God! It was I!* Waves of relief washed over him. He could leave London soon! His oldest son, heir to the earldom, was being married in four weeks. There was a great deal to be done, and then he would be free. *Bess,* he thought, *Bess! It was all my fault.*

CHAPTER 14

YOUNG Lord Francis Talbot was being married at Sheffield Castle on the twenty-eighth of June. In time young Francis would be the seventh earl of Shrewsbury, and it was a very important occasion, this wedding.

"I won't go," said Bess. "I will not go, Jane!"

Jane took pen and paper, and wrote to Lady Leche. *Bess refuses to attend the wedding of Lord Francis,* she wrote hastily.

Two days later Lady Leche's answer came, to Bess.

You must attend the wedding. If you do not, everyone will say you are guilty of lying with your daughter's tutor. Are you mad, Bess? You must come to the wedding. You shall come here first, with Jane and the children, and attend the wedding with me and Sir Francis, and all your family.

Bess said, "I'm going up to bed."

Propped up in her big bed, she refused to leave it till the next morning. In fact she was still in bed when Jane came in about eight o'clock. Bess looked over at her, and then she wailed suddenly, "But what shall I wear, Jane? I've been sitting here thinking of all my gowns, and none of them is suitable."

Jane said, "I think you should wear something very plain, Bess."

Bess said, "You're mad! If I go to that wedding—which I don't want to go to—I'm going as myself, Jane! Not some simpering saint!" She bounced out of bed, and started pawing through an upright wardrobe that she had had specially constructed for her best gowns. Head still uncombed, standing in a short, thin smock, she started throwing everything onto the bed, running from the wardrobe to the bed in her bare feet. Finally she threw on top of the heap a dress of palest green satin.

"I'd forgot I had it!" she exclaimed.

Jane said, "Bess, it is cut very, very low."

"Of course it is," said Bess happily. "I copied it from a gown of the queen's. It is perfectly beautiful. And what's more, my little green stockings will go fine with it."

June 28 was a beautiful day. Bess wore her pale green satin, and she wore her green stockings, and she had dressed the children in their finest, and she was so proud of them. But when the time came to leave for Sheffield, she began to get pale. She was sitting in her litter, with the Cavendish stags carved on the posts, looking, Lady Leche thought, as though she were setting forth to the Tower green to have her head cut off. She came up to Bess and laid her hand over hers.

"Bess, you look beautiful. Truly beautiful. I am proud of you." Lady Leche gazed into her daughter's eyes. She ran her own eyes over Bess for the last time. And then she asked, "Bess, where did you get that magnificent pearl collar?"

Bess grew even paler. Her eyes were enormous. "I bought it," she lied.

Lady Leche lifted one eyebrow, and gave Bess a long, level look. Bess thought, *Oh, lord, lord, I should never have worn it! What will Shrewsbury think when he sees it? But it is so beautiful, and looks so elegant with this gown. Anyway, he probably won't even see me, there will be so many people there.*

At Sheffield Castle, the greatness of the occasion and the marriage of the eldest son had put the immense power and wealth of the earldom on rare display. Bess was overwhelmed.

The castle itself was set in an eight-acre park, with the most magnificent oaks Bess had ever seen in her life. They were towering giants, so old, so massive, so proud. On the north, the River Don sped between its grassy banks; on the east the River Sheaf, and in every direction beyond, stretched the moorland, remote; to Bess it was a most beautiful sight.

There were hundreds of liveried servants, escorting the arriving guests, taking the horses away to the huge, huge stables and pasture set aside; silken tents blossomed colorfully on the spreading lawns and gardens; within there were

168

musicians on the gallery over the great hall, and flowers and greens everywhere, and rooms set aside for the comfort of the guests, with maids attending.

Jesu! Bess thought. *Someday I'll entertain like this at Chatsworth. Someday.* She looked around for her boys, who came behind; she had a daughter in each hand, and Jane right beside her, and then Sir John Thynne swaggered up and took little Mary's hand in his, to escort her, and Bess smiled at him, for she knew she was receiving hard looks, from many, many people. She lowered her eyes.

The ceremony would take place in the parish church of St. Peter and St. Paul.

"Shouldn't we go into the church?" she asked Sir John. She was suddenly afraid to meet anyone she knew. "I'd like my daughters to be able to see," she added.

Within the dimness of the church she breathed easier. She bowed her head and prayed for her children and Aunt Linacre and Jane, and she sighed, comforted by the church itself, listening to the music. She still held Elizabeth's hand, but Sir John was on the other side of her, and little Mary next to him. Bess whispered, "You're very brave. Everybody'll think you're my latest lover."

Sir John's lips twitched. "Flatterer!" he whispered back and squeezed her hand.

Bess flashed him a merry smile. Somehow she felt much better. She looked up at the balcony that ran around the church above. Here below the guests were jammed in; above, on the balcony, stood the castle's household. With Shrewsbury's usual thoughtfulness, they were not excluded, Bess thought admiringly. *He knows how to do things right, he does.*

The words of the marriage ceremony always made Bess cry. She wiped her eyes and thought, *How young they are, the two of them, how young, and how sweet! I pray they are happy.*

Sir John led her out, easing through the crush of people. And now outside in the gardens, there was entertainment for the children, a group of acrobats and a performing bear and a show in one of the tents, a funny puppet show. And there was food, food, food. Bess left her daughters with their older brothers and all their friends. She clung tight to Sir John's arm as he walked her toward the huge castle

169

doors; she could hear the music, there would be dancing, of course, and eating and drinking, and she hung back and slowed her steps, and she thought, *Oh, I wish I hadn't come!*

Bess looked around for her own family, her mother and Jane, and stolid Sir Francis Leche. There were so many gowns, she couldn't find her mother or Jane!

"Don't look so worried, girl," Sir John whispered.

Bess said please, let her find Jane, and perhaps she should go to one of the rooms set aside for the ladies. Sir John released her, with some reluctance. "I'll wait right here," he said.

Bess pushed between the crowds, she couldn't find her mother, she couldn't find Jane, she could not find her brother James or his wife, and desperately she pushed her way back to where she thought she had left Sir John. At first she didn't see him, and then, with a sob of relief, she did see him, and pushed her way back to his side, just as the horns blew and the musicians started to play. Somehow the floor was cleared, and the earl of Shrewsbury led his new daughter-in-law out for the first dance.

Bess, and everyone else, watched. The earl did, indeed, look exceedingly handsome, assured, and as though he were enjoying himself, too. Then as everyone clapped and cheered, he handed his partner into the arms of his oldest son, Lord Francis Talbot, who bowed briefly to his father and then led his bride onto the middle of the cleared space in the center of the great hall.

Now the earl himself stood watching, turning from left to right to greet his guests, moving about the edge of the hall.

"We can dance, now, I think," Sir John said.

Bess whispered, "Not yet, please." She was still searching for Jane or her mother; she would feel much safer standing next to them. But the music suddenly changed, into a gay galliard, and the insistent beat set Bess' foot to tapping and brought a smile to her eyes and face, and she was just about to turn to Sir John and say she wanted to dance when she realized the earl was standing right in front of her. Bess thought he was just passing by, and she hunted desperately for something polite to say. Only before she could speak,

he reached out and whirled her away into the middle of
the floor. He had been very impolite to Sir John Thynne,
something he would normally never have done. He was
smiling down at her, and everyone was looking, no one
more closely than Lady Leche.

Lady Leche had been very satisfied by what she saw. She
said to Jane, very low, "By my faith, Jane, we may be seeing
Bess' next husband."

The dance of the galliard was exceedingly fast and furi-
ous. Bess whirled and pirouetted and was tossed into the
air. When she came down again, she said breathlessly, "I
ought to thank you, Mother told me." She was going to add
she knew her mother had written to him, but there wasn't
time, as she danced away from him, and then back again,
feeling his touch, forgetting anything but the fun and
pleasure of the dance.

When the music came to a stop, Bess stopped just as
quickly, bringing both feet together in a final little stamp,
and then she laughed up at him and said, "Oh, I haven't
danced that way for a long time!"

Then she realized he should leave her, and she whispered, "It was good of you to dance with me first, m'lord,
it'll give the she-wolves something to howl about."

"Take my arm, Bess," he said. "I'm going to get you some
cooled wine."

"Aye, I'd like that," Bess said, tucking her hand inside
his cozily, just as if it belonged right there, forever and ever.
She was suddenly so dizzily happy, it wasn't decent to feel
so happy, she thought, trotting along at his side. But when
they had left the hall and the people behind, by a sudden
quick turn of an old passage, and a door closed behind her,
she looked up at him in surprise.

"Where are we?" She looked around the room, it was
fairly small, having been made by partitioning off part of
a much larger older room. It was hung with tapestries to
keep out the damp in winter. And she also realized that
he was reaching out for her, and she stepped back in a
hurry.

"Please, my lord, if you disarrange me, I'd never dare
show my face again." She put both hands in front of her
to fend him off, and then she moved sideways like a crab,

and sat down in a great big chair, by a littered table. Then, safely seated, she was suddenly shy and asked him for the wine he'd promised; she wriggled one foot loose of her shoe and dropped it on the floor.

The earl had gone to the sideboard to pour two cups of wine, and when he turned, he saw the green-stockinged foot she was massaging with one hand.

"Bess," he said, "you're wearing those stockings!"

There was a sudden and deep silence in the small room. After six months they were together again. After six months. The remembrance of the night in December swept back over Bess like a flood. She looked across at him, as if she were memorizing him.

"My stockings?" she whispered and looked down at her foot. "You remember my stockings?"

"How could I forget, sweetheart?" he said, absently setting down the wine cup and just looking at her face. Finally, he sighed and picked up a cup of wine and brought it to her. Bess took it from him, only their fingers touched, but it was like a delicious lightning, running through her body, just the same as before.

Bess didn't say a word; she held her wine rigidly in front of her.

The earl said softly, "Bess, it was your stockings that Henry Jackson saw, and it was how he identified you. My lawyer pointed out that he only assumed that your Aunt Linacre had actually given them to you; he didn't know it for a fact."

Bess heard his voice as from a great distance.

"So he is going to admit that he is guilty of slander."

Bess said, very low, "Thank you, my lord."

"Your name will be cleared, Bess."

Her brows drew together, just slightly; there was a question in her eyes. Did he mean that then the incident was closed? She said, "Your name—he knew it was you."

"He was afraid of me," the earl said.

Aye, Bess thought, *and even I, even I am a bit unsure.* But it wasn't fair! "That miserable knave," she said with sudden violence, and took a big drink of the wine.

Shrewsbury said, "That sounds more like you."

Bess' eyes flashed dark. Did he mean she was earthy—too

172

earthy for him? She was; she was. Once again she fastened her eyes on him, as though she would never see him again. She would remember him, just the way he looked now, today, out of reach. He was younger than she, he was enormously wealthy and he bore one of the oldest, proudest names in the realm. She had been a fool, just as Aunt Linacre had said.

But it was his fault, too!

Bess said, "I shouldn't stay here any longer with you. I won't have a shred of reputation left. The tongues of the gossips will be wagging by now, my lord." She reached down for her shoe and started to put it on the green-stockinged foot.

The earl said to her bent red head, "Bess, why wouldn't you see me, when I came to Chatsworth? Why?"

Bess finished putting on her shoe. She raised her head. She looked up at him, he was standing right in front of her. She tried to think of a good lie, and she opened her mouth to say that when she thought, *"Oh, be damned to lies! What is the matter with the truth? If I shock him—but how can a woman shock a man?*

"I felt bad!" Bess blurted. "I felt afraid and alone, and I was in bed, practically naked, and I wouldn't have been able to fend you away, I was afraid to let you in that room; it was my flux, and the bed would be all over blood—" She stopped.

The earl had come close to her while she was speaking; he took her hand and squeezed it. "Oh, Bess," he said, lifting her gently to her feet and scarcely touching her, "I am truly not such a monster."

"Well, I don't know," said Bess doubtfully. Her flux had never inhibited Cavendish. But for him coming again to Chatsworth, she would have to renounce him. "You mustn't come to see me, my lord," she said pleadingly. "I must be very careful, for the sake of my children and for my family. And for Sir John."

Shrewsbury said, "What? What about Sir John?"

Bess said, "Well, you see, I am betrothed to him. He asked me to marry him, again, last night."

"You are betrothed to him?" the earl asked.

"Aye," said Bess.

"I see," Shrewsbury said. "Come then," and he took her hand and led her to the door.

Bess followed him, almost hanging back; she didn't understand him at all. She thought had he truly wanted her, he would have said so. Cavendish would have. Bess regarded him, puzzled; he wanted only to be her lover, and that she could not permit, for the scandal that would then surely descend on her—she could never face her children; she would never live it down. Her slow steps had carried her almost to the door.

"Oh, I've done everything wrong," she said and looked up at him. The earl leaned over and kissed her cheek.

"No, no, my love," he said, low. "You haven't done anything wrong."

But he was letting her go, Bess thought despairingly. At the door she said, "Good-bye, my lord." There was, after all, nothing else to say.

CHAPTER 15

THE earl of Shrewsbury spent part of the summer on progress with his queen and part in the country, moving from one great residence to another. At thirty-eight, and a widower, he could have married any woman in the realm, and he should, he knew. He should marry a young woman, to bear him children; although his four stalwart sons were the envy of his friends, a round dozen sons would not be too many to ensure a rightful succession to the mighty earldom. He tried, during the summer, to find such a young woman.

On September 29, the high commission met, announced that the Lady St. Loe had been the victim of a vicious slander, and her name was officially cleared. Henry Jackson was pronounced guilty by his own confession of unprovoked slander. The earl thought that Jackson had been punished

174

enough, having been in prison since May, and Henry Jackson was secretly released, a chastened young man.

October passed, very slowly it seemed to Shrewsbury. And on the first day of November, having heard no news from Derbyshire of his own particular "great matter," the earl decided he had behaved like a fool and, with his customary efficiency, set in progress the plans that had lain festering in the back of his mind for three months.

A legal document was drawn up and sent to a lawyer to make sure it was correct. Saddlebags were packed, excuses were sent to the queen, all bills at the inn were paid, and in the late afternoon the earl set forth from London, accompanied by his usual retinue, all wearing the badge of the Talbot.

It usually took four days to reach Derbyshire. But this time there were to be no stops, except for fresh horses and perhaps an hour's sleep. The earl of Shrewsbury was in a tearing hurry. Less than two days later, he galloped through the gates of old Chatsworth. He never glanced at the towers of new Chatsworth, which had risen very high now. He took the four low steps all at one bound and hammered on the doors with the butt of his riding whip. This time he was not leaving Chatsworth without having what he had come for.

Bess had spent a miserable summer. All during July she had gone over and over in her mind the time they had spent together in that little converted room at Sheffield. She had said and done everything wrong. It must be, she thought, that she had been right from the very beginning. A powerful physical attraction existed between the two of them, and other than that, well—the earl thought she wasn't good enough for him. In short, she should marry with Sir John, and forget Shrewsbury. She should marry because Sir John had asked her and she had accepted. For the sake of her family.

On the fifteenth of July she had said to Jane, "I don't think I can marry him. It would be wrong."

Lady Leche wrote that if Bess didn't marry, she would probably get herself into more trouble, which enraged Bess, but which Jane thought privately was true.

Meantime the summer nights were sweet and warm, and Bess longed for her lover and damned him at the same time, for the rumors came thick and fast about the various women Shrewsbury was seen with and the high-born ladies whose names were coupled with his. Furiously Bess flung herself into the building of Chatsworth.

From her accounts it now seemed certain that the entire cost would reach eighty thousand pounds. Jane said, "By my faith, Bess, I cannot believe what you have accomplished! But what are you going to do when it is finished?"

"Live in it!" shouted Bess, whose temper was impossible these days. Jane packed up and left for three weeks with her mother.

Lady Leche was sincerely puzzled. "I could have sworn, from the tone of Shrewsbury's letter to me—there was an undescribable concern and anxiety in it—and from the way he looked at Bess, that he was in love with her."

"She told him she was going to marry with Sir John," Jane explained.

"Good God," said Lady Leche. "For all her wit, she can be positively stupid. In Shrewsbury's strict code it would be perfectly permissible for him to cuckold Sir John but not to deprive him of his promised wife. But now what is she going to do about Sir John?"

She was going to tell him she could not marry him. She told him that positively and sadly the last week in September. She thanked him for being patient with her; she confessed that she honored and respected him as a friend; she thanked him for coming to her rescue when the terrible scandal had swirled around her, and for his faith in her. "But my dearest John," she ended, "I cannot marry with you. You deserve someone nicer than me. I am an awful shrew. Even Jane has left me."

She thought, *It is true. Everything everyone says about me is true, even the scandal was true, I am impossible.* In this mood she took to her bed and gratefully wallowed in self-pity for the whole night, feeling very sorry for herself and very sure that at that very moment, while she had renounced the man who wanted to marry her because she was so in love, that the earl himself was probably in bed with somebody else.

At least Jane came back in October, to help her get the

176

boys off to school. Bess was so glad to see her she behaved herself well for three weeks; and the household ran smoothly and happily. Bess was so glad to have someone to talk to in the evenings that she put herself out to be sweet and accommodating, and she poured into Jane's ears all her troubles.

"I can't live this way the rest of my life," she told Jane. "It's so ridiculous. Yearning after a man like a girl!"

"Time will help," Jane said, which Bess resented heartily. She wanted Jane to reassure her, so she pouted and said sullenly, "I've been trying to think of an excuse to go and see him. Or I could write and ask his advice."

"About what?" asked Jane.

"I don't know, Jane. Don't be stupid. Anything." Then she quieted. "You're right, Jane."

"There are dozens of other men in the world, Bess."

Bess said, "There are hundreds. Aye, hundreds."

On the third of November, in the afternoon, Bess was in the kitchens, supervising the final stages of apple conserve. Jane, upstairs, heard the noise of hoofbeats and went to the window to look out. "By my faith," Jane said aloud, as she realized there must be at least thirty riders.

Downstairs Bess strolled out of the kitchen; she heard the noise plain now, too: the rattle of harness, and while she was wondering who could be arriving, the earl pounded on the doors, and Bess, electrified, ran toward them, alone, and threw them open.

He was dusty, disheveled, he smelled of horses and sweat, and she hurled herself into his arms like a bolt of lightning, uncaring who saw her.

"Oh, Shrewsbury," she sobbed. "Oh, my love, my love!"

The earl didn't care who was watching either. He hugged her tightly. He whispered, "You didn't marry Sir John!"

Bess whispered back, "Oh, I couldn't! I couldn't! Not after you!"

CHAPTER 16

BESS was going to be married to the earl of Shrewsbury. She couldn't believe it. She didn't sleep for three nights; she kept waking up and sitting straight up in bed as the fresh realization of what had happened bolted her out of sleep.

If she could only sleep with Shrewsbury! But she couldn't. Her reputation had been so badly damaged that now that she was going to be the countess of Shrewsbury, all must be most proper and correct, so the earl insisted she sleep with a maid in the room, and Bess had chosen a pretty bright young girl named Digby. Digby slept at the foot of her bed on a trundle. At least Digby slept quiet and dreamlessly, tender young thing she was. Whereas the earl had crowded into his room not only his body servant, who almost always slept in the same room, but his valet, who snored, which had an adverse effect on the earl's temper the following day.

Bess was learning that the great nobility had no more privacy than royalty. There were always swarms of attendants and friends and hangers-on, even the young sons of the gentry, who sent their children to be brought up in a great household. Shrewsbury had been accompanied by only thirty people, but that number, modest for him, made the walls of Chatsworth bulge. Men wearing the badge of the Talbot strutted proudly everywhere; Bess' household considered them thoroughly obnoxious.

But Bess was so happy she would have slept with a dozen people, all snoring in the same room. "What's sleep?" she said to the earl, her eyes glittering with laughter.

She sat up in her big bed, suddenly wide awake. She'd been dreaming, so vivid a dream it had been startling and sobering. She could see Cavendish's face so clear, it was as though he had been right in the room, and he was saying, "You'll make earls and countesses of them all."

And Bess had said, "Oh, Cavendish, how is that possible? Without you?"

"Don't ask me, sweetheart. But you'll find a way."

The smile with which the words had been said and the remembrance of the dream struck Bess to the heart. *I have abandoned him,* she thought. *In thinking of my new love I have forgot him.*

She leaned back among the pillows, pulling the quilts up around under her chin. Sir William had been her dearest, best friend in the world, and her lover, but he had not replaced Cavendish in her heart. Always deep in her the love she had borne Cavendish remained unchanged, forever possessed she had been. Now what had happened to her?

She lay back, squirming to get more comfortable. The one candle flickered. She was very weary, and she half dozed, two tears squeezed out from under her eyelids. Did she dream again? She was never sure. But she could hear his voice so plain, and see the smile that lifted the corners of his mobile mouth. "Bess, they're my children! Make countesses and earls out of all of them!"

Bess opened her eyes. "Oh, Cavendish, you knave," she whispered.

But how to approach the earl, Bess thought. *How?* He had been gone all day on a visit to his castle of Bolsover, where there had been trouble with his tenants. He had been annoyed by it, thinking he had been very generous about the rents and further annoyed by the fact that the queen had written sharply to admonish his handling of the trouble. It seemed to Shrewsbury the queen always sided with the tenants. He was weary, and he was stretched out in a big chair, with his feet practically in the hearth.

"It's the damnedest, coldest November," he said aloud.

"I know, my love," Bess said.

The earl grinned. "We agree on that, then. If it weren't so damned cold, I could take you off into the woods and rape you, and then I wouldn't be so irritable."

Jane glanced at the earl in alarm. You could never tell,

179

she thought, what his lordship was going to say. He seemed so strict; he was strict and unbending and he lived just as strictly by his standards. The trouble was, Jane thought, he made the standards himself, and no one could tell what they were.

The earl continued, "Don't fidget so, Bess. For God's sake, just sign that document; I want to put it in the packet to go to London tomorrow."

"Well, I ought to read it before I sign it!"

"Just sign it, Bess," the earl commanded. "It's a very generous marriage settlement; women have few rights and I wish to be fair. I won't make it more, though, Bess."

"Don't insult me!" Bess cried. As if she'd ask for more money!

"God's death," the earl said. "That's the first time in four hundred years that an offer of marriage from a Talbot has been considered an insult."

Bess giggled. She dipped her pen. In the silence Jane could hear its scratch. "There!" Bess said proudly. Then she said, "But, my lord, there is one matter on which I wish to speak."

Jane threw Bess a glance. What was coming now? Jane almost missed a stitch in the quilt she was making Bess for New Year's.

There was a pregnant silence. Bess didn't know how to continue; the earl had closed his eyes and seemed to be asleep. If she could only see him alone! But no, it would be better just to ask outright and not wheedle or appear to wheedle: That would be demeaning. *I will not demean myself,* thought Bess determinedly. *But if he only would not sleep.*

She wanted to pace the room; instead she held her hands tight in her lap and began. "My lord," Bess said steadily, "I have raised my children myself and I must look out for them."

The earl still seemed to be asleep. Jane stopped her careful stitches and listened, fascinated.

"Therefore, I am going to ask you, my lord," Bess went on, whether or not he was asleep, "to consent to a betrothal between two of my children and two of yours."

Jane gasped and tried to turn it into a gulp. The earl

180

opened his eyes and bent his steady blue gaze on Bess. She sat upright and stiff, waiting for his reply; inside her heart she was praying, praying. *Please, please,* her heart asked.

The matter of the marriage of their children was of immense importance to both Bess and the earl and to all their contemporaries. The earl had wedded his eldest son to an earl's daughter, nothing less would do. The earl now thought rapidly that of course it would be a step up for a Cavendish to marry a Talbot. But on the other hand, it was a healthy, strong stock; in the background of the Cavendish family was a famous judge, for instance, more than a hundred years ago. There was the brilliant George Cavendish, their uncle, whose long book about Wolsey Shrewsbury had read. Brows drawn, he considered her words.

Bess said, "The marriage settlements I make on my children will be most generous. At least five hundred acres of land, at least two manors, furnishings for the dwellings." Bess was bargaining as she would have with a stranger. But that was the best way. For a Talbot she would have to pay high. "And a thousand pounds in money or rent," Bess added.

Shrewsbury thought, *I have six children. This is a good offer.* He nodded. Then he scowled. "But I shall pick, myself, Bess," he said, "who should marry whom. I reserve that right."

Bess said levelly, "It shall be yours. Your decision has made me very happy." Then she added, "Very happy, indeed, my lord." She took out her handkerchief and wiped her eyes, and then sent him a starry smile. The earl untangled himself and got to his feet, and Bess threw her arms around him and kissed him and whispered, "Oh, my jewel, you've made me so happy!"

Jane bent her head over her needlework again. She couldn't wait to write all this to their mother; she couldn't wait.

My dearest mother, Jane wrote, *first more about the children: The earl refused to consider Elizabeth as a bride for his son Gilbert, but he has chosen Mary. Mary, he says, is a battler and able to stand up to Gilbert, who is, according to his father, a high-handed and exciting young man. Gilbert is to go abroad for two years when he reaches fifteen, and the earl will not change that plan under any condition. But Bess, too, feels Mary is right for Gilbert; they are both now so young that it will be years before they will live as man and wife, of course. Henry is to wed with Grace Talbot. The earl is adamant that the ceremony be performed in the church at Sheffield parish and in the presence only of the household and the immediate families. There is to be no show made of it. It will be solemn and private, he says.*

Jane nibbled at the end of her pen. *Last night,* Jane began, and reconstructing the scene in her mind, she saw it clearly. Bess had laid in front of the earl the marriage settlements she had made on both of the betrothed children. He hadn't even glanced at them. He'd received that afternoon, late, a package of mail from London. He had taken over Bess' big table, and it was strewn with mail and documents. Bess announced, "I'm going to dismiss your head groom."

Shrewsbury was reading; he'd been gone all day. A frown of incomprehension crossed his brow, and he laid down the paper and asked Bess, "What did you say?"

Bess said, "That knave of a head groom of yours has seduced my little maid Digby, of whom I am very, very fond. She is very upset, and so am I."

Shrewsbury said, "There's a fine of five shillings for seducing one of the maids. I suggest you fine Digby five shillings and we'll add ten shillings to our combined fortunes."

Bess said dangerously, "Shrewsbury, be serious! She's but sixteen, and a virgin, she's been with me only two months, and already she is an integral part of my household."

The earl now raised his eyes again from the letter he'd been reading. "Well, that's the problem, you see, Bess. There's no fine for seducing a maid in somebody else's household. That's free."

Jane, remembering this scene, smiled to herself. She wrote busily, trying to recapture it for her mother. Then she added, *But this morning the earl, having spoke with his head groom, discovered that the man was ready and willing to marry Digby, so all is settled happily. And we will all be settled more happily, too, when we get to Sheffield. Here, Shrewsbury's men are all over the whole establishment; the cooks quarrel, the grooms fight;*

182

Bess and the earl keep strictly apart, each sleeping with servants in their rooms. One last piece of news. The earl came to me yesterday and said how fond he was of Thomas [Jane's oldest son] and that he would like to have him enter his service, and of course I was very pleased, and Thomas will go to court next year. And the earl also told me that all of his residences would always be mine, to enter as an honored guest, then he laughed and said whenever I couldn't endure Bess, I should take a holiday. My dearest Mother, Jane ended, I shall see you soon at Sheffield.

Lady Leche laid down the letter after having read it twice to herself and then once to her husband. She wondered aloud, "Do you note the lack of any planned ceremony between Bess and Shrewsbury?"

Sir Francis said, why, he hadn't thought about that.

"I should like to see my daughter married," Lady Leche said. "But it looks as though his lordship has some other plan, I cannot imagine what."

Lady Leche and Sir Francis arrived at Sheffield castle on a very cold day, the first week of January. It had looked all day as though it would snow, but they arrived before the first flakes began to fall. Lady Leche was heartened to see that the whole combined forces of Cavendish and Talbot—the children—seemed happy, indeed exuberant. Gilbert Talbot and William and Charles were already inseparable, sleeping together with their servants in one bedroom, the walls hung with their gear and sporting equipment, a huge, messy room in which their servants vainly tried to keep order. Shrewsbury's two girls and Bess' two all lodged together in a large suite. Grace was already tall, slender, and with her father's elegance and his level blue eyes. Paired with Henry, the redheaded Henry, they were startling. Mary, who was ten, and Gilbert, who was fourteen, were good friends, Lady Leche thought, *Thank God for that.* She was very fond and proud of Mary; Mary, who, as the youngest of the Cavendish clan, had always more than held her own. Mary, who could ride like the wind, and whose merry laugh could always be heard—Lady Leche hugged her tight, then later went up to help her dress for the betrothal ceremony.

183

It was very impressive and very moving, the sight of the children solemnly reciting their vows in the candlelit church, plain and old as it was.

Their parents stood to one side, the light glittering on Bess' red head. Lady Leche thought, *She has done well for her children, allying them by marriage, two of them, to one of the oldest and proudest names in the realm.* She thought of Cavendish, she could almost see him nod his dark head and flash his brilliant smile. *Ambition,* thought Lady Leche. *I pray Bess has not too much of it, and let it spoil her life. . . .*

The short ceremony was over; the priest blessed the children and the whole company. Lady Leche went up to the altar to kiss the youngsters and wish them well; later they all filed from the chapel. Lady Leche, back at the castle, saw them all gathered about a table, ten children all talking, all eating, all laughing boisterously. She was looking around for Bess when a servant handed her a note.

It said only, *I have taken Bess away. She bids you good-bye. Shrewsbury.*

CHAPTER 17

SHEFFIELD Manor Lodge had been built by the fifth earl of Shrewsbury, as a retreat; now it lay in snow, and every morning the fresh tracks of forest animals bore testimony to its rugged hunting fame. The earl loved the lodge with passionate love. And it was here that he brought Bess right after the ceremony.

The bedroom where Bess woke in the predawn grayness was paneled in rough-barked oak. The bedcurtains were drawn closed, yet she could hear the crackle of the logs in the fireplace; someone had come in and replenished the fires while they slept. In her great fear of fire, she rolled over and stuck her head out of the curtains, to look at the fire. Satisfied it was protected by a heavy screen, she retreated among the curtains.

She put her hands under her head and sighed, drawing in her breath with exquisite delight, just to be alive and greet the new day seeping grayly into the room. *Think how happy my children are, and how fortunate! Under the patronage and eye of Shrewsbury. All the wealth and power and all the most famous schools will be theirs, and all the most famous people in this realm, and others they will meet. They will travel abroad and be easily familiar with Paris and Rome and Venice. My daughter Mary, my exciting Mary, will be a Talbot, she is already. My daughter Talbot. And Henry is married to Grace Talbot! What a household we have! Ten healthy growing children, ten of them.*

I wonder what they are all doing now, Bess thought. Shrewsbury hadn't even let her say good-bye. After the ceremony Bess had been so moved that she had gone up to her bedroom at Sheffield to sponge her eyes in cold water and compose herself. She had looked around for Digby, but Digby was gone, disappeared completely. Bess said again, "Digby?"

The earl said from behind her, "Digby is gone to the manor lodge ahead of us."

Bess turned, and he said, "Here, Bess, put this on," and she had looked at the cape he was holding; it would come down to her ankles, and it was lined with sable. She breathed, "I've never seen anything like that!"

"It's my present," said the earl, putting it around her shoulders. And then he put around her head its matching hood, fastened with wide heavy gold frogs. And Bess was transported back into the past, and out of the past Cavendish's voice reached her, she so young, and he all of a sophisticated twenty-four, saying patronizingly, "I'd like to put a sable with gold clasps around your head, someday."

And her own crisp retort, "Good God! I wouldn't want to wait that long!"

Bess looked up at Shrewsbury, and her eyes filled with tears again. They were for Cavendish, and her own youth. "Thank you," Bess whispered. "It's too magnificent a gift. But I have something for you."

She hadn't known what in the world to buy for Shrewsbury, who had everything he wanted. She had rejected any-

185

thing she could buy, from a horse to a hound; he was so particular about horseflesh and dogs she couldn't possibly please him. He wore very little jewelry; she had thought of giving him a ring, but she could well imagine he would never wear it, for he wore only an old, old ring with his crest, which had come down from one of the first Talbots.

But Shrewsbury loved cards and chess. So Bess had had her own cabinetmaker, whom she considered the most talented in the world, make him a gaming table. It was of walnut, inlaid with the Talbot impaled with the Cavendish stags, and inlaid with chessmen, dice, and musical instruments. Bess had designed it herself; she had thought of it when the earl had admired the rich chest, inlaid with his initials, that she had given to young Gilbert.

"I have a present for you!" she repeated.

"Not now," said the earl, and then, because he realized he had hurt her feelings, he said, quickly, "Bess, my darling, it is you I want, and I have been so damned patient. But now I'm not. Come." He held out his hand.

Bess drew back. "Come where?"

"We're leaving," said the earl.

"But," said Bess, "the children. I ought to say good-bye. My mother—"

"Come, Bess," said the earl, taking hold of her and opening the door. At the door Bess hung back, and so he picked her up and carried her down a short passage and out another door and deposited her in a litter with two horses already hitched and an escort waiting, already ahorse. In the frosty late afternoon the horses stamped and whinnied, their breath coming white like smoke.

The earl piled fur rugs around Bess and got in beside her. "It will take only fifteen minutes to reach the manor lodge, sweetheart. You're being abducted."

Now, early, early in the morning, it was five days later. Bess rolled over and lay close beside him, her lips at his ear.

"My jewel," she whispered. "My love and my lord, do you

186

realize—I had forgot all about it—but do you realize you haven't married me yet?"

The earl stirred, "I haven't?" he asked.

Bess' finger rubbed the side of his cheek. "And what's more, you haven't shaved for five days."

"Go to sleep," said the earl. "I promise to shave this afternoon."

Bess laughed, closed her eyes obediently, and went back to sleep in two minutes.

They had dinner at eleven in a big, raftered room with a fireplace twelve feet long, and five feet deep. After dinner Shrewsbury said, "I've changed my mind, Bess. I'm not going to shave. I think I'll grow a short beard, it's all the fashion." He grinned at her.

Bess regarded him, with her head on the side. "All right," she said, "but not a long, droopy one."

"And now I'm going out."

"Where?" asked Bess.

"Out," said Shrewsbury. "And you can't come."

"Be damned to you," said Bess good naturedly. "Goodbye."

I ought to go out, too, Bess thought, *and walk in the gardens.* The lodge boasted two walled gardens. But she was so full of roast quail and dove—which she loved, it was a fine treat—that she pulled a pillow down onto the fur rug in front of the fire and watched the flames contentedly.

Some fifteen minutes later Digby was tidying up Bess' table and putting away clothes when there was a knock on the door and she was informed that the earl requested her presence. She scurried out of the room and presented herself before him with a quick bobbed curtsey, looking up into his unshaven face with his blue eyes aglitter. Then Digby saw her husband was in the big room, too.

"You two will witness a marriage," the earl said. "Stand beside us." He took Bess' hand and then glanced over his shoulder. "You two should hold hands, too," he said, and Digby gratefully took her new husband's strong brown fingers in hers and squeezed them.

And so, in the presence of only two witnesses, standing before the priest, holding hands tightly, Bess and Shrewsbury repeated their vows, Bess looking up at the earl while she was saying the words after the priest. Then the earl took her in his arms and kissed her, and Digby wiped her eyes. The earl thanked them and gave them each a gold piece. Digby later looked at it in wonder, she had never seen one before.

Digby's husband, Archer, so neat in his blue livery, took Bess' hand and kissed it, and told her he would serve her for the rest of his life, my lady, and Digby curtsied; and when they had both left, Bess had to blow her nose.

"Don't cry," the earl said, smiling down at her. He hugged her tight. "I have something for you. Look."

He drew her over to the table where lay a chest of gleaming wood bound with silver. There was a key in the lock, charmingly wrought. The earl lifted the lid and handed the key to Bess.

"Yours," he said.

"Mine?" Bess stuttered, looking down at the box, which seemed literally awash with Oriental pearls.

"Those are the Talbot pearls and they belong to the countess of Shrewsbury," the earl said. "I believe you are the countess of Shrewsbury, are you not?"

"I don't know who I am," Bess said shakily. "It's a—they're a king's ransom, my lord."

"Permit me to correct you, madam," Shrewsbury said. "They're an earl's ransom. More important."

Bess was just standing there, looking, so the earl lifted the eight-strand mass of pearls and put them over Bess' head; they came down way below her waist. Shrewsbury stepped back to look at her. He nodded. "You're tall enough to wear them, my love."

Bess swallowed. "Thank you," she mumbled.

The earl grinned. "They belong to you, Bess." Then he went toward her and took her in his arms. "Bess, Bess, my love, these pearls were collected by the men in my family for the women they loved, as I love you, my Bess, my dearest love. There are none like you, sweetheart, none as beautiful, none as gay, none so alive and none so gallant; I'm going to call you None." He tipped up her chin and looked down into her eyes. "Now, today, I must do one more thing, besides getting wed. I must write to the Queen's Majesty and tell her I have married the Lady St. Loe."

Bess heard his voice from far away. He pronounced "Saint" like "Sint," she thought. It was such an elegant accent.

"I love you," she whispered. "I adore you."

Part IV

CHAPTER 1

November, 1568

THE fortunes of men and women lie not only within themselves but in the mirrored and pictured images of themselves that they project on their world. This fact was brought clearly into focus for the earl of Shrewsbury as he sat in the garden at Hampton Court, talking alone with his queen.

It was a pleasant afternoon, mercifully so, for it had been cold. But today, at two o'clock, the sun was shining. The earl basked in its warmth, throwing open his jacket, feeling the caress of sun on his face. The queen did the same, she who so eagerly welcomed every season and all the excitement of a wonderful world that somehow today let her enjoy warm sunlight in November.

"A gift of God," she said, smiling. "And you, my lord, are also a gift of God, to a needy sovereign."

Shrewsbury's blue eyes were instantly wary. He always amused her by coming straight to the point. "In what way, your Majesty?"

Elizabeth laughed; he had brushed away the compliment so baldly. "You are not a courtier," she needled him.

"No?" he said. "After all my long training?"

"I answer neither question," Elizabeth said. "But before

long you will well perceive how much I do trust you, as I do but few men."

"You will not tell me wherein, madam?"

She shook her head. "Not yet."

She had a pressing problem; she'd had it for almost eight months. She hadn't known what to do, but now, now, she thought she'd solved it. "Later, my lord."

The short interview weighed on the earl's mind all the rest of the afternoon and evening. When he finally escaped from the primero table, where he had lost, he sat down at his table and wrote to Bess.

It is midnight, sweetheart. He could feel her sympathy flowing over him; she knew he hated to stay up late. *Ah, Bess,* he thought. *And I lost more than a hundred pounds,* wrote the earl. *At primero.* He dipped the pen. Then he scribbled the sentence that had weighed on his mind all day, for he suspected well enough what Elizabeth wanted from him. *She declared she trusted me as she did few men, but she would not say wherein. But I doubt it was about the custody of the Scottish queen. However it falls out, I will not fail to be with you at Christmas, or else you shall come to me.*

Bess read the sentence twice. She thought, *He must mean doubt not; he was so tired he left out the "not." It must be: "I doubt not it was about the custody of the Scottish queen."* She raised her eyes from the letter and regarded Jane. "God's death!" she cried and drew a deep breath and read the letter aloud to Jane.

"By my faith!" Jane gasped.

The fire crackled and they both jumped. For the scandalous behavior of Mary Stuart, Queen of Scots, had been the most eye-popping and juiciest piece of news since Bess of Hardwick had caught and married the earl of Shrewsbury after a slightly less scandalous lapse. In Derbyshire they finally left off talking about Bess and how she had managed to catch the earl when the first piece of news came flying from Scotland: The Queen of Scots had a lover, Bothwell! Then she not only had a lover, but he had murdered her husband; then she wed with her husband's murderer. When Bothwell fled, and the nobles caught Mary and brought her to Edinburgh, she'd leaned out the window, half naked,

192

hair streaming, and called curses on her people, while they shouted back, "Burn the whore! Burn the whore!"

"Imagine!" cried Bess, who wished she'd been there to see and hear it.

Now Mary had fled to England, seeking aid, and the problem was: What to do with her? What? It was politically inconvenient to have a deposed monarch queening it in the north of England, a beautiful headstrong woman who claimed to be England's queen too, but was it dangerous? While the queen and council in London debated what to do, eight months had gone by.

"The custody of the Scottish queen." The sentence rolled around in Bess' head. Somehow it was very exciting.

It was not exciting to Shrewsbury. He wanted nothing to do with the Scottish queen. But his own queen leaned close to him and said, "Very well, my lord, But if you do not undertake it, who will? For it is you we trust. Deeply."

It was December 15. Troubled and liking this job little, the earl wrote to Bess. *Now it is certain the Scottish queen comes under my charge, at Tutbury. When I don't know. And if I should judge time, it is long since my coming here, my only joy. Since I married you, such is the love which I never tasted so deeply before. I leave tomorrow.*

"He will be home then," Bess said contentedly, "in time for Christmas."

Bess was so busy she forgot about Mary Queen of Scots. When the earl was away, it was Bess who took up the reins of the huge, huge establishment. The first time he had ridden off to court, she had said, "I can take over your duties, sweetheart," and he had smiled and said, "By God, I think you could!"

"I'll try," Bess had assured him.

It was like a small kingdom. There was a master of the wardrobe, for there were literally hundreds of liveried servants to be clothed, to say nothing of the big growing family. The wardrobe contained racks and chests of furs and cloth and carefully put-away, outgrown children's clothes, listed and inventoried.

There were nine immense dwellings, and the rents and

the produce and the upkeep were tallied and toted and salaries paid, even to my lord of Shrewsbury players, for the earl had a troop of players and was extremely fond of the drama. There was a master of horse for the enormous stables. There were bailiffs and overseers. And at the head of this was the busy Bess, but not too busy to keep her eye on the final stages of building at Chatsworth, not too busy to oversee with love the new great house the earl was building at Worksop, and not too busy to have suggested to the earl that they construct a row of small stone houses at Buxton Springs, to encourage more people to come and take the baths. That row of stone dwellings Bess had labored on with love, her neat drawings in pen and ink the picture of bucolic charm. And they were going up so fast!

"Winter cold never stopped me from building," she told the earl.

"I know that, sweetheart," he said, thinking of the first time he had come to Chatsworth.

The earl arrived at Sheffield on the twenty-first of December. And it was a happy Christmas, snowy, cold and gay. The earl was so glad to be home he almost forgot Mary Stuart, too. But on the day after New Year's, in his study, writing fast in his execrable handwriting, he made a final plea, to Robert Dudley, now Lord Leicester, the great earl. *The Queen of Scots coming soon into my charge will make me soon grayheaded.* He ran his hand through his short shaggy hair. *May it please Her Majesty to give me leave to come up to speak with her, though I tarry not past one day.*

One day. That's all he was asking for; if Elizabeth would permit his coming to court, he might be able to persuade her to let someone else do this job. But he scribbled on. *In any case Sheffield Castle itself is far more suitable than Tutbury for the keeping of this queen, but for God's sake let me know soon, for my energetic wife is fast removing everything from Sheffield.*

Leicester pleaded the earl's case well. But they had all forgot one important thing: that the Elizabeth Tudor knew very well indeed into whose hands to place this ticklish, many-faceted problem, her royal young captive cousin. Shrewsbury's head might ache, but Elizabeth's head would rest easier and sleep sounder on her goosedown pillows.

She said, "His lordship is not given permission to come to court! Tell him!"

Shrewsbury had written correctly; his energetic wife was rapidly emptying Sheffield of the stuffs needed when the household moved from one great dwelling to another. Bess was saying, "Now where in God's name did I put that red velvet for the dais? Open me that chest there."

"Bess . . ." said the earl from behind her.

"I must find that velvet," Bess said.

"The devil with velvet!" said the earl impatiently.

Bess turned, and then she smiled and thought: *I am really excited about meeting and hostessing a queen, But Shrewsbury couldn't be less impressed by what he had heard of Mary.* Besides that, to him the name of Talbot was more noble than either Tudor or Stuart; in the bottom of his heart he thought that, and Bess knew it.

"Bess," said the earl, "you are aware, aren't you, that all the children and most of the household will remain here? There will be no one with us, there can be no one with us; no one is to have access to this queen." Shrewsbury was already calling Mary Stuart by the words "this queen," in contrast to Elizabeth, whom he called the Queen's Majesty.

"Aye, my lord, I know. All this stuff is just for her chambers and ours. And her people. She has four ladies-in-waiting, for instance."

Shrewsbury groaned at the thought. He was thinking what Jane had said to him last night, when he had told her that Bess didn't seem to realize the difficulties ahead. Jane had said, "Oh, but you see, my lord, when Bess has a problem or something ahead, she rushes in and throws herself into the first task—readying a castle for royal visitors this time—and until it is done, she doesn't look ahead. Later she will, and later she'll plow through the next problem, just like harrowing the first field, and then the second, the way it is always done, every spring." Jane looked up at him, smiling.

Now Shrewsbury said, "Bess, Sir Francis Knollys writes to me that Mary Stuart is driving him mad."

"He does?" Bess inquired with interest. She cocked her head on one side, watching the men stagger out of the great hall with another loaded chest. "I hope it doesn't snow," she said, "till they get those chests to Tutbury."

"Damn the chests," said the earl. "I want to talk to you. I want to explain a few things. First, you must always address this queen as madam. Second, you are not a hostess but a jailor. Third, we have to leave tomorrow morning—"

"Well, then we can talk later," Bess interrupted.

"Talk later? I have about a thousand things to do tonight before leaving Sheffield!"

"Well, so do I! I don't want to leave Jane's feather bed, for instance."

"Jane's feather bed? Jane isn't coming."

Now he had got her whole and outraged attention. She had depended on Jane's being with her. Her mouth flew open. "I can't get along without Jane!" she cried.

Shrewsbury shook his head. "You can get along without anybody, None. I've never known a more self-sufficient person than you, my love. I told you but you don't listen. No one is to have access to this queen."

Bess frowned, her wits working busily. She'd write to Cecil, she would, and to Leicester; she liked the great earl; they respected each other. As soon as she got to Tutbury, she'd first write Cecil though, her old old dear friend. Surely they'd let her have her sister with her.

Shrewsbury looked down at her face. "Plowing the next field already?" he asked.

"What are you talking about?" she asked. "First I've got to find Jane's feather bed and keep it from going to Tutbury!"

When Bess first saw Tutbury Castle, from a distance, she was charmed. It was like a medieval village; it didn't look like a castle. The river Dove encircled the foot of the hill, and crowning the hill was a cluster of stone dwellings, chimneyed and peaked. In the center of the approach was an ancient drawbridge, an enormous gate in the stone ramparts, then the gray stone-walled village. Was it built on Roman ruins? Shrewsbury didn't know. Perhaps. They rode across the drawbridge, which in the old fashion could be drawn up by its massive creaking chains. The river rushing below was chillingly cold; Bess shivered as her horses' hooves beat against the wide oaken planks; she looked up at the huge portcullis.

The courtyard was small. The first hall very small, dank and dripping with wet. Bess was lifted from the saddle and stood looking about her. "Shrewsbury," she said, standing next to the earl, who was entirely clothed in heavy leather riding clothes, "I don't know if even *I* can make this place habitable. It isn't even fit for my horse!"

Bess kept on her heavy cloak. It took her five hours to inspect Tutbury. In the kitchens the cooks were outraged and horrified, throwing pots around and screaming at each other. Bess screamed back.

"Get those fires burning higher!" The head cook was so upset he banged one of his helpers on the head with a pan instead of the wooden spoon he usually used to bang heads. His victim fell onto the floor clutching his head and moaning. The head cook occupied a sacrosanct position, and Bess didn't bother to reprove him.

"You will have to do the best you can," she said. God knew when this queen would arrive; according to the distraught Sir Francis Knollys, who had Mary in his keeping, they had started for Tutbury on the twenty-fourth of January, and it was now the last day of the month. "But it is so cold," continued Bess, to the head cook, "that all possible fires in this kitchen will have to be kept going day and night, and for hot water, too."

Tramping through small halls, through the tumbled mass of dwellings, linked together by twisting stone corridors and low passageways, she finally chose a suite for Mary. It had three rooms, a great chamber, an outer chamber, and an inner chamber. Nonetheless, queen or no queen, the suite of two rooms she chose for herself and her husband were the best Tutbury had to offer; the rooms were higher, so they looked out over the earthen ramparts that towered up above the stone walls, and they had two huge fireplaces. *I'm not having my husband catching deathly colds if I can help it,* she thought.

There was no task Bess relished more than the impossible. For three days she labored like Job and Hercules, the earl remarked. And when Mary's room was hung with

197

tapestries—and the dais covered with the red velvet that had turned up in the bottom of one of the chests—and topped with a draped canopy and a scrap of Turkey carpet on the floor, and Bess' linen sheets on the fresh-smelling feather bed, she professed herself pleased. The other two rooms were also hung with tapestries, and there were beds for Mary's ladies-in-waiting.

She had finished none too soon. On the fourth of February, from the ramparts of Tutbury Castle, Bess held tight to the earl's hand as they watched the approaching cavalcade wind slowly toward them, half of it up the hill and half of it still streaming across the river meadows.

The wind blew bitterly. Bess reckoned swiftly and with sinking heart that there must be a household of a hundred and fifty persons with Mary, and behind them rumbled a jumble of carts, with baggage piled high and tied on.

Bess glanced at Shrewsbury's face.

"What are you thinking?"

He said, "I'm thinking the first thing I must do is inform her the members of her household will have to be cut by two-thirds."

The huge problem in a crowded castle was the sanitary problem. Within the castle, within the rooms set aside for the family and guests, were garderobes, usually set behind screens or in closets, kept clean and tended by the servants. Outside the castle were the privies used by most of the household. Bess had had a number of these constructed. Naturally in winter they were bitter cold.

But where, Bess thought, *would they all sleep, but crowded together in anterooms and hallways, sleeping cheek to jowl!*

"We can't give up our own two chambers," Bess said, and Shrewsbury said curtly he had no intention of it. Whose castle was it, anyway?

"Come," he said, holding out his hand. The time for greeting their royal prisoner had arrived.

Bess was wearing a gray gown, and two long strands of her famous pearls. At the bleak stone entrance to Tutbury, she and the earl waited; and now they could see the Queen of Scots, in the center of her people, riding alongside Sir

198

Francis Knollys. She watched Mary alight from her horse, her ladies then grouped themselves around her, her page ran ahead.

There was Lord and Lady Livingstone, the maids-of-honor, Mary Seaton and Mary Bruce, the bishop of Ross, John Beaton, the cardinal's nephew, a doctor, an apothecary, a crowd of lesser people, and now in front of Bess stood the Queen of Scots herself. Sir Francis made the introductions. Mary was very tall. Her dark eyes glowed underneath a wealth of chestnut hair; Bess didn't know it was a wig; she was twenty-seven years old. Bess dipped her a tiny curtsey.

But Mary Stuart hardly glanced at her; her eyes flicked over Bess and came to rest fully on the earl. *Here,* Mary was thinking, almost as though she were thinking aloud, *here is my antagonist, my warder—God's blood, that I should have a warder!* She could look Shrewsbury almost in the eye, for she was almost six feet tall. She was about to speak but the earl preempted her. In his most clipped and icy tones:

"In the name of the Queen's Majesty, we have been instructed to house you here and the said Queen's Majesty sends you greeting."

Then he made her a small formal bow, and Mary swept him a curtsey. Upon that, unappeased by the melting smile she was bestowing on him, as she drew up all her force to exert her legendary charm, he listened distantly while she thanked him in two tumbled sentences spoken in French. Her eyes gleamed a little as she watched his face, and she was annoyed that he obviously understood the rapid French.

The earl inclined his head. "I make no doubt you would seek your chambers now." He waved his hand in the gesture he always used to summon a servant, and a blue-liveried footman bowed in front of Mary. The earl turned away from Mary and spoke to Sir Francis.

"I wish a word with you, sir."

He held his arm for Bess, who took it, and trotted along at his side with Sir Francis tramping along behind them—the corridors and steps were so narrow, even here off the main hall. Bess whispered.

"You speak French?"

"Fluently," growled Shrewsbury, who had taken an instant dislike to Mary's manner.

When the door had closed to their private rooms, Sir Francis was saying with an admiring grin, "Well, by God, you will tame her, my lord!"

There was no answering smile from the earl, who looked grimmer than ever.

"How many of her people are there, sir?"

"Sixty, in her immediate entourage, plus eighty servants," Knollys said. "Her doctor, apothecary, embroiderer; her page Bastien and his wife, at whose wedding she had been dancing the night her husband was murdered; her tailor, a Willie Douglass who had helped her escape from Lochleven, the two priests—"

Shrewsbury cut him short. "Those numbers will have to be cut in half, and even then—" He shrugged and went to the sideboard to pour Sir Francis a cup of wine. Then he remembered. "Permit me, sir, to offer you my sincere condolences on the loss of Lady Knollys."

Sir Francis was silent a minute, and then he said, "As sure as God is in heaven, my lord, I don't know when I have suffered more than this winter! With my poor wife so ill and this she-devil, complaining constant, demanding, making life hell, always seeking to escape, I fear—" He shook his head as if to say words would not convey the least of what he had suffered. Then he looked over to the standing figure of the earl, and he repeated what he had said before, "But I doubt not you'll tame her, my lord!"

Bess thought, *I want my husband taming no woman.* She went over to the sideboard herself and helped herself to wine, sipping it by the fire, her back to the flames, she only half listened to the two men, busy with her own thoughts.

Sir Francis left thirty minutes later, declining food, anxious to shake all memories of Mary. The earl and Bess had gone with him to the gates, politely, to wish him Godspeed. He and his escort clattered over the drawbridge, and after that sound died away, Bess heard the heavy chains rattling and clanking as the bridge was drawn up, enclosing them within the ancient walls.

200

In this hall there were no windows. Torches had been lighted in the niches under the stone arches. Bess thought, *I think this was built by the Romans. It has stood here for a thousand and four hundred years or more.* She turned slowly around in a circle. *What have these walls not seen, what languages have they not heard? How fascinating are the dwelling places of man, how eloquent are they.*

Shrewsbury said, "I've ordered our supper upstairs, in front of the fire."

Bess said, "Should we go up and bid our guests goodnight, or—"

"She is not a guest, Bess; she is a state prisoner."

The cold words made Bess shiver. But she was hungry.

Bess ate roast venison; she liked the ribs. She was in bed by nine o'clock. By ten the whole castle was quiet. The Scots were exhausted by their nine days' trip. *Where are they all sleeping?* Bess wondered. *Crowded together in anterooms and hallways on pallets?* The wind moaned around the walls. The river, lapping so close, encased its lower ramparts in ice, along the banks. The castle slept. It slept uneasily, pursued by the past and the present and the recurring woes of generations of men.

CHAPTER 2

"SHE drinks only French wines," Bess said breathlessly.

Three days had passed; outside it was snowing and inside the earl was reading the long list of Mary's court and her attendants and servants. He damned her to hell and back with the pox thrown in. Mary had a train of one hundred and forty people. The crown allowed him fifty-two pounds a week for their maintenance; that sum wouldn't feed half of them, to say nothing of French wines. It would hardly feed the horses and the grooms. Shrewsbury thought he could write to Leicester and inform him that the Scottish

201

queen's stable should come under the aegis of Leicester himself, as master of horse. He scowled and made a note to write to Leicester about it today.

Shrewsbury studied the list.

Sir John Morton, priest. The earl would have liked to draw his pen through that name, but Elizabeth would not permit it, he knew. She believed in tolerance of another's religion. Mary would be allowed to have her priest.

Master of household, master of horse, a surgeon, a mediciner, six valets, fourteen servitors, a tailor, two wardrobe keepers, an embroiderer, three cooks, a pastry maker, a baker, two pantry men, three gentlemen's gentlemen, four boys, a farrier, three lackeys, ten maidservants—*Good God*, said the earl.

"She eats off nothing but silver salvers, she eats in bed and the whole room is in a mess! And all that chestnut hair is a wig; she cut off all her hair when she escaped from that island, and it didn't grow back properly. And she wants to borrow my portable bath."

The earl raised his head. "No," he said.

Bess' portable wooden bath, hinged in iron, was copied from the queen's. For though, in Bess' time, many went unwashed, the nobles and the gentry did not. For fear of offending the queen's sensitive nose, it was imperative to be clean and wear clean clothes. They said that Leicester, in his new town house, was constructing a hot room, for baths. *Wouldn't that be wonderful?* Bess thought.

"I will not have her bathing in your bath," the earl said positively, scowling. *What if she'd picked up the French disease from one of her husbands or lovers?* And Shrewsbury included her first husband, the king of France, in his doubts. "There is enough danger of illness here, without going to meet it," he said, pushing back his chair and standing up.

Bess thought, *How handsome he looks today!* She sighed in pure pleasure at the sight of him. He looked as healthy as a man could look, and as big and exciting. He had been able to ride out each day; but they couldn't go together. It was not yet a burden; Bess didn't realize yet how much of a burden that would become: the fact that one of them had always to stay with Mary Stuart; they could never leave her alone.

202

"I want you to come with me, Bess," he said. "I've allowed her three days. Now we are going to make a beginning, and reduce the numbers of her household."

Mary Stuart, her prettily capped head bent over her desk, was writing to the French ambassador in London, picturing her plight, so that he could immediately protest and send her letter to her brother-in-law, the king of France, for these unendurable conditions would have to cease.

I am in a walled enclosure, she wrote, *on the top of a hill, exposed to all the winds and inclemencies of heaven. Within the enclosure, resembling that of a wood in Vincennes, there is an old hunting lodge, the plaster cracked, and situated so low that the rampart of earth, which is behind the wall, is on a level with the highest point of the building, so that the sun can never shine upon it, and it is so damp that the furniture molds; in short, the greater part of it is more of a dungeon for base criminals than a habitation fit for a person of much lower quality than I. The only apartments that I have consist of two miserable rooms, excessively cold, that but for the curtains and tapestries that I have had made, it would not be possible to stay in them.*

One of her Marys, Lady Livingstone, announced his lord-ship the earl of Shrewsbury and Lady Shrewsbury. Mary put away the letter and went to her dais. She was prepared to do battle.

There was first an exchange of frosty good mornings, the earl managing to imply that it was hardly morning, being half past twelve, and implying also he disapproved of Mary's late-morning arisings. He proceeded immediately to the matter at hand, tapping the list he held and laying it in front of her, with thirty names checked off.

Mary studied the list. "But where will they all go, my lord?" she asked, as though he were going to cut off their heads forthwith. She leaned forward, fastening her great eyes on him. "They cannot go back to Scotland!"

"It's not necessary they go back to Scotland, madam," the earl explained, annoyed. "They can be sent, with your recommendation, north to some of your friends." His emphasis on the word *friends* was openly derisive, for Shrewsbury did not approve of the action of the northern earls, who had welcomed Mary into England and came to

203

pay her homage on bended knees. In Shrewsbury's opinion they were a pack of fools.

"They should be happy to do you a little service," he added. "You hardly need three cooks, a baker and a pastrymaker, six valets, and ten servitors; what's more, madam, in these cramped quarters, they'll freeze to death, or get sick, and we shall have an epidemic sweeping through these halls."

Mary started to speak, but Shrewsbury cut her short. He knew what she was thinking. "It is the Queen's Majesty who decides, madam, where we lodge. Not me, nor you."

Mary looked at him with twin daggers in her eyes. The reminder that Elizabeth Tudor was in charge did not sit very well. Mary would never be able to understand the loyalty and admiration of the English for their queen; Mary was sure her surface charm could win any man; she was proud, very proud, she was a queen. Elizabeth Tudor was proud, too, but she was proud of her Englishmen, every man jack of them. And they knew it.

How can I win him? Mary was thinking, studying the earl's face. But he had had enough of her silence, and he continued: "Your master of horse will be replaced by one of Lord Leicester's choosing, and the grooms also."

Mary said, "Being a bit fearful of your requests, I carry here in my hand a good luck token sent me at New Year's, as a gift from Lord Leicester. It is a piece of the horn of a unicorn."

This sentence did not take Shrewsbury aback. Leicester had always been an opportunist. There was little doubt but that Mary was Elizabeth's heir, and if anything happened to the queen, God forbid, England might have to suffer through such a queen as Mary had already shown herself to be. Leicester was backing all the horses.

"Madam," he said, "in my capacity of lord steward of England, it is my duty to take good care of you. I might remind you that your very name comes from that office, which your ancestors held in Scotland. Give me leave to discharge my duties as well as I can. If Lord Leicester takes over the charge and cost of your stable, it will be well for both of us."

"I count on Lord Leicester as a friend, my lord," Mary

said. "And I do not consent, my lord, to the reduction of my household in any manner or form whatsoever! I forbid it!"

Bess, standing at the earl's side, was fascinated by this confrontation. Her eyes went from one to the other; Mary's ladies watched; the room was silent, waiting for Shrewsbury's reply.

Shrewsbury said, "Madam, I have been placed in charge of you and your household, by the Queen's Majesty. As I've reminded you just now, I must do as I see fit to ensure the health and well-being of you and your people. Thus today those thirty people of yours will depart. You shall be permitted to bid them good-bye."

Mary went rigid with fury. How did he dare? But this time she managed to keep her temper. "I shall protest your action, my lord!"

The earl bowed. He thought, *God, she'd have my head; if she ever ascends the throne, Cecil and I shall be together on the gallows before the wink of an eye.* Only Elizabeth's heartbeat stood between him and a bloody death. But what could he do about it? Nothing. Except what about Bess? The earl took her hand and left the room, saying nothing to Bess, turning over in his mind that this danger was involving her. And what should he advise her to do?

Bess, at his side, clinging to his hand, whispered, "She will come to respect your integrity in time, my jewel."

In time? Shrewsbury wondered. *How much time?*

How much time? Bess began to think about that, too. The first weeks of warding Mary Stuart were like a very slowly boiling pot; there was little roiling of the water and little steam, just wispy curls across the top of the still water.

How much time? thought Mary Stuart. *How much time—to be a prisoner in this frightful ancient ruin of a castle?* Already almost a year had fled since she had escaped from her Scottish captors and come running to her cousin, Elizabeth Tudor, for aid.

She was being dressed for supper. It was seven o'clock. Her wig was set carefully on her head and tugged into place and settled firmly. Her reflection in the mirror was comforting. *My lovely face,* she thought, *my lovely face! Surely all*

205

the men who believe in me will come to my aid. How the northern gentry in England had flocked to see her, their admiration obviously shining from adoring eyes. *My very misery will bring them riding to me from all over.*

It was bitter cold. She said, "Tonight we'll have music and dancing to keep us warm. And we shall be happy, for the future cannot be worse. It could only be better!"

"She will be the focal point of rebellion," Cecil said bluntly. He was already tiring of the problem of Mary Stuart. "She is a born troublemaker."

There seemed to be no doubt that she was writing and receiving letters from the duke of Alva, the Spanish soldier that all England despised and feared. Furthermore, the council was considering the matter of Mary's marriage to the duke of Norfolk. Leicester was for it. Elizabeth was hesitant but not against it; perhaps it would be best for Mary Stuart to have an English husband. But Cecil knew that Norfolk's first task would be to undermine Cecil himself and oust him from the council, and from his place at the queen's side. Cecil had long ago learned to live with all the nobles who wished him out. Out! And thoroughly dead. He leaned back in his chair. The first thing to do was to find out how Mary was conniving with the Spanish Alva, the greatest enemy England had, with the exception of his master Philip himself. Philip, the king of Spain, whose distant presence Cecil never, never forgot; it was always at his shoulder, just behind him, in the back of his mind while he slept. Now Mary Stuart was intriguing with this man, this king, and as the wife of the richest noble in the realm, the Duke of Norfolk, she would be able to deal abroad with England's enemies, in fact to do anything she wished.

But even that night Leicester himself had said to the queen, "Mary Stuart would be less dangerous married to an Englishman."

Cecil had said slowly, "It is not a crime for Mary to marry Norfolk, yet how dangerous might her very liberty prove to be."

"I have one more letter to dictate," he said aloud to his secretary. The image of Mary Stuart and her suitor and the great earl and Shrewsbury himself were replaced by Bess.

Suddenly he could see clearly that flashing smile, and those huge eyes brimming with laughter. The memory made him feel better. But:

"To Lord Shrewsbury," he dictated. "I give this advice: There should be very few subjects in this land to have access to this queen. Glory joined to gain might stir men and women to adventure much for her sake. And as for Lady Shrewsbury, the Queen of Scots may see the countess if she is sick or for any other cause, but rarely. No other gentlewomen must be allowed access to her."

"I shall wait for that letter," Cecil added, and when it was set in front of him, he picked up his pen and corrected a word or two. "Don't bother to rewrite," he said. "Just send it, tonight."

Bess read it six days later. She could imagine Cecil, there at his table, correcting the letter in his own hand. She sighed. "No other gentlewomen," she said. "That's like condemning me to prison, too."

She looked over the earl's shoulder as he wrote back to Cecil. *March 13,* the earl wrote. *This queen does daily resort to my wife's chamber, where, with Lady Livingstone and Mrs. Seaton, she sits working with her needle and the talk is altogether of indifferent and trifling matters. I think there can be no danger, but rather more surety of safekeeping, yet if the Queen's Majesty is not pleased, I will make such restraints as she orders.*

It seemed to the earl that day after day, when he came into his quarters, there would be those women, grouped around, sewing, chatting endlessly, until he got to hate the sight and smell of them. They used some kind of heavy musky perfume, whereas Bess, learning from her mother, used flower fragrances; she smelled like rosewater, violets, or lavender, even strawberries, for she made a kind of lotion for her face from strawberries and thick cream.

But Bess was fascinated by their talk. Mary Stuart, brought up in the French court, having the exquisite Diane de Poitiers, the king's mistress, as her example, could bring to life and recreate for Bess the continental scene, with its grace and beauty, its delicate refinements in all the arts, its careful protocol, even its sparkling wines and rich, rich food.

Florence Brossier, the embroiderer, was sketching Bess,

who would stand patiently for hours, it seemed to Shrewsbury. And yet what annoyed him most was Mary's habit of
staying up, he thought, all night.

Mary seldom retired before one in the morning. All evening would be spent at supper, with French wines, with
Scottish and French ballad singing, with endless, the earl
thought, silly chatter, for passing by her rooms, one could
hear the gab of women's high-pitched voices and bursts of
laughter.

"God's death," he said, "they don't even play cards!"

He considered them brainless and silly. But he wouldn't
have minded it so much had they not had the disconcerting
habit of intruding on the earl's own chambers at any hour
of the night. Either a page or a lady would come aknocking
on the earl's door, waking him out of a sound sleep, with
a trifling personal request, in what the earl called the middle of the night.

He came back to the very present, this night itself. What
a frustrating experience! A March snowstorm had kept him
within these walls for three days. And he suddenly realized
he was freezing cold.

"By God," he said aloud, with such force that Bess
jumped almost out of her chair by the fire, "I can't even
feel my own feet!"

He was wearing three doublets and his warmest boots.
Bess was wearing three petticoats, he knew, and a furred
gown. And any minute one of those damned Scots would
come aknocking on the door.

The bedroom was the warmest room in Tutbury. The
earl shoved back the papers on the desk.

"We're going to bed!"

He seized Bess in his arms and carried her into the bedroom, stood her on her feet, and said to Digby, "Prepare
the countess for bed."

He came back in a few minutes, dressed in his heavy bedgown, carrying himself a tray with wine and glasses and
cakes. He put a few more logs on the fire and poked them
with the iron. Bess was sitting in bed, all washed and her
hair wound up and bound with a tiny cap. Digby curtsied,
she slept in the adjoining room on a pallet, and the earl's

body servant slept in the hall outside the door, so crowded was the castle.

The earl said to Digby, "On no account do I wish to be disturbed." Before the door closed, he said to Bess, "Do you realize I never see you, or that we are never alone?"

"Aye, my lord," Bess said. "I know it."

"Well, we are now, and we're going to forget this damned queen, and pretend we are back at Sheffield Manor."

Bess smiled.

He poured her a cup of wine and brought her a plate with a confection on it that one of Mary's pastrymakers had baked that morning. Bess laid her napkin over the counterpane, so it wouldn't get dirty, for the washing at Tutbury was a big problem.

"Today she talked endlessly of Norfolk," Bess said.

"Damn Norfolk," said the earl. "Bess, even when we are alone, all we think about is this queen!"

"Well, let's forget her," Bess said, "and drink all the wine!"

An hour later, after his lovemaking, she lay wrapped up in his arms; now they were talking about themselves and not about Mary Stuart. Bess was happy, and there came a knock on the door. Shrewsbury sat up in bed, and in a very calm and controlled voice he said, "Digby, what is the matter?"

Digby's voice came through the closed door.

"The page Bastien says that this queen is having a chill and needs strong wine and more hot water and another heavy quilt; she says it is as cold as a dungeon in her rooms."

As Digby talked, the earl's temper rose and rose, yet politely he waited for her to finish.

Then he roared, "Digby!"

"Aye, my lord?" came Digby's quivering voice.

"Tell the page Bastien that there are still dungeons in Tutbury, and if he doesn't take himself off immediately I'll put every Scot in the castle into the aforesaid dungeons!"

Then the earl lay down again and pulled up the quilts, while Bess lay there and laughed helplessly and delightedly. She shook with laughter.

The earl hugged her tight. "To hell with all of them," he said. "To hell with them!"

Four days later a hasty letter arrived from London. It hinted at danger: The Queen of Scots was to be removed to the earl of Shrewsbury's manor of Wingfield.

CHAPTER 3

ON the third of April, Bess came to bid good-bye to Mary Stuart. She was dressed in soft brown velvet riding dress, and hat with a black feather, she looked slim and excessively elegant, and Mary felt real jealousy. She was riding out and away, and the Queen of France, Scotland, and England was shut up in a dingy old castle! But Bess didn't notice.

"I shall prepare Wingfield Manor for your people and you, madam. You shall enjoy the spring there."

The earl went to the doors of Tutbury, to see Bess ride off. Her escort was ready, her litter was piled with baggage. He leaned down and kissed her good-bye.

"I won't be able to endure this place without you and with all these damned women hounding me," Shrewsbury said. "Believe me, Bess, I'll be at Wingfield with this queen by the twentieth of the month." And since it would be the fifth before Bess would reach the manor, that would give her only fifteen days.

"I'll be ready for you," she promised.

She was going first to Sheffield to get Jane and to pick up her two young daughters and Shrewsbury's two daughters and young son, Edward, and take them all to Wingfield. And she must ride over to see her new granddaughter!

"I'm a grandmother, my lord," she had said, the first day the news had come, a week ago. She peered at herself in the mirror. She didn't appear to have changed. So she

210

guessed it was all right. And she decided to be proud of it. Now she waved to the earl, put spurs to her horse, who had whinnied and danced at the sight and smell of her. Her head groom rode just behind her; he was leaning forward in the saddle, talking to her, and Bess turned and Shrewsbury saw the brilliant smile on her face and he frowned. It boded ill: Bess was leaving him and she was happy.

Bess, accompanied by Jane and the five children, arrived at Wingfield Manor on the fifth of April, as planned. Wingfield lay eight miles south of Chatsworth. It had been built in 1440 by Ralph Cromwell, chancellor of the exchequer to Henry VI, and had been purchased from him by John Talbot, second earl of Shrewsbury, in 1445.

It was a fortified manor house.

Bess saw from the distance its four-story-high tower, which protected the southwest side of the manor. She clattered across the dry moat and entered the first courtyard, for Wingfield had two courts. She decided that Mary Stuart should have the rooms off the inner court, from which it would be difficult to escape—or be rescued, for that was suddenly what everyone was afraid of now. Rescue.

But when she stood in the great hall of Wingfield and looked down its length of seventy-two feet to the great oriel and the bank of windows on the north side, she was lost in admiration.

The room was entered through a porchlike balcony, which led to more rooms. "These shall be our apartments," she said to Jane, and she ran up the stairway and through the porch to look out over the hills.

April had greened the land, and the fruit trees were a sea of white and pink. Bess' heart filled with joy at the beauty of the land, and she cried, "Oh, Jane! We shall be happier here! All of us!"

"I hope so, Bess," Jane said.

"And even though you and the children can't be here, you will be near."

Jane nodded. She and the children were to go to Chatsworth the next day. Jane thought they should have left today. Everything was ready; an army of servants—some from the village—had helped ready the manor for guests.

"I couldn't bear to part with you before I actually saw them coming," Bess said.

It was eleven o'clock. The children had gone to bed; Jane and Bess had had their late supper together, and on this last night with Jane, Bess refused to go to bed. "I hate to think of tomorrow," she said. "Except for seeing my jewel, of course."

In the last fifteen days, Wingfield Manor had seen floods of Bess' friends from the surrounding and far-away manors. The unpredictable countess of Shrewsbury was at Wingfield, and the Queen of Scots was actually coming to dwell among them. Bess sighed. All the fun would end tomorrow. But then she returned to the thought of Mary. So did Jane.

Jane spoke first. "But then, you see, Bess, she hasn't anything to do—but make trouble."

Trouble. The word hung in the air. "Oh," said Bess, "it can't last much longer. Maybe they'll let her marry Norfolk. She talks of him endlessly, and sends gifts and notes. Let's forget her!"

Bess slept later than usual the next morning. She wakened and stretched and rubbed her head. *I had too much wine last night,* she thought, annoyed with herself. She sat up in bed, sunlight was flooding the room. She rubbed her head again. *But it was worth it,* she decided; they'd had a wonderful evening of talk.

After she was dressed, she and Jane went up to the tower to look out. "I won't let you and the children start for Chatsworth until we see them coming," she cried.

It was such a beautiful day they all went out riding and took a picnic, for Bess' last day with the children. They returned at three o'clock, and they were just in time. From the tower Bess and Jane could see the cavalcade coming, stretching out far behind the lead riders. Jane glanced at Bess. *Such an enormous responsibility,* she thought, *for all those people and a captive queen.* She sighed. "We'll be very near," she said comfortingly. "Very near, Bess."

"I'll come over often," Bess promised as she kissed Mary and Elizabeth good-bye. She hugged Edward. "My lord

212

your father will soon ride over to see you." The children were riding in a litter because they had ridden far that day. Bess stood at the entrance gate, over the old dry moat. She waved and waved. When the last cart with the children's baggage jolted out, she turned and went back, alone, into the manor.

CHAPTER 4

THE page Bastien hammered on the closed door of the bedroom of the master of Wingfield.

"The queen is desperately ill!" His voice, a moan of fear, jolted Bess out of a sound sleep.

"I'm coming, I'm coming!" she shouted back.

She rolled out of bed, grasping her bedgown. Digby had laid her slippers on a stool beside her bed. Her hair was tied back, she fastened her robe; the earl was swearing under his breath; he watched Bess go to the door. They'd only been here a week, and now this. "Send for me if you need me, None," he said. But how the devil could he sleep with all these constant upheavals? Due to this queen he never got a good night's sleep. And perhaps he'd best send to London for a doctor.

My God, thought Bess wildly, *what if she should die? They'd blame us.* She stood in Mary's bedroom, watching the writhing figure on the bed.

"Every bone and muscle in my body aches," Mary cried, "and I am so weary with exhaustion I think I shall scream and scream and scream!"

Instead she began to vomit. Her maids rushed around and brought towels and basins; and when that was finished, she staggered out of bed to sit on her garderobe behind the screen and Bess heard her groaning.

God's death, she's going to die, Bess thought. She sent other servants for more hot water and clean sheets, and herself

213

began to strip the bed of its smelly linens and even the quilts; she dragged them off the bed and threw them out into the hall, to be gathered up and taken away quickly, before the stench reached every room in this wing.

In the outer courtyard, two men were ahorse and carrying a scribbled message from the earl to Cecil, telling of this queen's illness, and urging him to send two doctors immediately.

Cecil, upon reading this call for aid, thought privately it would be much better if she did die, but knowing the earl was right, he dispatched Drs. Caudwell and Francis to Wingfield immediately.

But before they arrived, Bess thought she would go out of her mind with worry.

The first night she stayed up all night, watching by the bedside. After the terrible attacks of vomiting and dysentery ceased, the room was cleansed as well as possible under the circumstances, with Mary tossing and crying out in pain, muttering about the old pain in her side, which she had had for years now. Bess packed her body with hot bricks wrapped in soft clean linen, the bed had been changed, and quilts were piled on her to keep her warm. She shook from head to toe.

The next night the earl relieved Bess, and the following night they took shifts of two hours each, waiting on this queen, trying to comfort her and to do their duty as her guards. There was always a suspicion in the earl's mind that Mary's illnesses were not real and that somehow she was planning to escape; and if she did escape from his guard, he would be eternally suspect, if not for treason, for incompetence.

By the time the two doctors arrived, both Bess and the earl were exhausted, their tempers at short leash. The earl greeted the two men with his usual restraint, and when they left him briefly, to wash up after their journey before they saw their patient, Bess said, "You should have made them more welcome!"

Shrewsbury scowled and said it was their duty to come, and he didn't have to greet them with flowery phrases.

"You're so unbending," Bess said. She took them to

214

Mary's inner quarters, on the second quadrangle courtyard.

Mary, propped up in bed, pale and wan, greeted them with grace; and both men, Bess saw, were impressed with her pitiful charm. Poor, poor Scottish queen, a sick prisoner. Bess thought, *This sympathy is what Cecil fears.* She excused herself, and almost ran to her own room, so glad was she to be relieved of the responsibility. A great load was off her shoulders, and when she closed the door behind herself, she said to Digby, "Let no one in! I'm going to have a bath in peace."

But when she had had her bath, she decided she would go mad if she didn't get outside; and so Digby dressed her quickly in a new close-fitting doublet, over her underdress, and off she went. The earl saw her disappearing in the distance, riding with that damned groom he disliked so much.

The earl had dinner alone with the doctors. They had spent the afternoon writing their report to Cecil, and when Bess came in, they had finished it, and it was lying on the table ready to be sent off to London. The earl handed it to Bess to read. While she read, the three men watched. No visible expression came into her face till she finished it and threw it down on the table in disgust.

"Of course there are sickening stenches in those rooms!"

Bess, eyes flashing, then went on to explain that she had placed a garderobe in each chamber, and the servants, passing through them, would relieve themselves, instead of going out to the privies, and that the filthy Scots never emptied the pots till they were overflowing, that even her servants had to clean up after them, and the floors, too.

"God's death!" Bess ended. "Those damned Scots piss all the time and they can't even piss straight!"

There was silence.

Bess said, "We'll have to move all that household over to Chatsworth, for a few days! And we'll have to scrub that whole damned wing, all the apartments, and all the floors! Put that in your report, and tell Cecil if he won't agree, I'll not be responsible for the health and well-being of anyone in Wingfield. No one. Tell him that!"

Dr. Francis meekly took up the report, and said he would add Bess' words and, overwhelmed, the two doctors filed out, clutching their papers. When the door closed, the earl said, "You sound as though you were brought up in the Banks."

Since that was the section of London inhabited mostly by thieves and whores, Bess took it as the deadly insult the earl had intended. Breathless with anger, she stuttered, "How dare you?"

"Try to remember," the earl said, "that you are the countess of Shrewsbury."

He started for the door himself, and when he had opened it, Bess shouted, "By God, I'm trying to forget it!" And she hurled the sander off the table at him because it was the first thing that had come to hand.

It was their first serious quarrel. To get some fresh air and exercise, the earl rode out for a few miles with the one departing doctor, for Dr. Francis was staying to look after Mary. When he returned, it was late afternoon, and as he passed through the great gallery the sun lit the whole length, through the oriel, lighting it into beauty. But he didn't notice, and went through the porch to his and Bess' apartments.

"What are you doing?" he asked curtly.

"Packing!" Bess answered. "And I've given orders to the Scots to do the same. As soon as permission comes from Cecil, we can be out of here in an hour."

Since there were three maids in the room, the earl contented himself with a muttered "uhm," and stalked out; but Bess, still angry, followed him onto the porch.

"Where are you going? You should pack, too!"

The earl said calmly, "Don't give me orders, madam. As a matter of fact, I'm going to check on this queen, which is what you should have been doing in my absence."

"I didn't even know you were gone, and care less! And second, I'm not going to set foot in those rooms! You can do it! You go chat with someone who's worthy of your high status!"

"You might learn something from her," the earl said. "Like dignity."

"And how to murder my husband, too?" Bess whispered silkily.

The earl went on down the stairs. Seething, Bess returned

216

to her packing, while Shrewsbury satisfied himself that Mary was safely in her bed and well guarded. He had supper, and at twilight himself made the round of the gates and watched while the new guards were posted. Meanwhile, exhausted by both her anger and the lack of sleep through Mary's illness, Bess withdrew to the inner bedroom and got ready for bed. Still too annoyed to eat, she had some wine and a cake. Digby lighted a few candles, and Bess decided she needed something to cheer her up and forget her husband. She said to Digby, "I think I'll wear my new nightgown."

She slept either naked or in her smock. But it was suddenly the fashion to have a silken gown, and Mary had given Bess some French silk, and Bess had embroidered the long, slender thin garment with black needlework, around the neck and arms and the hem. She slipped it over her head and looked at it. Digby was enchanted.

"Oh, madam!" she cried, touching its softness with her fingers.

"I feel very luxurious," Bess said happily, forgetting Shrewsbury entirely, in her admiration of this new fashion, which Elizabeth Tudor had espoused also. She sat down on her stool, and Digby began to brush her hair, while Bess had another cup of wine and another cake. So she was chatting happily with Digby about how Chatsworth, while not quite finished, would at least hold them all till she could have this queen's chambers thoroughly cleaned, how, too, living at Chatsworth she could keep an eye on the painting and the last of the beautiful plasterwork that would decorate the ceilings. And she had just finished saying, "And imagine, Digby, how beautiful the gardens will be this last week in May," when the earl came into the adjoining room. Hastily she drank off the wine. While Digby finished tying up her hair, Bess remembered that she had not only hurled insults at him but also the sander, and while she was thinking this the door opened. He loomed in the doorway, looking grim, and Digby, seeing the incline of his head toward the door, fled hastily, and Bess was alone with him. He shut the door and bolted it.

The earl himself had had some varying changes of mood

217

during the afternoon. When he had escorted the one departing doctor a few miles, he bethought himself that he couldn't leave Wingfield long without its master, considering the seriousness of his custody of the Scottish queen; and he had galloped home as fast as he could over the muddied roads, which had enabled him to let off some of his anger. By the time he reached Wingfield he was beginning to think it was comical, for he remembered the stark look on the faces of the two physicians confronted by Bess, and her lurid account of the Scots' sanitary habits. But this his second quarrel with her had fanned the flames again rather high, and he had stamped off and assuaged some of his feelings by dismissing thirty of Mary's servants, regardless of what she or Elizabeth should say at such high-handed action. He felt a lot better after it was done. The departing Scots would leave tomorrow in a body, and he had written to Cecil that in view of the conditions at Wingfield, there was no help for it.

When he had apprised Mary of this, she had been angry, too; he had taken her unawares, for she was up and at her desk writing. The earl had looked casually at the paper and seen immediately that he had intruded at an awkward moment for her, indeed, for she was writing in cypher. He took the paper and crumpled it in his big hand and told her curtly that if she continued to use cypher, he would forbid any correspondence.

Mary leaned her head back on her chair and closed her eyes as though she had fainted, whereupon the earl said to Mrs. Seaton, "Your mistress appears to be swooning," in an icy tone, and left the apartments.

"Women," muttered the earl as he went up to get ready for bed. From the inner bedroom he could hear Bess' voice, and the very sound of her artless chatter sent him into a sudden fury.

So when he closed the door after Digby, he did so with a tremendous clap of wood against wood. Bess jumped to her feet and turned around to face him.

He ran his eyes over her, scowling. "What's that thing?" he growled.

Bess said, "It's a night rail."

218

"It sounds like a new species of bird," Shrewsbury said, coming toward her, implacably. "Where's your smock?"

He liked her smocks; they barely concealed her buttocks, and she looked seductive in them, he thought.

"The queen has these to sleep in," Bess said, backing away toward the bed.

"The queen doesn't have a husband," said the earl. "It looks like a nuisance to me."

Bess climbed onto the bed and inched away from him. "Now, Shrewsbury," she said, "be careful. Don't pull at it, you'll tear it."

"I'll tear it to bits," he said, "and throw away the pieces."

"Oh," cried Bess, "you wouldn't do that! After all my work, look at the embroidery, it took me hours to do it! It came from France! Please, my lord—" She broke off as the earl was watching her with grim eyes, and he started toward the bed, taking off his bedgown, tossing it onto a chair. Horrified, Bess tried to back away from him, scrambling across the bed on her haunches, when Shrewsbury gave a shout of laughter and leaped for her, throwing himself across the bed, seizing her, and rolling her over, coming to a stop with Bess lying beneath him.

"Now," he said, "we'll see who really is the master of this castle."

When Bess wakened in the morning, it was ten o'clock. The sun was shining bright, and the windows were wide open, with the fresh spring air pouring into the room, sweet-smelling from the acres of orchard on the hillsides. Before he had left the room, much earlier in the morning, the earl had thrown them open as wide as possible, and covered Bess up warmly with another quilt. She never stirred.

But when he came back at ten o'clock, she opened her eyes.

"Good morning, sweetheart," he said, "I gave orders you were not to be disturbed."

"Good morning, my own love," Bess murmured sleepily. He sat down on the edge of the bed and gathered her into his arms and smoothed back the hair from her cheek and brow.

"I'm as worried as you are about the conditions here, Bess."

"Um," said Bess, putting her head against his shoulder.

"This place must be properly cleaned before someone gets sick. We'll go to Chatsworth for a week, at least."

"Aye, my lord," said Bess.

"I worry about you," the earl said, having no notion it was not Bess who was going to be sick, but he himself. "You will go to Chatsworth today," he ended. "And we will follow tomorrow."

With or without permission, he had decided to leave Wingfield. That morning he had written to Cecil: *I have taken it upon myself by the advice of the physicians to remove this queen in a litter to my wife's house at Chatsworth, eight miles hence, and to remain there for four or five days until her lodgings here be made sweet and better, returning next week.*

Chatsworth was not quite ready to be lived in, but as she went from room to room, from one great gallery to the other—for Chatsworth had two galleries—Bess couldn't look at it enough. This was her dream and Cavendish's dream, and it was alive. No tapestries yet hid the color of the painted wood, no Turkey rugs took one's eye from the polished floors and the massive heavily leaded windows soared two stories in the galleries, flooding the chambers with light. Although there was too much lead, Bess thought; that's the only wrong note; there's too much lead between the lights.

But outside, on this day, the first of June, the gardens were another tribute, this time to Aunt Linacre, whose genius was very, very plain. Everywhere one looked, everywhere the delighted eyes rested, past the series of ponds, within the enclosed yew walks, with their unexpected sudden opening out, to show a fountain or a rose garden, everywhere, it seemed to Bess, Aunt Linacre was saying to her, "Look, Bess! Look and smell the eglantine!"

Bess sat down on a stone bench beside the fountain. "Dear Aunt," she whispered, "it is all so beautiful that never, never will I forget to thank you."

220

The roses were budding, and she gathered a great basket of them, to take up to the chamber where the queen would sleep on a pallet bed, to be sure, and be without her dais. But it should be clean and sweet-smelling, and the rooms of Chatsworth were so perfect in proportion that just the flowers and the June skies peering in the huge windows and shining on the new floors should be beauty enough, even for a queen, Bess thought proudly. Bess stood back and looked at the window seat piled with bright cushions and the table before it with an enormous bowl of roses. There was something to be said for complete simplicity. One single magnificent hanging would complete the room. She sent a groom over to old Chatsworth to bring one of the copes that she had reembroidered herself, with the head of the Greek god Apollo looking forth with all his handsome bright gaze.

Bess went to the bedroom that she had originally intended and planned as her own. The rage nowadays was for black and white, and Bess suddenly decided she would use black velvet and black damask, enlivened only with thick gold lace and fringe; it should be truly elegant and luxurious. She went out of the room, which held now only two pallet beds, a table, a garderobe, behind the inevitable screen, and her portable bath. She was conscious of unreality, almost; she was actually going to live and sleep in Chatsworth. After eighteen years. And eighty thousand pounds. *It is almost done,* Bess thought. *What will I do?* If I weren't building, I'd probably fade and die, I would.

The earl arrived the next day, with his prisoner in a litter. He rode slowly at her side, and by the time the eight miles had been accomplished, and Mary's litter came through the gates and the lovely curtain walls of Chatsworth, there was fresh color in her cheeks; she looked, Bess thought, a thousand percent better already. If Shrewsbury worried about what Elizabeth would say at his abrupt taking of matters into his own hands, he didn't show it. Everyone dined on trestle tables in one of the great galleries; Mary's inevitable silver salvers, platters, water ewers, had been left behind to be newly scoured and scrubbed, along with everything else in her suite. Empty though the gallery was, the

221

chamber was decorated with wainscotting and colored wood marquetry, and the enormous fireplaces, with their huge overhanging mantels were examples of the plasterer's art.

Because formality had been abandoned, everyone was gayer and there was more laughter and talk; somehow everyone felt free. Mary walked in the gardens with Bess attending her. One day she climbed to the roof of the bower Bess had had built and sat on its flat roof in the June sun and professed herself more content than she had been since she left Scotland.

But it was over all too soon. Five days went by so quickly Bess couldn't believe it. And they started back, all of them, to Wingfield.

CHAPTER 5

BESS rode ahead, for Mary was still confined to her litter. She clattered into the courtyard at Wingfield and went right up into Mary's quarters, stood in the center of Mary's bedroom, and sniffed. A slight frown crossed her brow. Still sniffing, she proceeded from room to room in this inner suite off the inner quadrangle.

The hangings had been removed, and she had forbidden them to be rehung, she wanted them aired in the sun for at least three weeks, every day. Mary's dais was bare; its red velvet coverings were also outside. Bess inspected the garderobes. She detected nothing with her sniffing but the odor of strong soap.

It was a cold day for June, so she had small fires lighted, and on these she threw herbs, freshly garnered from the gardens of Chatsworth. Soon the rooms were smelling sweet of applewood and lavender and rosemary. Satisfied, Bess went off into her own room to change out of her dusty riding clothes.

But in the end it did no good. Three days later, Shrewsbury rode over to Chatsworth to see his younger daughter and his two stepdaughters, to bring them messages from Bess, to get air and exercise, and to supervise the transport of fresh meat and fowl. On the way back—it was a warm day—he felt unduly hot and removed his doublet, tossing it to his groom. When he dismounted at Wingfield, he was conscious of extreme thirst, and by the time he reached the bedroom to wash, his linen shirt was soaking wet, and he was shaking with a severe chill. One look at him terrified Bess. He was suffering from what she called the ague, a severe shaking chill, which often preceded a dread illness. She knew what to do: First, she commanded his body servant to strip off his clothes and sponge him with warm water and cover him up warmly. Bess then fled to the kitchens for what she called metheglen, a spiced mead served boiling hot.

When she reappeared, the earl had indeed been sponged off with warm water, but he was still white as a ghost and shivering. She started to hold the hot, hot cup to his lips —she had wrapped it in a napkin—when he said, "I can hold it."

He started to sip the hot drink, and then he said, "Listen carefully, Bess," for he too knew he might be coming down with an incapacitating illness, something he had picked up from these damned Scots. "Tell Archer to place extra guards at the gates and on the tower in four-hour shifts." He shivered and tried to drink more of the hot mead. "Send for Francis and a hundred extra men from Sheffield immediately. Do these two things first!"

He drank off the mead and passed her the cup, which she filled. "I'm so damned thirsty, None," he muttered.

Bess clung tight to his other hand.

"Listen, I've changed my mind. Have Archer close the gates, have them guarded at all times, let no one in who isn't authorized. Don't open the gates in the mornings."

"Aye, my lord," whispered Bess.

"Do it now!" He gestured with the cup. "Now!"

"I don't want to leave you," Bess cried.

"Now," he muttered. "Go, Bess, please!"

Bess did go; as she was crossing the porch outside their

apartments, Dr. Francis came hurrying along, and she cried, "Oh, thank God, where have you been? Go into his lordship while I carry out his orders!"

She ran down the stairs and across the great gallery; she stopped at the earl's table and picked up a piece of paper; on it she scrawled, *Do as this man, Owen, requests.* Then she added her initials, *In haste. E.S.*

With this paper in hand, folded, she told her head groom to ride immediately to Sheffield Castle, using all speed, and tell Lord Francis Talbot, who was in residence there, to bring a hundred men, well armed, to help guard Wingfield in his father's illness. She pressed the note into his hand; he rode off with three grooms, also armed, and then the huge gates clanged shut. Bess said, "And they're to stay that way, until we get aid!"

By the time she climbed the steps again and crossed the porch, there were extra guards at each gate, and at each entrance to the courts, lookouts were placed on the tall tower, and armed guards stood outside Mary's suite of rooms, in the west quadrangle, and Bess could report, "Everything has been done!"

"One task more," the earl said, "you must write Cecil and tell him I am ill."

He leaned back against the pillows, and he could feel the fever rising quickly, for now his head ached badly, and his chest ached, and there was pain between his shoulder blades, a knifing pain. He had drunk a quart of the mead. *Maybe it was too much,* he thought, but now he knew he wasn't thinking straight.

"Let no one in," he muttered, "even my kin." He kept dreaming about the brief talk he had had last week with Lord Dacre, a distant relative, who had actually approached him slyly, to see if there was the faintest hope the earl would connive at freeing his prisoner. The earl had been so astonished he had contented himself with calling Lord Dacre an ass. But it had showed Shrewsbury how true it was that men would indeed try to rescue Mary for the glory and gain involved; not many Englishmen, but enough to worry about, and if he, Shrewsbury, were one of them, he would certainly choose this time, right now, when the earl lay sick, to get into Wingfield and get Mary out.

He kept hearing Bess saying, "The gates are shut."

Then he would say, "None, I can't breathe."

He knew he was propped up on big bolsters and pillows. He knew his body servant kept laying cool cloths on his aching brow. He knew Dr. Francis was there and that night had come and that Bess was there, too.

Bess was frantic with fear. At midnight the earl seemed to be on fire with fever, and his mutterings were delirious. His body servant wept at his side. "He will not live the night," he said to Bess.

Bess' mind ran around like a creature in a cage. The night, the night. It had hours more to run. By now Owen should have reached Sheffield, and young Lord Francis should be ahorse, at the head of the one hundred men his father had requested. Bess knelt by the bed, leaning over the earl to sponge off his face and forehead.

Then she thought, *The priest!* And she slipped from the room and through the porch and down into the blackness of the great gallery, whose seventy-two-foot length shimmered in the moonlight coming through the five huge windows at its end.

Bess stopped, suddenly, in fear. *What stirred there, in the far shadows, under the oriel?* They said Richard III had stayed at Wingfield. *Was it he, wrapped in his black velvet cloak, the archvillain of English kings?* Bess fled through the long, long gallery, pursued by the soundless ghosts of the past; she fled to Mary's rooms and pushed past the astonished guards.

"Sir John Morton, where is he?" Bess asked and when the priest arrived, hastily summoned, she said, "Lord Shrewsbury is dying!"

Sir John looked horrified, everyone gasped, and Mary cried out as though in terrible pain.

Sir John took Bess' hand. "Do you want me to go to him?"

"Aye!"

"For the last rites?" the priest whispered.

"No!" cried Bess, jerking her hand away. "No! I want you to come with me and kneel and pray to God to save his life!"

Bess and Sir John knelt together at Shrewsbury's side, the

earl knowing nothing of their prayers; his recurrent nightmare persisted—someone burst into Wingfield and rescued Mary Stuart.

But no one did. At four, just before daylight, Francis Talbot arrived, to come to his father's bed and hold his hand. Shrewsbury suddenly opened his eyes and saw his oldest son and managed a smile, and said, "Thank God, Francis." Then the earl closed his eyes again and drifted off into his feverish painful world again.

In London Elizabeth and Cecil were horrified and frightened to receive Bess' letter. Posthaste, messengers were sent flying back to Wingfield—and also to Lord Zouch, who lived nearby, to go to Wingfield and lend his assistance. When Lord Zouch arrived, he stepped back into Bess' life, a figure from the past.

She hadn't known Cecil had sent for him; she saw him coming across the long gallery toward the steps, and she cried out as though in pain, holding onto the stairrail.

She hadn't slept in six days. *She looks like a ghost,* Lord Zouch thought. *My God, Shrewsbury has died.*

He held out his hands as he came nearer. "Bess," he said, "oh, Bess."

She came down the last three steps like a sleepwalker. She seized his hands in hers. "My lord," she mumbled, "you shouldn't be here."

"Aye, Bess," he said, "I have orders to be here."

She drew a long shaky breath. "They don't permit us any guests," she whispered. Then she realized what he had said. "Orders?"

"From Sir William Cecil, to come to help you." He looked down at her. "Bess," he asked, bravely nerving himself to ask the question, "how is his lordship?"

He thought, *She's going to faint.* He put his arm around her, and suddenly she gave him her old starry smile. She said, "He's better! The fever—it is gone!" Lord Zouch took her in his arms and hugged her, while Bess wept and wept on his shoulder.

By the next day the earl was able to drink milk and thin soup. But Shrewsbury was the worst patient in the realm, Bess thought, and next to him was Mary Stuart. Although

Bess was able to write to Cecil on the twenty-sixth of June that her lord was recovering fast, by July Mary was sick again, and the earl, who hadn't given himself enough time to recover, had a serious relapse and was back in bed with another attack of fever and bone-chilling ague. As July passed, Bess thought she didn't have one single night's unbroken sleep.

She lost ten pounds, she was frantic with fear over Shrewsbury. And Mary Stuart moaned and complained throughout the whole month, needing special foods and needing to be carried outside in her litter to take the air; she bribed Bess' servants to carry letters; she sent jewels with messages inside; and she had to be watched constantly. Meantime, the earl was, Bess thought, coughing his life and lungs away.

On the first day of August the earl had been out of bed for two days. Mary had recovered. That first week in August Bess slept during the nights. But she still worried over Shrewsbury. She wrote to Cecil and the queen, to permit her husband to go to the baths at Buxton for ten days, to recover from the terrible illness.

Nothing happened. No permission came. But all at Wingfield was quiet; Mary was recovering and seemed full of lassitude; she had some swelling in the hands and arms, and she was pasty and rather bloated, Bess thought. She was curiously quiescent.

Bess said, "My love, I am going to order you to Buxton Springs! If you wait longer, it will be September and it will be cold. You know the cold winds that blow about there in September!"

Shrewsbury did know.

"Your health is the most important thing in your life, and in mine," Bess said. "I pray you, my lord, please go! To Buxton!"

Shrewsbury was silent. He still felt weaker than he admitted to Bess. He waited a week longer, and then, on August 11, he set forth for Buxton Springs. Bess insisted he go by litter, and she knew it was an indication of how bad he was feeling that he agreed.

Bess sent for Jane. And then, two days after Jane had arrived, with minute instructions on how to run and watch

and ward the establishment at Wingfield, Bess, regardless
of Elizabeth Tudor and Cecil, started out for Buxton
Springs at five in the morning, to take care of her husband.

The earl was so glad to see her he didn't reprove her.
Bess fed him pieces of bread steeped in currant juice, or
a few stewed prunes. Then he would take the baths, and
she would make sure he didn't stay in them till he felt weak.

"And pay no mind to me, my love," she'd say. "You are
to be chaste when you take the baths!"

She stayed five days, overseeing his diet, which was excessively simple and full of the natural purging foods. Bess
firmly believed the baths and the diet would rid his body
of the poison of his illness. On the sixth day she galloped
home to Wingfield. The following day a blasting letter
arrived from Cecil. She had left her post! She had betrayed
her trust! The Queen's Majesty was outraged! Cecil was
sending Lord Huntingdon.

She wrote to Cecil that they would be pleased to have
Lord Huntingdon, and she added that there had been no
cause for alarm; Mary Stuart was perfectly safe, and if he,
Cecil, thought someone else would be more faithful or
trustworthy than she, then she was more than willing to be
replaced. Cecil pondered over this letter and held his peace.

CHAPTER 6

"WHY? Why? God's death, why?"

Bess stood in the cold darkness of the hall at Tutbury;
here they were again, in this old, dank, miserable prison.

"Stop shouting," Shrewsbury said curtly.

"I can't endure it," Bess said, turning away from him.

Mary had preceded them up to her quarters, gasping
with the old pain in her side. Her two secretaries followed,
clutching bundles, and her priest, who walked with head
bowed, praying silently.

"We'll all die," Bess said flatly. "We'll all catch the ague or the pox, and die." She marched along. "Then I hope Cecil and the Queen's Majesty will be satisfied we've done our duty." Bess stopped suddenly and pointed to a part of the stone wall that overhung the narrow stairs. "Ice, by God! Ice!

"You should have refused to come here. Lord high steward. You're the lord low steward of all England."

The earl, his patience gone, gave her a whack on the behind. "Get up there and be quiet."

Bess would have spoken, shouted, in fact, but he was speaking and she was curious.

"You're well named, I've named you well, you're the worst *shrew* in England. Now get up there and be quiet."

Bess was so angry she ran up the rest of the stairs, flung into their own apartments, and whirled to face him. But the earl was in a true and towering rage.

Bess backed away from him. "You beast," she muttered.

"Aye!" he roared. "And don't cry!"

"I'm too old to cry," Bess said coldly.

She thought drearily, my beautiful Chatsworth, standing there empty, ready to welcome us, and here we are, back again in this horrible place; what did the Talbot pearls matter if she had to wear them here? "I'm going to leave you," she said.

He swung around to face her. "Don't do it, Bess," he said in a flat tone. "I warn you, don't do it."

"I'm sorry I married you," she said. "All I want is to be back at Chatsworth." She went on into the bedroom, her red head high. The earl heard her start to talk to Digby, giving quick, curt orders to get another petticoat out of her chest and to warm it a bit in front of the already blazing fire. When he came into the bedroom, she turned her back and began to struggle into the petticoat, pulling it up over her bare thighs, for her stockings came only to her knees.

Then she fled to the garderobe and whisked up all her petticoats and sat herself down. Imitating Mary, she groaned and grunted. "I think I have the dysentery," she moaned. *Let him tell that to Cecil!*

The earl banged the door as he left the room. Bess sat on the garderobe vowing to stay there an hour, if need be, if she didn't freeze to death. Only in ten minutes the earl knocked loudly on the door.

"This queen is deathly ill," he shouted through the heavy oaken panels.

"Jesus Christ!" said Bess. She stood up, grabbing her cloak, and started forth.

In the meantime Lord Huntingdon had decided that since Mary's effects had all been neatly packed to be transported to Tutbury, it was a propitious moment to search her rooms and the packed chests. Huntingdon despised Mary, for the principal reason that he was descended on his mother's side from the duke of Clarence, and of royal blood. The men who were searching Mary's rooms were armed with pistols, so when Bess arrived on the threshold of Mary's suite, she paused just for a moment to see what was happening. Then with full vigor, she flung herself into the fray.

Huntingdon whirled in surprise as Bess advanced on him. Mary's women were screaming in fright, Huntingdon's men were tossing clothes and linens and hangings about the room, looking under the beds and even under the garde-robes, waving their pistols. From Mary's bedroom came more noises, and above it all Mary's own cries.

Into the midst of all this strode Bess, unleashing her fury on Huntingdon. "You fool," she shouted at Huntingdon. "Do you need pistols for a few women? The damned things will go off and kill somebody. Maybe it will be you!" Bess shouted in his face.

Huntingdon retreated momentarily before this onslaught.

Bess grabbed one of his men by the arm. "Get out of here! Get out of my way!" She pushed past him, bumping up against another man who was bent over a chest. Bess gave him a shove in the middle of his back, and he fell forward into the chest. Bess gave him a good kick as she went by into Mary's room.

Two men were in the room, emptying the contents of her writing box onto the table. Mary lay on the bed screaming.

"My heart!" moaned Mary, rolling from side to side.

"God's death, you've given her a heart attack." Bess picked up the fireplace poker and advanced on the two men. "Out! Out!" They backed away to the door, and Bess looked past them to Huntingdon's outraged face. The men were waving two papers, and Huntingdon seized them.

"They found cyphers!"

"Get them out of here before I brain them," Bess said. She started to close the door in their faces when she thought of a final word. "You're a cipher, Huntingdon, and a big fool too!"

Bess banged the door in Huntingdon's face. "There!" she said, with great satisfaction. She turned to Mary. "Calm down, madam." She shot the bolt. "There's nothing the matter with you that a big fire and Kennedy rubbing your legs won't cure. You're just sick of Huntingdon, and by God I am, too!"

"And I'm going to get rid of him, too," she announced to the earl as they were finishing their supper.

Shrewsbury said, "I've already written Cecil about it, Bess. I've told him all, you don't need to write. I also added that if he said anything about your being too tender with this queen and aiding and helping her, it was a lie."

Bess said, "Let him say anything he wants. It's I who have the final say."

The earl frowned.

Bess pushed back her plate. "I'm going to write, too." She pulled a piece of paper toward her. They were eating on the only table in the room, which held also the writing implements. Bess dipped the pen; the earl watched her write, her red head bent over her paper. She wrote only two sentences. She handed the paper over to Shrewsbury, waving it, not bothering to sand it. "You can read it," Bess said. "And then put it in with yours."

Shrewsbury read: *My dear Will, if you don't remove Lord Huntingdon from our sight, I will go back to Chatsworth. I will not dwell in the same house as that pompous Plantagenet. Your friend and servant. E. S.*

She picked up her cup and drank her wine. "If he doesn't want me to look after Mary, he can find somebody else," Bess said with finality.

Bess could avoid Huntingdon for the next three weeks, but Mary Stuart could not. She was quite pitiful, Bess

231

thought. Guards stood at the doors and within her chambers, only withdrawing when she undressed or bathed. She was not permitted to stay up at night, for the lights had to be extinguished at ten; and if they were not, men rushed in and confiscated the candles. Mary tried to write her letters in the dark, the only time she had privacy. Huntingdon now had been with them four weeks, and the last ten days of October, the earl didn't trust himself to stay in Tutbury and was out all day. The newly augmented garrison he set to work building winter quarters, he organized hunts and set the men to cutting wood and endeavored to keep everyone busy, including himself.

He looked well now, Bess thought, remembering with fear and horror that he had almost died. And on the first of November, a messenger from Cecil pounded in with Huntingdon's recall.

"Thank God!" Bess exclaimed. "Now I hope we have seen the last of that loathsome toad!"

It was Saturday night, and the castle celebrated. Mary had supper at eight, with her ladies; they had their music, their ballad singing, and everyone was happy until midnight.

Then word came from the north that the great northern earls had gathered up an army of 20,000 men and were marching on Tutbury to rescue Mary.

In Bess' bedroom the candles had been lighted, the fire freshened, and some food and wine brought. Shrewsbury wouldn't let Bess get up, she sat against the pillows, her face white with fear.

"God's death, they'll kill us all, my lord," she whispered, fearfully.

"I expect they are completely incompetent, Bess," the earl said. He sealed the letter he had written, and handed it to his body servant to be given to the waiting horseman. "And there will certainly be other advices besides mine coming into London. They've been on the march for three days now and have been celebrating mass at the various cathedrals along their path and gathering more strength as they come. But once they leave the north—" He shrugged; he didn't want to worry her any more than she was worried But because of the uncertainty of news and information, he had got dressed and left Bess and gone down through the icy halls of Tutbury to send out a detail of men to watch from ten miles out, just in case. He was pondering what else he should do and decided there was nothing else to do tonight, except double the guard on Mary's doors.

But he was up at six in the morning.

So was Bess. They worked well together. *A good team,* he thought proudly. She was extraordinarily efficient. The castle had to be provisioned, in case of siege. It also had to be fortified. The earl set his garrison to digging fresh earthen ramparts and created three lines of defense. He rounded up an extra hundred men from the nearby country. They cut wood and stacked it and dug wells, within the new ramparts.

Bess supervised the organization of the huntsmen and sent to neighboring dwellings for flour and grain and beans and all the staples. Within five days the castle was ready for as good a defense as could be managed. And every hour Bess checked on Mary to make very, very sure no one had access to her, except those who were trustworthy.

Mary's eyes burned with excitement. Bess said, "My Lord Shrewsbury orders you to pack a few necessaries, madam, in case he has to take you south."

Shrewsbury had in the back of his head a plan to spirit Mary out of Tutbury and south to Nottingham Castle, whose defenses were more secure. His duty to Elizabeth meant to him that he must prevent Mary from being rescued—if he died doing it.

Mary's smile held triumph. "I shall so order," she said.

Shrewsbury had sent out horsemen as lookouts, posted ten to fifteen miles out. On the twenty-first of November the rebel army was fifty miles from Tutbury, and nothing lay in their path. That night, a cold miserable November night, the mists from the river Dove enveloped the ancient castle, rising wraithlike and ghosty and chillingly damp. Within, the moisture formed on the stone walls and ran down in droplets.

"We couldn't see an army if it were coming right outside the walls," Bess cried.

She imagined the menacing forms of men scaling these

233

walls, the outer walls of Tutbury, ready to rush at the castle with bone-chilling screams, like the sieges she had read about.

"For all we can see," she whispered, "the whole countryside out there is crawling with rebels!"

The patrols on the battlements could see nothing through the mist. The water ran down their armored chests and arms. The castle waited for its enemies, and Mary waited to be rescued. Sick though she claimed to be, her cheeks burned with color and her eyes with excitement. From the latest reports, smuggled to her by her very capable servants, she often knew the news before Bess herself; there were twenty thousand loyal north Englishmen coming to rescue her and to set her on the throne of England!

"I never lose faith. I never lose heart," Mary exclaimed after Bess had left the room.

Outside and inside, great torches burned and flared, showing only the thickening mist. They frightened Bess more than the darkness because they showed her how truly deep the fog was, and how well it could conceal the men who marched and rode toward Tutbury. Frantic, she rushed to Shrewsbury and excoriated Cecil and the queen.

"They are mad not to have called out, sent out the levies!" cried Bess, stumbling over the words. "They've deserted us, the fools! We huddle here, with a few hundred men, in the path of these madmen! They'll kill us, my lord! You know they will!"

The earl said, "Bess, hysteria won't help. I've told you, they are most likely hopelessly incompetent."

"The sheer force of numbers will overwhelm us," Bess said more calmly, and the earl thought that this was probably the truest statement, and yet—suddenly he began to fear for Bess' life too. He had no illusions about his own, if the rebels should capture him, but he thought that Mary would intervene to save Bess, although one never could be sure, nor sure that Mary would be able to control the men who marched so recklessly to save her. The plan in the back of his mind, he now resolved to put into action.

"Bess," he said, taking her in his arms, and squeezing her hard, "tomorrow we will leave Tutbury. Now go to bed, and try to sleep."

He had formulated his plan carefully, but he wanted to again go over the maps and the list of trustworthy men who would accompany him; he had not undressed but was in a riding habit, a heavy dagger in his belt, and in front of him, on his table, the candlelight winked on the loaded pair of pistols.

Bess lay in bed and watched him. "It is as though we've retreated a full century," she whispered.

He looked over at her and nodded. "I would like to send you to Sheffield, Bess," he said. "But I don't dare." It was ten miles to the north. "Speaking of a hundred years or so," Shrewsbury said, "it was to Sheffield that the Talbots always retreated." He sent her a grin.

The smile was so appealing that Bess got out of bed and came over and put her arms around his neck, leaning over him to see what he was doing. She reached out to touch the gleaming barrel of the pistol.

"Don't touch!" he said. "They're loaded!"

Bess withdrew her hand hastily. "Why, my lord?"

Shrewsbury lifted his head and glanced at the door. "One never knows, when one watches and wards a castle full of Scots, when one of them might gain entrance. It would be very, very wise of them to send a couple of men to dispatch me. In the ensuing confusion," the earl went on placidly, checking off a name on his list, "Mary could escape and ride north to join her rebels."

"God's death!" Bess hadn't thought of treachery; why she didn't know, for it was so obvious.

"I wish," he continued, "that you'd get back in bed and go to sleep."

"Aye, my lord," Bess said, for she was cold. She clambered back into the big bed, and drew up the quilts. After a few minutes the earl glanced over toward the bed. She slept peacefully. He sighed and was content, for it showed him plain that she had perfect trust in him, and that was exactly what he wanted from his wife.

The mists still lay deep and impenetrable about the castle as the dawn slowly, inevitably came. The torches were extinguished, for fuel was running low. As the day lightened, the mists retreated, the landscape looked innocent and empty. At eight, two lookouts rode in to report the enemy troops had passed through Knaresborough. They were on their way to Tutbury. At ten two more lookouts riding madly reported the rebels had already swarmed through Tadcaster.

"Why don't we leave?" Bess cried.

"Because I want to arrive in Coventry after dark; I most certainly don't want to escort this controversial queen through the streets of Coventry and start a riot. We're not taking a large escort; we can ride faster with a small, carefully chosen troop of men."

Bess had followed him onto the castle roof. She swept the bare cold landscape with anxious eyes. Suddenly she cried, "There are riders coming!" She hung onto the stone coping in terror.

"They're coming from the south, Bess. Not from the north. This is some kind of help."

Bess thought, *Of course he is right.* And she relaxed. She was wearing riding clothes, and she was warm, in her heavy cloak. Suddenly the sun came out, and she gratefully drew deep breaths of the fresh air, for inside Tutbury it was damp and smelly. Bess was positive there was something wrong with the water at Tutbury, too. Joyfully she watched the horsemen who were coming closer, until she saw that it was a small troop, and, annoyed again at Cecil and the queen, she muttered that if this was the kind of help Cecil had in mind, he was just as stupid as the rebels.

"They must have sent all of twenty men," she said.

"They should have sent out the levies!" Bess repeated. She was staring at the men who were now very close, and she could see, she could sense, she was sure! "It's that fool Huntingdon," said Bess, "there's one consolation. If the rebels catch us, his head will roll, too. I hope I live to see it."

Shrewsbury laughed but said to come on now and see what news Huntingdon had brought. He was crossing the old moat, and they could hear the castle gates creaking slowly open and then closing again. By the time they reached the inner doors, Huntingdon was striding in. The two earls shook hands, and Huntingdon blurted out that he had come to help escort Mary to safety! And that the crown had called out the levies, and in every county the men were beginning to gather, but that there wasn't time to wait for that. They must ride south with Mary!

Shrewsbury nodded. He told Huntingdon to get something to eat, and the same for his men, they would start in thirty minutes: All was arranged.

Mary had been given orders an hour before. She was ready. She was dressed in man's clothing, her long, pretty legs encased in hose and Spanish boots.

"I shall ride astride," she announced, giving Bess a triumphant look.

"You will ride with me, madam," the earl said. In the courtyard, he and his men surrounded Mary. Behind them came Bess, with four sturdy rogues whose loyalty Shrewsbury accounted the highest in his employ. In the rear rode Huntingdon and his men.

The earl lifted Bess into the saddle. He said, "Now, listen, my dearest None. If there is any trouble, you have orders to escape. Don't crouch over my body, and daub your fingers in my blood, None. I forbid it."

Bess looked at the scant sixty men.

The earl said, "One hundred more will follow us, thirty minutes behind, as rear protection, Bess."

The small scouting force that was to ride ahead now trotted out of the gates. Bess was already ahorse; she followed the figure of her husband with her eyes as he went to the Queen of Scots, who, dramatically attired in her man's doublet and hose, was waiting for him as a true queen waits for a subject. Quickly the earl assisted her into the saddle. Now, leaning forward, one hand on the high saddle, she patted him on the shoulder with the other gloved hand.

Mary possessed a sensuous charm; the drama of the occasion heightened it; Mary was at her best in moments of crisis, whatever kinds of crisis; all the high excitement of her Gallic nature flowed out from her face and eyes and body; she knew everyone was looking at her, and she glowed.

"My dear lord," she said, using French, "are you saving me, or yourself?"

The earl replied, "I am desolated to tell you that you are

237

being hurried away from the consequences of your own folly, madam. For when blood is spilled, who knows whose blood it might be?"

"I would gladly spill all my blood to welcome my friends and clasp them to my heart!"

Shrewsbury swung up into the saddle. For a moment he looked across at her. "Madam, you have been placed under my care. Under that care you will ride to safety."

He raised his hand, the horns blew, and the sixty men trotted out the gate of Tutbury castle. A thin icy rain splattered into their faces.

Bess hardly felt it. She had been near enough to hear Mary's conversation with the earl, but she had not caught the rapid French. She was seething with anger at the way Mary had leaned over and practically caressed the earl's shoulder. She looked at the two of them up ahead of her. She rode behind, while Mary rode with Shrewsbury.

Bess hardly noticed that the thin rain had almost stopped and since it was coming from the north, it was at her back. The business of riding in close formation kept her busy, so gradually her anger lessened; the problem, in essence, was that Mary had a prior claim over Shrewsbury. She would have to learn to live with it. If it had to be done, she could do it. As her mother had always said, there's many a way to skin a cat.

So Bess rode on. Ahead lay Coventry, ahead the landscape was empty, safe. Behind Bess, by some thirty miles, came the straggling host of the northern earls. But the margin of time and distance was enough.

When darkness fell, the pace was slowed. It was late in the evening when Bess entered Coventry. Now the torches were lighted, and the pennons unfurled; the streets were empty, as the earl had wished. The householders peered out at the passing horsemen, and they said only, "Why, 'tis the earl of Shrewsbury; naught to fear."

At the Bull Inn, the courtyard was lit well, for the earl had sent riders ahead, to warn of his coming. Without giving Mary a chance to be the center of dramatic attention, he took her upstairs to the best bedroom the inn had to offer, set two guards at the door, and left her in the care of a single little maid.

"Good-night, madam," he said, and Mary was left alone with the one servant. It was anticlimactic. Mary could feel one of her wretched headaches coming; the pain in her side began to throb. She was safe, indeed, and out of the way, and demeaned by being lodged in the bedroom of a common inn! And it was due to the earl of Shrewsbury! Mary felt the manacles of his care tightening around her relentlessly. But she would fight it, and him, with every means at her command.

Eyes flashing, as the pain ached at her side, she said to the little maid, "Do you know whom you serve?"

"Aye, madam," quavered the girl.

"You can go out later and tell everyone that the Queen of Scotland is held a prisoner in a common inn."

The girl shook her head. "I am not permitted to leave this room, madam. His lordship so commanded."

At that moment his lordship was wolfing bread and meat and cheese, and washing it down with strong ale.

"My love, you've drunk almost a quart of ale," Bess said. "You'll have gout."

"Aye, I probably will," the earl agreed cheerfully.

Bess laughed. It was so good to be away from Tutbury! It was so good to be at an inn, just like ordinary people! It was so good to be normal and forget that the next room held the Queen of Scots. She was already weaving a web around them, but tonight they had broken it, and were ordinary travelers, glad to have arrived, on a cold November night, and at a comfortable inn; it was blissful.

CHAPTER 7

IN London, Elizabeth and Sir William Cecil had pondered long and laboriously the problem of Mary Queen of Scotland and the Isles. The uprising in the north had underscored the dreadful fact that while she lived in England, she was an ever-present danger to the crown and the peace of the realm. True, it had been put down with ease, but that had been partly due to the incompetence and hesitation of its leaders, who now would suffer dearly with forfeiture and death. The duke of Norfolk had promised on his oath he would not seek to marry Mary. But to offset that, the new Spanish ambassador arrived and Cecil smelled a troublemaker, a nasty one.

"Well, Your Majesty?" Cecil asked.

"Let them hie themselves to Chatsworth, then," Elizabeth said. "It is deep in the uncharted countryside, and it is walled. And I suppose it is more suitable. Suitable for a queen. God's death!" she exclaimed. "I wrote myself to reprove Shrewsbury for lodging Mary in a common inn!"

Cecil smiled slightly. *Poor Shrewsbury,* he thought.

"He demeaned a queen," announced Elizabeth, angrily.

"He kept her safe from her would-be rescuers, madam," Cecil pointed out.

"Aye, but in what manner? Why, I told him that when I journeyed there, to Coventry, I lodged at a place called the Frears! There was no excuse for a Bull Inn!"

She spit out the two words, and Cecil tried not to laugh. But he could imagine what the earl had thought of the reproof he had received. Yet who else in the whole realm could do this job, this awful task? Who else? *Nobody,* Cecil thought, *nobody but the earl and countess of Shrewsbury.*

He wrote to Shrewsbury that day. When he had finished dictating, he thought, *He'll be glad to read this. But I wonder what he thought when he received the reproof for the Bull Inn?*

The earl had exploded in wrath. "My ancestors are writhing in their graves! Ah, if only it were a hundred years ago! Then I'd deal with both queens, and you, too!"

Bess laughed. But now, she was watching him read Cecil's letter. There was no explosion, thank God. It must be good news. Her face brightened, and the earl looked up from the last page. He said, "None, we can stay at Chatsworth, and Cecil is coming to see Mary."

And this, thought Bess, *standing on the threshold of the beautiful room, this is the chamber of the countess of Shrewsbury, and it is fit for a queen!*

Huge windows with deep-cushioned seats looked out over the rising hills behind Chatsworth. The bed was hung and covered in lustrous soft black velvet, with gold fringes, a perfect foil for her red hair. The tapestries she had labored on for years hung over the paneled walls, and above them the elaborate plaster work of the white, arched ceiling, touched with gold paint, set off the color of the whole bedroom. *And I did it,* Bess thought. *I did it all!* A mansion, new in concept, with its twin galleries, and its soaring windows, the perfection of its setting, its gardens, a hundred beautiful rooms, and its sparkling river. *Wait till Cecil sees it, now almost finished!*

What a sight! William Cecil thought. He was mounting the shallow graceful steps that led up to Chatsworth's first gallery, and there Bess was waiting to greet him, she and five of her children. They were all redheaded. Cecil smiled as he came toward them. He kissed Bess, and greeted her children.

"Bess, it is magnificent, and you are magnificent, and how proud Cavendish would be."

"I think so."

"Eighteen years, Bess, and this is a house fit for a queen."

"Aye, the bitch," said Bess, and she grinned at Cecil companionably. "She is out in the gardens with my jewel. We don't dare leave her walk alone out there. She'd put a letter in the shrubbery or under a stone, or someone might be hiding out there to have a hasty word."

Cecil hesitated. Bess knew he had come to see Mary.

She went right on. "I don't know what you want from her exactly, Will, but I can tell you you won't get it. She won't be content till she has your head and mine, plus the Queen's Majesty! And that the mass will be said all over England."

Cecil looked at her gravely. "She says that to you, Bess?"

"No. But that is what she thinks. I know. I know from the little ways she has and how she speaks. Slyly. In praise of the butcher, Alva!"

The duke of Alva was indeed drenching the Netherlands in blood. But at least Cecil's mind could be at rest about

241

Bess. She was not one of Mary's adherents, despite the gossip.

"Bess," Cecil said slowly, "remember she is a task that you do for the Queen's Majesty!"

"That's what my lord says. I'll try. Tell the Queen's Majesty that I will try."

But she thought, *All I really want is to get rid of her, rid of her forever and ever, rid of her out of my house! But I won't think of her now, I'll think about Lady Cecil, who arrives tomorrow.* Lady Cecil was reportedly the most brilliant woman in England, outside the queen. An intellectual of the first water. Shrewsbury had said, "I hope she won't overwhelm you, Bess." Bess shook her head seriously.

"Why should she?" she asked.

The sun shone on Chatsworth and its distinguished occupants. The sun of royal favor was shining on them and on Mary, too. To entertain guests in new Chatsworth was to return to normal living, without the shadow of the imprisoned queen falling impartially on all of them. The very presence of Cecil, representing the crown, made Bess' tasks fall away. She could be mistress of Chatsworth, and nothing else.

Cecil had brought permission for Mary to ride. Now when she walked or rode, for she was passionately fond of being outdoors, Cecil and Shrewsbury, or Cecil alone, rode with her. *Thank God for that,* Bess thought. For try as she would, she was jealous of Mary's claim to Shrewsbury's time; she couldn't help it. There was her husband, eternally with another woman.

And every night she prayed Cecil would be successful in his mission, whatever it was. They all knew it was important; only Mary did not realize how important it was.

Mary's rooms were in the east wing of Chatsworth, sumptuously furnished. She could walk in the gardens, she could ride. The return to more normal living, planned carefully by Elizabeth, was supposed to tempt her to sign away her claim to the English crown; and when she signed it, Elizabeth would promise to install her as queen regnant of Scotland. But Mary refused. She could not be tempted. And in fact, she felt triumph, for she thought the favor bestowed

242

on her meant that her cousin Elizabeth was weakening. Poor Mary, who would not perceive the realities.

Cecil set them forth very clearly. "Would it not be better, madam, to return to Scotland as queen regnant than to be nourishing the hope of something you cannot have, nor have the right to?"

"Are you questioning my birthright?" Mary asked. "Am I not the great-granddaughter of Henry VII of England?"

"Aye, madam, but—"

"How can I resign, resign my very ancestry?" Mary asked prettily.

Cecil did not smile. After five days of this, he gave up. And he thought, *I pity Shrewsbury! I wouldn't want the custody of this woman, either.* Suddenly he realized the blight she cast, and he wanted to leave quickly, before she roused him to a frenzy because of her stubborn complacency and her inability to care about the people in whose name she claimed her sovereignty.

And yet, in spite of Mary, Bess had made them so welcome that Cecil had luxuriated in the benevolent warmth. He had many envious enemies. How good it was to be sincerely loved, as an old trusted friend. How wonderful not to have to guard the tongue. How precious was generosity warmly bestowed. Plainly Bess showed her dismay at their leaving.

"And I have tucked in two freshly plucked birds and this basket of fruit and herbs. And for you, my lady," Bess said, "a parting gift."

It was a needlepoint panel of herbs and flowers that Jane and Bess had worked, which Lady Cecil had much admired.

"Bess!" cried Cecil. "We shan't be able to repay you!"

Bess said reproachfully, "Will. It brings my love to you both, and so you shall remember me thus."

Lady Cecil hugged Bess and kissed her good-bye and made her promise to come and see her and the new house they were building, a house called Theobalds.

After they had gone, and the last of their train wound down through the curtain walls, Shrewsbury put his arm around Bess. "Everyone loves you, None." he said. "And one of the reasons is you have no envy. Of anyone."

Bess said, surprised, "Why should I be envious?"

The earl smiled. "I'm not quite sure, but everyone else seems to envy someone."

Bess said, "I forgot to tell Will that I think this queen is up to a new trick. I forgot to tell him."

The earl said somberly, "I'll write." He glanced at her sharply.

Bess said, to exonerate herself for forgetting, "It's just a look in her eyes, a hint of triumph and complacency."

CHAPTER 8

THE plot was simple: the assassination of Elizabeth, the arrival of the duke of Alva with his bloodthirsty Spanish soldiers from across the channel, and the placing of Mary Stuart on the throne. The duke of Alva, however, a sensible man, refused to come to England until Elizabeth was dead, by a bullet or a quick knife thrust or perhaps poison. It didn't matter which. In London a man called Ridolfi was weaving this web, with the help and connivance of the duke of Norfolk, who was to be Mary's husband. Had Bess known of this, she wouldn't have slept at all that fall; neither she nor Shrewsbury would have survived this plot, had it been successful.

When Norfolk's servants were arrested, they confessed quickly, and the duke himself was sent to the Tower. Messengers galloped hastily to Chatsworth with the news and also the orders that they were all to remove instantly to the safety of Sheffield Castle. When Bess read the letters, that was at least a small consolation. At least it wasn't Tutbury!

Outside Chatsworth it was snowing. The earl said quietly, "It will be a difficult remove, for you, Bess. But we should start tomorrow morning."

She never failed to admire his calmness. She drew a deep breath. "We might all have been murdered in our beds!"

The earl smiled. "What better place for you and me?" But he was thinking, *When the duke of Norfolk, that misguided man, comes to trial, I shall have to preside over it. But I shan't tell Bess about that yet.* The immediate problem was to tell Mary. And which of them should do it?

"You do it," said Bess. "You can be so icily controlled and disdainful."

But Shrewsbury held out his hand to her. "You come with me, None."

So, trembling a bit, from emotion she didn't quite understand, Bess stood at his side.

The earl said, without preamble, looking across at Mary, who was still in bed, for she never rose early since she stayed up half the night, "Madam, three days ago, the duke of Norfolk was arrested and placed in the Tower, for treason against the Queen's Majesty."

There was an immediate uproar. All Mary's ladies screamed. Mary cast aside the whole tray on her lap, so that everything spilled and clattered, and threw her hands high in the air, and cried, "Oh! Oh! God have mercy on us all! God have mercy! God help us!" She began beating on the overturned tray with her fists.

One of the ladies fell onto the floor on her knees and started to pray in Latin. Mary's maid, Kennedy, of whom she was so fond, threw herself on the bed to quiet her mistress.

"Jesu," Bess breathed, hardly moving her lips.

Shrewsbury shouted, "Silence!" He was standing close to Mary's bed, and he leaned over and dragged Kennedy off the bed.

"Silence!" he roared. "You shall all pack; we move to Sheffield Castle tomorrow morning!"

"I shall spend the day in prayer." Mary shouted at him.

"Madam," said Shrewsbury coldly, "you may spend the day on your knees, and tomorrow you may go to Sheffield still on your knees, if you so desire." He turned his back and marched Bess out of the room.

"They're all mad!" he said.

The next day Mary and her ladies wept all the way to Sheffield. They protested and shivered and shrank and cowered, as though they were all going to their immediate deaths.

When they rode through the great park that surrounded

245

Sheffield, with its century-old trees, and when the great massive pile came into view, Mary gave a gasp of dismay. The earl smiled. "Aye, madam, look well, for you will never escape, nay, nor be rescued, from Sheffield."

If Chatsworth had a hundred beautiful rooms, in the modern style with painted woodwork and elaborate plaster ceilings, gilded and colored, Sheffield had three hundred rooms, and it was so huge that some years later one of the young Talbots could say that he had not seen Mary Stuart for six months, even though they dwelled under the same roof. Shrewsbury placed Mary in an inner suite, with doubled guards and men outside her windows, on the rooftop and on the ground.

Part of it was done for Bess. For Sheffield was so big that she was afraid someone might have got in and be in hiding. It was so vast, so intricate, with connecting stairs hidden in walls and rooms that one never suspected it until another whole wing would open out from a narrow passage.

"But all those passages are guarded, Bess," the earl would say, still not telling her he would have to leave the day after Christmas. In the meantime, for the children's sake—for there were still young children, Mary and Elizabeth were fifteen and sixteen, young Edward was eleven, and George ten—Bess made their own living quarters as comfortable as she could.

But, Bess thought, *if anyone does creep in, they'll murder me and my children.* When they had first got there, she had gone from suite to suite to see and pick which were best, but the earl said it had been planned. She would have the suite next to his, and the children next to her, and to ease her mind he placed guards at the passages and stairs that led to these suites. Bess devoted herself to combing the castle for the prettiest beds for the girls, and the coziest hangings, for she had not had time to bring much from Chatsworth, they had come in such hurry and haste, in obedience to the orders from Cecil and Elizabeth.

Shrewsbury waited two weeks, then, and at night, on Christmas Eve, told Bess he must leave the day after Christmas. She uttered a cry of fright.

"You're leaving me here, all alone!"

246

Shrewsbury laughed. "Bess, there are five hundred men here to protect you."

"What if one of them is a traitor?" Bess whispered.

"And besides that, Bess, Cecil is sending—"

"Not Huntingdon? God's death, not Huntingdon?"

"No, no," Shrewsbury calmed her. "Sir Ralph Sadler."

"But he should be here already." Bess wailed.

"Aye, he should be, and I don't know why he's not," Shrewsbury said.

"Perhaps he's been waylaid and murdered."

"Bess," the earl said, "you are letting these silly women make you hysterical."

"I'm not, I'm not. She plots and plots and weaves webs of deceit. How do we know Sadler hasn't been intercepted by her friends? How do we know he isn't a secret friend?" She put her hand on his arm and tugged at him. "Look at me, my lord, and tell me you're sure he isn't a traitor."

Shrewsbury looked deep in her eyes. "I know him well, None. Don't fret. Bess, for the children's sake, I want to have a happy Christmas."

It began to snow Christmas night. When Bess stood at the threshold of Sheffield Castle the next morning, to watch the earl ride away to London, the castle park was white with four inches of snow glittering in the early sunlight. He hugged her and kissed her good-bye. He looked down at her face and—she was forlorn. He said, "When I leave you, you are quiet and tame. I must remember that."

Bess said, "Don't tease me. Now."

"I'm not jesting with you, None." He smiled down at her and said, "Now do not fret. You have much, much to do; thank God you're kept busy; most people don't have enough to do."

"My duties are onerous," Bess cried.

"That's what you think now," Shrewsbury said. "Later you will retract those words. Good-bye, Bess."

"I'll miss you," she whispered.

"Good," he said. "That's exactly what I want to hear."

Astride his horse, he waved good-bye, and slowly, because of the snow, the troop of thirty men trotted out the big gates and through the snowy park. When she finally turned, the huge bulk of Sheffield Castle loomed before her. *Hundreds of people to care for and a queen to guard. God's death! Who could be glad of that? Shrewsbury is mad. I am responsible for all these people and the Queen of Scots. And likely Sir Ralph Sadler will never come, and probably his dead body lies in the snow somewhere. Or he'd be here.*

Bess said, "Those gates are to remain closed. And guarded. Since my lord is gone."

Caps were touched, and Bess suddenly smiled dazzlingly on the trim, liveried guards. Their blue jackets fitted so neatly, and they smiled at her so admiringly. Bess thought, *I'm really quite happy. I wonder why?*

The December day passed slowly. Each time the gates were opened, Bess would fly to the entrance to see who entered. Messengers with letters and gifts were not permitted within the great castle and had to open their saddlebags and give over the contents to the guards on the outer doors.

If it weren't the season for gift giving, Bess thought, *we'd be left more alone.*

In the afternoon, the sun came out. Mary sent Kennedy to ask permission to walk outside, or even on the leads. Bess refused. "No! Tell her no! She is not to leave her suite!"

And then Bess thought, *The leads!* She would go up there herself and look out across the park. Maybe she could see Sir Ralph Sadler coming! For where was he? Here she was, all alone in this castle, with a frightened queen, who would assuredly climb out any window to escape and ride to freedom! She had done it before! Why wouldn't she do it again?

The day before New Year's, packages and letters arrived from London, and included were some from the earl.

Bess tore open the earl's letter, in haste. Maybe there would be an explanation of Sadler's whereabouts. But there wasn't. Shrewsbury wrote only that the trial of Norfolk would open the sixteenth of January.

Oh, my God! Bess thought as she read. *That's more than two weeks away. He'll never get home!*

By now, the earl had written, *Sir Ralph must be with you.*

248

"He's not, he's not!" said Bess aloud, just as though the earl were right in front of her.

And my dearest None, I miss you so very much, my only joy; this is a grim business, to see an old friend in such case as this, traduced by his own dreaminess. I fear very much that the gallows which haven't been used, thank God, since Her Majesty's accession, will have to be used now, and in point of fact, rebuilt. For Norfolk is really not a traitor, but misguided and unable, yet the letters in his possession are irrefutable proof that he knew this plot was to begin with the murder of the Queen's Majesty. And here there is much talk that if Norfolk suffers on the gallows, he should be joined by Mary of Scotland, for why should he be punished and not she, who aided and prodded him? The Commons are hot for her blood. Dearest None, good-night; it is after midnight, and as you know I turn into a bear after ten. May your New Year be the happiest you have ever had, and as soon as I can, I'll be with you, my dearest.

Bess put down the letter and looked around the room; it was darkening with the swift early winter night. "Digby," she said, "the children and I shall dine up here in my bedroom, before the fire."

That night she placed extra guards at her door, the children's doors, and at the foot of the twin stairways that led up, up through the massive walls of Sheffield Castle. Bess was sure that Mary's friends knew the gossip Shrewsbury had written and that Mary's life might very well be in danger, and that recklessness might be the order of the day. What better time to try to rescue her than when the castle was commanded by only a woman?

On New Year's Day, 1572, Bess wakened early, determined to present her gifts to her children as happily as possible. She wakened and turned in bed; had she heard something? The sound of an arrival? No, she must have dreamed it. On her chest were the new knitted stockings for her two daughters and the handmade silk smocks, trimmed in black silk on white, and for each, a new close-fitting doublet, clasped down the front with pearls. Shrewsbury had left each of them a new velvet bedgown and matching shoes, for they both had grown so rapidly. Gilbert had sent Mary a string of pearls. *They'll be married soon,* Bess thought. *Imagine! A year or so and they'll be wed.* For young Edward, who was home from the Shrewsbury school, a leather jacket with matching hose and boots, a new red and a new blue doublet, again with matching hose, and a new book on horses and their care, from his father.

When all the gift-giving was over, it was still early in the morning. Bess' bedroom was a welter of empty wine and water cups and half-eaten food on trays and piles of gifts and letters. Outside it began to snow again, but within, it was a fine New Year's and Bess said, "Now I'll open your father's present to me!"

Bess had the habit, when she and the earl were separated, of keeping his last letter in a flat box on the table beside her bed. When the new letter came, she would replace it and put the next to last letter away, safely, in a large box. Now with excited fingers she opened his gift, wrapped in silk, and it was the most beautiful box she had ever seen in her life. It was gold and silver, which was all the rage and fashion now, to combine the two colors. It was sprinkled with gems. Bess opened it to look inside and to place inside it his last letter. But when she opened it, she gasped, in such delight that Edward, who had been sitting on the foot of the bed, climbed across the tumbled counterpane to look.

"It's a clock!" he cried to Mary, who was sitting by the fire in her new bedgown.

It was a ruby and diamond bracelet with a clock. Bess started to blubber. Edward patted her hand. "I miss him so, Edward," Bess said, taking the napkin Edward proffered.

"Wind it," cried Edward.

Bess picked it up gingerly. She could just hear the earl saying, "Now be careful, Bess, don't attack it. It's a delicate contrivance.

She turned the tiny stem carefully. She held it to her ear. "It's ticking," she cried in delight. "It's actually ticking."

Everyone gathered around to look and exclaim. Bess sat cross-legged on the bed, her head bent over the clock, and gently set it and put it on. She wore it when she went to Mary's suite to wish her a Happy New Year and to present the earl's gift to Mary. She came to Mary with the children, so they could properly give her their New Year's greeting.

Mary, before the children, was her most charming self, gracious, appealingly pathetic. She exclaimed over Shrewsbury's gift, which was a copper and silver warming pan, with a packet of sweet-smelling herbs to sprinkle over the coals. Bess thought it was typical of him, because it was something she needed.

"But the gift you could give me, my lady," Mary said, "which would mean the most, is permission to walk outside."

Bess shook her head. "I am sorry, madam."

She knew her children thought her harsh.

"When Sir Ralph arrives, then you may ask him," Bess said. And she thought, *Will he ever arrive? Ever?*

She watched from the leads that day and all the next day, and then, just as she was turning in her walk, in the blowing wind, up on the top roof of the castle, she saw horsemen. She turned and ran down, down into the great hall, and when Sir Ralph came striding in, to greet her, she cried, "Oh! I'm so glad to see you here, sir."

"My lord Shrewsbury tells me you're equal to ten men!"

"Be damned to his lordship," Bess said, "I thought you'd been waylaid and murdered." And then she asked direct the big question on her mind. "Are you going to take over her custody, sir?" Breathless, she hung on his answer.

"No, my lady. My orders are to leave when his lordship returns."

She was obviously disappointed, he knew. Perhaps this could cheer her up. "The Bishop of Ross—this queen's priest—he was with her first when she escaped; you remember him?"

Bess nodded.

"Well, he has confessed and implicated her."

What would that mean? Bess wondered, as she escorted him up to Mary's chamber after he'd washed and eaten.

It was early evening, and Mary looked exquisite; wax candles burned, Mary's spaniel lay before the fire, and she sat on her dais, with a canopy above her, her ladies grouped about at her feet, and her page Bastien, playing his lute.

Sir Ralph bowed.

Mary reminded him: "You held me in your arms when I was a babe, sir."

"It was my honor and pleasure, madam."

"That pleases me to hear," she said. "Now you must sit, sir, and tell us the news."

Sir Ralph, bearing news that was not good, hesitated. He contented himself with: "I bring you a letter from your countryman and ambassador to the court of the Queen's Majesty, the bishop of Ross."

He proffered the letter. One of Mary's ladies took it, and Mary laid it on her lap. Sir Ralph decided to mince no more words.

"The bishop in his letter tells you, madam, that he has confessed his part in the plot of Norfolk and Ridolfi to murder the queen and place you on the English throne. He advises you to stop conspiring."

The scene changed, like lightning. Mary was enraged. For a second no sound came from her, then she managed to spit at him, "Jesu!" She sat there, trembling in her chair. "He lies! The bishop is a flawed and fearful priest. He has done as *you* would have him do." She rose to her feet and pointed a shaking finger at Sir Ralph. "But you will find me to be a queen and to have the heart of a queen."

She had stepped down off her dais and was facing him. "The heart of a queen!" And she pressed her hand over her heart, which was indeed beating madly, hammering inside her chest.

"Throw that lying letter into the flames, and that is where I will put the bishop. When I am free. I came here as a free princess and now I am in prison. Aye, I'll let my dearest cousin Elizabeth deal with Norfolk, he's her subject, but you may tell the whole of both realms I'll deal with the bishop, the lying priest, when I am free."

Sir Ralph was backing toward the door.

But Mary had the last word. "I'll wash my hands in his blood!"

Bess slept that night, deeply, relievedly, and woke in the morning refreshed and happy. She was able, that sunny January morning, to ride out through the great park. Sir

252

Ralph walked with Mary on the leads; he was afraid to take her outside.

Bess said to him, "She plots to go out and then to faint, perhaps, and to be carried in, and then another female could take her place in the bed, and she will disguise herself and slip out—she has all kinds of plots, plans and connivings; remember how she escaped from Loch Leven—and that was an island!"

"Jesu, what a task you have!" Sir Ralph lamented. And Bess said, "Oh, now it is your task, happily. I'm not going to see her whilst you're here. I need a respite, sir." But how long would it be? she wondered. How long?

But for two weeks she kept her word. She didn't see Mary until the day the news arrived from London that the trial of the duke of Norfolk was over, had consumed but twelve hours, and that Lord Shrewsbury had pronounced the sentence of guilty, slowly, in his clipped tones, and with bright tears standing in his blue eyes. Sir Ralph shuddered and said to Bess, "Madam, I can't tell her. I honestly can't tell her. I can't face another of her storms. I pray you, Bess, do it for me."

Bess slowly climbed the steps to Mary's room, and she could hear the weeping and loud lamentation going on within.

Jesu! Bess thought. *They—she knows—already. And how? She knows things before we do.*

When Bess entered, Mary was dressed in mourning, and so were all her ladies. They were praying on their knees, Mary at her priedieu and the ladies behind her, kneeling on cushions. With a final mumbled Latin prayer, Mary rose and faced Bess.

"It was the earl of Shrewsbury who pronounced sentence."

"Aye," said Bess. "But he was moved and wept."

"I weep," Mary said. "And it is my fault."

Bess was surprised, to hear her admit fault.

But Mary went on. "It was the fault of a letter I sent to my sister queen, begging her to spare him."

Bess scowled. "Your letter could have made no difference."

253

Mary took this as an insult, but she decided not to deign to answer it. She said, "My whole body weeps with me, I am ill, and I shall fast and pray. Today I eat nothing. Nothing then on Wednesday, nothing on Friday. I shall pray and fast."

"As you wish, madam," Bess said.

But that night Mary went into a fit of hysterics and moaning. Finally, Bess was summoned to calm her.

Bess thought, *She is afraid. She is afraid for her life.* But she cried out it was her letter to Elizabeth that had cost Norfolk his life.

"Madam," Bess said, "it was not your letter. Norfolk confessed." She called Kennedy; Mary's bed was readied for the night, the pillows plumped, and Mary's short hair brushed and her nightcap tied on. Kennedy kneaded her legs and feet and washed them. The candles guttered low. *Oh, lord, lord,* Bess thought, *I'm so wearied of her.*

That night Sadler wrote to Cecil. *We look hourly—hourly—to hear some good news from you, of his lordship's coming, and my return.*

And they did look hourly. Every hour either Bess or Sir Ralph checked with the lookouts and returned sadly; there was nothing to report. And Bess would sigh deeply because she had prayed she and the earl would be relieved of Mary's care, and now it seemed as though no one else would do it. After a bare three weeks Sir Ralph couldn't wait to leave. Even Bess was depressed, as February arrived in a deep swirling snowstorm that turned the park into a beautiful and hopeless sight, for who could arrive now?

Bess took to her bed. Let the whole castle, tense and unhappy, go to hell. She had logs piled high on the fire, she had a bath, she put on her most beautiful nightgown and bedgown; she had marchpane and sweet Alicante wine; propped in bed, she read aloud the psalms from the black velvet-covered book that always lay on her bedside table.

The next day two messengers from London struggled through the storm, three days late. They brought a letter from the earl, which Bess ripped open, ripping the seal apart so the paper tore, too. But all it said was that he had asked advice about a personal dresser and maid for her from the most fashionable lady in London, Lettice Knollys. Lettice had recommended a woman whose services Shrewsbury had been able to procure; when he came home, he would bring her and all the things Bess had asked for; and Mary, too, for she had given him a long list of necessaries from London. As a postscript the earl had added, *This worthy woman's name is Mrs. Battel, a name I deem suitable for your personal servant.*

Bess swore, and then laughed.

When the letter arrived, Bess had been doing the household accounts. When she finished, she was appalled. No wonder Shrewsbury complained and fretted over money. Bess, in a flurry of indignation, seized a fresh piece of paper and wrote to Cecil.

My exceedingly good friend, as I hope I shall always be able to call you, this queen is beggaring my lord, my husband. Her servants and she request all manner of things, which we must supply, from laudanum to fancy purges—this queen takes many medicines, prescribed by her mediciner and this is one of but many instances. Her servants, sloppy and careless, break all manner of things, from knives to pots, and lose things and burn the bottoms out of containers and soil quilts so bad they must be discarded, and now, my dear lord, we have Sir Ralph, with all his train—to say nothing of thirty-six horses of his—to feed and care for. You know together my lord and I have twelve children to provide for, to maintain their dwelling places, etc., and this queen is herself a terrible charge, without its beggaring us. Pray you tell the Queen's Majesty that fifty-two pounds a week for this queen's diet is woefully inadequate.

Bess nibbled at the end of her pen. Money flowing out for Mary Stuart. Instead of into the further decoration of Chatsworth or a dowry for Elizabeth. Then she forgot the money. She added, *Sir Ralph grows more tense and woeful every day. Please send my jewel home to me.*

She was about to add that only Shrewsbury could handle Mary when she realized what such words would entail to Cecil.

A coldness enveloped her. Was Mary beginning to respond to the earl, to lean on him? For better or worse

255

was he beginning to be the male figure in her life? The very fact that it was he who had pronounced sentence on Norfolk was but another link in the chain that was binding them together. It made Bess feel sick. So she shoved the thought aside and banished it swiftly, and told herself it was not so. The earl's absence had made her fanciful and silly; the confinement was bringing everything too close, so a proper view could not be taken. Bess sealed the letter to Cecil and went up on the leads to look out again.

The next hour, Sir Ralph ascended the twisting stairs, to pace on the leads, and they took turns all day. Mary did not ask to go out; it was Friday, and she was fasting, saying prayers for the life of Norfolk, her dear suitor, who had wished to marry her and whose letters and gifts she treasured in her heart, she said. And at five o'clock in the afternoon, when Bess had given up hope, and another long, long night stretched before her, she heard Sir Ralph shout and come running down the steps. "My lord arrives!" He seized Bess and gave her a kiss.

Bess and Sir Ralph did a little merry dance together in the hall, laughing and happy, then rushed to the main gates and were standing there waving and shouting greetings when Shrewsbury rode in.

"I brought everything, None. Mrs. Battel, wigs, red wigs and black wigs, and everything else from bane to vinegar!"

"Oh," cried Bess, "it was only you I wanted, only you." He squeezed her so hard he was crushing her, and it was sheer heaven. "My jewel, my darling," whispered Bess, as though she were drowning in a sea of happiness.

At dinner, during which the earl devoured all the food in sight, he told them all the news; and Sir Ralph, his good humor restored, told the earl all his travails. Afterwards, Shrewsbury said that he would go up to Mary and greet her. Bess frowned. Sir Ralph said he would go, too, because he was leaving early, early in the morning to get a good start and would say his good-byes to Mary tonight.

"You come, too, None," Shrewsbury said.

Rebelliously, Bess pouted. As soon as he was back he had

to go see that wretched queen! Still, it was best she go with him. At his side, she marched up the steps.

Mary, of course, had known of his arrival and was dressed, perfumed, and waiting anxiously, her hands busy with her needlework, her ears alert for the sound of his step.

"He comes!" she said to her ladies and gave a final glance around the room to make sure again it was pretty and neat, and that the warming pan he had given her was strewn with herbs, and that the room smelled fresh and aromatic. She bestowed on him a wonderful smile; she looked beautiful. The fasting had thinned her face and figure, and her eyes shone with their unusual glowing colors, gold and green and hazel.

The earl bowed and came to her dais. She drew a deep breath of pleasure and gave him her hand, which he took in his big one and kissed.

"Your gift, my lord, pleasured me much, and your thoughtfulness, but to see you is the most pleasure."

Bess thought, *I'd like to strangle her. And shake her head off.* Her eyes blazed.

Sir Ralph then came forward and greeted her, and graciously she tendered her hand, which Sir Ralph kissed gingerly, as though he weren't quite sure. He stepped back, and said, "Madam, I came to bid you both good-night and good-bye. I leave tomorrow early, to get a good start for London."

Mary glanced at him, her eyes shining golden, as they often did when she was deep in thought. They penetrated Sir Ralph as if they knew what he was thinking and what he would report to Cecil and her hated cousin Elizabeth.

"A safe journey to you, sir. God go with you," Mary said. And then, because she was happy and excited, she gave him one of her entrancing smiles. She looked from Sir Ralph to the earl; she was happy because their arrival was an event. Prisoner that she was, her days and nights stretched before her in endless boredom. To have guests here at night was an exciting event. She asked them all to sit, and then she leaned forward in her chair, fastening her eyes on Shrewsbury.

257

"The news, my lord," she said. "What news?"

Shrewsbury was conscious of warring emotions; her eyes, her body, were telling him that she was truly delighted to see him, grateful to see him; somehow she had bestowed her trust in him and on him. In some oblique way he was her only cavalier. How narrow the course, the earl thought, between warding a prisoner and taking care of her. He took refuge in his cool manner, which always put a distance between him and the person he wanted kept at that distance.

"Madam, the news is not good, as you know. Saturday night the Queen's Majesty signed the death warrant for His Grace the Duke of Norfolk."

Mary gave a cry of horror.

The earl said, "Surely you are not surprised. But you may be surprised when I tell you that Sunday night the Queen's Majesty rescinded it."

Mary said, "I have prayed!"

"Ah, madam," the earl said, "but many pray otherwise. For the safety of the realm."

Mary said softly, "When you pronounced the sentence, you wept."

The earl said, "Aye, madam; I was much moved. It is the first execution of Her Majesty's reign."

His blue eyes regarded her steadily, and she knew he had left unsaid what he was thinking: You, Mary of Scotland, have caused it; it is your fault, and on your conscience. Her eyes glittered with tears.

"You shall see, my lord," she said, "someday you shall see and recognize, that I am a queen and have the heart of a queen. Therefore, I must accept with gratitude what my subjects sacrifice for me. But pray allow me to weep and ask God to intervene, in mercy."

Shrewsbury was not appeased. "Your part in the plot, madam, is well known. There are many in the Commons who would desire you to suffer as Norfolk will. But the Queen's Majesty said to me, 'How can we be the hawk to the bird which has flown to us for succour?' " Suddenly he was tired of Mary. Elizabeth had been filled with horror that it should be by her command and her signature that Norfolk die. This queen had no such scruples.

Mary sensed his withdrawal. She whispered, "I am sunk in grief."

"So also is the Queen's Majesty, madam. And I, too, as an old friend of Norfolk. I bid you good-night."

Sir Ralph thought, *Now is the time for royal rage.* But it was not forthcoming. Instead, Mary said, "My lord, God keep you as you sleep, and watch over you. And I pray you, my lord, to let me walk outside with you tomorrow. I pray you!"

"I shall consider, madam," the earl said. He bade her good-night, and Bess also, and Sir Ralph, and then gratefully they shut the door on the imprisoned queen.

Early in the morning, Sir Ralph rode off; Bess had been up very early to see him off. Sir Ralph was full of smiles. Bess thought, *Now everyone is glad to leave; it used to be otherwise. It is Mary's presence, of course.* But the sun was slanting across the park, lighting the snow into such glittery beauty that it was breathtaking.

"Look!" she said to the earl.

He was so happy to be home. Back home. "I suppose I must take her out today," he said.

"Why?" cried Bess.

"She is pathetic. She is caged."

"Snakes should be caged."

"I know," the earl agreed. But later he went up to Mary and escorted her down into the great hall and through a postern gate into the park. Bess went along with them to the door. Cold as it was, she watched from the doorway, seeing Mary cling to the earl. Mary was laughing and drawing in deep breaths of fresh air; she was so excited she ran forward and stepped over her shoes in the snow, so glad was she to be outside. The earl leaned down and brushed her shoes off with his gloved hand, and then she put her hand on his arm, and they walked together. In the doorway Bess said aloud, "Snakes shouldn't be caged. Snakes should have their heads cut off!"

259

CHAPTER 9

BESS' head revolved with plans. They could move Mary to Sheffield Manor Lodge; it had two walled gardens. Or they could build a place for her, a pretty new smaller dwelling, and Bess set to work to draw the plans. All during February's cold and stormy nights, when icicles hung over the stone copings, she fashioned the neat architectural drawings she loved so much to draw. And Shrewsbury approved. They'd start building as soon as the ground unfroze. Bess rode out and inspected the park to see where it should be built. If they must ward this queen, it was imperative they get some relief from her constant presence.

Mrs. Battel was still with Bess. She had brought all manner of delightful soaps and perfumes and brushes and combs; and she washed and dressed Bess' hair and took care of her clothes and made sure her mistress was a model of fashion. Digby was promoted. Digby had less to do.

Gilbert was coming home, after more than two years traveling and study at the University in Padua. Charles and William were returning, too; for of course Bess had sent both her sons abroad, too; if Shrewsbury thought it correct, Bess would follow his example. Mary was so excited she could hardly wait to see him; she knew she would be married soon. By late April, the whole family was in residence at Sheffield, and Henry and Grace Talbot were wed in a small private ceremony in the presence of the immediate family. Off they went to lodgings in London.

"Write!" Bess cried. "Write, like your brother Gilbert." Gilbert loved nothing more than to sit down at his table and delight his father and Bess with all the gossipy news from everywhere.

Gilbert and Charles were inseparable. *Charles,* Bess

260

thought. *Charles.* Her youngest son. There was only one word for Charles—dashing.

He was handsome, with auburn hair and a magnificent figure. Charles was an expert shot, and expert with the rapier and sword; he rode like a centaur, and Shrewsbury said he had already seduced enough women in Derbyshire to more than double the population. He was betrothed to a charming well-dowried young lady named Margaret Kitson.

William Bess adored. He was not as brilliant a personality as Charles, but he too was gay, and, along with it, he was dependable and thoughtful. The earl disapproved of their escapades, and when he did, Bess rose like a tiger in their defense.

"God's death!" the earl said angrily. "They were caught poaching last night, along with young Edward and Stavely." Stavely was a servant of the earl's.

Bess giggled, and the earl said it was no laughing matter to set such an example. Bess gave them both a lecture, and the eighteen-year old Charles just laughed and kissed her, and said, "Aye, mother."

They ran up enormous bills for their clothes, their jewelry, their horses, dogs, weapons. Charles paid such a price for a falcon, the earl almost exploded with rage.

Charles said, "My lord, I'll give him to you, then," in such a disarming fashion that Shrewsbury had to smile, and said, "Jesu! Charles, what makes you think I can afford the damned bird myself?

"Charles," continued the earl firmly, "you're a bad influence on Gilbert, to say nothing of young Edward and George. You must curb your recklessness, or you'll never survive in the queen's service."

Charles said, "Aye, my lord," in such a penitent manner that Shrewsbury patted his wide shoulder and said, "Heed my advice, young man. It'll do you good."

"You're always after them," Bess said.

"I have to," the earl replied irascibly. "They all need a firm hand."

On the first of May, he was passing down the corridor outside the suite all five young males occupied when Gilbert, in his shirt only, burst out of the door waving a piece of paper, shouting with laughter, and also shouting for Charles.

"Charles is in the stables," Shrewsbury said. "At least he's up and dressed."

Gilbert was still laughing and waving the paper, and the earl said, "What is that?" and seized it.

"It was pinned to the curtain of my bed," Gilbert said, "as a May greeting!"

The earl read, printed in big, bold letters,

HAPPY HAPPY FIRST OF MAY
OUTDOOR FUCKING STARTS TODAY.

Shrewsbury said, "This is the fruit of his studies in France and Italy?"

"Give it back, Father, I'm going to frame it!"

The door behind Gilbert opened, and William appeared.

The earl said, "William, don't you know better than to appear in the hall naked?"

William backed into the big sloppy bedroom. "I didn't know you were here, my lord."

"Obviously not," snapped Shrewsbury. "Now both of you get dressed, and go out riding, or something."

Later in the day he discovered Gilbert and Charles moving furniture into a far unused room under the eaves in the west wing. "What the devil are you two doing?" he asked.

Gilbert said, "Charles is helping me pick the furniture for my lodgings in London."

"I've a good eye for furniture," Charles said, "just like Mother."

The earl looked at the bedstead in question, with its red testers. "That bed is not going to London."

"Oh, Father," Gilbert said. "It's just an old bed. If you'd let Mary and me have the town house—"

The earl was so annoyed he was speechless.

Gilbert went right on. "Charles helped me make a list of all the things I need, and I need money, Father, for linen. . . ."

Shrewsbury said, "Gilbert, you have your own money.

262

Use it. And for your information, the town house is rented, to help me support you and Charles and Edward and George and Henry and Grace and Mary and Elizabeth."

But Shrewsbury had to concede that Charles was dependable and loving. He was leaving for London two days later by himself. He refused to take Gilbert with him for he said if he did, he would never accomplish what he was trying to accomplish before his marriage. "I can't spend my time in baiting bears," Charles said. He was going to wait upon the powerful earl of Leicester, the queen's favorite, who was close to Walsingham, whose service Charles wanted to enter.

Bess bid him good-bye at eight in the morning. So at four in the afternoon, when she saw him coming through the park at a fast gallop, by himself, she knew something dreadful and ominous had happened.

Charles flung himself off his lathered horse and came bounding in to her and took her in his arms. "Mother," he said, "the Queen's Majesty is very, very ill!"

He held her and looked down at her face and thought what, what would happen to Mother and the earl if the Queen's Majesty died and this queen took her place? Then he was conscious of the earl standing next to him saying: "Charles. Calm yourself. Tell us clearly what you know."

Charles thrust out a letter, which he took from inside his doublet. "From Leicester, for you." He caught his breath and said, "Briefly then, I met couriers from London, from my lord of Leicester. They told me that the Queen's Majesty lies ill, with pains in the chest and heart, and that Leicester and Cecil have been with her constant, and all the doctors and ladies crowded in her bedroom, she sits propped up on cushions; she looks very, very frail and thin."

The earl ripped the seal off Leicester's letter and read. Written hastily, it carried the same news Charles had just told them, and then the earl of Leicester had added plaintively, *I hear talk that Mary of Scotland bears me ill will. I pray you, my lord, find out why, if you can, and let me know the cause of this evil.*

Shrewsbury said, "Leicester is fearful."

"You should be fearful, my lord!" Charles was thinking that living with Mary Stuart was like living with a loaded pistol. He added, "This is not a game, my lord! And I am

263

going to stay here with you and Mother till we have better news from London!"

"That boy," said Shrewsbury, after Charles had departed the room and left Bess and him alone, "that boy will probably found a dukedom."

"And William will, too," said Bess.

CHAPTER 10

THE whole realm of England trembled and waited upon the health of their beloved queen. A week passed. Within her crowded bedroom, earls and statesmen and friends and doctors tiptoed, knelt and prayed and took as good care of her as the rude medicine of her age permitted. And suddenly one morning, the strangely colored eyes glowed again, and Elizabeth stepped from her bed, thin as a lion's cub, but just as powerful.

When the news reached Sheffield, Charles saddled up his big horse and galloped off for London with Gilbert and William. Bess, with all the rest of the children, left for Chatsworth; the earl wrote for permission to take Mary to Chatsworth, so her quarters at Sheffield could be given their quarterly scrubbing; spring unfolded, the sun was shining warmer every day, and everybody was happier.

But Bess had a problem on her mind that she didn't confess to Shrewsbury; in fact she had two problems, and she consulted him about only one.

The one she divulged was Elizabeth, Elizabeth, who was so beautiful that people stared at her; Elizabeth, who was trained so well that her French was perfect, she played the virginals and the harp and the organ, she sketched, she read voluminously, and yet—"Yet with all these accomplishments, she is drifting through life." Bess flung out her hands, and the earl looked down at his dusty boots, for he'd just come back from a day's trip to his castle of Bolsover,

264

to check on affairs there, and looking down at those boots, he said nothing.

Bess continued. "I've just had her adamant refusal to even consider Mister Bertie." (Mr. Bertie was the very attractive son of one of Bess' dear friends, Katherine, the dowager duchess of Suffolk.) "He is the third suitor she has refused."

The earl asked, "What reason does she give?"

Bess said, "No reason! She just looks at me, and says, 'Oh, Mother! I will marry, maybe. Later. Or when the heart inclines!' She repeated that, and looked at me and smiled. 'When the heart inclines. A beautiful phrase, Mother.' Then she went to the virginal, and played for two hours!"

The earl smiled. He said, "She is—she has been created and born just to be loved, Bess. She should be the beloved mistress of a great king or an oriental potentate." He sighed. "She is not born to be somebody's wife, Bess; she is a jewel."

Bess snapped, "You're mad, my lord! Born for love!"

"Exactly," said the earl. "Gentle, devoted, beautiful, a treasure for a king. Never a housewife, not a bit like you, Bess."

Bess said, "You sound as though you'd like to bed her."

The earl raised his eyebrow. "What man wouldn't?"

Bess looked at him in horror. And he said quickly, "Oh, come, Bess. I feel for Elizabeth as a father, but I can see only too clearly what sort of child-woman she is. And if I were you, I shouldn't worry. Don't push her. Suddenly, somewhere, she'll find her love, and she will go to him, willy-nilly, and you won't be able to stop her. She'll go to him like an arrow from a bow, straight into his arms."

Bess stood. "Well, that's a great deal of comfort, my love! A great deal!"

The earl patted her on the shoulder. "Don't fret. And I take one thing back. She is a good deal like you, and yet as sweet and gentle as a dove."

Bess pondered these words as she rode at Elizabeth's side on their way to Chatsworth. Bess wanted to gallop, but Elizabeth shook her head and said she just wanted to amble and enjoy the beauty of the country. At the head of each hill she would pause and check her horse and look out and draw deep sighs of satisfaction. "It is so beautiful I want to imprint it on my mind," she explained dreamily.

Bess' other problem was her brother James. Lady Leche had worried about James for ten years now; old Hardwick Manor was drifting rapidly into decay. James was a good son, good natured, kind, and completely incompetent. At Chatsworth Lady Leche and Jane explained it all to Bess, after, that is, Bess had inspected the purple room, for she had been anxious about the color; it must be just the right shade of purple, so the tender blues of the woodwork would set off the purple ceiling, arched with plaster cornices and decoration.

The color was just right. Bess listened to her mother and Jane, and suddenly she said, "Well, of course, there's a solution, Mother. I'll buy Hardwick, and—"

"You'll have to tear it down," Lady Leche said.

"It's almost fallen down, Bess," Jane said.

Bess scowled. "Let that go for now. What if I buy Hardwick, and set James up in one of my manors, with an income for life, instead of paying outright, for Hardwick? Will he do it? That way?"

"Yes," Lady Leche said. "I think so. Only don't order him or push him, Bess."

But when Bess saw Hardwick, she was so appalled she blurted, "Oh, my God, James! How could you?"

It was in ruins. Windows gaped, the steps were broken; one whole wing sagged so badly that its roof was only eight feet off the ground. The stable doors hung awry and wouldn't shut. The fields were wild with weeds. Bess, taut with anger, said, "You ought to be ashamed! How can you look at this? I'll buy it from you, and I'll show you what you should have done!"

The good-natured James was annoyed. "I'm not the man you are, Bess." Bess sighed and remembered her mother's words. She tried to be temperate.

"James, I'll give you a good fair price, but I'll give it to you yearly, for the rest of your life, and you can live in Oldcotes. Will that suit?" James was about to turn down Bess' offer, only he met his wife's pleading eyes. Still, he

266

shook his head. Then he asked, "Will you tear down Hardwick, Bess?"

Bess shook her head. "I can't," she said. "It's me, it's where I was born; it's alive, James. Houses are alive, you know. I'll tear down those two drooping little wings and keep the manor house, and attach new wings to each side, to make a quadrangle."

He said, "You decided very quickly."

She said impatiently, "It's my profession; I know a great deal, James, about building. And about design."

"So you won't tear it down?"

"No," Bess said. "I can't."

James smiled then. "All right, Bess! I accept! You can have Hardwick!"

And when he said that, Bess suddenly smiled tremulously; and she hugged James and kissed him, and only then did she realize how much she had wanted Hardwick.

"Oh, James," she cried, "you've made me terribly happy. I love it, I love it, every stick and stone of it. And I'll make it into the most beautiful manor house in all of England, retaining its past and promising its future. Oh, how glad it will be to see the carpenters come. I can just hear every old board saying welcome home, Bess! Welcome home!"

"What is this?" Shrewsbury asked, leaning over Bess' table and looking at her drawing.

Bess bit her lip. "It's the architectural sketches for the additions to old Hardwick Hall."

Shrewsbury sat down on her stool and pored over it.

"I bought it from James, my lord," Bess said tremulously.

"I hear it is in virtual ruin," the earl commented.

"Aye," said Bess. "But—"

"Don't you have enough to do without rebuilding and remaking a ruin, Bess?"

"No, my lord," Bess said. "I think I'd die if I weren't building."

Shrewsbury grinned and stood up. He looked down at her face, and then he patted her shoulder, and he said, "They're beautiful plans, Bess. Jesu! You are a clever girl."

Bess flung her arms around him. "Oh, thank you, my love! Thank you!" She was thinking, Cavendish said that to me, in just the same way. But men are strange. Cavendish had meant it. Did Shrewsbury?

He seemed to. He seemed to take pride in her capabilities. He had placed Buxton Springs in her hands, for instance, and it was prospering as never before. Bess had introduced a sliding scale of charges. From five pounds for nobility, less for a knight, and very little for a yeoman, and the consequence was it was literally jammed. Bess said the baths were so healthful that it little behooved them to keep out the poor. So everyone flocked to Buxton, including the famous great earl of Leicester, to whom Bess had written to bring a very small retinue, for there could be no overcrowding tolerated at the baths, for sanitary reasons. This letter made Shrewsbury smile, for who but Bess would give orders to the great earl, except the queen?

Mary loved the baths. It was the highest spot in her summer. But this year, in June, on the second of the month, the duke of Norfolk was executed; Elizabeth had finally brought herself to sign the death warrant. It had made her ill, the thought of Norfolk's dying by her signature; now his death made Mary ill, so ill that the earl couldn't believe it was an emotional sickness.

Bess did. "Take her to the baths!"

Shrewsbury wrote Cecil that he didn't think the baths would do Mary any good, she was too sick. And she had turned away from him, too. It was he who had presided over Norfolk's trial, he who had pronounced the sentence of death, and Mary recoiled from his presence. Shrewsbury was thankful for this; the knot between them was obviously broken. He was relieved.

Bess was not, for now the burden fell on her. In revolt, she wrote to Cecil that she was going to entertain that summer, at Chatsworth. All her family were with her, and although she didn't say so, the presence of the famed Scottish queen was drawing the counties from miles around, like bees to a pot of honey. After all London was two hundred miles away, but here, in their midst was not only the Queen of Scots, but the earl of Shrewsbury and their own exciting Bess of Hardwick! Plus the exciting young males of Talbot and Cavendish. The food bills soared. Tuns of wine disappeared overnight. But it was very gay, and Mary got better.

Bess often escorted her to the bower through the fragrant gardens. She had had the doorway to the bower decorated with the carved lions of Scotland and the Talbot hound, and when Mary passed through the doors, she would look up to see the crouching lions and smile proudly. On the roof she reclined and drank in the fresh air and listened to music and did her needlework. Bess escorted many, many guests to her there. And by September Mary was recovered. Recovered enough to buy a most expensive falcon for Shrewsbury and present it to him, on her own wrist, her hand trembling slightly as she rested it on his tanned forearm, for it was a hot, sunny day, and he had pushed up the sleeves of his shirt.

The look he received from her eyes was almost imploring. He thanked her stiffly. "He is a magnificent bird," Shrewsbury said.

Mary cried: "The finest in England. Especially for you, my lord."

The earl murmured his thanks again.

"I look forward to the day when you would take me with you when you hunt."

She stood very close to him, and looked directly into his eyes.

"I will, madam." And then he added in his stiff manner, "It is the least I can do."

She was not taken aback, for she knew him very well now. She simply smiled and clasped her hands together in joy. "Oh, thank you, my lord!"

Shrewsbury showed the bird to Bess. Bess said, "I wish it had bitten her."

Shrewsbury grinned. "But I'll have to take her hunting, tomorrow."

Bess was about to say he didn't have to do anything he didn't want to do for Mary. But then she bit off the retort, for she knew it wouldn't do any good. It was all too clear to her that Mary needed the earl, and that he was responding to that need.

The following day, when they rode off together, Bess called a pox on Mary; her own horse was saddled, and off she rode, alone, to Hardwick.

Nonetheless, in spite of Mary it had been a wonderful summer. She had had all the children with her, and perhaps for the last time. Charles and his Margaret Kitson, and Mary and Gilbert were going to be married, and William and Ann Kighly. William, in his own quiet way, had found his own bride; he was deeply in love, and Bess' heart glowed for him; he was very, very like his father. And as for Ann—she clung to William's hand, and her eyes followed him everywhere. Bess was satisfied. "There is nothing better," she told the earl, "to make a mother's heart happy than to see her son's wife truly, truly adore him."

So Bess said to Elizabeth, "Now, my girl, are you going to stay at home, with your mother and father, when everyone else has left?"

Elizabeth laughed. "They'll all be here, singly, separately, and in groups, Mother!"

Bess sighed. "Elizabeth," she said, "you are being extremely foolish." Then she asked, "This summer, with all the young men here, didn't you find a single one of them to your taste?"

Elizabeth said disapprovingly, "I don't like the sound of that question. I'm not in the market for buying a chicken!"

"Oh, Elizabeth," Bess cried. "Maybe I phrased it wrong! I meant wasn't there anybody who—"

"No."

"Is that all you are going to say?"

"There was nobody. Nobody. I wouldn't have let any one of those men even touch me."

Bess looked at her in amazement. Was there something wrong with her? she wondered. And when she repeated the conversation to the earl, he smiled.

"There's nothing wrong with her, Bess. She's waiting."

Elizabeth always went with her to Hardwick. Elizabeth was planning the gardens; from Aunt Linacre she had inherited the books and from Aunt Linacre she had inherited her love for the art. When they rode up the hill to Hardwick and saw it after only three months' work, Elizabeth's face always shone with pride and pleasure.

The tumbled old wings had been shorn off and the

270

foundations for the two new ones lain. And in their center the old manor house welcomed them.

Its windows glittered with new panes. Its rebuilt chimneys, each one different, stood bold against the sky.

When they came, they often stayed the night. Elizabeth had picked a room on the second floor, looking west over to the setting sun and the lake. "It was Aunt Linacre's room," Bess said.

"I knew it was," Elizabeth said. "You can feel it; it has love in it."

Bess started to cry.

Elizabeth said, "When I need her, I shall come here." She had brought all her mementos of Aunt Linacre. On the walls she hung her aunt's needlepoint gardens. Every day, as soon as she came, she gathered flowers to put on the table by her bed and the table before the window seat and before the fireplace. And she put Aunt Linacre's embroidered pillows on the window seat.

Bess wiped her eyes and hugged her daughter. "Oh, Elizabeth," she said, "you are so sweet."

"I'm not sweet, Mother," Elizabeth said. "I need the remembrance of her love for me."

Bess looked at her. Then she said, "Well, so do I. Maybe that's why we're here."

Elizabeth said, "Not entirely for you, Mother. You must rebuild; you must create." Then she smiled, "But I will, too. You leave the gardens to me! And Mother, I'm seventeen. From now on, I want a room of my own."

With three weddings planned for November, the entire household lumbered back to the vastness of Sheffield Castle. Mary and all her train, Bess and all the children, Jane and the earl, and great carts of baggage, streaming through the great park, back to Sheffield. And with all there was to do, Bess still kept her finger on the rebuilding of Hardwick. On the grounds of Sheffield, she and Shrewsbury were building what they called Turret House, which was shaped like a turret and adjoined the lodge. It would be a safe place to keep Mary and give her a change of scene. The earl told Mary, "From your windows there, you will

271

be nestled among the mightiest oaks in England! One, quite near Turret House, can shelter two hundred horsemen under its branches!"

After the flurry of weddings was over, he took her riding in the park to see the half-finished Turret House. It was a cold day, but it was only about a mile's ride from the castle. On their way back, as they drew near to Sheffield, Mary was thrown from her horse.

She lay sprawled on the ground, and the earl knelt beside her, turning her gently.

"It's only my ankle, I think," Mary said tremulously.

The earl drew a deep breath. "Are you sure?"

She moved, she was sitting up now, shaken and white, but when he lifted her to her feet, she said almost gaily, "There's nothing broken, my lord, I'm sure."

They were both relieved, but she couldn't bear the weight on her right lower leg and ankle. Shrewsbury lifted her easily and carried her through the huge doors.

"It's good we were near home," he said.

Her arms were around his neck, and she smiled at him.

"To think I boast of my horsemanship," Mary said. "Now you won't take me anymore." Then she sobered. "Oh, what would I do if you didn't take me out once in a while, my lord!"

These words were so genuine that the earl found nothing to say. How pitiful she was in her strait confinement. He set her down on her feet gently. She bore her weight on one foot, holding onto him for support. He was about to say that if she would only stop her conniving, when Mary said, "I pray, every morning, that you will come and say I may go out with you."

The earl said lightly, "Why don't you try my faith, sometime, to pray to?" Mary recognized the appeal for her to compromise her fierce stand, as the true and Catholic heir to England. And she bent her head. Then she said, "I shall, my lord. I shall try." She raised her head and looked him straight in the face. "During a Lent, I swear, I'll attend church with you."

The earl held her steady. "Does your ankle hurt?"

"Aye, my lord. But it's truly nothing. Just a good excuse to have Kennedy bathe my feet and legs."

Bess had designed Turret House, and it was two years in building. Perfectly round, pierced with many, many windows, it rose like a slender column among the giant oaks and adjoined the manor lodge's second walled garden. It was just big enough to house Mary and her staff and no one else, so it was really Mary's house. All the spring of 1574 Mary labored happily on all kinds of needlework, from needlepoint pillows to bed hangings, table covers, and chair covers. And each room, paneled in oak, was painted in color, then, soft glowing colors. Sitting in church alongside the earl, in the early spring, (she had kept her promise to attend the church during Lent this year) she was as happy as she could be, under these so difficult circumstances. When Turret House was finished, she was enchanted with it, when she sat in the deep window seat, she could reach out and almost touch the fluttering oak leaves. "The round rooms are delightful," she exclaimed. "Delightful. It's like being outside, up in the trees." Since above all Mary loved being out of doors, this was a great compliment to Bess. But Bess was tired of seeing Mary's head next to the earl's in church.

Bess said stiffly, "I'm indeed happy you like it, ma'am."

Later she said to Shrewsbury, "I'm so sick of seeing her bewigged head next to you in church every day. I'm going to move her over to Turret House today."

Shrewsbury said, "Well, she can't help her wigs, None."

The whole household knew Mary's hair, which she had shorn off when she escaped from Scotland in men's clothing, had never properly grown back, and she had a huge wardrobe of different colored wigs. "Don't fret at her, Mother," Elizabeth said. "She can't help it."

"No, she can't, Mother," Frances chimed in.

Frances was visiting the earl and her mother. Now everyone helped Mary move over to Turret House, except Bess. When Frances and Elizabeth returned late in the afternoon, little Bess, who was five, was not with them.

"Where is she?" Bess wanted to know.

"She adored the house, Mother. She truly did. It's like a doll's house to her. And Mary insisted," Frances corrected herself hastily, "*this queen* insisted that she stay."

"But there's no place for her to sleep," Bess cried.

"She's going to sleep with the queen, share her bed."

Frustrated, Bess cried, "Be damned to this queen! Be damned to her!"

Elizabeth said, sighing, "Oh, Mother."

Bess started to retort and held her tongue. *And if I don't get that chit married soon,* she thought, *she'll drive me crazy.*

It was a beautiful warm summer. Mary, with her new house and a trip to Buxton Springs, was healthier and looked ten years younger. Mary and Frances were both at Sheffield a great deal, for each was expecting a child; Elizabeth was happy because she had their company. Mary Stuart was enjoying them, too. They all sat in the gardens in the afternoon, sewing, Mary and Frances on baby clothes, and Elizabeth was making each of them knitted blankets. But Bess, restless, suddenly left for Hardwick and stayed there two weeks. The two new wings were going up fast. It was September when she returned, and there was a great deal of mail for her.

Bess said to the earl, "My lord, my dear old friend Kate, the duchess of Suffolk writes that she and the duchess of Lennox will be passing near, the end of the month."

Shrewsbury frowned, "They can't stay here, Bess."

To his surprise, Bess agreed. "But what if I met them at Rufford Abbey, and they could break their journey and refresh themselves there with me for a few days?"

The earl looked at her, long. Then he said, "All right, Bess."

"The duchess of Lennox writes she has permission to visit her estates in Yorkshire, but she has promised the Queen's Majesty she will not see this queen," Bess explained. "And it has been so long since I have seen my friend Kate!"

Shrewsbury knew she was referring to Katherine the dowager duchess of Suffolk; Cavendish had been very friendly with her, and she had been Frances' second godmother, but Shrewsbury thought her officious; she was always telling everybody else what to do, which he found extremely obnoxious.

"I certainly don't want to see that woman," he said. "I don't know how you endure her. It's a pity that so witty a woman has to be so pushing."

274

Bess laughed, and said she didn't pay any attention to that, that she just let her talk and did as she pleased. Nonetheless, she didn't show the duchess of Lennox's letter to Shrewsbury; instead she burnt it. While she watched it burn, she knew the plan she had in her head was dangerous. The plan, if it succeeded, would probably land her in jail. But then, it was just a plan, it probably wouldn't succeed, there were too many *ifs*. And she hadn't truly decided, anyway. She figured she had about two and half weeks before the decision was necessary. For what Bess had kept secret from Shrewsbury was the fact that the duchess was bringing her young and only son with her. Lord Charles Stuart. Bess' eyes gleamed when she repeated that name in her head. The most noble lad in the kingdom, cousin to the queen of England and uncle to the young king of Scots. Bess sighed.

"Well, Elizabeth," she said, off-handedly, "I'm going to Rufford Abbey in about ten days now, and you may go if you wish."

Elizabeth frowned and shook her head. "I don't think so, Mother."

"Have you ever been there?" Bess inquired, knowing very well that Elizabeth had not been there.

"No," said Elizabeth.

"It lies on the edge of Sherwood Forest; it is very romantic, three small rivers wind through the grounds. The architecture is quite interesting; the gardens and fish ponds are enchanting. The borders against the walled gardens are five feet deep, and are planted with the most magnificent and rare plants and trees. Of course, it will be October, but you will find it fascinating."

Elizabeth shook her head. "I don't think I'll go, Mother. If you don't mind."

My God, what a silly twit, Bess thought. *Why not say yes, once in a while? Everlasting no's, that's what a mother gets from her girls! Everlasting no's!* These last eighteen months since her brothers and sister had been married, Elizabeth had turned down four more young men, till the earl himself said, "No more matrimony plans for Elizabeth, Bess. I refuse to do any more."

275

"Well, suit yourself, Elizabeth," Bess breathed through hardly parted lips, afraid to speak further for fear she would explode. So the next week, she resigned herself to thinking that Elizabeth would not come with her to Rufford, and perhaps it was just as well, and yet—all that week, Bess managed to hint she would be lonely on her journey, till finally Elizabeth said, "Mother! Do you truly need or want me to come?"

Bess stuttered, "Of course I don't need you, Elizabeth."

"All right, then," Elizabeth said.

"You'll have to make the choice by yourself," Bess said darkly, leaving Elizabeth to wonder what on earth she meant. What was so important?

Bess was leaving early in the morning of the fifth of October, for she expected her royal and important guests on the eighth, and she wanted to be properly ready. She intended to set forth at daylight, so she went up to Elizabeth's suite to bid her good-night and good-bye. She climbed the steps, almost a bit relieved, too, for Bess really didn't like secrets, she preferred being direct, ploughing her way through obstacles. She found Elizabeth packing.

"I changed my mind, Mother," Elizabeth said brightly. "I think I need a change, and a change like Rufford."

Bess was dismayed; she looked at the small bag that Elizabeth was packing.

"Is that all you are taking?" Bess asked.

"That's all I shall need," Elizabeth said.

"Men's clothes?" cried Bess, in acute horror.

Elizabeth shrugged her elegant shoulders. Bess thought, *She's had that idea from this queen—her and her men's clothing for riding.* Elizabeth rode astride now, whenever she could. "I think you should take one dress," Bess said in a faint voice.

"What for?" Elizabeth asked. "I hardly care about impressing the duchess of Suffolk; she's a tiresome woman, I don't see how you endure her."

Bess started to reply and held her tongue. Elizabeth's clothes and Elizabeth's actions were her own. Bess had done enough now; it was up to Elizabeth. Bess smiled beatifically. "Wear what you please, my love," she said and tripped off down the hall, wondering what would happen, and now a bit afraid to put another finger in this pie. Elizabeth would take care of it from now on.

By the time they arrived at Rufford the next afternoon it was raining. Bess was tired and wet, Elizabeth was gay and quite dry in her leather boots and hose. She reined in her horse and cried, "Why, it is beautiful, Mother. Completely a romantic image in weathered stone."

In the rain it looked very dreary to Bess. She was anxious only to get inside by a warm fire and change her clothes. But Elizabeth lingered in the hall, making little puddles, and went out to walk along the cloister walls before she came upstairs. Bess heard her in the next room. Elizabeth called, "You brought the portable bath, didn't you, Mother?"

The next day the sun was shining, so Elizabeth rode out, and Bess supervised the readying of guest suites and chambers. Carts piled with featherbeds and quilts and linens and extra cushions arrived, and by nightfall all was ready. And it began to rain again.

It rained all night; on the morning of the seventh it was still damp, and mist wreathed the meadows. Elizabeth looked pale.

"You've ridden too much in the last two days," Bess said. "Stay in bed." *Elizabeth is frail,* Bess thought. *She's the only one of my children whose health I worry over.* "Stay in bed," she repeated, and Elizabeth, sighing, said she would. When Bess looked in on her at noon, she was fast asleep.

Bess fretted all that day. And she didn't sleep too well that night. Turning restlessly in her bed, she thought, *Well, at least the rain has stopped. It is so quiet here, so unearthly quiet.* But in the morning, it was a perfect morning, the sun brilliant, and the air fresh and warm and no wind. Elizabeth took her meager breakfast outside by the fish pond, sitting there in the sun, her long legs crossed, her white, man's shirt open at the neck.

Elizabeth disdained jewelry; she wore one ring, the ring Cavendish had given Bess during her pregnancy with Elizabeth, a cluster of pearls set with rubies; Bess had given it to her on her fourteenth birthday, and she wore it like a wedding ring, always.

277

All morning Bess was nervous. "I hope they arrive by dinner," she kept saying, and it was about eleven o'clock when they heard the distant sound of horses and harness. Bess looked around for Elizabeth, but she was nowhere to be seen. No one could find her; she hadn't taken her horse, so she must be walking.

So Bess greeted her guests by herself. The long line of jolting carts and litters and horsemen hove slowly into view. Both ladies were in the litter. They had finally alighted from it and kissed Bess and exclaimed how glad they were to have arrived and how weary they were, and Kate, the duchess of Suffolk, was already explaining to Bess how she could improve the looks of the hallway, and that she really needed a brilliant rug, there, expensive as they were, rugs, but she, Bess, could afford anything she wanted in the world, Kate continued, laughing, when the duchess of Lennox suddenly turned pale as a ghost and clapped her hand to her breast.

They got her upstairs fast, two servingmen carrying her, and laid her on her bed, while her women fussed and removed her shoes and stuffed pillows behind her and tucked quilts around her. Bess thought, *There's something wrong with her heart!* She breathed shallowly, just as Cavendish had.

"You must stay in bed and not move!" Bess cried.

The duchess leaned back, her face fearful.

Bess took her hand. "I'll take care of you," she promised. "You must not lift a finger!" Then her eyes fell on the duchess' son, Lord Charles Stuart. *Why, he's perfect,* she thought, *for my Elizabeth. Very very tall, very darkly handsome, very very masculine, and with all that he looks intelligent.* Happily Bess tripped upstairs after him and his mother and into the room she had set aside for the duchess.

Charles knelt by the bed, on the other side from Bess, his mother's hand in his.

"Lady Shrewsbury is right, Mother," he said. "Don't move, just rest!"

"I think it would be best if Her Grace were relieved of this much company," Bess said.

Charles agreed. He leaned over and kissed his mother and started for the door, shooing some of the other women

278

before him, including the duchess of Suffolk. Charles went down the wide shallow stairway, following the duchess, and when he reached the bottom step, Elizabeth came in the open doors.

She was about twenty feet from him. As she came closer, he could see the perfection of her face, the elegant grace of her walk, and her body. And when the duchess of Suffolk presented her to him, he heard nothing, not his own name, Lord Charles Stuart, not anything but Elizabeth. Her eyes met his, and she smiled.

"How can I curtsey to you, my lord, in man's clothes?"

He reached for her hand and raised it to his lips. "I like this better," he said. And then, ignoring the duchess of Suffolk as if she didn't exist and was not there at all, he kept hold of Elizabeth's hand and drew her toward the open doors.

"Please show me the gardens."

CHAPTER 11

LATER, the earl would accuse the duchess of Lennox of pretending an illness and keeping Bess in constant attendance at her side. But that was not true, the duchess had a failing heart, the trip had exhausted her, and she lay pale, breathless, dizzy and wan, propped up in her bed, with Bess supervising her diet, a very light diet, with natural purging foods. Her chamber was always kept scrupulously clean, constantly aired. The duchess of Suffolk, a bit bored by all this, kept Bess informed. "You're such a fine doctor, if we stay here much longer, you'll have to learn midwifery."

Bess shot her a long look.

"I try to keep my eye on them, but they disappear," the duchess added.

Bess said, "Kate, my daughter is a perfect young lady, and I trust her perfectly."

"The more fool you," commented the acid-tongued Kate,

"he's a very likely long lad, charming as all the Stuarts."

That night Bess knocked on the door of Elizabeth's room. There was no answer. Bess hesitated, her hand on the latch. Then she drew back. If she accused Elizabeth of anything, Elizabeth would be properly outraged.

The next day, they had been at Rufford four days, it began to rain again. After she had bid the sick duchess a good morning, Bess went down the steps to the paneled, cozy former study of the bishop, and there, within the room, sitting hand-in-hand before the hearth, were Charles and Elizabeth. When Bess came in, they both turned and stood up. One brief look at her daughter's face was enough, and Bess could hear plainly the earl's voice, as he had said, "And when she finds her love, she will go straight into his arms like an arrow." *God's death, she's lain with him!* The knowledge rushed through Bess' head. There couldn't be any doubt, for she had that look in her eyes as they touched: Charles the tenderest adoring look, a secret adoring pride. *I'm going to have heart failure, too,* Bess thought. *My dear lord, what will I do?*

Meantime Elizabeth was saying, "Good morning, Mother," in the sweetest, most loving tones.

"Good morning," Bess choked out. "You're both up early this rainy morning," she continued.

"We got up before dawn and took a long walk in the misty rain. It was beautiful."

"And won't you have anything to eat, my lord?" Bess asked Charles.

"I'm not hungry, Mother, but Charles is," Elizabeth said, sending him another starry glance.

"I can imagine," said Bess, thinking savagely that seduction was hungry work. But then Charles suddenly put his arm around Elizabeth. And holding her thus, tight against him, and ruffling her hair with his hand, he said, "My lady, I am going to ask your permission to marry Elizabeth." He turned Elizabeth toward him, and he said, really to her, "We love each other." There was dead silence. *I'm going to faint,* Bess thought. *Leave it to Elizabeth, that's what I thought! Well, she has done it, and now what are we going to do? What?* The shadow of Elizabeth Tudor stalked into the room, Bess could feel, as though she were right there, the terrible wrath of her sovereign.

"Jesu!" Bess breathed. She hesitated. "My lord," she whispered, "your marriage is a state affair!"

Charles was not perturbed, he simply contradicted Bess. "Indeed not, madam; I think it a truly personal affair."

Bess sank down into the nearest chair. Charles had spoken with all the assurance of his nineteen years. Elizabeth stood proudly at his side. Finally Charles said, gently, as if to soften the intractability of his words,

"My lady, I love your daughter, and I will have no other woman."

"But your mother," Bess said, following Charles down the upstairs corridor, "but your mother, she is not well, my lord!"

"She is well enough to hear me," Charles said, and gave Bess a smile.

"You'll give her another attack!" Bess cried.

Charles shook his head. "No. I won't."

Within her room, the duchess mercifully, was feeling much better that morning. Her heart was beating stronger, it seemed to her, regular and even, and she had no pain.

The duchess had borne eight children. Of those eight, she had but one son, Charles, left to her. Most of her children had died in infancy, but Charles' older brother, Darnley, who had married Mary Queen of Scots, had been murdered. This terrible blow the duchess would never recover from, nor would she sleep without nightmare, and the memory would never give her rest. So when Charles, her only surviving child, her tall, handsome son, came into her room, he knew as well as the duchess that there was nothing she could or would deny him. His peccadilloes she had always largely ignored. Last year she had thought to send him to Cecil, to be schooled in Cecil's household. But the canny Cecil would have none of that terrible responsibility. He had recommended a tutor for Charles, and the duchess had kept Charles with her.

He leaned over the bed and gave his mother a good-morning kiss. She squeezed his hand and sighed at him,

281

lovingly. Charles stood third in line to the throne. And
Mary of Scots was not well, and neither was little James of
Scotland, her young son. Every time the duchess looked at
Charles she saw a king. As tall as her own uncle, Henry
VIII, and so marvelously young!

Charles said, "Oh, Mother, you look so much better this
morning!"

"I am, I am, my dearest Charles."

Without more preamble, then, he proceeded to tell her.
He was in love; he would have no other woman in the
world. And she was eminently suitable.

The duchess said, "Charles, you could marry a princess!"

Charles grinned, the lazy grin that always enchanted her.
"I could, but I shall have no other but Elizabeth Cavendish!"

The duchess could deny him nothing. In the end, she
recovered her own share of the Stuart lazy wit. "God's
death, Charles," she said, "I've gone to the Tower twice
before on matters of love! It seems I'll have another sojourn
there!"

In the chapel of the ancient Abbey, Charles and Elizabeth
were married on the fifteenth of October. Before the ceremony began, Charles asked the priest for permission for
his mother to sit, he established her gently in the front pew
and put a cushion under her feet and gave her a kiss. Then
he took his place at Elizabeth's side.

They repeated their vows, and Bess cried. The three
ladies gave them a wedding breakfast, with the finest of
French wines, which Bess had brought with her. The
shadow of Elizabeth Tudor, the Queen's Majesty, was
banished temporarily from the festive board.

But the earl wasn't absent from Bess' thoughts; not at all.
She felt as though she could almost physically feel the
glowering anger smoldering alongside her. And even
Elizabeth's father. What would Cavendish have thought?
Would he have raised one black eyebrow and reminded her
that what he himself had said about Will Herbert? "It is
an old, old gambit to wed one's daughter to an heir to the
throne."

Bess squirmed. During the breakfast, she suddenly

resolved to be proud and happy while she could, so she laughed, and kissed Elizabeth good-bye, for Charles would have none of Elizabeth's going back to Sheffield, to get clothes, for instance. No, Bess could pack and send her things; she had her very own personal maid with her; Charles would provide her with anything and everything she needed. He would take her to a place of his in Yorkshire and then to his London town house in Hackney.

"Good-bye, good-bye," they called.

But the next day, when the duchesses rode off, everyone was a bit subdued. All the ladies were again pondering the results of their high-handed action, for Charles' marriage was a crown affair and not theirs. Bess rode off alone to Sheffield. She missed Elizabeth, and she felt alone and fearful and uncertain. When she arrived at Sheffield, the great castle hall was empty. She fled upstairs to her own chambers. She had a bath, and she was standing in her little smock when the inner door flew open and banged against the paneling. In the doorway stood the earl. He advanced slowly. "Where, Bess," he asked, "where is Elizabeth?"

CHAPTER 12

IT was late at night. It was cold. It was snowing. Great drifts were forming under the mighty oaks of Sheffield park.

The earl sat at his table, writing. When he lifted his head and glanced at the clock, the hands pointed at four. The very dead of night. He stretched. He felt inexpressibly weary. *Oh, Bess,* he thought. *Bess.* He had finished one page of his letter and drew a fresh sheet.

Although I had no knowledge whatsoever of the matter until it was accomplished— He broke off, startled, as Gilbert burst into the room.

"Father!"

The earl pushed back his chair and stood up.

"Father, it will be soon!"

283

The earl smiled and patted Gilbert on the shoulder. "Don't worry so, Mary is a healthy wench like her mother."

"But come, Father, come!"

The two men went off down the hall. Gilbert led him down to the suite he and Mary occupied, for Mary had come back to Sheffield for the birth of her first child. She had wanted to come home, to the safety of the great castle and all its familiar faces, and she had planned to come home to Bess. But Bess wasn't there. Bess was lodged in the Tower, in London.

There was deep silence in this anteroom. But suddenly the earl and Gilbert heard Mary cry out, and then there was a moment's silence, again. And then there was the cry of a child. Gilbert's eyes filled with tears.

"Oh, Father," he muttered.

The earl patted his shoulder, again. "Congratulations, my boy." He went to the sideboard and poured two generous cups of wine. "Drink deep," he said.

Gilbert did. And now he suddenly bethought himself, *What is the sex of this child?* And while that occupied his mind for a minute, now that he had heard the cry of his first child, the door opened, welcome warmth from Mary's bedroom came in with an aproned nurse, who cried, "My lords! There has been a boy child born this night!"

Mary held her son in her arms while the two men peered down at the tiny red face. "He's a big boy," Mary said proudly.

Gilbert thought he was the tiniest little thing he had ever seen. But Mary must know better than he.

"We are going to name him George," Mary said. "In honor of his grandfather!"

The earl was pleased. But it was impossible for Gilbert's and Mary's thoughts not to fly ahead—*Since Francis, the earl's eldest son, has no sons, is our little red-faced creature the eighth earl of Shrewsbury? Is he the heir to the earldom?*

Shrewsbury was wondering that, too. He was also wondering whether there was an earldom. For the greatest fear of the old landed nobility, with their vast holdings of lands and castles and lesser dwellings, the greatest fear was forfeiture.

Shrewsbury's thoughts were interrupted. Mary said, "Oh, you must write to Mother, my lord!"

The earl said, "Gilbert, we cannot invite one single soul to the christening of little George. In fact, the Queen's Majesty has just written—" He waved a sheet of paper before Gilbert's nose— "that she objects strongly, strenuously and completely, to you and Mary being here at all!"

Gilbert scowled. The whole family was feeling the weight of the queen's massive displeasure. The Talbots were in great disgrace. Thus, the earl continued, "I shall myself christen the child, and young Edward and young George will stand as godparents."

There was no question of taking the baby to the church. Mary quickly converted her small anteroom into a tiny chapel, with bowls of holly and pine branches and candles and a tall table with an open Bible. There the family gathered, and the earl, holding his first grandson, christened and named the baby, and read from the Bible, and asked the Lord to bless and keep this precious child. Mary wept and later hugged the earl and kissed him. "It was beautiful, my lord," she whispered. "Thank you. I thought it was beautiful." She kept hearing in her ears the reading he had chosen:

"And Jesus said, suffer the little children to come unto me, for theirs is the kingdom of heaven. . . . We ask our Lord Jesus, to watch over and keep this child; we christen him George, and the Lord bless him."

Young Edward, his voice breaking a bit, promised that he would guide and teach this child and pray for him.

Everyone in the little room was so moved by the simple ceremony that the earl blew his nose and announced that now they must all drink to the mother, for after all she had had something to do with it.

And Mary wiped her eyes, and tried to smile; the earl had laid the baby in his decorated cradle, and suddenly the baby took charge and let out a long wail.

"Well," said the earl, "that's a lusty cry." He put his arm around young Edward. "You may find, my boy, that your godson will soon be teaching you a few things."

And so, wrote the earl that night to his angry queen, *I christened the child myself, and two of my younger children stood as godparents. No one has had access to this queen, neither Mary nor Gilbert have even seen her. Mary had long planned to have her lying-in at Sheffield, and indeed I appreciated her desire to have her firstborn child born at Sheffield; it is right and proper.*

The castle, which has sheltered us for so very many years, he thought. God, it was lonely without Bess. And what could he say to Elizabeth that had not been said on her behalf? He himself had been so outraged and angry, it had been easy for him to understand how angry Elizabeth had been. *As for the other matter, my wife scarcely knew more than I did, until they stood before her, and Lord Charles claimed he would have no other bride, he could not and would not live without Elizabeth.* He reread the few words. Useless to keep repeating the same words, the same excuses, for Bess' reprehensible conduct.

But he had to get her out of the Tower! She was being questioned daily, he knew. His mind flew back to the first time he had seen her, when he himself had questioned her so relentlessly. Vividly he remembered. *I should have known better than to marry her,* he thought. *I was warned well enough. She will always be in trouble. Always.* What was she saying to her questioners now? He heard she was unrepentant, as she had been that day with him. Standing there, pregnant, shouting back at him. *I should never have married her,* the earl thought, *and yet how much I wish, how much I would crave, a son by her. A lusty son, just like her. Cavendish was lucky.*

The earl sighed, and called his servant. He got into his lonely big bed. *I could use,* the earl thought sleepily, *I could use a pretty compliant woman, who said always, aye, my lord.*

On the seventh of April, 1575 Bess was packing. She was, as Shrewsbury had guessed, completely unrepentant. She had flinched and cried before the earl's wrath, but that was because she was afraid: he had been so coldly and furiously angry with her. To think that she, his wife, could have jeopardized the mighty earldom, the integrity of the name of Talbot, to marry her daughter to royalty! In secret! At one of his own estates!

Before she left London, Bess called on her daughter in Hackney. Elizabeth and Charles had partly escaped the royal anger, but only partly. They had been confined straitly to their home, and it was guarded.

Elizabeth thought that was rather amusing. "It shows she is a virgin queen, Mother," she said gaily. "She didn't seem to realize that all Charles and I wanted was to be alone!"

"I see it has had results," Bess said.

Charles laughed. "Aye. In about four months. Elizabeth would like, my lady, to come to Chatsworth for her lying-in."

Bess was so pleased she couldn't speak for a moment. Then she said, "It will be a great honor, a great pleasure—why, I think it would be the greatest pleasure in the world, my lord."

Charles said, "The Queen's Majesty will receive us next week. I think that if anyone can charm her, it will be your daughter."

Bess thought, *I may have plotted this, but they love each other! They adore each other! They are so happy. If I've spent time in prison, it was worth it.* She hugged them both and kissed them good-bye. Seated in her carriage, she waved.

Now back to Sheffield, she thought. *And what reception shall await me there?*

By the time she reached Sheffield, she was riding, and the carriage was left behind. The park, the giant oaks, were all green with April, and suddenly Bess was so excited at coming home that she galloped up to the great doors and reined in with a flurry of pounding hooves and flying gravel. The earl was standing in the courtyard waiting, and Bess threw her one hand in the air. "I'm home! I'm home!"

He lifted her down from the saddle, her brilliant smile enveloping him, and she threw her arms around him. "Oh, I've missed you so," she cried truthfully. "I've missed you so, my jewel, my love!"

Nothing must do but that she run upstairs as fast as possible to see her new grandson George. Bess held him in her arms and looked across to the earl.

"Isn't he beautiful?" she whispered in awe. She didn't dare kiss him till she had bathed away the travel dust. She

287

held him gently, a little away from her and studied his face. "How intelligent; look at his eyes." She laid him back in his nurse's arms. "I must have a bath," she said.

When she entered her own rooms, Digby and Mrs. Battel both cried and curtsied and fussed around her. The earl shooed them out; he wanted a moment alone with Bess.

"It's been almost four months," he said.

"Aye, I know, but it was worth it."

She shouldn't have said that, she knew it as soon as the words were out of her mouth. "Oh, my love, I didn't mean it the way you are thinking! I meant if you could see Elizabeth. She is so radiant, so happy, so youngly happy, so in love." She came close to Shrewsbury and put her hand in his arm. "I missed you so, I told you that and it was true."

He looked down at her. Then he gathered her into his arms in a close grip. "I missed you so much, Bess, so much."

Bess smoothed back the shaggy hair from his forehead. "You had no dealings with any other wench, I hope," she teased.

"No," said the earl, "but I considered it."

Bess laughed. It was a warning, and she didn't heed it.

Mary Stuart had lived with Bess and the earl for more than six years now, and her very proximity was conspiring to make her a member of the family. Unwanted, deplored, annoying, but always there. There to be watched, waited on, aided in sickness, warded in health, considered, a family burden like the willful uncle, or the black sheep. Sometimes hidden away, sometimes paraded before guests, she was always there. She depended on the earl's meticulous consideration of her plight, political and human, and she depended on Bess for her care. For although Bess could fly out at her in anger, when it came to need, Bess was at her side. Bess, with her practical help. A long time ago, when Mary had writhed on her bed with taut nerves, Bess had said, "I think it would do you good if Kennedy bathed your feet and legs and rubbed them." Now Kennedy did that almost every day for Mary; it soothed her nerves. When Mary was sick, Bess would hurry in, her concern showing plain, her warmth to anyone in need was very evident. Nonetheless, Mary was now very annoyed with Bess.

Hadn't she had the impudence to wed her daughter to Mary's own brother-in-law? Lady Elizabeth Stuart! The daughter of this common redheaded creature was going to bear a child who would be first cousin to her own son! Bess had struck a telling blow to Mary's grandeur.

"Aye," said Bess. "My grandson will be cousin to your son! Elizabeth expects her baby in the late summer!"

Mary clung desperately to her queenly stature; it was all she had left. She said, "Oh, someday I too hope to be a grandmother."

Bess caught the dig, but she replied good-naturedly. "Aye, when you're old enough. Time enough, later."

Mary was a born troublemaker. Every day she prodded the earl, "It is spring, my lord! Please let me walk outside!"

Shrewsbury frowned at her. "The Talbots are in disgrace, madam. Disgrace has fallen upon the whole household. The Queen's Majesty has forbidden walks."

"But it wasn't your fault," Mary said hotly.

The earl said bluntly that Elizabeth thought it was his fault because he hadn't stopped Bess.

"Who could stop Lady Shrewsbury?" Mary inquired.

The earl grunted. It was true but galling that Elizabeth Tudor was more inclined to forgive Bess, whom she admired, than Shrewsbury, who was not the culprit. But Elizabeth kept insisting that he should have kept better surveillance of his willful wife. What kind of man was it who permitted such connivings and royal marriages to go on right under his nose? In one of his own dwellings?

Mary said softly, "My lady is overjoyed at the prospect of a child by this marriage. She talks of nothing else. But you have little George," Mary continued. "I think little George an unusual baby, my lord."

Manlike, the earl rose to Bess' defense. "Bess loves little George as much as I do, madam."

"Oh, I am sure," Mary said. "She doesn't speak of him very often though." That was a lie, but Shrewsbury didn't know it.

Mary was stitching busily on a beautiful petitpoint square that was to encase a pillow for the queen. "I have almost finished this," she said. "When it is done, I pray you will send it to the Queen's Majesty, with a letter asking for per-

289

mission to ride and walk abroad." Shrewsbury nodded and excused himself. He was very annoyed with Bess.

He was more annoyed later that day. "It isn't necessary you go to Chatsworth."

"Why, I must," said Bess. "Elizabeth is expecting her baby in August. She cannot travel too late, she should come in July, at the latest."

"And you must be present when the child is born, I suppose?"

"Oh course!"

"You weren't here when George was born."

Bess looked at him, then dropped her eyes. She sighed.

"You weren't here because you are more concerned with the advancement of your children, because of your soaring ambitions. An earldom is not enough for you now; royalty is glimmering in the distance." Shrewsbury said then, "I have contempt for people who want titles they don't deserve."

"God's death!" Bess was trembling with anger. "They loved each other!"

"You are guilty, Bess," Shrewsbury said calmly. "You connived to bring them together. It is your fault."

"I'm going to Chatsworth now," Bess cried.

"Go, then," the earl said shortly.

"If you loved me," Bess mumbled, "you would tell me to stay."

"I do love you, Bess," he said. "But I want you to love me and put me first. Not your children, not Elizabeth, not a Stuart grandchild, but me."

Bess, very upset and distraught, said that all she wanted was for everybody, everybody in the whole household to be happy and gay! And that she tried to please them all! And she had failed. "Damn the Stuarts," she shouted suddenly.

Shrewsbury grinned. "You are mad, Bess," he said. "But I do love you!"

So Bess stayed at Sheffield till July, and then the whole household journeyed to Buxton for the annual stay at the springs. Mary Stuart had looked forward to the springs since May, counting the days, it was such an outing and holiday for her. But then the earl took Mary back to Sheffield; they didn't dare have Mary at Chatsworth with her brother-in-law. Bess clung to Shrewsbury and hugged him.

"I don't want to leave you, my jewel," she said.

"Then don't," Shrewsbury said implacably.

"Oh, I must," she whispered. "Elizabeth would never forgive me! Mary wouldn't have forgiven me if I hadn't been in the Tower!" Shrewsbury sighed. He kissed her good-bye, and she rode off, away from him.

But when Bess saw Chatsworth, gleaming and glittering like a jewel, she forgot the earl. There was still decorating to be done, and every day she rode over to Hardwick to watch the new wings rise. She felt free. Every day stretched before her, in a shining array of hours, in which she could build and supervise and indulge to the hilt her great passion. When she sat on the grass at Hardwick in the summer afternoon, munching her bread and cheese with a bit of onion and some ale, the sound of hammering was the sweetest music in the world. The smell of paint finer than the most subtle perfume. The smell of new timber was heaven itself. The lumbering carts, with their load of stone, more exciting than the greatest of painting. *Oh,* said Bess to herself, *during these sunny summer days, I am so happy. I don't deserve it. I am so happy.*

But every night she wrote to the earl. Even though she always asked for something, perhaps malt for her workmen's ale, she always sent something, too, such as fresh lettuce, which the earl loved. And he was very good-natured about sending all the stuffs she required, from wood to stone to beef, until he finally added a note to one of his letters. *I find the lettuce I receive the most expensive I ever ate.* Bess laughed when she read it.

Chatsworth thronged with guests, and callers, for everyone wanted to come and pay their respects to Lord and Lady Stuart. Every day when Bess came home, it was like coming home to a party. Frances was there with her new little son Robert and Charles and William came and went with their wives. Bess had no compunction about leaving every morning; they were all grown up, and they were used to having a mother who was busy, and anyway, she was always home at night. One August day she came riding in, and William was in the courtyard. He helped her from the saddle.

"William," Bess said excitedly, "I've found a new plasterer who is a genius. His name is Abraham Smith. And he is a genius."

Charles came clattering down the stairway out into the court. One glance at his face told Bess that Elizabeth's time had come.

"My lady, Mother," Charles began, his eyes wide and fearful.

Bess picked up her skirt and ran.

Elizabeth had talked endlessly about a son just like Charles. She was so in love that all she wanted was a boy, like his father. So when Bess laid her daughter into her arms, she didn't know whether Elizabeth would scream, as people said Anne Boleyn had screamed, or what she would do. Elizabeth, in Bess' eyes, had turned somehow into a royal being, unaccountable to ordinary mortals. But Elizabeth took the baby gently and lovingly and kissed it, and Charles wept. They told Bess in hushed tones they had discussed it and they had a name ready, a beautiful name, picked by both of them. An old name, Arabella. No one knew whence it came; it was like their love for each other, made in heaven. Elizabeth said the four syllables softly, like music.

"The Lady Arabella Stuart," said Bess. "Oh, it is beautiful, and she is beautiful." After all, in these modern times, one needn't be male to rule a kingdom.

CHAPTER 13

ELIZABETH and Charles went back to London in late September; and in October, Elizabeth, in the queen's chamber, talked alone with the queen, everyone else in the big, beautiful room being out of earshot.

Elizabeth was dressed in a tawny colored velvet, and she wore one single magnificent diamond pendant at her throat, which Charles had given her when Arabella was born. It was an ancient family piece.

Elizabeth, leaning forward, her huge eyes fastened on the queen, asked the Queen's Majesty to tell her in detail of all the training and education she had received. And smiling gently, the queen answered every question. Elizabeth's honest admiration for the queen's brilliant mind pleased the queen, naturally; she could never receive too much assurance of love and pride from her subjects. Elizabeth gave this so willingly that the queen was more than mollified, she was pleased. Later in the month word was received at Sheffield that the stringent care of Mary Stuart could be relaxed; she could ride and she could walk out in the great park.

"That Elizabeth!" said Bess proudly. "She can charm anyone!"

"That Elizabeth," said the earl crossly, "and you, my wife, are responsible for the whole contretemps." When he thought of the sleepless nights when he had dozed off only to dream that the great earldom had been forfeited to the crown, he shivered.

He had been away for ten days, riding from one great dwelling place to another, overseeing the finances and talking to tenants, and getting away from the parcel of women. Frances was at Sheffield with little Bess and her baby son, Robert.

"And Robin is a most remarkable baby," Bess said. He looked like Cavendish, Bess thought. Everytime she held him in her arms and crooned little songs to him, she told him that his grandfather would be very, very proud of him! Being only six months old, he just looked at her with a glint in his dark eyes, and Bess would squeeze him and laugh.

Mary and Gilbert had gone back to London. London was gay, and so was Gilbert. He wrote often, detailing all the court gossip, who was in love with Leicester, that the queen was kinder to him and had actually flipped him on the cheek, teasingly, last week, and that young George was growing bigger every day. He was ten months old. Both the earl and Bess talked endlessly of these children, and worried too, for the first two years of their lives were the most dangerous; there was so much sickness that could come in the night and snuff out a tiny life! Bess wrote endless letters to Mary and Elizabeth about the care of their infants; the necessity of cleanliness, clean servants and warmth, and good, good food.

With the rules of Mary's care relaxed, the whole castle prepared for Christmas, and everyone in the family who could come did come. Shrewsbury had always been a fine patron of the drama, and his players were preparing entertainments. Mary, with all this talk of children, had sent her son presents, including a pony; and when she received word back from Scotland that he was not permitted to accept them, she was stricken and woebegone. The earl felt very sorry for her, and so she was allowed to witness the plays and be part of all the festivities.

"You have her fairly well in hand, like a good falcon," Bess said.

It seemed to Bess that Mary was plotting less; under the earl's eye she was quieter.

"Even her dress," Bess continued, "I note that she wears plain gray wool, now, most of the time, like a nun. She has retreated in a way, but under your wing, my lord."

The earl thought, *She is encased in a silken web, like a cocoon, she can see through it, but not escape. She cannot escape because of me.* And yet she reached out to try to hold his hand. He said, aloud, "It's a damned difficult position, Bess."

Bess nodded.

Then the earl said strongly, "She needs you too, Bess. Never forget we are both her caretakers."

This was very important, and he didn't know whether she perceived it or not. "I take care of her because it is my duty, Bess. And yours, too," he added.

"Aye, but I hate it, and you don't."

Shrewsbury didn't like that answer.

"You feel sorry for her."

"She has just had a gift returned from her only child."

"She left her only child when he was six months old," Bess snapped, "to marry her husband's murderer! She

294

wanted Bothwell between her legs so bad she gave up a kingdom, and worse, her only child!"

Bess knew he didn't like her language. She turned away, and when she was by herself in her room, she sat down at her table, leaning her chin on her hand. She thought, *Oh Aunt, what shall I do about this damned queen? She's ruining our lives! I know what you'd say, Aunt,* Bess thought. *You'd say, "Think, Bess! How fortunate you are, beside this imprisoned queen, who is suffering for her selfishness; do as your husband says, treat her like a charge, like a duty."*

Bess said aloud, "I'll try, Aunt. I'll try."

But when she tried to explain to the earl what she had decided was the right course for her, he said, "But, Bess, you can't forget that she is a human being."

"I can," said Bess. "I must; that's the difference between you and me."

"No, Bess," he said, "It's not. You are full of warmth and love. That's what's causing your problem."

And problem it was, for them. Yet during the coming months, it would solve itself through unwanted solution; there was tragedy ahead; it would serve to bring the earl and Bess close, and Mary would be almost forgotten between them.

The first herald of disaster was a lathered horse and courier from Jane, who had been at Sheffield and had gone to visit her mother in the spring.

"Mother is sick!" Bess cried. "I must go!"

"Of course," Shrewsbury said, and made all the arrangements, in his usual precise manner. A litter for Bess, in case of inclement weather and all the gifts of food and drink the great castle could produce.

Bess set forth early the next morning. When she came along the hall toward her mother's room, Lady Leche could hear the quick click-clack of her heeled boots. *It is Bess,* she thought, *no one else walks quite that way—lightheartedly yet purposefully going forth to meet life head on.* She smiled as Bess opened the door.

"I knew it was you, my love, by your walk," she said.

Bess thought, *Oh, she doesn't look too sick; she looks as lovely as always.* Her blue eyes were enormous, the heavy lids adding mystery to her thinned cheeks. Lady Leche's bedroom was pretty and her comforters and quilts were a blaze of color and luxury. Bess was pleased to see her so well taken care of; she sniffed, the way she did when she entered Mary's rooms.

"It even smells good in here, and you look as beautiful as ever!" She leaned over and kissed her mother.

"You can't talk with her long, it's her heart," Jane had warned her.

So Bess excused herself, after just a few minutes, to get washed and into another dress. She closed the door gently behind her. Jane was waiting for her, to show her her room.

"Mother is astonishing," Bess said. "She must be over seventy and she looks beautiful. The bones of her face are perfect."

Jane smiled at Bess. "You look just like her, Bess," she said. And Bess shook her head; she didn't look like her mother, at all. Anyway the important thing was her mother's health.

"Just what is the matter, Jane? How does it affect her?"

"Severe pain," Jane said, "in her chest and sometimes in her lower back." Jane looked very white when she said that. Bess stopped in the middle of taking off her doublet; half unbuttoned, she stood facing Jane.

"It is serious, then?"

"Very," said Jane flatly.

"But she's never been sick in her life."

"Aye. And isn't that fortunate, Bess?"

Lady Leche died three weeks later. When Bess returned to Sheffield she was dressed in black. The earl gathered her into his arms. "I'm so sorry, my dearest love," he whispered. "I'm so sorry."

"It's a turning point," Bess said. "Mother is dead, and I am getting older."

"So am I, None," the earl said.

"I am beginning to realize that I am mortal," Bess added. But then the earl laughed and said, "Oh, no, Bess. Not you."

Bess looked askance at him.

"You don't look a bit different from the first day I ever saw you," he said, in some wonder. "It must be my lovemaking," he added.

Bess was thoughtful. "Do you suppose there's something wrong with me?"

"Whatever it is, I approve," the earl said.

But the next blow in December was entirely unexpected. The letter from Elizabeth came as an ordinary letter, only the news it contained was so shattering that at first Bess didn't believe it. She read the letter again, and then she looked at Jane and the earl and said, "Lord Charles Stuart died last week."

She said the words flatly, unemotionally, and Jane cried, "Oh, no! It cannot be!"

Bess said, "He was just twenty-one."

The earl came over to Bess, who was sitting straight and stiff in her chair. He got her a glass of wine. "Drink this," he said, watching her.

Suddenly Bess began to sob. "My poor child, my poor child," she cried over and over. "He was sick only three days! He died in the night, while Elizabeth watched. There wasn't time to send for me or Jane. There wasn't time; it was so quick."

"Oh, Bess, oh, Bess," Jane kept saying over and over.

Bess still sat there in her chair, swallowing her sobs and biting at her lip. Shrewsbury handed her his handkerchief. Finally, Jane asked timidly, "But the funeral, Bess? Shouldn't we go to London? Shouldn't we—"

Bess cut her off. "It's all over, Jane. All over. It all happened so quickly."

Elizabeth wrote again two days later. She was very firm. She would not come home, nor should anyone come to London. She and little Arabella were trying to set their lives straight, without their beloved father and husband. They were all right. They needed time alone, even at Arabella's tender age, Elizabeth thought the child needed safety and her mother's continual presence.

The earl read Elizabeth's letter. He laid it down. He said, "She is more like you than I thought. Let her alone, Bess. She knows what she wants, and no one can force her."

297

But the thought of Elizabeth alone in London with her toddling daughter kept Bess fretting until the earl lost patience.

"Don't try to tell her what to do. No one can tell you what to do."

"Well, then don't try to yourself!" snapped Bess.

In the spring, Gilbert and Mary arrived, with little George, who was two. He couldn't say grandmother, he called Bess Lady Danmode. She adored him. The earl was restless and decided to ride out for two weeks and make a tour of inspection. Bess said, "While you're gone, I'm going to move over to the manor lodge and refurbish it; it needs it sorely."

Shrewsbury looked up from his accounts. "I can't afford it."

Bess snorted. "The chairs are falling apart. You're finishing up a huge house, and you—"

"It has always been the custom of the earls of Shrewsbury to build another house." The earl had almost completed the construction of a new mansion called Worksop. "I do as the Talbots have always done."

"A pack of hounds," Bess said.

"And I've spent thousands on Chatsworth, too. Thousands."

"You have not. It's my money."

"Your money! And you've furnished Chatsworth with dozens and dozens of objects from Sheffield, from Bolsover, from Rufford! Everything you see that is pretty or valuable—it's whisked off to Chatsworth!"

"Oh, go to hell," Bess said.

Shrewsbury raised his head from the ledger he was studying. It didn't help matters that he was reading a list of the goods Mary Stuart had required and got from him. Three hundred pounds of goods. Buckram, damask, canvas, sheeting, live quails in cages, vinegar, paper, hempseed, comfits, sugar works, and that damned French wine, hogsheads of it, for Mary and her household still refused to drink any ales or beer. When he spoke to Bess, he was so angry he didn't bother to swear.

"Don't use your common language here in my dwelling!"

298

Bess got to her feet. "You know what you are?" she asked. "You're a fart! And what's worse, you're a stinkless fart! Too proper to be human!"

She marched to the door and slammed it.

In a flurry of passion and anger, she moved Mary Stuart over to Turret House and established herself in the manor lodge. And since it was only about a mile or so from the castle, she could hear the next morning the noise of the departure of the earl, who galloped off in a cloud of dust with thirty-five retainers.

"I'm glad you're gone," Bess shouted from the garden of the lodge, even though he couldn't possibly have heard her.

She set to work immediately. The upholsterers had already been summoned; she hadn't told Shrewsbury that. When they arrived, Bess set them to work; there was a whole crew of them. By nightfall a great deal had been accomplished, and Bess was pleased. Many chairs had been re-covered, with needlepoint and embroidery done by Bess and Jane and other embroiderers, even though Bess always told the earl that she actually employed steadily only one embroiderer. But of course they were not finished. She gave orders they were to be put up for the night. Since there was not as easy accommodation at the lodge, Bess sent them over to the castle. In an hour, John Dickenson, the keeper of the earl's wardrobe, appeared. Dickenson had had strict orders from his master.

"These men will not be permitted to remain overnight," he informed Bess.

Bess said, "God's death, fellow! Do you dare to give me orders?"

John Dickenson blanched, but he was more afraid of Shrewsbury than he was of Bess.

"His lordship issued strict orders."

And he had.

"I have sent them away on his lordship's orders. I sent them away an hour ago."

Bess advanced on him in helpless fury. "Get out!" she screamed. "Get out of here! You little ball-less turd, you! Get out!"

Dickenson ran.

He had no sooner showed his heels than from the nearby Turret House, where Mary and her staff were lodged, came cries and screams and wailings.

"My God, what is happening?" Bess shouted as she ran through the walled second garden of the lodge and flung herself into the garden surrounding Turret House.

Bess paused for just a moment as the garden door banged against the wall. Mary was there! She was safe! She was sitting in the garden, by the little pond, for it was a warm evening, and Mary loved to be outside and would never go in until dark, for her nine o'clock dining hour.

It's the Tower of Babel, Bess thought. From each window of the round house Mary's servants and ladies were hanging out, and each seemed to be speaking a different tongue, French, English or Scottish. Bess tried to make out what was happening, and she ran across the grass to Mary.

Mary cried, "I've been robbed! My jewelry! My jewelry!"

Bess didn't care whether Mary had lost every jewel in her box as long as she was safe. Shrewsbury would never forgive her if something happened to Mary in his absence. The thought made Bess angry. After all, why should she be held to account about this queen? But still some sense had to be made out of this, for the earl also fastidiously abhorred anyone's losing anything in one of his own dwellings; he would be outraged, that Mary had been robbed under his roof. And he'd blame Bess.

Bess said, "Madam, just what has happened?"

Mary's ladies had ceased shouting from the windows and had streamed down into the garden again. This was the tale: that one of them had gone up to Mary's chamber to get her a knitted throw, and when she had entered the room, Mary's jewel box was open and some fine, fine pieces were missing!

Bess said, "Well, madam, you know that within Turret House there are none but your own train."

Mary digested this. "Someone else must have got in. Your upholsterers, for instance."

When Bess heard this accusation of her hardworking upholsterers, she denied it instantly. "They are honest and good; they were under my eye the whole time, anyway."

"You spent the whole day with upholsterers?" Mary

smiled at her pityingly, as though if she had, she was a fool.

"Madam," Bess said dangerously, "I spend whole weeks with my plasterers! We shall have to search everyone in Turret House."

"I forbid it," Mary said. "I trust my people."

She did. And she always had treated her servants very, very well. They loved her. Bess frowned. It was a puzzle. Then she saw the answer. "You may forbid it, madam, but I am in charge here. I shall order a search."

"It will be in vain," Mary said. Then she rose to her feet. Her legs were swollen, and she stood gingerly. "I forbid a search!" She had suddenly realized a search meant the disrobing of her women and maids. Her mind recoiled from such indignity to her own train, not ordered by her. "Madam, I forbid your guards to touch my women and servants!"

Bess was about to shout back that it would be done forcibly then, if they didn't consent. But she didn't. She thought, *Oh, it's not worth a fight, a few jewels that aren't mine anyway.* She threw out her hands just like Cavendish and used one of his expressions. "Christ's blood, madam, if you don't want your jewels back, I shan't quarrel with you." She turned and left the garden. *Let them all wail now and count the precious jewels and find out exactly what was missing.* She was sick of the sight and sound of them. *I'll leave,* she thought. But she didn't dare. If she left Mary alone, the earl would be angry enough to—to what? Bess wondered. *I can't leave,* she thought. *The truth of it is I don't dare. And I let her win this fight. It will lull her into security,* Bess thought. *Just wait till the next one.*

She was back in the lodge with the half-finished chairs, standing around forlornly. She said aloud, "But I won't be here when you come back, Shrewsbury! I won't be here. You can have your castle and your precious queen. All to yourself!"

Gilbert rode over to Bolsover castle the day his father was leaving there and coming back to Sheffield.

"My lady Mother has left," he said.

Shrewsbury looked at Gilbert in true and helpless amazement, and he looked so unhappy that Gilbert blurted, to help soften the blow, "She did say for you to come to Chatsworth, if you wished."

The earl was now so suddenly angry with Bess that his face grew white and his eyes blazed. Gilbert stepped back and away.

I, come to Chatsworth! he thought. *I've come to hate Chatsworth, the very name.* His jaw set, he growled out that Mary was thus now alone, and the earl started shouting orders: They must leave immediately for Sheffield.

Gilbert wrote to Bess. He knew his father would not.

After we had mounted, Gilbert wrote, *he said, and I was surprised that he confided it to me, he said, "Is her malice such that she would not tarry one night, for my coming? I fear the effect on the household. All the house will discern her feelings against me by her departure before my coming. Gilbert, what quarrels you and Mary have, keep them secret from your household."* *Then later, when I reminded him you have said to come to Chatsworth, he said, "Her going away gives me small cause to go to Chatsworth. Gilbert, you know how often I have cursed the building of Chatsworth for want of her company, but you see she cares not for my company, by going away."* *Then later he said to me, "I would not have done this to her for five hundred pounds!"*

Bess laid down the letter. *He is worried about money, too,* she thought, *or he wouldn't have used that analogy.* Then she turned the page and read on.

But George rejoiced greatly in my lord's coming, as I could not have believed, if I hadn't seen it myself. George is very well, thank God.

The letter was dated August 1. Bess tried to blot the earl out of her mind. She was beginning to feel guilty. *I should not have left him.* She thought of him there, at Sheffield, alone. But instead of going home, she went to Hardwick and spent a week; she returned to Chatsworth on the eleventh of the month. At five o'clock in the morning a rider with the badge of the Talbot pounded on the lodge gates of Chatsworth, rousing the sleepy gateman.

Bess ripped open the seal of the letter he carried. Shrewsbury's distinctive scrawl leaped out at her. *None, come home. George died last night.*

302

Bess cried out in acute and tragic pain. That darling, gifted boy. And she hadn't been there. She had deserted them. She pressed the letter to her cheek.

"Oh, my love, my jewel, I'm so sorry," she whispered.

CHAPTER 14

BESS had made such a great success of Buxton Springs that literally the whole of the realm happily journeyed there, the great and the small. Leicester himself, the great earl, thought them so beneficial he came every summer that he could and then proceeded to Chatsworth for a week. The Queen's Majesty wrote to Bess: *Being given to understand from our cousin of Leicester how honorably he was lately received and honored by you, our cousin the countess, at Chatsworth, and how his diet is supervised by you at Buxton's, I suggest, seeing his growing fat, that on festival days, as befits a man of his quality, you allow him for his dinner the shoulder of a wren and for supper the leg of a same.*

Bess laid down the letter. "She loves him," she said to the earl.

But the next letter from the queen was not so happily received. Bess had thrown herself into the rebuilding of old Hardwick Hall and had decided to mask the two old wings —she and her daughter Elizabeth had decided this on one of the girl's visits, and Elizabeth had sketched out two tall masking walls and graceful towers. The costs were soaring. The earl's great project at Worksop—the new mansion—was almost complete. Turret House—with its enclosed stone staircase leading to Mary's beautifully decorated round chamber and its flat roof for sunning and taking the air—was famous. Seeing the Shrewsburys were so wealthy, the queen thus wrote and cut the allowance for Mary's diet almost in half, reducing it to thirty pounds a week.

Bess said only, "I'll manage."

In three weeks Mary wrote to Elizabeth that she was starving. The queen then reprimanded Shrewsbury; and the earl, waving the letter in Bess' face, received the reply that Mary needed to diet anyway, she was becoming stout.

"You take everything so seriously, my lord," Bess said gaily. "She's truly not starving. There just isn't enough money for fancy confections with almonds, et cetera," said Bess over her shoulder, trotting away to find Gilbert, with whom she was going riding.

"Come back here!" roared Shrewsbury, and Bess turned in surprise. "When I try to talk to you, you always turn your back, and—"

Bess said, "But you knew I was going out with Gilbert. We planned it yesterday when it was raining." She paused. "I must get out once in a while—you know that!" Unrepentant, she went out the door. Shrewsbury, fuming, thought she acted as though he were her jailer and that she was forever trying to escape from him, while his true prisoner, Mary Stuart, was pleased and delighted when he appeared. He now went up to see Mary, who was back in her quarters at Sheffield. She was watching at the window as Bess and Gilbert and Elizabeth rode out.

"Where is my little darling, Arabella?" she asked the earl.

"She's having her portrait painted," the earl said.

"Her mother and grandmother are out, I see," Mary said sadly.

Mary had fallen again from her horse and hurt her back, and Shrewsbury was afraid to let her ride. Now impelled by pity for her, he said, "I'll have a carriage built for you."

Mary turned and smiled so sweetly and came over to him and put her hand on his arm. "Oh, thank you, my lord," she whispered. "Thank you!"

Elizabeth and Arabella were staying at Sheffield for a visit; so also were Gilbert and Mary, Francis, and two of the Cavendish males; it seemed to Shrewsbury that his dwellings were always crowded with Cavendishes, laughing, boisterous, leading Gilbert astray, to say nothing of Edward and George, if they were home. The Cavendishes swarmed over and around Bess and him like bees. *He never had Bess alone,* he thought, *but he had Mary Stuart.* She clung to him and clung to every word.

Bess brushed his protestations aside. "How would we endure it, if we didn't have our families here?"

"They're always here!"

"Elizabeth is going back to Chelsea next week," Bess said. For Elizabeth refused to live with them; she insisted on her own place in London with Arabella. Gilbert refused also, insisting on living in London, too; and when the earl's town house in London became vacant, he moved in. He and Bess designed stained-glass windows to be inserted into the dwelling. When Shrewsbury got the bill, he was outraged.

"We told you about it," Bess said in defense of Gilbert.

"You did not!" shouted Shrewsbury, throwing down the bill on his table. "Charles must have suggested this to Gilbert. You and your brood are beggaring me!"

Gilbert said placatingly, "Lord Leicester thinks the new windows are beautiful, Father."

"Let him pay for them then!"

But later, when they were alone, he said to Bess, "Oh, None, what is happening to us?"

"It's because of this damned queen," Bess said sturdily. "This damned queen! How can normal people live with her? We must get rid of her! We've warded and watched her for eight years!" She was silent then, thinking. *Eight years, and it's made us prisoners, too.*

"She's our duty," Shrewsbury muttered.

"Damn duty!" Bess cried. "We've done enough!" But she knew that his deep sense of responsibility had allowed Mary Stuart to capture him in this oblique way. She was his charge, placed there by fate and his queen, and she was dependent on him.

"Well," said Bess, "this queen has been the death of many men, so be careful, my lord."

The relations between her and Mary had grown steadily worse. Mary, with her sweet air of martyrdom, her plain gray gowns, her eternal stitching, and the lugubrious mottos that always appeared on her embroidery.

"En ma fin est ma commencement," Bess jeered. "How *tragique!"*

305

"She is a tragic figure," Shrewsbury said.

Bess made a rude noise. "Go weep along with her, then," she said and stamped out. Then she stuck her head around the door. "But she has you, after all! She has you!"

In March that year, 1578, Elizabeth's mother-in-law, the duchess of Lennox, had a tete-à-tete dinner with Leicester; she wined and dined the great earl in the manner to which he had become accustomed. He left her about ten o'clock, and an hour later Lady Lennox collapsed and died before midnight. Of course, the great earl's enemies said gleefully he had poisoned her.

"Of course, he didn't," Bess said, defending Leicester, whom she liked. "She had a weak heart, I know that well enough."

But now Elizabeth was left alone in London without the comforting presence of Arabella's other grandmother. Bess wanted her to come home.

The earl shuddered at the prospect, for Elizabeth was as extravagant as the rest of the Cavendishes, to say nothing of his own son, Gilbert, who spent money like water. And Elizabeth had a train of servants and tutors and maids for herself and Arabella, who was now, since the duchess' death, directly in line to the throne. He sighed with relief when Elizabeth refused to come, except to visit.

Nonetheless, the great duchy of Lennox was left vacant; of course, it belonged to Arabella, in direct line it belonged to her. Even Shrewsbury, with his strict eye for proper procedure, avowed that indeed it did belong to Arabella Stuart, three years old. One of the Shrewsburys should go and give battle to the Queen's Majesty, and urge Arabella's just and proper claim.

Elizabeth herself was aware of the need for petitioning the queen. She did so, she sought help from Leicester; and all the family talked of nothing but Arabella's rightful claim. Mary Stuart grew sick of it, and then plunged in, too, and left the duchy to Arabella in a new codicil to her will.

"It's not worth the paper it's written on," Bess said contemptuously.

"You never know, Mother," Henry said, looking portentous and stroking his red beard.

"Henry, you've lost your brains," Bess snapped. She gave him a sudden sharp glance. "Don't let this queen take you in, Hal," she added, warningly.

"Mother, you never know," Henry repeated.

Bess said, "Don't keep saying something so stupid! You've been around this queen for so long, you forget she's dangerous. You want to lose your worthless head, Hal?"

The earl lost patience. "Stop quarreling!" he roared. "Stop bickering, and do something!"

Charles and William laughed, but Henry said placatingly, "My lord Father, why don't you go to London to plead Arabella's cause? It would be best in your hands."

"Such flattery, my lord," Charles said. He had risen and poured some wine, which he tossed off, and he commented, "This isn't the finest of French wines, Mother. This is inferior stuff." He made a face.

Shrewsbury roared again, "It offends your palate, no doubt?"

Charles, unrepentant, bowed. "It surely does, my lord. Anent the discussion, however, before we lose track of the subject, I think our lady Mother should go to London."

"Aye, Mother," William said. "The Queen's Majesty truly admires and likes Mother, no matter if she did wed Elizabeth to Charles Stuart. And Leicester adores her!"

"Aye," said Gilbert, chiming in.

The earl glanced at his son with distaste. "All of you go to bed," he ordered. "Your lady Mother and I will decide." With enormous impatience he paced the room while William and Charles kissed their mother, bade her good-night, reminded her about the wine. Then all four of them stood in the doorway, and Bess said sweetly, "My blessings go with all of you, my dearest sons." She smiled at them so dazzlingly and heaved a great sigh of pride and love. The door closed, and the earl could hear them all striding off down the hall like a herd of cattle, there seemed to be so many of them.

"God's death!" he muttered. "They're driving me insane. Why the devil did you have so many children? And why are they always underfoot?"

"They're not," cried Bess.

"Well," said Shrewsbury, more quietly, "perhaps they are right. You should go to London."

"No, my lord," Bess said, "I don't believe they're right. I think you should go."

But the Queen's Majesty wouldn't permit it. First, she sent word that she would receive the earl; then she contradicted herself and gave orders he could not come, because of Mary Stuart. In the end it was Bess who rode off to London, in October, to do battle for her granddaughter and her beloved daughter.

The court was at Richmond because of the plague in London. There was no room for visitors. So the earl of Leicester found two rooms for Bess. And in some magnificence, with bulging jewel cases and bags full of beautiful clothes, plus Mrs. Battell and Digby, Bess moved into the quarters of the great earl and made herself at home.

But there was something much, much bigger at stake here than the duchy of Lennox, and no one realized it more than Bess. So, when the Queen's Majesty, all aglitter with jewels, her red hair piled in curls and the great golden eyes gleaming, told Bess that she had taken the little Arabella under the protection of the crown, under her own protection, Bess didn't disagree. She pointed out that Arabella was an unusually brilliant, healthy child. She was being tutored in the same manner that the Queen's Majesty herself had been. Next year she might begin a bit of Latin, for instance.

"My daughter Lennox," said Bess, "is devoting her life itself to the Lady Arabella, as Your Majesty knows."

The queen agreed to a grant of five hundred pounds to Arabella, and two hundred to Elizabeth, her mother. The queen and Bess than exchanged one direct glance, and Bess knew it was useless to protest that this was not enough, for the queen would simply remind her that she, Bess, was the wealthiest woman in England. That understood, then, there was the matter of Lady Lennox's jewels. This was also a very difficult question, for there was doubt as to the whereabouts of the jewels, and furthermore, it must be remembered that the young king of Scots himself was the grandson of Lady Lennox, the same as Arabella.

God's death! Bess thought. *I'm playing a game of chess lacking a king, so I've already lost.* No, the hope was that the Queen's

Majesty would come to like and trust the little Arabella as she matured. That was the big hope, and it lay truly in the hands of the child. *What will she grow into?* Bess wondered as she made ready for bed. *Who will she be? A great queen, a brilliant gifted woman, like the Queen's Majesty herself? What a pity,* Bess thought, candidly admitting to herself, *what a pity there is no child, no issue, by* that *splendid strain. But what if, by some mysterious alchemy, little Arabella has a bit of it, enriched by the Cavendish and Hardwick strength and doggedness? Is Arabella going to be a queen?*

Bess was not despondent. Much was going well. The devil with the jewels of the duchess of Lennox. The true jewels were Elizabeth and Arabella. Propped in bed, the candles burning, Bess pondered what she had accomplished. She had prodded little of material value from the Queen's Majesty. She had accomplished something more: She had won, once more, the admiration and liking of her queen. Happily, she sipped her wine and heard in the distance the arrival of Leicester. Doors banged, voices rose and fell, and then suddenly the great earl himself appeared, in slippers, with a servant carrying wine and cakes. In the next room his musicians began to play softly.

Digby and Mrs. Battel left on a waved command. A chair was placed for the earl by Bess' bed. The doors, of course, were left wide open, so from their position at the wide doors both ladies could see into the room, but they could not hear what was said.

"Ah," said the earl, stretching out long legs, "it is good to talk with you, Bess."

They understood and admired each other; both were supreme opportunists. They began to speak candidly of Mary Stuart.

"When she first arrived in the realm, I was perfectly willing to see her remain," Leicester said.

Bess, speaking rapidly and low, told him in detail how Mary plotted and how only Shrewsbury was able to control and watch her. "But it is too grave a responsibility for us to do this forever," Bess ended. "God's death, my lord, imagine the burden! There are times when I'd like to poison her!"

309

Leicester committed himself by pursing his lips, and nodding, then smiling slightly. Their eyes met. Bess said, "Not under my roof, my lord."

Leicester grinned. "A pity," he observed, thoughtfully. "Bess," he said, then, positively, "she cannot go on living indefinitely; I thought she was a thorn; more and more I perceive she is a dagger."

Bess said truthfully, "Not under Shrewsbury's care."

But Leicester shook his head. Walsingham was pressing him daily with the reports of his spies here and abroad. "She is a dagger, poised at the heart of the Queen's Majesty."

Bess saw he truly believed it. She didn't know whether she did or not, she knew Mary too well, and she deemed her incompetent. But Bess had drunk a lot of wine. "I hate her," she said. "I hate her. But, my lord, at the same time, I feel sorry for her!"

When Bess returned to Sheffield, she was careful not to betray Leicester and say bluntly that he would be delighted to see Mary poisoned. Instead, she told the earl that Leicester, Walsingham, and all of the principal members of the privy council would look the other way if Mary should die and were convinced she was becoming more and more of a danger as each day passed.

The earl had understood this himself; the reduction of Mary's diet from fifty-two pounds to thirty told him which way the winds were blowing. What Bess didn't understand was that it bound him even closer to his royal prisoner, for now the earl felt deep and sure in his heart that he was the keeper of her very life itself. And finally, one night, he said as much after a long argument.

"But without me, they would kill her."

"Let them," said Bess. "Let them."

"No," said Shrewsbury. "No."

CHAPTER 15

ELIZABETH, although she refused to live with Bess and the earl and maintained her house in London, nonetheless visited often; and she and her mother became closer and closer. During the next years they flung themselves into the rebuilding of Hardwick and the layout of its gardens, which decended down the sloping valleys to the lake and river. Flowerbeds bloomed all through the valley until they comprised acres and acres. For now Bess was so wealthy in land that the fat cattle and sheep could graze far, far from the dwellings themselves.

Rare plants were ordered from distant lands. And when the two women weren't at Hardwick, they were at Chatsworth or Worksop, spending the earl's money to improve his own gardens, his own houses. Bess was very proud of Worksop, for she had taken over its building almost entirely. The accounts were sent home to Sheffield to the earl, who would read in Bess' own hand, *Changed mind, changed the stairwell, and added another light to the windows.* And *Ordered a new gaming table for Chatsworth, engraved in fives at the corner.*

The earl could almost hear Bess' voice. "I love fives, they're so sturdy and reliable. Five, ten, fifteen, twenty!"

But she was not here at Sheffield. No, Mary was here. The earl wearily shoved back his chair and decided to take Mary out in her carriage.

But one day, when Bess was with him, they received a letter from Elizabeth; and when Bess finished reading it, she handed it to him, looking surprised and a little shocked. For Elizabeth had written simply that she was closing the London house and coming home. It was the late fall of 1581.

For a week Bess had recurrent feelings of disquiet and

311

dread. To dispel them, she occupied herself in the decoration of a huge suite for Arabella and Elizabeth. Elizabeth's bed was draped in green and white brocade. But all week, as she waited, she was irritable and edgy. "I'm afraid something is wrong," she would cry. Then, "But she is only twenty-seven!"

And when Elizabeth climbed from her gilded carriage, Bess' whole body stiffened in alarm and fear. Elizabeth was suddenly and painfully thin. Her beautiful face was white and drawn, shadowing even her indestructible beauty. Bess was frozen with fear and terror.

"My love, my love," she whispered, drawing Elizabeth close in her arms. "Oh, my love, you are ill!"

Elizabeth's eyes filled with tears. "Aye, mother. I'm afraid I am."

"It's the long journey," Bess said. "It's the journey, my dearest. I'll put you right to bed, and you'll get better. With me and your Aunt Jane! I'll send for Jane! She will come, my love. She will come."

Elizabeth tried to smile. But what she said terrified Bess. She sounded just like her father. She said, "Mother, I am afraid I am going to die."

Elizabeth ached with pain in every gland in her body. The doctors could give her laudanum, but it rendered her unconscious; she would shake her head and then finally give in. Jane and the earl and Bess took turns, during the late fall, by her bed. They promised to care for and look after Arabella in exactly the way that Elizabeth had laid down for them, to follow the rules, which were so important. Her sister Mary came. Mary was carrying another child, but Elizabeth was too sick to see it, and no one told her. Mary, calm and competent, told her sister she would love and comfort Arabella as she would the dearest of her own children. The words made Mary think of her little dead son, George. She put her head down onto Elizabeth's hand, and Elizabeth could feel the tears she shed.

"I vow it, my dearest, dearest sister," Mary said.

When Elizabeth died, in January 1582, the earl was fearful for Bess' sanity. She shut herself in her room. It reminded Jane of when little Temperance had died. Fran-

312

tic, the earl wrote to the queen that he was taking Bess—and Mary, of course—to Chatsworth, because his wife was so inconsolable. It didn't help.

"The memory of my beautiful, beloved daughter will follow me in each of my houses," Bess wept. "Nowhere, nowhere, never can I find consolation for my grief."

Shrewsbury lifted her from her bed. She struggled. He carried her into the hallway. Trembling with passion and tears, she tried to fight him; and when he set her on her feet, she pulled away and tried to run back into her room. He caught her arm and jerked her around, put one arm around her waist and literally dragged her to an open doorway.

"Look there!" he commanded. "Look! While you cower in your room weeping!"

Little Arabella also lay on her canopied bed. Face down. Supine, a handkerchief balled in one little fist.

"Arabella," said the earl softly.

The child stirred. She turned her head.

"Ar'bella" the earl repeated. He said the contraction of her name tenderly, lovingly.

"Aye, my lord?"

"You miss your mother so much, do you not, my little Ar'bella?"

"Oh, God," Bess whispered. She stood stock still. And then suddenly she ran to the bed and gathered the child in her arms. "Oh, my dearest darling," she said, "I love you! I love you so! My little love! Come weep with me, and we shall try to comfort each other!"

Holding the child tight, Bess crooned over her granddaughter, until the earl, satisfied, left them together.

CHAPTER 16

BESS, with her customary single-mindedness, now threw herself into the task of raising a child, who might—she never forgot it—be heir to the throne. And no one else in the realm forgot it either. Mary of Scotland didn't, for the little Arabella was growing up under her nose, chattering in French with her, showing her dolls, and demonstrating her ability to read.

Both Charles and William Cavendish were climbing rapidly into positions of importance; the inimitable Charles was already a member of parliament, to the great delight of his constituency. Both were the parents of healthy sons, a reproach to Shrewsbury, whose four sons had none of their own, now that little George had died so prematurely. It seemed to the earl that his nine dwellings swarmed with healthy loud-talking Cavendishes, who pushed all the world in front of them, like so many chessmen, to suit their winning gambits. If only Mary and Gilbert would have sons instead of daughters!

Bess was busy with the rebuilding of Hardwick. She labored over the outlines of the gardens Elizabeth had laid out, and she kept to the letter of them. She and Arabella traveled about from one great estate to the other, with a mass of retainers, servants, and tutors. Whenever a good piece of land came on the market, it seemed to the earl that Bess bought it.

The great earl of Leicester wrote often to Bess; he had got himself married to the most bewitching of the ladies in the realm, Lettice Knollys, and she had presented him with a son. Bess and Leicester wanted to betroth the little Arabella to Leicester's little boy, Lord Denbigh, who was one year old; the two children exchanged rings on a chain. The queen was annoyed. Mary of Scotland was very annoyed, and Shrewsbury was derisive, and Bess and Leicester waited until March the next year, 1584, to formally betroth the children.

"Arabella can have no finer friend at court than the earl of Leicester," Bess said positively. And of course it was true. Bess was writing to Cecil, and at the end of the letter, to show Arabella's prowess at eight, Arabella had added a postscript, recommending herself to the queen's principal secretary. Bess watched her write, the pen clasped close in her dimpled hand.

Je prieray Dieu, monsieur, vous donner en parfait et entiere

314

sante toute heureux et bon succes et seray toujours preste
a vous faire toute honneur et service.

Each letter was so carefully formed! Bess was very proud of her.

Since Arabella was eight now, Bess thought it would be good for her to spend the winter in London, at Shrewsbury House, with its great new stained-glass windows that the earl still complained about. There, Mary and Gilbert lived in splendid fashion; and Mary had two little girls, it was a proper place for Arabella. Bess had not forgotten that Elizabeth had asked Mary to help with the upbringing of her orphaned daughter.

"She will be happy in a household with other children," Bess said.

"You speak as though there were no other children here," the earl said.

Bess paid no attention. "And Gilbert and Mary entertain so much and so lavishly that Arabella will be in a suitable environment, too."

The earl snorted.

But when Arabella had gone and Christmas—the Christmas of 1583 had passed—with the earl's players giving a wonderful play, followed the next night by a pageant— closed into the great castle with Mary, as always, Bess began to fret. Mary's barbs were endless.

"I've told de Mauvissiere [the French ambassador] that you have been so affectionate to me that I might have been your own queen, you would not have done more for me."

Bess said stiffly, knowing these words would be repeated to the Queen's Majesty, "I cared for you, when you were sick, madam, as I would have any sick person in my charge!"

She banged out of Mary's room.

That night Mary was sick. "She says you upset her," the earl said crossly. "She said she had merely thanked you for your kindness and you slammed the door in her face!"

"Aye, and I'll do it again!" Bess shouted. "The piss-head!"

"She's ill," Shrewsbury said quietly. He thought, *How she has changed, the poor thing. She came to Tutbury a young woman, and now she is puffy and stooped and lame.* "The poor thing," he said, and Bess realized he wasn't paying any attention

315

to her, Bess, at all. His thoughts were completely on Mary.

That morning he had received a gift of a puppy, brought from one of his relatives in the north, a New Year's gift. He suddenly said, "I know what will cheer her up."

Bess was so angry she screamed at him. "You fool, you knave!"

The earl brushed by her. "You keep quiet," he said, only.

The puppy was a Skye terrier. The earl bore it in his arms, up to Mary's room. She lay back on her pillows, the candles burning, her face white and pale.

Shrewsbury set the puppy on the richly embroidered counterpane. Mary sat up straight and uttered a cry of real delight. Her old smile flashed out.

"Thank you, my lord! Oh, thank you," she said, her big eyes suddenly filling with tears of gratitude. "You are so kind to me, my lord." She petted and hugged the puppy, while her ladies exclaimed with little cries of joy at the squirming mass of gray fur. They brought Shrewsbury wine and a chair. The puppy barked, a little high bark, and Mary laughed. The earl raised his glass.

"A Happy New Year," he said, smiling.

The ladies and Mary made much of him; they were so grateful and happy that he was with them and had brought such a wonderful gift for their beloved mistress. When he finally left the peaceful, pretty room and its occupants, who had hung on his every word, he went down to his own bedroom, passing by Bess' suite with an even tread. Within, Bess sat before her fire alone. For almost fifteen years she had endured the presence of another woman, alien, in her house. For fifteen years. And for all that time, Mary of Scotland had repeatedly thrown down a gauntlet and challenged her. Now the struggle between them had emerged into the open. The battle had been joined a long time ago. But now there was need for action, and an end to the fight.

Early the next morning, Bess left Sheffield. Mary's challenge had been accepted. It was a fight to the death. And there was no doubt in Bess' mind who would win. She would.

316

CHAPTER 17

AUNT Linacre had always said, "When you're angry, work!"

And Bess did. For a week—between Chatsworth and Hardwick, with her carpenters, her masons, her plasterers. Bess fell exhausted into bed every night.

But she didn't sleep well.

Jane said, "You've abdicated."

"I?" cried Bess, astonished.

"You," said Jane. "You've left him with Mary. And you know how deeply he hates the idea of the household knowing there is a rift between you."

Bess knew well enough. Appearances were very important to the earl. Bess had not only struck a blow at his pride, but she had struck it publicly. The county loved nothing better than to gossip about its principal peer and his countess, the unpredictable Bess.

Bess fretted then. When Charles and William arrived to see her, she was glad. But they had come from Sheffield and brought a letter from Gilbert.

Gilbert wrote that the earl had been at Worksop, for just a day, and had entertained the earl of Rutland there, in the privacy of his study. Rutland was related to Shrewsbury by marriage, but just the same he was known to be a sympathizer to Mary's cause. Was Gilbert worried? Hastily Bess scanned the letter again.

Charles asked, "Mother, would my lord do anything foolish to help that queen? Could his sympathies be enlisted?"

"No," Bess said, "absolutely no!"

But the suspicion of it would be enough. Cecil and Walsingham watched Mary like eager slit-eyed hawks, anxiously waiting for a chance to seize their victim in their claws and display her to the world as a conniving traitor. If they had to sacrifice Shrewsbury to catch her, they would.

Sudden fury at Mary seized Bess. It was all her fault! The

fault of the Scottish queen, whose demands on her husband had bound him to her side so securely. Bess' dark eyes blazed. "Listen, Charles . . ." she began.

After a leisurely dinner Charles and William, laughing, had ridden out of Chatsworth, making straight for a tavern and its garrulous owner, whose hospitality they had enjoyed before. After they had been there about an hour William remonstrated with his brother.

"You're drinking heavily, Charles."

"That's the plot."

"But you aren't supposed to get drunk."

Charles grinned. "Why not? It will make the whole thing more realistic."

"Don't forget you have to ride home," the practical William reminded him.

So, although his servant, Henry Beresford, who had accompanied them, had to help Charles into the saddle, he managed to ride home, hunched over the reins, every once in a while bursting into loud laughter. When Bess saw him, she reproved him sharply. He made her a low bow.

"The deed is done, Madame la Comtesse," Charles said and was swiftly aided out of the room by William and the faithful Henry Beresford.

"*In vino veritas.*" the gossips said, nodding their heads sagely and repeating with relish the incautious drunken words they had been intended to overhear. "It must be true. The Cavendishes would know."

London was two hundred miles away. The third night after Charles and William had spent their busy time in the tavern, Bess sat propped up in bed, her wine cup full, pondering what was going to happen next. And almost at that very moment, in London, William Cecil was listening with astounded countenance to the earl of Leicester. Ten minutes later they both arrived at the queen's chamber, and into Elizabeth's ears they poured the whole tale.

Elizabeth listened in stony silence. She didn't believe a word of it. But there was need for action. She said slowly, "Write to Lord Shrewsbury, and inform him of my decision to replace him with Sir Ralph Sadler."

318

When the messenger reached Sheffield Castle, Mary heard his news. She cried and raged. Taut with anger, Bess' face kept swimming before Mary's hate-filled eyes. Mary screamed out wild threats at the absent Bess. But when the earl arrived at her door, she quieted and began to cry soundlessly. *Alone and friendless, I am,* she wept. In her plain gray gown, she seemed shrunken and old, finally devastated before the deliberate malice of the shrewd and implacable Bess. She wept and whispered, "I shall write my dear cousin, the queen, and beg for redress! Ah, my lord, that you must bear this for my sake. Ah, all we can pray for is that justice will finally triumph."

She was sitting in her chair, and Shrewsbury sat down on a stool before her, and took her hand. He waited for her to calm herself; she wiped her eyes and blew her nose. He was thinking, in the silence, of a day long ago when he had warned Bess, before she had even seen Mary. Never, never say or impute or jest about any relationship between me and this queen! It might be the ruin of my house.

And she had remembered that too, well enough.

"Write the Queen's Majesty, of course," the earl said. "But she does not believe it, madam."

"But what can we do," Mary sobbed, "to save our honor?"

The earl said calmly, "Since the tale is out of whole cloth, is must be required that Charles and William and Bess herself testify before the council that they were lying."

"Will they do that?" Mary asked, wiping her tear-stained face. She was trembling from head to toe, and Shrewsbury was fearful. Was she going to be very ill?

"I am trembling with nerves and fear, I think," Mary said, apologetically. The future stretched before her, frightening her badly. She fastened her eyes on the earl's well-known face. What would she do without him? Without the knowledge of his presence, without the sudden sound of his steps, which she knew so well, without his big figure seated beside her in her carriage on the way to Buxton Springs, or without the sight of him riding beside her, his men protectively surrounding her, the pennons flying. "Oh, God in heaven," Mary suddenly cried, "what shall I do? What is going to become of me?"

And in her extreme distress she whispered, "How could she have done this to us?"

How indeed? the earl thought. But Mary was so pitiful he forgot himself.

"We never harmed her. And for her to say we are lovers —and that there was a child!"

"I think that rumor was added on, as more and more tongues repeated the tale," the earl said.

His words didn't help because Mary thought then of those endlessly clacking tongues. And she was vulnerable, of course, because of her legendary charm and her behavior in Scotland.

"I've lived like a nun," Mary said. "A nun. I've lived like a nun, the virtuous life. And all set aside by the lying tongue of a lying woman and her lying sons."

"Madam, all is not lost yet. Bess will retract her words. And you may be permitted to remain at Sheffield."

"No, I shan't," Mary sobbed. "All is lost, now, even my honor. It was the only thing I had left. Your friendship and my womanly piety. Aye, if I didn't know that the Lord my God stood ever beside me, I should think even He had deserted me, his faithful and virtuous servant."

Shrewsbury could see plainly that her shivering had increased. He said, "Get on your bed, madam, and have Kennedy bathe and rub your feet and legs."

These words reminded Mary of Bess. And now Bess had struck her lethal blow, coldly and cruelly. Bess was gone, forever. Bess who had been kind and on whom she had leaned. Mary's thoughts went full circle from anger to despair that she had lost Bess.

She staggered over to her bed, Shrewsbury leaping up to help her tottering figure. "All is lost," Mary wept. "All is lost."

CHAPTER 18

ALL was indeed lost, for Mary. Elizabeth wrote that Sir Ralph Sadler would take over her custody. Elizabeth was perturbed by the scandal, she who hated scandal, the merest breath of it, touching one of her principal peers and her royal prisoner: What would they say abroad? So to show that she believed none of the lurid tales of love in dark corners, and two babies somehow disposed of secretly and horribly, she permitted the earl to take Mary to Buxton for one last time; and then he was to escort her to Wingfield and hand her over to Sir Ralph. This was the final annoyance for the earl—that Wingfield, one of his own manors, should be used.

So the two of them journeyed for the last time to Buxton. The ride that used to be undertaken so gaily by Mary, the high spot of her year, now was part of a final journey.

Sadly she climbed up into her carriage, assisted by her servants, for her leg grew more lame every month. And when the horses trotted sedately out through the great park, the towering oaks seemed to say good-bye, good-bye; symbols of honest and earthly strength and beauty that they were, good-bye, good-bye, they called, their leaves trembling in the light wind and the sunlight falling dappled through their mighty height. Good-bye, good-bye.

Shrewsbury, as he rode alongside her, felt there was something portentous about this leavetaking, for Mary had with her now only a small train, much reduced from the first time he had seen her riding toward Tutbury, on that winter day so long ago.

Then he had deemed her a dangerous woman; now the price had been paid over and over. Do old sins never cease taking their inexorable toll? He said, leaning over the high saddle, "Come, madam, smile! You'll enjoy the baths, the waters."

Mary was always at her best in deepest adversity. She smiled back, "Aye, my lord! And the fresh air. Oh, what balm it is to my soul and lungs, as you know, my dear friend."

During their five weeks at Buxton, his admiration for her queenly courage deepened. The only time she did not control her emotions was when she rode into Wingfield, on September 6. She blanched then, and, knowing he was looking at her, she said hastily, "The memories rush back, my lord!" She turned to him, looking up at his face. "How sick you were! How we prayed, on our knees! Is it possible it was fifteen years ago! How young we were!"

She climbed the twisting stairs to her old quarters on the inner quadrangle. At the top, she turned to the earl.

"Good-bye, my lord. God go with you."

She could not say more. The earl bowed and kissed her hand. "I shall send Sir Ralph up to greet you, madam." He stood over her looking down. Was it for the last time? Unease and fear gripped him. She was so vulnerable, he thought. *Without me, what will she do?* But what was there to say? Neither could say what was in the heart.

"Good-bye, madam. I hope you are happy here at Wingfield."

"Aye, my lord," said Mary, not trusting her voice. She thought suddenly how happy we would truly be if Bess would come bursting in, as she used to, and say, "Why, what's all the gloom for?" Bess, who was never afraid, never unsure, always sweeping all difficulties aside with scorn. Mary and the earl stood there together, saying the ordinary parting words. If Bess had seen them, she would have thought with surprise, *Why, how forlorn they are without me.*

The earl went back down the twisting steps. He called from the bottom, trying to be hearty. "I'll put your letter into Her Majesty's hands myself. I should reach London in four days. Good-bye. Good-bye."

The echo of his voice died away. Mary went over to the tall and overhanging mantel; the hearth was bare now, in September. She leaned her elbow on it wearily and looked around the disordered room, for boxes lay piled up and the whole room was awry. When Bess had moved her, somehow it was neat and swift and orderly. Suddenly she choked back a loud, gasping sob. "I must get out of here!" she said aloud. "I'll do anything to get out of here!"

When the earl reached London, he stopped briefly at Shrewsbury House. The sight of the enormous stained-glass windows roused momentary and impatient anger; they'd cost a fortune. Bess and her preoccupation with light. She was beggaring him. The damned windows would remind him of her constantly. He resolved not to stay there and went on to one of his old haunts, a comfortable tavern. Perhaps tomorrow he would get a room at court.

How long it had been since he had come to London! It seemed part of another life. *B.B.*, he thought. *Before Bess.* Now, thought Shrewsbury grimly, he would start anew. *A.B. After Bess.* Before he went to court he saw his lawyer and talked with him about a legal separation.

But when he arrived at court, he was amazed and astounded to find that everyone—literally everyone— blithely absolved Bess from any guilt, excused her, and said, "Why, after all, she made amends!" Even the queen! Even the queen!

Not that Elizabeth Tudor had not been kind, gentle, understanding and had listened to him fondly. When he entered her room, crowded as always, she had bade him sit close to her on a stool; and the others had drawn away, so they could converse in private low tones, together. Long ago, when they were young, both in their twenties, she had teased him about his conservative views. "My dear old man," she had purred at him, smiling. Since then she had called him that often, as was her way. She did so now, leaning over to him.

"It pleases us to see our dear old man, my lord."

She looked magnificent. Her eyes glowed with the old fire. For an hour and a half they talked together. She told him that Bess and her two sons—who had stood tall and protecting and redheaded alongside Bess—had all appeared humbly before the council and admitted their guilt and retracted their words. The retraction was generously made, openly made.

Bess had said, frankly, "I said it, my lords, because the burden of this queen's care was becoming insupportable for my lord!"

So after all, shouldn't Shrewsbury forgive?

"No," said the earl. He mentioned a legal separation. The queen was horrified. One of her principal peers and, she intimated, her dear Bess, her own cousin the countess, separated? *No.* She was adamant.

So was Shrewsbury. It was as though he had longed for such a confrontation with her. This principal peer had had enough. Enough.

Unconvinced, stubborn, he left her after that hour and a half. He spent the night with a pretty blond woman. The next afternoon he presented himself again at court. Once more the queen commanded a stool to be brought to the side of her chair. The earl sat down, preparing to renew the fight when in the opened white-and-gilded doors he saw Bess.

She had been stopped in her entrance by Leicester, who had kissed her hand and was standing with her; Bess threw back her head and laughed at something Leicester had said. Then she came toward the seated figures of her husband and the queen.

She was dressed in yellow satin; her walk was as inviting as always; there was something sinuous about Bess' figure that nothing, no clothes, could disguise. And of course she was wearing, flaunting, the Talbot pearls. In a brief moment the earl could visualize Bess before the council making her confession, absolving him and Mary. God! She was always in trouble! And yet she came toward him and the queen, looking just the same as always. *If we were alone,* the earl thought, *I'd probably strangle her.*

He knew he should rise. Every eye in the room was on him and Bess. How the tongues were clacking, he thought. The earl rose, slowly, obviously reluctant. He stood very tall, he bowed very briefly; his eyes, in his very stern face, swept her as coldly as only he could do, with his correct and distant manner.

Bess curtsied before the queen. The queen waved her hand. Another stool was brought, and Bess sat down gracefully; her little slippers and her wickedly expensive silk knitted yellow stockings just showed as she arranged her gown. She leaned toward the earl. "My lord," she said, very very low, "in her Majesty's presence, I ask you to forgive me."

The earl's eyes blazed with sudden fire, and the oath that ran through his head was left unspoken owing to the presence of his queen. And of course, every eye in the room was on them, everyone knew of what they spoke, and in fact everyone was unconsciously so eager to hear what was being said that there was a dead silence.

Elizabeth looked about the room, and one of her ladies immediately began to chatter to her neighbor. Elizabeth said, low, "My lord, your wife is making amends which we think you should hear with the kindness of a husband."

The earl said then, "I should have preferred to hear her say that on her knees, madam." A little smile accompanied these words, to lift them into irony, as if to imply, too, that it really mattered nothing to him, what Bess did or didn't do.

Bess looked at him, but he refused to look at her, and had spoken directly to the queen.

"Ah, my lord," Elizabeth said with reproof.

Bess didn't dare say anything. She sat straight, her dark eyes fastened on his face, imploringly. And then she suddenly realized that Shrewsbury was enjoying himself. *At last,* she thought, *he has got the two women in his life at his mercy. For fifteen years he has had to cope not only with Mary Queen of Scots but the Queen's Majesty and, not the least, with me. Now he is coming into his own. He is going to lay down the rules. Well, I'll let him, he deserves it.*

She said in the silence, "I'll do anything, my lord, to make you truly understand that I am sorry for everything I have done. It was because I was jealous." *There,* she thought, *that's the worst confession a woman can make, and I've made it.* She leaned toward him. "I was jealous of you and that queen!"

Elizabeth's admiration for Bess rose. She smiled at her, approvingly.

Shrewsbury said, "You were jealous of my duty, my duty to the Queen's Majesty, to watch and ward Mary Stuart?"

He shook his head. "I do not find that a reason for scurrilous lies touching my honor and I do not condone it in any way."

"But I wasn't jealous of that," Bess said. "I was jealous of that queen."

Elizabeth bit her lip to keep from smiling. "My lord," she said with severity, "it is our wish that you take back your wife, as a proper loving husband, to take care of her and to love her."

Oh, that isn't the way, thought Bess. *He'll be crosser than a bear.* "But if I cannot ask for your love and care, my lord," she said, "at least I can ask for forgiveness! I only did it for you!"

"Nonsense," said the earl sharply. "You did it for yourself."

"Aye, my jewel," Bess said, forgetting and using her own endearment for him. "I guess you're right." She said, "Your Majesty, I'm trying not to weep in front of everyone!" She set her jaw stiff and blinked her eyes.

Elizabeth leaned downward to touch her hand, and Bess said, "Oh, don't do that, Your Majesty! I shall weep!"

Elizabeth said, "My lord, you should be ashamed of yourself!"

Shrewsbury now gave his queen an incredulous glance. And Bess blurted, "He's had so many females to deal with, Your Majesty, that he hates our sex—or my sex," she added hastily.

Shrewsbury thought, *God's death! If she says any more she'll get me in deeper trouble with my queen.* "Bess," he snapped, "be quiet!" He turned to Elizabeth, "Your Majesty, will you dismiss my wife? I should like, I beg, to talk to you privately, and I will try to do as you command." Then he added, for her and for Bess, "In my own way."

No one at court that week talked about anything but the earl and Bess. It was a perfectly fascinating subject. Rumors flew in all directions, spilling from mouth to ear, with exclamations and wonderings. They said the earl had taken up with a blond woman called Eleanor Brittain and had sent her to Sheffield lodge to await his pleasures. They said that he was going back to Bess, as the queen commanded, and

326

that he was going to provide for her. They said he would never live with her again or speak to her again. But the person who gauged the situation most correctly was the earl's brother-in-law. Sir John Manners was saying in London, to all who asked him, "It's a simple matter of being the master of the castle. His lordship is determined to be it."

Shrewsbury had been staying at his favorite inn; anxious to shake the dust of London, he had sent word to Bess that she should be ready to leave in two days, and he would call for her.

She was ready. She hadn't seen him alone for ten months; she was diffident and shy as she came down the steps to the waiting carriage; the earl bowed a little, and helped her in; it crossed his mind fleetingly that she reminded him of the first time he had come to Chatsworth, when he had teased her about being tongue-tied in his presence. He closed the carriage door without saying a word.

He's going to ride, Bess thought. She said to Mrs. Battell, trying to be cheerful, "His lordship hates carriages."

They jolted off. Bess felt very forlorn. She sat in the corner of the seat and tried not to cry.

The first night they stopped at an inn, Mrs. Battell was brushing Bess' hair when the earl walked in. Mrs. Battell dropped the brush; she'd been wondering the whole day whether the earl would seek out his wife or not. Quickly she fastened Bess' hair back with a ribbon. "Good-night, my lord, my lady," she murmured.

The earl didn't answer her. He was looking at Bess with an unreadable expression. Bess blurted, "Oh, my jewel, if you really want me to go on my knees to ask your forgiveness, I will! I was just trying to be brave before the Queen's Majesty. And Jane told me you'd never forgive me. That's what Jane said. You'd never forgive me."

There was silence.

Finally Bess whispered, "Will you, my lord?"

Shrewsbury said, "I don't know."

"It's been months and months since I saw you," she said, starting to cry. "And I've missed you so, I've missed you so," blubbered Bess. She put her hands over her face. She was thinking rapidly she was far too old to cry, it just made her look older than she was. "Oh, hell's fire!" muttered Bess, wondering now how she had got herself into this dreadful situation. "I did it on the spur of the moment."

"Don't excuse yourself," the earl said wearily. "You're so officious and shrewish, I am tired of it."

"I wanted to get rid of this queen."

"You were determined to get rid of her at any cost."

Bess wiped her face. She sat straight. "And what is the cost?"

"I don't know, Bess," Shrewsbury said. "Come on, let's go to bed."

"Go to bed?"

"Aye, None, I'm weary, and it's late. And we have to get up early. I left orders for us to be called at six."

"Go to bed?" whispered Bess, hopefully. Maybe everything would be all right after all.

The earl smiled slightly at her tone. "None," he said reasonably, "we've been married for seventeen years. And marriage is a habit you don't outgrow in a hurry. Don't you want to go to bed?"

Bess smiled. "Aye!" she said.

They arrived at Chatsworth four days later. *Chatsworth?* wondered Bess. *Why Chatsworth?* He hated it. Why hadn't he taken her to Sheffield? Or to Bolsover? She fretted. She talked endlessly to Jane when the earl rode out, which he did almost every day, either for duty or pleasure.

"I think he's deciding what to do with me!"

"He ought to chop your head off," Jane said.

"Oh, Jane," Bess wailed. "I'm afraid of what he's going to do. They say he sent that Eleanor Brittain to Sheffield Manor, and she's young and blond and has big breasts! Do you suppose it's true?"

"I don't know, Bess," Jane said. She sighed. "I feel very, very sorry for you, Bess."

"Oh, by my faith," Bess whispered, stunned at Jane's words. Did Jane know something she didn't? No, she couldn't. She could only observe, and it had brought her to the conclusion that Bess deserved her pity. "Oh, what is going to happen?" Bess cried.

The earl had been at Chatsworth four weeks. About eleven that night, after his lovemaking, Bess lay with her hand under her head, her eyes half closed. She sighed. She said, "You know, I feel just like a bride, and we've been married seventeen years. Do you suppose there is something wrong with me, my love?"

The earl stirred, and she heard his chuckle, just as she used to hear it, and he rolled over and hugged her. "Go to sleep, None," he said, just as he always did.

Bess slept late the next day, and when she came down the steps later, he was standing in the big doors; there was baggage about and at least thirty horsemen waiting in the court. Fear struck Bess. Was this the blow she'd been waiting for? Tense, she asked, "Where are you going?"

"I'm leaving," he said.

"Well, I see that! But where?" She took a step forward.

"Bess," he said, "for more than fifteen years I've been tied to Mary Stuart. Now I'm free." He was pulling on his gloves.

Isn't he going to say anything else? Bess thought. "But," she began, "but when are you coming back?"

He shrugged. "I don't know. I'm leaving you, Bess. I'll be back sometime, maybe. I left you three hundred pounds."

"I don't want your money!"

The earl laughed. "That's a silly statement, coming from you."

"Well, I don't," Bess said. "I want you!"

The earl said, "Bess, a long time ago I learned, without knowing it, how to keep you well in hand. It was by leaving you. And that's what I'm doing."

He started to walk away. Bess, stunned, stood silent, watching. He went out to his big horse, there was a man holding the reins, and quickly the earl was up in the saddle. Then the spell broke, and Bess rushed to the doors. She shook her fist at him.

"Shrewsbury!" she shouted. "I wish you in hell with your deep-uddered whore!"

The earl grinned. He waved to her. "Good-bye, None," he called cheerfully.

CHAPTER 19

A FEW miles south, Mary Stuart, at Wingfield Manor, was slowly weaving the web of her own destruction, amiably assisted by the spies of Walsingham and Cecil. Beady-eyed, they watched and abetted her every move; and she, willy-nilly, was securely placing herself into their hands.

What the earl had feared for her was happening week by week, month by month, during the next twenty-four months. She plotted under the curious sniffing noses of the planted spies, who aided her to her scaffold.

Every night Mary dreamed, and couldn't sleep because she thought at last she was succeeding. And when the day came that she was permitted to ride out and suddenly saw a troop of horses coming toward Sir Ralph Sadler and herself, she gave a little cry of joy. Her rescuers had arrived! And on time!

She was disabused swiftly. The men riding toward her were the queen's men, and they arrested her and took her away with them. The tragedy of Mary Stuart was rapidly coming to a climax.

The news reached the earl at Bolsover. He read and reread Cecil's letter. Slowly he laid it down. Mary Queen of Scots was going to be tried for treason at Fotheringhay castle, a crown castle, where she was now held close and strait a prisoner.

Who is with her? the earl wondered. *Kennedy? Kennedy certainly. Lady Livingstone? Andrew Melville?*

He brought his hand down on his table and realized he had made a fist and that he had hurt his hand. *I'm getting old,* he thought.

Suddenly, he found he couldn't with equanimity recall one by one each of Mary's little train of servants and friends. The past rushed back too painfully. That faithful little band, who loved Mary, and who had depended on him for so long, now they were lost. In an alien wilderness. Sick at heart, the earl left Bolsover and rode to the great healing embrace of the park and castle at Sheffield. When Gilbert came out to help his father from the saddle, he tried to cheer him with a hug. The earl's face was white and strained.

"Do you realize, Gilbert," he said, "that if and when sentence is passed on Mary Stuart, that it is I who shall have to preside?"

Mary couldn't sleep. She lay on her pillows. Kennedy was bathing her feet and legs. The candles burned against the plain stone walls. Over and over in her mind floated pictures of the past, the days of her youth, the happy exciting days in France, the comfort of her mirror as she looked at her pretty face; there was not much time left to recapture life, soon it would be ended for her, as the dark hours of the night fled. Who could sleep if they knew the coming dawn was the last dawn? Alongside her, on the bed, the Skye terrier snored. She put her hand on the rough fur and pulled at his ears, gently.

Her ladies were bent over their sewing. They were putting the last stitches into her gown and underclothing. Kennedy kneaded her swollen legs.

"Ah, that soothes me," she said.

Her mind wrestled with approaching death. Even now, as the night hours fell away before the inexorable turning of the earth, the precious earth, it was impossible to accept the fact that she would die. *Not I,* she thought. *Not I.*

Kennedy was weeping. "You are so brave, madam," she sobbed.

Mary gave her a swift smile. "I cannot believe it is really true," Mary said. "That's why I am so brave."

At five o'clock she rose, and they began to dress her. She had worn her plain gray gowns so long they had had to improvise a gown for today, her last entrance upon the scene and her bloody exit from the world stage.

In another part of the castle of Fotheringhay the earl

tossed restlessly; he finally rose and, wrapped in a warm bedgown, sat at his table reading, his body servant watching him anxiously, while Gilbert dozed in the bed.

They had arrived at Fotheringhay that February morning. Already the great stone pile was surrounded by crowds. Contemptuously the earl had ordered his men to ride through, scarcely bothering to call "Make way! Make way!"

"Father!" Gilbert had remonstrated.

Shrewsbury scowled. He despised the morbid curious who thronged outside the gates. "Do they expect the thrill of the smell of death?"

"They want to see the great pass by, great men like you, my lord," Gilbert said. Gilbert thought, *Father is so old fashioned, so conservative.* But he thought also, *Father does look like the great lord he is.* And he sighed. So much trouble; Gilbert was even forbidden to see Bess. And he hated that whore Brittain, as he called her.

The earl, as lord marshal of England, was carrying with him the warrant for Mary's death, smuggled from under Elizabeth's nose by her secretary Davison and placed in the earl's hands. Shrewsbury himself didn't know that Elizabeth was unaware the warrant had left London. Although she had signed the warrant, she did not know it had been taken to Shrewsbury; and he had no notion of the storm that would break when she did find out. Now he had before him the task of reading aloud to Mary Stuart her sentence of death for treason.

Inside the castle he was met by the earl of Kent; preoccupied, Shrewsbury acknowledged him by a mere inclination of his head. He said curtly, "Summon this queen," using his old name for Mary.

And when Mary stood before him in her gray gown, when their eyes met, he was afraid there would be unspoken appeal in her eyes; he was afraid she would be saying silently—though his ears could not hear but his eyes ferret out the truth—he was afraid she would reach to him, once again, for help. *If I had never left her, she would not now be left alone and naked before her enemies,* he thought.

But she sent no appeal. She heard without emotion the warrant, and then calmly she went to the table in the small

332

anteroom, where there lay a Bible. She placed her hand on it.

"I swear, my lord, on this book, that I have never sought the destruction of the Queen's Majesty."

In his capacity Shrewsbury could not reply to this. He said in his most clipped tones that she would be summoned at eight the following morning.

"Ah, my lord," Mary said, as though she was telling him she wasn't fond of that kind of meat, "Why, I need a little time to put my affairs in order."

"Tomorrow morning at eight, madam. That is all the time that can be permitted to you."

The earl bowed briefly and turned his back; Mary, accompanied by two guards, was escorted from the room.

She will have worked fast and hard, the earl thought. She hadn't realized that more time would simply prolong her agony. He knew very well what she would do. She would summon each servant and bless each one, and thank them, and give them each a jewel. She would read over her will and add something here or there. She would write to her relatives in France; she would write to her son. She would prepare herself for death. *In my end is my beginning.* How many times had he seen her embroidering those wavy letters.

At seven—and it was a bitterly cold February morning—he went into the great hall at Fotheringhay to see the preparations, grim as they were.

Along the side of the hall, against the stone walls, were the rows of chairs for the witnesses, the gentry from the country about, and Shrewsbury and the earl of Kent.

The evening before Mary had sent a request for her priest. It was forbidden that she see him. Shrewsbury did not intervene. He knew that she had a eucharist wafer blessed by the pope, if she should need the last and divine unction and be denied a priest of the Catholic Church.

In the center of the hall was the draped platform. At that very moment, as Mary was being dressed, she was saying, "These shoes, of very soft leather, thank God I had them! How dreadful it would be to go squeaking up the steps to the scaffold."

Those shoes of white Spanish leather barely peeked forth under her scarlet petticoat. Her women put on her now a black velvet overdress. On her head they pinned deftly a white net veil that fell to her feet. She was ready.

On each side of her plodded a stolid guard, and thus she came into the hall, crowded with two hundred of the gentry.

There was absolute silence. Mary looked about the hall, her eyes flicking over the faces of the men and the platform to which she would climb for her last few steps.

She looked up at Shrewsbury. "But, my lord, I have a request that some of my people be with me at this time."

The earl of Kent said brutally, "No, madam. We can't have your women sobbing and screaming in here."

"I can assure you," Mary said evenly to Kent, "that such things will not happen."

Shrewsbury suddenly took charge. "Your request is granted, madam. You may pick five persons."

When Mary said their names, they were each name like a hammered nail in a coffin. Each name so familiar and each face so familiar. The face of Andrew Melville, for instance, his lips white with fear for Mary and his eyes full of sorrow and pity.

Her ladies came. She prayed, and the ladies removed her black overdress, and she mounted the steps where the executioner waited.

She knelt in her scarlet petticoat, and now all could see she had dressed completely in red. Even her arms were covered with red silk. A figure in blood, she stood, then knelt.

Shrewsbury closed his eyes. Under his breath he repeated: "Into your hands, oh Lord, we give this queen, and may your mercy extend to me, who am guilty, too." His eyes filled with tears, and, unashamed, he took out his handkerchief and wiped his eyes. Blood was streaming from the severed corpse. Mary's women were kneeling and praying. The executioner leaned down to pick up the severed, dismembered head.

Anyone who had lived with Mary knew that she was always wigged. Shrewsbury tried to signal the executioner, but he was too late. The head, lifted by the wig, rolled from his grasp, onto the floor. A little grayed grizzled head.

But for Shrewsbury the horror was not over. For when they gathered up Mary's lifeless trunk, there, cowering close to her, was her little faithful Skye terrier. It was covered with blood.

The earl had not permitted Gilbert to witness the execution. Gilbert was waiting, booted and spurred, his escort ready, in the hall. It was Gilbert's job to ride posthaste to London, to carry the news. Gilbert, at the signal from his father, started for the doors. Then he came back and kissed the earl.

"I know what it cost you, Father," he said, tears in his eyes.

Shrewsbury said, "Judge not, that ye be judged. Godspeed, my son. Good-bye."

After Gilbert left, the huge gates were closed again, and no one was permitted to leave the brooding royal castle, with its burden of the dead Scottish Queen.

Five days later it was snowing in Derbyshire. Through the afternoon cold and the whirling white flakes, the earl rode up to the doors of Chatsworth. When he dismounted, one of the grooms placed the Skye terrier in his arms. Bess was only twenty feet away, but in the dark, snowy afternoon, his figure was blurred.

The badge of the Talbot was the dog, of course, but the badge pictured the man carrying the dog.

As Shrewsbury came toward Bess, as the first Talbot had come, many many years ago, exemplifying fidelity and service, a huge sob rose in her throat, for she had thrown away, willfully, the love he had borne her. In the last months she had thought him gone forever, forever. Bess rushed toward him. His shoulders were covered with snow; he was cold, his face drawn. She touched his arm. She hadn't seen him for more than two years.

"My lord," she whispered, "I thought you would never come! I've longed for you so, I—"

He paid no attention to her words. He put the wriggling wet dog in her arms. "She is dead, None," he said. "I had to watch her die."

CHAPTER 20

"IT was my fault," Bess said, over and over.

Patiently Shrewsbury contradicted her. "It was my fault, too, Bess, and it was her fault. Because she was the one to suffer, it is natural to exonerate her, but she was guilty, too. We were all trapped."

"I deserted you, and her," Bess sobbed, "and you depended on me."

"Don't fret so, None," he said. "You'll make yourself ill."

Bess blew her nose. "We're getting older, my jewel. You are fifty-eight. It is time we settled down and were close as we were."

Shrewsbury sent her a slight smile. "I'm aware of my age."

"But, it is true!"

"I've stayed here six weeks, None. I'm going to leave soon."

"You can't!" Bess burst out.

"We won't argue about it," Shrewsbury said.

"He means it!" Bess said to Jane. "I thought he would stay! But he is going to leave me again."

Jane said sadly, for she was indeed sad at the thought of the earl riding off, away from them, "Oh, Bess, if he has made up his mind, there is nothing you can do."

"That is what he wants," Bess said, nodding her head. "To make me realize there is nothing I can do to make him change!"

The last night before he was to leave, Jane spoke with him. "She misses you so woefully, my lord," Jane said.

But Shrewsbury made no reply. In the hall the next morning, he bid Bess good-bye. Bess said, "You'll write, my lord?"

"Aye." He gave her a quick kiss. Then he was gone. Jane watched the troop of thirty men ride away from Chatsworth.

Bess stood alone in the big doors, waving. She turned to Jane. She said, worriedly, "I hope he doesn't catch cold! It's so bitter out today! And he isn't strong."

Jane thought, *He has tamed her, this way. And that is what he wants, and he is willing to pay any price for it.*

But Bess wasn't always so compliant; she struck back and fought like a hooked fish at the end of a relentless line. When Mary had arrived at Chatsworth, to have her latest child, the earl wrote that Gilbert would not be permitted to stay at Chatsworth.

Furiously, Bess wrote back.

Shrewsbury, unmoved, reiterated that Gilbert would be allowed to visit Mary and Bess, but he didn't want Gilbert staying there. His reason? Simply that Gilbert had been under Charles' influence long enough.

Bess had stamped about and swore, and drank three glasses of wine, and went to bed, putting the earl's last letter into the box beside the bed as usual. As she placed it inside the gold and silver box he had given her years ago, she banged the lid down angrily. "A pox on his lordship, pooh!"

But three days later she wrote back meekly that Gilbert had not stayed, but had just ridden over to Chatsworth to see his newest and third daughter, and wasn't the earl ashamed of himself?

The earl wrote back that it now came to his mind that Chatsworth was filled with precious stuffs from Sheffield, Rufford, and other principal dwellings, and these precious stuffs included, for instance, the jeweled Order of the Garter, which had belonged to the fourth earl of Shrewsbury, to say nothing of that pair of embroidered cambric and lace sheets from France, and where were they?

Bess sat at her table writing back and said had he forgot all the stuff she had lavished on him and his? The Order of the Garter was displayed in a glass case. As for the sheets, did he think she was going to provide sheets for his whore? Anyway, the sheets had worn out long ago.

Bess then carefully put his last letter into the gold and

silver box and climbed into bed between the beautiful precious sheets. Smiling, she smoothed the fine lace between her fingers. *Give Eleanor Brittain these sheets? He must be mad.* Then she hopped out of bed and added a last line to the letter.

"If you want the Order of the Garter, come and get it, my dearest jewel, and I'll send some fine spring lettuce with the messenger."

The will that Cavendish had written long ago had left Chatsworth to his oldest son, Henry, who was at the time of his death but six years old. Bess and the earl had, by law, revised the will; since Henry was marrying Grace Talbot, Bess had instead lavished upon him and Grace much other land near Chatsworth and a manor they could occupy by themselves. So now she took up her pen and wrote that she had been thinking of removing to Hardwick Old Hall, since it was nearly finished and giving Chatsworth to William.

This produced a flurry of mail from Shrewsbury. Before Chatsworth passed into William's hands, what about all the furnishings filched from the Talbots?

What things? Bess wanted to know.

The earl enclosed a list.

Bess flung back the challenge. Charles and William were both at Chatsworth now, in her absence, and she had ordered them not to permit him to enter.

Wife, Shrewsbury wrote back, *if you use force, I will employ the law.*

I am back at Chatsworth, Bess replied, *and we shall all be glad to see you.*

Then suddenly all was forgot in the startling news that raced from one end of England to the other. The Spaniards were at last sending the long-feared armada against their shores, an armada so enormous that the great ships were like floating castles, jammed with helmeted soldiers, and they were going to sail right up the Thames, to London, to capture the queen, and lay waste to England in blood and fire.

Bess tore open Gilbert's letter, the chatty Gilbert who kept Bess informed. *And my lord my father sat down and wrote the*

Queen's Majesty a wonderful letter, Gilbert wrote. *My lord said: "Your quarrel has made me young again!" And so tomorrow we start for Tilbury with five hundred men.*

Tilbury was the site of an old Roman fort, in a strategic position on the Thames, a position that would permit the troops to protect the capital and their queen.

The summer days slowly passed. On the coast the beacons burned bright, on the coast the people could see the formidable array of slow-sailing, towering galleons. But in Derbyshire all Bess could do was wait. Each day she and Jane—the men had gone, naturally; William and Charles with all available men had joined the men at Tilbury—accomplished the tasks of summer, the gardening, the cooking, the continual airing and washing and cleaning, until finally the news arrived. The swift, agile English fleet had wreaked a dreadful vengeance: When the Spanish ships heeled over, under the gunfire, not water but blood poured from the scuppers.

Bess and Jane gasped. "Ah," cried Bess, "not for nothing did our blessed queen build up our fleet!"

Jane poured wine. They drank to their absent men, and their queen, and their realm, safe now. And Bess said, raising her glass high, "To our brave seamen and our mighty fleet! And our men coming home!"

Would he come, she wondered? Would he? All the next week she waited, until one beautiful September day, they heard the sound of horses and men, many, many men, a big troop. And when the earl rode in, past the curtain walls, up to the courtyard, Bess felt her heart would burst with pride and love.

"We didn't do a damned thing, None," the earl said, as they sat in the garden. "The sailors and the Queen's Majesty did it all, spending thirty long years lavishing all available money on the ships."

Then he told her that the queen herself had come to Tilbury. "I wrote down what I could remember of what she said." He dug in his doublet and brought out a piece of paper.

"She came in a jeweled coach, at least it looked jeweled, the colors were so bright. She reviewed the troops on foot.

339

Then to speak, she rode a white horse, the following day. She was bareheaded, a page carried her silver helmet with a white plume, and a steel corselet covered the upper part of her body. She said—" Shrewsbury smoothed the paper—"When I remember how she looked and how she spoke to us, the tears spring to my eyes, None!"

He smoothed the paper again. "This is what I remember she said. First she had been warned not to come, to trust herself to an armed multitude. But then, I can recall exact. She said: I am come to live or die among you, to lay down for my God, and for my kingdom, and for my people, my honor and my blood even in the dust. I know I have the body of a weak woman, but I have the stomach of a king—and a king of England, too—and think foul scorn that Parma or any prince of Europe should dare to invade the borders of my realm!"

Bess looked at the earl. Bright tears of emotion shone in both their eyes. The earl put his arms around Bess, and she held his hand tight.

"How proud we should be, my love," Bess whispered shakily, and she rested her head on his shoulder. "How proud we should be of our queen and our country. But I am so proud of you!" And they sat there together, content, in the garden, till the sun sank over the rising hills.

Shrewsbury couldn't stay at Chatsworth and he wouldn't let Bess come with him. It was his duty, he told Bess, to return alone with his men, to ride into the great park at Sheffield, the horns blowing and the pennons waving. Bess imagined how it would be. . . . It was impressive enough the next morning when he rode off. But she was a bit worried. He looked thin and pale. She waved and waved, till she could see him no longer. Then she turned and, with her brisk purposeful walk, came back into the hall of Chatsworth. She was standing as straight and tall as always. But Jane said, "What is the matter, Bess?"

"I'm worried about him," she said. "But he wouldn't let me come with him."

CHAPTER 21

THE earl woke slowly and turned over in his bed at the manor lodge. He frowned and stretched. He lay there, thinking. Then he got up and put on his bedgown and went to his table. He dipped his pen. Outside the window, in the gray dawn, the trees were almost leafless; it was the first week of November. Then suddenly he drew the piece of paper toward him and dipped the pen again.

None, he wrote, *I am coming home.*

He laid down the pen, a sudden pain stabbed through his head, and he felt dizzy. He stood up. He swayed. His body servant, who was bent over the fire, poking at the logs, heard him call out, and he was in time to catch the earl as he fell.

His last letter was carried to Bess. She dressed in black and set out immediately for Sheffield.

"I know exactly what he wants done," she told the stricken Gilbert. "And I shall do it. It is very important that your father's funeral be carried out just as he would wish."

The mourners were not only all the gentry and nobility from far and near, but the faithful servants from Chatsworth and Sheffield, Tutbury, Wingfield, and Worksop. And the townsfolk.

A gentleman led the earl's horse.

Then came the men in the family.

They made a procession to the church where Bess and the earl had witnessed the marriage of their children. Within, it was lit by torchlight. Within, Bess waited for the funeral cortege, and the closed coffin.

And when it was over, numbed and white, she rode back to Sheffield. She went to her old rooms; standing with her back to the fire, she waited for Gilbert. When he came, she said, "Gilbert, I will return to Chatsworth tomorrow. That is all I wanted to tell you. I think your father would have approved of the services."

Gilbert clenched his hands. "Aye! But it is well that you should leave!"

Bess raised her head imperiously.

"Aye!" said Gilbert, his well-known temper flaring now. "You leave!"

"How dare you?" whispered Bess.

"He died alone with that whore! You never loved him!"

Bess advanced on him, her hand upraised. "God's death, you fool!" she shouted. "You fool! I adored him!"

She picked up a brass vase. "You fool, Gilbert! I adored him! And he knew it! He knew it!"

Standing there, with the vase poised, she saw through her tears that Gilbert had left her. She set down the vase. She said to the empty room, "You fool, Gilbert, not half the man your father was, nor ever will be. Ever will be," Bess repeated. She turned around and shouted to the other closed door, "Digby! Battell! Bring me some wine!"

CHAPTER 22

"WE are leaving Chatsworth," Bess said to Jane. "Leaving."

"At our time of life, Jane," Bess said, very serious, "we must begin again anew. Chatsworth is finished; I am going to give it to William."

"Bess," Jane said, "if you don't stop working so hard, you'll collapse." Bess had spent four months now going carefully over every article in Chatsworth, deciding which precious hanging or picture or memento to take, and which to leave.

Bess shook her head. "Work is the only antidote I know, for grief and fear and uncertainty."

How many times had she gone up and down the stairs, Jane wondered. Nonetheless, by spring, everything was

342

packed; and on the first of May she and Bess and the household set forth for Hardwick Old Hall.

"Back to where we started, Jane," Bess said.

Jane said, "Oh, Bess, it seems as though you are leaving everybody and your whole life behind you."

Bess said sturdily, "Well, I'm not. I think about them all the time. I even talk to them, Cavendish and Sir William, and my jewel. And Aunt Linacre and Mother. And Elizabeth. All of them." She flashed Jane a look as they jounced along in the carriage the earl had built for Mary. "Do you think I'm mad, Jane?"

Jane put her gloved hand over Bess' hand. "No, I don't," she said. "When I'm gone, Bess, please talk to me, too."

But the first thing Bess did when she got to Hardwick Old Hall was to call in her favorite cabinetmaker. Jane was amazed. They didn't need a single piece of furniture, surely. "What is it you want?" she asked.

"For the whole of my life," Bess said, "I've never had a proper table for my drawings. And now I'm going to have one."

Jane had never seen her so impatient for a piece of furniture to be finished. When it was done—and it was plain, large, and slightly tilted—Bess stood in front of it, rapt with admiration and excitement, running her hand over its smoothness. "Ah," she sighed in true joy, as though Shrewsbury had presented her with the biggest emerald in the world.

For a week Bess crouched on a stool in front of her new table. On a flat table nearby, the sheaf of papers grew. She permitted Jane to look at some of them: sketches of rooms, sketches of stairways, sketches of towers floating upward from a roof. Then one day she worked till nightfall, wolfing down beer and bread at her table. When Jane came in to tell her dinner was ready, she was staring in rapt excitement at the large sketch of a house. She drew a long, deep breath.

"This," she tapped it, "will be the finished mansion."

Jane looked at the black and white ink-drawn sketch. She said involuntarily, "Why, it's nothing but glass, Bess."

Bess roared. "God's death! I never should have shown you!" She banged her hand down. Then she said, "I'm

343

sorry, Jane; it is my fault. No one can understand how this will look, how arrogantly magnificent it will stand, how regal, glittering with light and glass. No one can see it now, but me. I can see it. Plain!"

Her eyes shone.

Jane whispered, "You're going to build another house?"

"Aye." Bess was looking at the sketch.

"You decided so sudden?"

Bess shook her head. "I've been wanting to build another house for four years. But I didn't dare. Shrewsbury would have had my head. He'd have killed me! And you know what they say about me: If I stop building, I'll surely die!"

She pushed back her stool, stood up, and laughed and then she remembered. She leafed through the neat stack of plans, and drew one out. "Look, Jane! Look. Mistress Kniveton's room!"

Jane said, "If you don't come and eat dinner—" she said, then "—it's beautiful, Bess."

Bess laughed. "Oh, Jane, you know nothing about proportions. But it will be a beautiful room, cool, and peaceful, a retreat, but a comforting combination of beauty and quiet." She took Jane's hand. "I'll come now."

They went down the steps, and at the bottom Jane said, "But Bess, where are you going to build this house?"

Bess went to the front doors and flung them open. She pointed. "Up there. At the very top of the hill. Where all England can see!"

Bess employed three hundred and seventy-five men to build Hardwick New Hall.

"I don't have time to waste! I'm almost seventy!" Then she gave Jane a merry glance. "But don't tell anybody."

Jane thought, *No one would ever believe her age.* Every day, after her meager breakfast, she climbed the hill like a young woman, brisk, head erect. Her red head was lightened by gray, yet it melted into the red and it was a beautiful color.

"I hate wigs," Bess said.

Mrs. Battell clucked. "You don't need a wig, my lady. Your hair is the fairest color."

Bess said, looking into the mirror, "But sometimes I think

344

I'm not myself, Mrs. Battell. I'm my mother." She laughed. "But then inside I'm still myself!"

The foundations of Hardwick Hall were laid by the next fall. Carefully, Bess used native stone; the lead came from her own mines; the marble would be quarried from nearby Ashford; iron came from Wingfield and alabaster from Tutbury. The earl had left Bess an income of two thousand pounds a year, a great sum. In all of England there was no wealthier woman than Bess, save the queen.

Bess, climbing the hill that fall, watched the walls begin to rise. On bitter days she would cry as of old, "If water is freezing, use beer!" And then she remembered the earl's lazy voice from behind her, that day long ago at Chatsworth. "Why not warmed ale?"

They warmed the beer in huge kettles over a fire, outside in the thin snow, and slowly, slowly, the shell of Hardwick New Hall rose, day after day, week after week, month after month.

Everyone around came to see and to stay and to be entertained. The house, Jane thought, was always full, always bulging with nearby friends, the Manners or the Thynnes, or the many, many relatives, children, grandchildren. Letters came from all over the world. Henry was in Italy, Charles in France and then in Germany, then later in the Netherlands, and Gilbert in France. Bess was so proud of them. They were all accomplishing what their father wanted them to accomplish. And at home, William, her sturdy right hand, with his quick humor, was the husbandman.

"I am like my lord Shrewsbury, Aunt," he said to Jane one time. "Many's the time I heard my lord say he was happiest on his estates."

Bess, who in the old days had taught her grooms to work at embroidery, to help along the many projects, now put her efficient chaplain, Master Jenkinson, in charge of the accounts. Every two weeks they would sit down together and go over them. The great mansion was rising, and so were the costs.

Bess was working on a new piece of needlepoint, which she had just designed. Jane looked down at it. At the bottom of it was a device of tears falling on quicklime. There was a motto.

Tears bear witness that the quenched flame lives.

Jane gave another glance at Bess' face. "Why, Bess," she said.

"I've been so unhappy for the past week," Bess blurted. "I'm going up and getting into bed."

Jane sighed and sat on by the fire. After about an hour she too went up the stairway, pausing at Bess' door; she could hear Bess' voice, so she knocked and went in.

Bess was sitting up in her huge bed, with her mass of satin pillows behind her back, while Mrs. Battell was holding up various gowns for her to see. Amazed, Jane saw Bess was smiling.

Bess said, "Sit down by the fire, Jane. I was lying here, thinking about my jewel, and I suddenly thought, why, he left me the London house on Cheyne Walk to use. And so I decided, Jane. We're going to London for the rest of the winter!"

Bess sent all manner of bedding, hangings, linens, quilts, household goods ahead of them to Cheyne Walk, so that when they arrived, the big house would be properly beautiful and comfortable. They set forth on November 18, 1591, wrapped in furs, and with fur rugs, six wagons coming after. It was like a progress, Jane thought. As though the queen herself were moving through the land. And when thus they entered London, with outriders, footmen, grooms, guards, personal servants; with the Cavendish stags and the badge of the Talbots flying; and Bess and Jane in the coach the earl had built for Mary, with the fleur-de-lis of France, people said, "It could only be Bess! It could only be Bess of Hardwick, come back to London!" By the time Bess' coach had drawn up before Shrewsbury House, the street was jammed with people.

The queen sent a personal invitation to Bess. The court buzzed. For the young who didn't know, all the tales were told again and again.

"Certainly she was poisoned! By her brother-in-law, who

346

wanted her out of the way, because Sir William had left her all his money and estates! Twice she had been in the Tower! It was a terrible scandal, about her daughter's tutor and other men. Lord Shrewsbury stopped it and wed with her in secret. To this day no one knows where or when they were married. No one. But he left her. He left her."

The day came when Bess was to come to court. The court waited. The queen waited. Elizabeth was now fifty-eight. Before dinner that day she had danced five galliards. But as she looked about the crowded room, there were many beloved faces missing. The great earl, her love, her Robin, had died before Shrewsbury. Walsingham had died. Sir Christopher Hatten, the wit, the bon vivant, had followed them. There were many gaps in the familiar scene, and so many young.

She must be seventy, Elizabeth thought.

And suddenly there she was. In the open doorway, her head high. Her hair almost undimmed—for Bess was wearing apricot velvet, carefully chosen to match her hair. And there were the pearls, the collar Shrewsbury had given her, boldly telling the world that no matter what Shrewsbury had done or not done, she was his countess and she defied their gossip.

When she stood before Elizabeth and curtsied deeply, Elizabeth stood suddenly and took her in her arms and kissed her. What dread were the advancing years when Bess of Hardwick stood like a bulwark against them? Here was tonic. How could anyone be afraid, who lived in the same world as Bess of Hardwick?

"My dearest cousin of Shrewsbury," the queen said, "it warms my heart to greet you!"

She is a legend in her own time, Elizabeth thought. *How proud I am of her, a woman.* A stool was brought for Bess, and the two women, queen and countess, talked. They talked of the earl.

"I used my lord too hard," Bess said. "I forgot how tender men are."

Elizabeth smiled.

Bess told the queen about the new house; if anyone could imagine the arrogance of the design, Elizabeth could.

They talked of the past; they talked of the great earl of Leicester, and of Mary Stuart, and of Sir William St. Loe; they talked of the times of their youth.

Then Bess spoke of Arabella. "She is sixteen, Your Majesty. It is my dearest wish to see her married, with your blessings."

Elizabeth's face was stern. She peered across the room with her eagle eyes as if to see the future, clear.

Arabella has made the wrong impression, Bess thought swiftly. *It is her Stuart waywardness.*

Bess went back to London by water, in the queen's own barge. She knew she must talk in private to Cecil.

The queen's great secretary was stooped and gray, but as vital as ever. Bess hugged and kissed him. After a sumptuous dinner, with the finest of French wines, they sat by the fire together, free to talk.

It was Arabella's lack of humility that annoyed the queen. It was also Bess' daughter Mary Talbot, who was pushing the girl. It was Mary who had asked for two ladies-in-waiting for Arabella; the queen had snapped that Arabella was not a princess.

But of course there were only two heirs, now, to the throne of England. Mary Stuart's son, James of Scotland, and the Lady Arabella Stuart.

"Thus, extreme care must be taken of her, her person, her life," Cecil said.

"I shall bring her down to Hardwick with me," Bess said.

Cecil nodded. "It would be well. The Queen's Majesty is going to charge you with her care. She will be safe with you." *It will be a burden,* he thought, *more than Bess realizes. She only realizes that she will have her granddaughter with her; she sees only the immediate future. Perhaps,* he thought, *she is right.*

"What are you thinking, Will?" Bess asked.

"I was deducing your philosophy, which is ofttimes a dangerous thing to do. First things first, it is with you. In that case Bess, now, here in London," he continued, "you should enjoy yourself and have a merry time."

Bess did. She went to the Royal Exchange; she went to the theater. She bought paintings and rugs and all manner of material, silks and wools for her needlework and her clothes. She entertained and was entertained; night after night she went to bed at midnight and after. And she bought thirteen pieces of fifteenth-century Brussels tapestry, telling the story of Gideon. Bess would design a room in her new house for them.

After a farewell visit to the queen, when Bess left London with Jane and Arabella, twelve lumbering wagons bulged with her purchases.

In the wagons were two gifts from the queen. Two portraits. One of herself, in a brilliant gown embroidered with jeweled snakes and lizards, and one of her brother, Edward VI, an appealing portrait painted when he was ten years old. Forty-eight horses were hired for the journey, a journey that was once again a progress, for they had many invitations to stop at country homes.

One of the stops was to see Frances, at Holmes Pierrepont. They stayed a week. From there they made a last stop at the new home of Sir Francis Willoughby, an old friend of Bess'. His new house was called Wollaton. Bess explored every inch of it with him, even tramping through the gardens, literally mile after mile, to see Sir Francis' unfamiliar yellow flower, called "woad."

Charles had said to her, "Wollaton looks as though it ought to be floating alongside a canal in Venice."

I ought to build Charles a house, Bess thought. *I will build him a house at Oldcotes.* She would start it soon. Sitting in her carriage, alongside Arabella, the coach climbed slowly up the hill to Hardwick. Bess could hardly breathe from excitement. She had missed the sight of that standing shell of a house; she had been aching to see it, to start work again; she had fretted and fussed this past week; every night she had wakened, thinking, *Oh, what joy is mine, so soon! To see its beginnings built solid of stone, standing proud in its naked beauty.*

And there it was! Bess stood up in the litter to see better. Her eyes glowed. It was not a dream at all; it was real.

CHAPTER 24

THE years go around throwing out months as fast as a wagon wheel kicking up dirt, Jane thought. It had taken Bess seven years to build Hardwick New Hall; and even Jane had often to look out the window to make sure it was actually standing there on the top of the hill, just as Bess had said it would stand, the most wonderful new house in England.

Jane wasn't sure whether she liked it or not. Day after day she had come up the hill to stand at Bess' side, to watch the work. "By my faith," Jane would whisper, "you can't add another row of lights to those windows, Bess!"

"I can and will! I must!"

Bess scowled upward. The ground-floor windows had two rows of lights; the second floor three. The third floor four, and the towers—there were six of them so designed that on a gray stormy day they seemed to float—had three rows of lights; they were almost entirely glass.

So was the façade of the house.

"The reason the towers seem to float is that they are built —the end ones, in the rear, and the front ones, baying out from the front—twenty feet from the end towers," Bess explained. She looked up at the towers. Across the top of them was stone fretwork, and her initials. Huge, bold, they said, ES. From where Jane and Bess were standing they could see four of them. Jane thought, *She has signed her house like a painting. And she should.*

Sir John Thynne rode over every month. He kept trying to suggest that Bess put some ornamentation around the windows. There was none. They were set into the Derbyshire stone simply. Yesterday he had laughed and agreed that Bess had been right.

"You were right, Bess," he roared. Sir John never said anything in an ordinary tone of voice.

There were eight low pillars across the ground-floor entrance. Flanking the double doors were stone pots with flowers. The ivy, planted two years before, had begun to grow; it was carefully trimmed to weave its way between a few of the lower windows.

Arabella picked her way across the lawns and onto the brick entrance where they were standing. Bess waved to her. Sir John had a handsome grandson, and Bess was forever hoping Arabella would fall in love with him. If she didn't hurry up, she would lose his interest; there was a whole bevy of pretty girls after him. Bess sighed and brought her thoughts back to the present.

"And you see I was right about the towers," Bess said. She had designed them originally with only two rows of lights. She had changed her mind after it was done. At enormous expense they had been ripped out and rebuilt. "But come up and see the high chamber," she said. "Yesterday the Odysseus tapestries were hung."

She had designed the proportions of the room around that magnificent set of tapestries that told the story of Odysseus. She had bought them in London in 1587. The four of them entered the house, and Sir John said, as he always did, "Bess, that's the damnedest stairway I ever saw in my life!"

It was stone. It was very, very plain. The steps were so shallow they looked as though they'd been worn by the centuries. There was no true balustrade, just a stone coping. From where the four of them were standing, the stairway rose straight, then stayed level, under a plain passageway, wide, went off at a slight angle, and then turned even more slightly and disappeared upward, as though there was no end to it at all. It reminded Jane slightly of the fanciful pictures of a stairway to heaven, disappearing toward the clouds, substantial and yet insubstantial.

William had remonstrated with Bess about the stairway. "The weight of it, Mother. The weight's going to pull the house down."

Bess had just laughed. Then she said, "In the upper reaches of the house it will be wood, William. Don't worry about the weight."

"Remind me not to ever get drunk here, Bess," Sir John

351

said as he went up the shallow steps. "I'd never get down."

But when he stood on the threshold of the presence chamber, he was quiet.

The Odysseus tapestries were eight in number. The room was on the third story. The windows soared almost from ceiling to floor. Yet the colorings were somehow muted; the room held peace; it held beauty. At the very end of the long chamber a huge bay, formed by one of the towers, beckoned. Sir John leaned down and kissed Bess. Then he roared, "You're a genius, Bess!"

Bess shook her head wonderingly. She was very sure of her own talents, but the room defied her; she didn't know how she had created it. "Sometimes I think it is a gift of God," she said, looking to Sir John as though he might explain how the miracle had happened.

They turned and wandered down the stairway, through its meanderings. Outside, the curtain walls around Hardwick were set at close intervals with the fleur-de-lis of France decorating their top. Gardeners were busy at the beds underneath. Sir John thought the fleur-de-lis comical, even though they were effective.

"This queen would choke you if she saw those, Bess!"

Bess glanced at Arabella, who had heard. Arabella said, "But I admire your house at Longleat more than any other house I've ever seen, sir."

Sir John frowned down at her lovely face. "Kind of you," he muttered and looked at Bess. Arabella had turned away and was following Jane back into Old Hardwick. Bess said, "One is never a prophet in one's own household."

Bess is accustomed to Arabella's discontent, he thought. *The whole county knew of it; it must be difficult, living with Arabella.* "Good-bye, Bess," he said aloud.

"I'm so glad you came!" She looked up at him ahorse. His rakish beard was gray, now. *We are all getting old,* she thought. "Take good care of yourself, my dear friend. Godspeed."

He waved. Bess' liveried guards closed the gates after him. They wore the Cavendish stag on their sleeve. *Imagine,* Bess thought, *when I was growing up here, did I ever dream I would live like this? Did I? And now I am accustomed to it and*

352

take it for granted. Imagine, and I did it all. I did it all. Myself.

Bemused, she sat down on the brick walk—very wide it was—that led to the entrance of Hardwick New Hall. She leaned her head back against one of the twelve-foot-high pillars. The sun was high in the west; the skies were dotted with clouds. All around were the curtain walls, with their graceful fleur-de-lis. *Mary Stuart wouldn't mind,* Bess thought. Bess used the crests of her four husbands and Mary Stuart, too, when she deemed them artistically suitable. *I've a right to them,* she told herself stoutly. *If I don't, who does?*

From where she was sitting, she was looking straight at Hardwick Old Hall, about a hundred yards away. It made her think of Elizabeth, for Elizabeth had designed the four masking towers. At right angles to the hall were the stables and outbuildings, with pointed roofs and mullioned windows. The afternoon sun glanced across them, starring them. And all about were the gardens: first the green, green grass, clipped to perfection; and then the borders, and the trees, and the shrubs, and sprawling yews. *Oh,* Bess smiled in delight. *Such a wonderful afternoon.* And in a moment, she would turn and look up at Hardwick New Hall. The afternoon sun would turn it into a place of arrogant and blinding beauty.

From her windows, Jane could see Bess. *What in the world is she doing?* Jane wondered. *Sitting there hugging her knees like a girl.* Jane was supervising her packing. Arabella was curled up on the window seat across the room, looking out the other window. It seemed only yesterday the last time she had packed for Arabella, Arabella going to court. Last year the queen had summoned her; the queen wanted to see Arabella at twenty-one. How Bess and Jane had labored over her wardrobe, even to the careful dressing and accoutrements of her personal servants, down to her grooms. Bess and Jane had watched her proudly as she rode off with her entourage. Going to court, going to London! And Bess and Jane couldn't help predicting a glorious future.

If the queen recognized Arabella's talents, what might not happen? Arabella herself could be the queen of England, if Elizabeth Tudor named her as her successor.

353

"I pray the Queen's Majesty finds Arabella a young woman to her liking," Bess said, when they could no longer see Arabella and her train.

"How could she help but admire her? She is gifted and so well trained! In languages, in music, in history, in etiquette!"

Bess lowered her eyes. Jane adored Arabella. And Arabella had formed the same relationship with Jane as Bess herself had with Aunt Linacre.

"Well," she said, "we'll see, Jane."

They saw, soon enough. Charles brought the news.

"She's making eyes at Essex," Charles said bluntly.

"God's death!" Bess clenched her hands. "Didn't you warn her?"

"Warn a Stuart, my lady Mother?" Charles inquired lazily. "Aye, I warned her. I gave her a lecture. She was so angry with me she didn't bother to congratulate me on my knighthood." Charles thought that was amusing and grinned. He had been knighted for his bravery in Holland.

"Charles," said Bess sternly, "what did you say?"

"I said, 'Arabella, don't be a fool. Lord Essex is beloved of the Queen's Majesty. And he is the stepson of her Robin, the great earl. Leave him alone, Arabella, on peril of your life. Or at least your life's ambition.' " He thought, *What else did I say?* He had stood over her, tall and commanding. "Your life's ambition is to get married, isn't it? And you can't do that without the permission of the Queen's Majesty. Annoy her, be arrogant in your youth, and you'll never get it, Arabella. Never."

"Oh, God!" Arabella jumped to her feet. "I'm the prisoner of two old women! Two old women!"

"Arabella," said Charles patiently, "you know your history lessons. Remember and never forget, the conduct of the Queen's Majesty with her sister and her brother. She was retiring, loyal, quiet in dress. She not once looked at a man, she did not ask for favors, she was studious, cautious, she made good sturdy friends, who never deserted her. In short, while her brother and sister reigned, she was a loyal subject. And that is what she expects from you."

Charles looked across at his mother. He didn't tell her

354

the words he and Arabella had spoken. What was the use? It would only hurt Bess' feelings, and might even somehow get back to the queen. If the queen ever knew that Arabella had called her an old woman, she would never crawl back into favor. So Charles said, "Mother, see if you can't instill some humility into this child of the Stuarts."

And then he added, "You may expect Arabella home soon. The Queen's Majesty is going to send her back to Hardwick." He knew how disappointing his words were. His Aunt Jane, dear Aunt Jane, looked stricken and white. His mother sat there with clenched hands, her eyes flashing dark fire. Charles couldn't help but smile.

"God's death!" Bess cried, and Charles laughed then outright and got up to pour Bess a cup of wine.

"Don't be hard on her, Bess," Jane implored. It was two weeks later and they were expecting Arabella that afternoon.

"Jane! She must be told how to behave!"

Jane shook her head. "It won't do any good," she said.

"But we must try to help her. Otherwise, what will happen?"

"I don't know," Jane said. But she thought, *My darling Arabella. If only her mother and father had lived. If only the great earl and his little son, to whom Arabella was betrothed in infancy, if only they had lived. They would have helped Arabella.* Now she had only herself, her Aunt Jane.

Bess didn't understand. Bess was saying, "There are many others who have suffered far more than Arabella. Look at the Queen's Majesty herself."

"Well, you see, Bess," said Jane, "Arabella isn't the Queen's Majesty. How could she be? Where are you going to find a woman like the queen?"

Bess was silent.

"Arabella is just Arabella. And when she comes, let me comfort her, Bess. Let me try to help her."

Jane shook herself free of the past. Arabella was lying on the window seat now, her head propped up on her hands. Arabella spent increasingly more time with Jane.

In the beginning, six years ago Arabella thought, she had

355

been happy here. In the beginning, close by, at Chatsworth, were her Uncle William and his three sons. At Sheffield were her Aunt Mary and Uncle Gilbert and their three daughters. Cavendish and Talbot and the young Lady Arabella Stuart herself, why, they were the honey that drew swarms of young people and older people from all about. Hardwick Hall burst with guests. Hardwick Hall was a hive, and Arabella was the queen bee.

But now—and it had seemed so sudden—all had changed. Every one of her three Talbot cousins was married, and married to a peer, or the oldest son of a peer. William Cavendish, oldest son of William, was eighteen. No longer could she confide and complain to him. When she spoke to him of Bess, he grew silent and unsympathetic; William adored Bess.

"God's death, Arabella," he said, annoyed. "It's not Grandmother's fault! Where else in the whole world could you find a woman like our grandmother!"

And her Aunt Mary's girls drove Arabella wild, with their incessant talk of their husbands and clothes for court, and the near arrival of an heir, to the precious earldoms to which they were all so finely wedded. The countess of Pembroke, the countess of Kent—Althea was married to the eighth earl of Kent and she didn't let Arabella forget it for a second—and the countess of Arundel. I hate them, Arabella thought, despairingly. And I hate them because I'm jealous.

She rose and went over to the other window to look over the lawns and the distant court. She'd heard the noises that heralded an arrival.

"Who is it, my love?" Jane asked.

"It's Will." Arabella leaned out the casement. "He's leading Grandmother's horse. She must be going riding with him."

"They are probably going over to Oldcotes."

Bess was building a new house at Oldcotes. Arabella watched as Will helped Bess mount.

"Why don't you go with them?" Jane asked.

"No," Arabella shook her head. She thought sullenly that Will would ride sedately alongside Bess, and talk and laugh with her. "When I ride, I want to gallop," Arabella said. "I'd rather go with Will by myself."

She turned to face Jane. "You know what they say about Grandmother, Aunt Jane? They say she will not die while she's building. Does she believe that?"

"No, Arabella," Jane said, and smiled.

"I think she does! I am the prisoner of two old women who will never die!"

Arabella stood with arms outflung, like a statue. There was silence in the room.

Arabella cried, "Aunt Jane, if I can't talk to you about how I feel—there's no one else but you!"

"Well, I'm right here," Jane said practically. "Why don't you go and see if your packing is proceeding?"

"Because I don't want to move over there!" Arabella started to weep soundlessly. At least she'd been content at old Hardwick Hall. At least she'd been content in her mother's suite, with all her beloved books and mementos. The ghosts of that frail happiness wouldn't follow her to New Hardwick, she was sure. Arabella felt alone and frightened. The slow tears rolled down her cheeks. "Aunt Jane," she said, "please don't ever leave me."

Jane handed her her handkerchief. "Wipe your eyes, my love," she said. "Of course I won't leave you. In fact, if Bess won't die while she's building, I promise you I won't die till you are free, free of Hardwick."

Arabella sniffed and gave Jane a wavery smile. "How silly we both sound."

Jane said, relieved, "Well, I'm glad you realize it, Arabella. Very glad, indeed."

Jane said to William, "Stay for supper, and stay overnight. Arabella is distraught."

"Arabella is always distraught," William said.

But he stayed. After supper they played cards, the four of them, around the table that Bess had given to the earl as a wedding present. It amused William to see, surrounding his grandmother, the spoils and plunder of all her marriages. He thought of the county gossip, which proclaimed blithely that Bess would never have given up the Talbot pearls in her lifetime if it hadn't been that Gilbert had inherited the earldom on the death of Francis, the earl's oldest son and she was still wearing her pearl collar. The county said that Bess had reminded Mary she would never have had a hope for the Talbot pearls if it hadn't been for her, Bess. "Not a hope, my girl, without me," Bess had said.

"Are you going to play or not, William?" Bess asked.

William grinned. "Certainly, and I am going to take this trick."

"You knave," Bess said. "I didn't think you had the queen."

Bess was very happy. Tomorrow night, she would sleep, actually sleep, in her new bedroom at Hardwick New Hall. Of course, it was hardly furnished, but that didn't matter. They would move in slowly, to make sure everything was perfect, and perfectly placed, from the portraits to the hangings. "Tomorrow, William," Bess said as Jane dealt, "I shan't go to Oldcotes. You must take Arabella out."

"Now don't spoil their first night in New Hardwick," William said. "Don't spoil it for them, Ar'bella."

She looked flushed and happy after their long ride. She loved to ride out with her escort, all the pennons flying, to show the county its most important beautiful and royal resident was abroad among them.

"I'll try, Will," she promised.

"Do more than try, Ar'bella," William said sternly, as though he weren't four years younger than she. He looked down at her face. Should he stay?

Arabella said crossly, "I won't spoil anything!"

"See that you don't," he retorted, just as cross, and started away from her. "Open me those gates," he shouted, for the big gates were always closed when Arabella was within them. These curtain walls, beautiful as they were, were also close protection for Arabella.

"I shouldn't be harsh with her," he thought then, for she is a prisoner of her own royal blood. I'm glad it wasn't my own father Grandmother mated with a Stuart. "Good-bye, Ar'bella," he called. "Good-bye."

Arabella waved. She turned and went slowly into Old Hardwick and up to her rooms. Her maids were all busy, chattering. Glumly she allowed them to undress her, out of her riding clothes, and bathe her. She got dressed. She had supper, eating almost nothing. And then she and Bess and Jane walked the hundred yards across to Hardwick New Hall.

Arabella knew where she was going, of course. Her bedroom was on the second story. But first she entered Bess' huge bedroom.

"I'm going to hang the copes here, I think," Bess said.

Arabella scarcely heard her. She went by Bess' huge bed and over to a carved doorway. Within lay her new bedroom, entered only by this one door. It was decorated in blue and gold damask, for Bess had wanted it to be pretty for Arabella. It was all blue and gold, with tiny yellow flowers. It was gay and young. Arabella stood, in the center of the room, and tried to smile.

The candles were lighted. Arabella's personal maid fussed about. She prepared Arabella for bed; she brushed her hair, and then she washed Arabella's feet and legs, and drew over her the white embroidered sheets.

"You should be weary after your long ride, my lady," she said.

"Aye."

One by one the lights in New Hardwick went out. Only the night lights burned. Arabella lay in bed.

"I'm in prison," she whispered to herself. "There is only one entrance to this room: through my grandmother's bedroom. I'm in prison."

Lying there, Arabella clenched her hands. Her body grew rigid. Then she began to scream.

CHAPTER 25

DURING any season when the weather was inclement, Jane and Bess took their twice-daily exercise in the gallery, walking back and forth, back and forth its long length. In the winter snow beat against the huge windows, ice clung to the roof; in the spring rain streamed down the glass, veiling the greening gardens and hillsides in shimmering, misty beauty. Very often Arabella walked with them; sometimes gaily, walking twice as fast, so they passed each other midway, Arabella laughing to see when they managed it just perfectly, to meet in front of the colored marble chimneypiece. When she walked too fast, she ended up under the portrait of the earl, and when she walked too quickly she ended under the portrait of her grandfather, William Cavendish. And when she passed the portraits of her young female cousins, all countesses, she kept her eyes averted.

Bess and Jane kept Arabella as busy as they could these years with endless books sent down from London, with hours at French conversation with her tutor, with lessons in Latin for William and his younger brothers, Arabella herself doing the tutoring. They entertained as much as possible, family and friends. Henry and Grace, who had no children, came often. Henry spent hours with Arabella; they talked forever, Bess thought, coming upon them in the high presence chamber, in the far glassy room formed by one of the towers. They talked of the inequities of the realm, the need for reform.

"What reform?" scoffed Bess.

Arabella shook her head pityingly. Grandmother is so old, she doesn't realize times are changing. And the queen. The queen is old, too.

Henry brought news of the court; Arabella listened eagerly. The Queen's favorite, Essex, was gathering about him a party of the young. Arabella's eyes gleamed. The young. She belonged in London, with them.

"Well, you stay well away from Essex, even in your thoughts," Bess said.

Arabella and Henry exchanged glances. Arabella thought, *Uncle Henry is so sympathetic. What would I do without him, without his coming? He brings me hope.* Her two other uncles, William and Charles, were just like Bess, giving her lectures.

Uncle Henry said, "Don't despair, Arabella. Soon it will be a new century, and you shall blossom."

Bess pushed aside the thought of a new century. "The

360

old one is good enough for me," she said, laughing. She tried to enlist the help of her grandson Robin Pierrepont, who was Frances' son, and who was almost the same age as Arabella.

"Bring your friends over; take Arabella out."

But Robin was not as patient as young William.

"She snubs my friends," he said, annoyed. "She wishes a splendid marriage, I think, Grandmother, an alliance with an old royal name. She talks of the Seymours."

"God's death, I know it." Bess was sure that if only Arabella would fall in love, she would stop conniving to ally herself proudly and would forget about a royal marriage.

That fall, they had lived in New Hardwick for two years. Arabella was twenty-four. The new century would be born on the first of January. Bess and Jane had planned a party, and Arabella seemed happy. Bess thought, *She seems to firmly believe the new century will bring her what she wants. I hope it does.*

Arabella was keeping in as close touch as possible with the antics of the earl of Essex. Then he was gone to Ireland, to settle that rebellious country; and when the news of his colossal failure there reached Derbyshire, Arabella ran to her room, threw herself on her bed, and began to sob.

Bess stood over her. She asked, implacably, "Arabella, how deeply are you involved?"

She was involved deeply enough to have the queen send down a Master Brounker to interrogate her. Arabella lied. She denied she had written to the Seymours. Yet how convenient it would be for Lord Essex, in his treasonable endeavors, to have a handy heir to the throne, Arabella Stuart, and a Seymour husband.

Master Brounker stayed four days. Bess and Jane were frightened of him. Would he take Arabella away? Essex's trial for treason was already underway in London. There was no doubt but that he was guilty. Bess and Jane were frightened; the Queen's Majesty was sad, stricken.

Master Brounker finally departed, the gates shutting after him. He would be back, he informed them, after consulting with the queen.

Arabella lay on her bed, crying out with nerves stretched taut.

"Undo her gown and bring hot water," Bess cried, distraught and shaken.

Arabella's maids obeyed quickly, and bathed her, and rubbed her legs and feet with lavender water, and tied back her beautiful hair, and laid cold cloths on her aching head. *Just like Mary Stuart,* Bess would cry in her heart. *Just like Mary Stuart.* Bess could hear the earl saying implacably, "You deserve it, Bess. You did it!"

After the ordeal, when Bess came back to her own room, through the one carved door, Bess cried out in despair, "But what can I do, Jane? What can I do?"

"Nothing," said Jane. "Nothing, God help us, but what we are doing."

Bess thought, *When one is old, the years fly by. Fly by. But for Arabella the earth turns so slow. So slow.* "My poor darling, my sweet darling," she would cry, sitting on the stool by Arabella's bed.

Then the next day, she and Jane would turn their wits to find some entertainment, a new arrival, a dinner party, a hunting expedition. Another letter to the queen, another present to the queen, another letter to Cecil's son, who had taken his father's place as the queen's secretary. Whenever she wrote to young Robert Cecil, Bess felt the lump in her throat, she missed her old friend so much.

And sometimes Bess got angry, too. "God's death! And if something happened to me, and if you weren't sleeping there," Bess pointed to the carved door between their two rooms, "where then would you sleep? In the Tower?"

"I'd rather be in the Tower!" shouted Arabella.

"Hah!" Bess threw back her head and snorted. "That's what Mary Stuart thought, when I had her care!"

Over and over, Jane thought, *the same endless quarrels.* Arabella, trapped by her birth, born with her fingers touching the side of the throne, and Bess trapped by the queen's faith in her, trapped into becoming a guardian for a lovely young woman who bore the blood royal.

"Freedom! I want my freedom!" Arabella would cry.

"You must have permission to marry!" Bess would shout

362

back. "I cannot give it! Only the queen can give it! Only the queen!"

Otherwise they would put Arabella in prison, in real prison. "I'm going to keep you from committing some outrageous folly if it costs me my life!"

Arabella screamed back, "Aye! But it will cost me my sanity!"

Then Jane would intervene. "No, it will not, my Ar'bella," she would say in her soft voice. "You are far too sane, my love. Now, you come with me."

Taking Arabella by the hand, she would lead her to the plain chapel. And there they would kneel together.

"Nobody listens to me," Arabella sobbed.

"God does, my child."

Arabella quieted. Jane's deep faith helped Arabella. If Aunt Jane believed it so thoroughly, maybe it was true.

Thank God for young William and his two brothers, Bess thought. They were younger than Arabella and none of them yet married. Bess called on them constantly when they were at Chatsworth.

When the news came that Essex had been executed for treason, Arabella took it with more fortitude than Bess had expected. That was because of Henry, who had come down with the news. He and Arabella spent hours, heads close together, commiserating, speaking of the loss of the earl of Essex, and the cruelty of the queen. Contemptuous of their talk, Bess said, "Keep your treasonous whispers from my ears; it makes me want to vomit."

She thought, *They are waiting for the queen to die. They are waiting.*

"God's death, Henry!" she burst out. "Even were she to die tomorrow—why, stone dead she would be more than a match for you and Arabella!"

CHAPTER 26

BESS was not only worried about the queen, she was worried about Jane. The queen was seventy, Jane was eighty-three.

Jane's hair was still deep, deep brown, dashingly streaked with white. It made Jane angry to hear that anyone suspected her of dying it. But she was getting thinner.

Bess spent long mornings with the head cook, devising new ways of cooking nourishing foods and tempting Jane to eat. Bess was still building at Oldcotes. Her will was written. Hardwick and Oldcotes and Chatsworth to William, in strict entail. Charles' affairs were flourishing. He had bought Welbeck Abbey, and Bess was helping with the restoration. He had leased Bolsover Castle from Gilbert; the two were still the same fast friends; nothing would ever break that firm friendship. But it meant to Bess that Charles was close to her, too. When he was not at court or abroad, he rode over every week to see his mother. It was Henry she worried over.

Henry was brilliant. He was charming; women adored him. He had no legitimate children; he'd made up for that by fathering a swarm of bastards. He was recklessly extravagant. And he had sold some of the Chatsworth lands. Bess would never forgive him for that.

"He wants to use you, Arabella, as a means of furthering his mad ambitions."

It was March. Early in the month there came the dread news that the queen was ill.

William—young William—had galloped over with the news. Charles and William were both in London. Bess thought, *And where is Henry?* Bess found out soon enough. Henry was on his way to Hardwick. The next day Bess looked up as Jane came into her anteroom, where she sat at her table, her spaniel at her feet. Bess saw Jane was white, her eyes snapping. Bess leaped to her feet.

Jane said, "The queen! The queen, Bess! She lies ill unto death! And Henry is at the gates!"

Henry came running up the steps; he burst into Bess' sight, Arabella's hand in his.

For a moment no one spoke. Then Arabella said, "She may already be dead!"

The words hit Bess like a blow. All the love and respect she had ever borne Elizabeth Tudor came rushing back like an avalanche; all the times she had talked with her; the times when Elizabeth, the beautiful princess, had first smiled at her. Bess put her hand to her heart. "Oh, God," she whispered.

Arabella looked so uncomprehending that Bess blurted, "I loved her."

Arabella herself looked white and shaken. She said, "Grandmother, Uncle Henry has brought an escort for me."

The room swirled around Bess. "He's not going to take you away!" Suddenly the implication of an escort, a wild ride to London, who knew what mad schemes might be in the minds of madmen, to use Arabella like the little Lady Jane Grey. Bess ran toward the stairway. She ran down those shallow steps and out the huge doors. She ran through the courtyard and toward the gates. Without the gates were at least forty horsemen. Bess raised her voice to the top of her lungs.

"Bar the gates!" she shouted. "Bar them!"

She stood in front of them while the heavy iron bars clanged down. Henry was running toward her.

"You bad son," gasped Bess. "You bad son! Get out! Get out! With your men! Push him out. I command you!"

And Bess stood there and watched as the armed guards on the gates hustled Henry through the postern door, a little door set in the wall, and banged it shut again.

Slowly she climbed back up the stairs. She could hardly get her breath. Mrs. Battell came to her, and Digby, summoned by all the shouting and excitement.

"Where is the Lady Arabella?" Bess gasped. Why hadn't Arabella come running down the steps with her uncle, as

Bess had fully expected? When they reached the gallery, Bess saw why.

Arabella was on her knees on the floor, holding Jane, crying helplessly, "Aunt Jane! Aunt Jane!" And in the distance the bells of Ault Hucknall church began to toll, sonorous and remorseless, sounding the knell and the passing of an age.

CHAPTER 27

BESS was dressed in black. It was two weeks later, it was still March, and cold. In the lower hall, at the foot of the stairway, her precious stairway, stood Arabella's boxes, Arabella herself, and young William.

Ten days ago, in spite of her deep grief, Bess had written to the young king of Scots, and now king of England, too, a letter inviting him to stop at Hardwick on his way to London through his realm. She had received a polite letter back, thanking her, but His Majesty had accepted an invitation from Gilbert, Lord Shrewsbury, to stop instead at Sheffield Castle. Bess said, "Arabella, it will be proper, in your uncle's dwelling, to present yourself to your king and cousin. Pray give my love to Gilbert and my dear daughter."

So much has happened, Bess thought. *In just two weeks, so much. Arabella is free. Pray God, James will be like a true cousin to her.* But she couldn't help a last word.

"Be careful, Arabella! Be humble!"

Arabella bit her lip. *How can it be,* she was thinking, *how can it be? All this time I wished to be free, and now I am, and all I want to do is to cry? Oh, Aunt Jane,* she thought miserably, *I'd rather have you back than be free!* She seized Bess in her arms and hugged her. "I'm sorry," she whispered. "I'm sorry. Every day, Grandmother, put flowers in the chapel for her! She loved them so!"

William said, practically, "Arabella, maybe you'd better ride than sit in that coach. Maybe it would be best for you."

"I can't, Will," Arabella said, wiping her eyes. "I'm not dressed for riding."

She had been dressed for this momentous occasion so lovingly, only Aunt Jane hadn't been there to see. "All will be well with me, Will," Arabella mumbled.

"Good-bye, my love," said Bess.

Arabella went to the doors; her coach waited. *The Lady Arabella Stuart,* Bess thought, *going to court, going out to meet her king.* William looked down at her face. Arabella and her three women had gone past him.

"I've a bit of news, Grandmother," he said, to take her mind away from this parting. She would be all alone, without her dearest Jane, here at Hardwick. "I heard that the first thing that the new king is going to decree is that Fotheringhay Castle, where his mother died, is going to be taken down, stone by stone!"

Bess looked up at him, in surprise. "Truly, William?"

He nodded. "Aye. It's true."

Bess thought of the day when the earl had come back from Fotheringhay with Mary's terrier in his arms, coming through the snow. Now James, her son, was going to tear down the infamous castle in which his mother had been executed.

"William," Bess said, "when you return, you must go over to Fotheringhay. Maybe there's something we can salvage. Not only stone, but maybe a mantel, or some fine paneling. Whatever."

She frowned slightly. William gave a shout of laughter. "Oh, Grandmother!" He put his big hand on her shoulder and squeezed it. "Jesus, what a girl you are!"

Bess sent him a look from her brilliant eyes. "Oh, Cavendish," she said, "you knave."

February 13, 1608

Bess had asked Digby to bring her some soup for supper. But that was before she knew that young William had come. So now she decided to get up and Mrs. Battell did her hair and fastened her collar of pearls around her neck. Bess told

367

her she would sup with William in the withdrawing chamber, off the high presence chamber.

"I think I need another petticoat," Bess said, feeling the drafts as she stood up.

"Aye, my lady," said Mrs. Battell, getting out a satin-lined velvet petticoat. "But this will keep you warm."

Bess put her hand on Mrs. Battell's shoulder as she stepped into the petticoat. "I do fairly well for eighty-seven," she said, smiling.

"Aye," said Mrs. Battell, "I wish I did as well!" She thought, *It's young William that's put the sparkle in her eyes. It's good he came. But it's so cold,* she thought, *it's a record cold, they say.*

Bess took her arm. They walked to the door, Bess' spaniel following close behind. At the entrance to the high presence chamber William waited.

The candles burned. The fireplace threw out wavering light. The tapestries shimmered, palely blue.

William said, "I was admiring it again, Grandmother."

He kissed her. Bess looked up at him. "It's a terrible night; you shouldn't have come."

"I brought a letter from Arabella."

He thought, *Will that satisfy her? Will she ask about the building? She is very old; maybe the letter will divert her.*

"How is the building?" asked Bess.

"Splendid," muttered William. "I think, Grandmother," he went on, forcefully now, "that it will be the fairest row of stone buildings you have ever done. Better than at Buxton Springs, for instance."

Bess nodded. "Yes, I think they will be." She took his arm. "Shall we walk the length of the chamber before dinner? I've been in bed, and it will do me good."

William sighed. The snow beat against the great windows. Bess clung to his arm. *She walks more tenderly,* he thought. He was silent. He couldn't think of what to say, and the only thing in his mind was the thought of the deserted buildings; they stood alone in the snow and cold. There were no carpenters there, no plasterers; the sound of hammering had ceased; there was only the snow and the silence. William glanced down at Bess.

They were standing in the far bay of the room, made

by one of the glassy towers. They turned, and Bess looked back across the long, long room.

"It's beautiful, Grandmother," William said, low. "The color of the tapestries—" His voice died away.

"Your grandfather loved the story of the great Odysseus." William put his hand over hers.

"But now you must come and eat and read me Arabella's letter."

They sat down to eat at a table before the fire, in Bess' withdrawing room, off the high chamber. The walls were hung with the green velvet hangings Mary Stuart had embroidered. *Imagine,* thought Bess, *how many years ago I saw her working these, in Tutbury. That dreadful Tutbury.*

The table was laid before the great fireplace. Abraham Smith had designed and made it. The overhanging mantel was held up by the Cavendish stags.

William poured the wine.

"You ordered only bread and meat?" Bess asked.

"There's cheese, too," he said. "I had a late dinner." He had had a late dinner because he had been at the building site, to see if it was possible to continue the building. "Eat, Grandmother; it will do you good, and I'll read Arabella's letter." He was anxious to keep Bess' mind from that damned building. "First she thanks you very much for the very, very beautiful gold bracelet."

Bess swallowed her soup. "My New Year's gift," she explained.

"Then she says: 'And would you like to know how we spend our time at court? In everlasting hunting. While I've been here at Winchester, there were certain children's plays remembered by the ladies. As *I pray, my lord, give me a course in your park; rise pig and go; one penny, to follow me!* Childish games. By princely example we play the child from ten o'clock at night till two or three in the morning.' "

"The Stuarts are all fools," Bess said. "Imagine what the Queen's Majesty would have thought. Is there any more?"

"Yes," William said. " 'Despite the cold, there are rumors of the plague. So we are going to leave and go to the earl of Hertford's castle. My dear Grandmother—' "

"Hertford?" cried Bess. She shook her head in despair.

369

"William, if Arabella doesn't stop her hankering for one of the Hertford sons, there will be trouble. That young man is the grandson of Catherine Grey, and I was in the Tower when his father was born to her."

"Eat, Grandmother," William said. "Don't worry about Arabella."

"I am eating!" Bess retorted. "I'm drinking, too," she added, her smile flashing out.

William laughed.

"Tell me about your boys," Bess said.

"They are all well, sturdy, healthy, horrible. When I was leaving, they were in the schoolroom. William had built a castle of blocks, and Gilbert had knocked it over. A royal fight ensued. William is always building, Grandmother. I wouldn't be surprised if he rebuilt Chatsworth!"

"Rebuild Chatsworth?" echoed Bess, putting down her spoon. "If he does, I'll either haunt him or help him."

But she looked white to William. She had picked up a cake and was nibbling it.

"I'm going to take you to bed," William said.

"Wait till I untie the dog," Bess said. She had slipped the end of the leash over the knob of her chair. "Remember when your Aunt Jane gave Arabella and me these puppies? How she loved her dogs! And you and she used to reproach me when I tied him to my chair to keep him from pissing on the rush matting."

But when they stood outside in the hall, beside the meandering stairway, Bess started into the long, long room. "Let's walk in the long gallery. I always say good-night to all my loved ones."

When they entered the great gallery, they could hear the wind more plainly.

Damn, thought William, as they walked past the first of the thirteen Gideon tapestries Bess had bought from Sir Christopher Hatton's heir, her last visit to London.

But Bess said nothing about the weather. They walked slowly down the great length. Bess paused before Jane's portrait. It hung next to the portrait of the queen in her gown embroidered in jeweled snakes and lizards.

"I am the only one left, William," she said, "except for

370

Lettice Knollys. How the queen hated her! Ah, the only ones left are the wicked ones."

"I wish you wouldn't talk like that," William said.

Bess laughed. "What's the matter with you, William? You're not usually so serious."

William took his eyes from the portrait of Mary Stuart, who stared at him with unseeing eyes. They had reached the end of the gallery, and they turned.

"You should have a cane, Grandmother," William said.

On their way back Bess stopped once more, opposite the portraits of Cavendish and the earl and Sir William. The wind threw a rattle of snow against the windows.

"But in the morning, the sun will flood the valley and the whole world will glitter and shine," Bess said.

William held her arm carefully as they descended the stairway. Mrs. Battell was waiting.

"I'll call you when my lady has retired," she said.

William nodded; Digby was coming up the stairs, and he wanted a word with her. When she came up to him, William whispered, "Does my lady know how severe is the weather?"

Digby said, "She ordered that the men lodged in the towers were not to sleep there tonight."

William was silent.

Digby said, "Master Will, have you stopped the building?"

William nodded.

"You didn't tell my lady?"

"No, Digby. No."

"Then she may guess. But we will not know, Master Will, if she does."

She opened Bess' door and then, seeing Bess ensconced on her satin pillows, she motioned William to come in. He went to the bed and took Bess' hand in his.

Bess said, "Don't be so worried, William. I am just weary. I'm building, am I not? And nothing will happen to me while I'm building!"

Bess settled herself comfortably.

Her eyes met William's but they were unreadable to him. She was tucked luxuriously in a mass of puffy satin quilts. She reached out one white and slender hand and picked up the Bible from her bed table.

371

"Read to me, William. John fourteen."

While he found the place, Bess continued, "It's my favorite reading. How your grandfather and the earl used to tease me about it."

William found it and a small smile tugged at his mouth.

"Here now, Cavendish," Bess said. "Don't laugh at your grandmother!" She sent him a long sparkling look. Then she sobered.

"My dearest boy," she said, very low, "read."

William cleared his throat, for there had suddenly been a big lump in it.

He began: "In my father's house are many mansions."

Bess leaned back against her pillows and closed her eyes.